What We Pass on to Our Daughters

MANISHA

D1091668

Leadstart
INKSTATE

ISBN 978-93-90463-58-9
Copyright © Manisha Yadav, 2021

First published in India 2021 by Leadstart Inkstate
A brand of One Point Six Technologies Pvt. Ltd.

123, Building J2, Shram Seva Premises,
Wadala Truck Terminal,
Mumbai 400022, Maharashtra, INDIA
Phone: +91 96999 33000
Email: info@leadstartcorp.com
www.leadstartcorp.com

Disclaimer: This is a work of fiction. All the names, characters, businesses, places, events and incidents in this book are either the product of the author's imagination or used in a fictitious manner. Any resemblance to actual persons, living or dead, or actual events is purely coincidental.

Editor: Kavya Shree
Cover: Rakhee Khadbadi
Layouts: Kshitij Dhawale

This book is yours to dedicate, once you finish reading it.

I dedicate this book to _____

About the Author

Manisha is a content writer based out of Hyderabad. She was a Miss India 2008 finalist, and has about a decade's experience in corporate communication and advertising. She loves to travel to explore the cultures of the world and yet, has come to the conclusion that the best, most important stories that need to be told are ones that exist in our homes.

Contents

CHAPTER I
Maya & Manish

She lay corpse-still on the dark brown sofa, wearing a green nightie with sorrow seeped into her eyes, ocean deep. Like a green leaf yanked from a branch and fallen too soon, she rustled between withering away and the last moments of life. Her mind limped back to that happy day that marked the change in her life.

She'd woken up with a smile that morning, had truly felt the water on her skin like she'd never before, and after getting ready, had flaunted herself to her parents all complete with a customary twirl. She remembered walking down the aisle without even looking at the groom waiting for her ahead; she was just happy to be. It was indeed one of the happiest evenings of her life.

And now, a year later, if someone looked at her, they wouldn't be able to guess she was thinking of happy times. She thought about that time harder like a child clings on to the mother on the first day of school. But all she felt was helplessness and sadness. She remembered the feeling but couldn't feel it, just like you can remember the sun but can't feel the warmth of it during winters. Why then do they say happy memories provide strength during tough times? Framed pictures on the walls, folders of videos filling up space on our computers, love letters of an ex stashed away in a secret place, souvenirs lining the shelves — we pathetically try to *capture* memories, only to realise later that they just remind us of what we've lost. Falling deeper and deeper into a whirlwind of these feelings, at some point, she fell asleep.

As her eyes shut away from the only light, dreams played clearer in the darkness. It was like watching a long, long play of several acts, the curtain constantly rising and falling. If staying awake was a struggle, sleeping was an even bigger one. She saw the red of her wedding dress even more clearly, heard her laughter distinctly and actually felt the happiness too. But soon as that happened, the present would spring up suddenly to yank her down, dragging her into the bottomless pit of sadness until something happy from her past would pull her back up. In this stomach-wrenching roller coaster of sleep, something inside her wanted to rip open her chest and escape to a state where there wouldn't be happiness, but no sadness either; a state where there was nothing at all, but just it — the thing inside her body. And then she felt it: sharp nails on the inside of her stomach, placing themselves on the wall and slowly digging deep into her flesh. But there was no blood. There was only pain; a pain that the body was more than willing to take as if wanting it all to end in one swift motion. Once completely in, the hands started sliding, slowly but decidedly and the light pierced effortlessly into her stomach. The light was healing. Strangely, the it inside her that was cutting through her body, started becoming one with the light.

Slowly, she felt the pain fade away from everywhere but the part of her stomach where the cut was being made. She didn't feel happy or soothed, she just felt fine. She felt like she's always known this feeling, rather, felt it. The pain from the cut became even more difficult to bear near the chest. The it combined with the light, pushed harder, becoming more painful. And so slow, she could feel her skin tearing molecule by molecule. It was so overwhelming, her brain couldn't comprehend it. She started sweating, her palms and feet went cold, the sweat from her armpits soaked her green nightie turning it into a darker shade that became almost one with the brown sofa. Her teeth clenched, her palms turned into tight fists, her toes curled and her knees bent to reach her stomach, shutting off the white light. Her entire body tightened into a ball and she felt the it inside her screaming while pushing harder. Her jaw hurt and she knew if she clenched any tighter, her teeth would shatter into a million pieces and cut into her gums. She felt something, another presence within her beginning to rebel the it. This *something* pulled the body out of the slumber, while the it dug its nails deeper to keep her inside. The tug of war went on for minutes until her flesh started to tear from the nails of the it and her body started sliding towards the *something*.

A shrill noise suddenly pierced her ears and made her jaws snap open in shock, drawing in a long, sharp breath of air as if she had just surfaced above the water. Gasping for a few seconds, she came to her senses and felt her stomach to see if there were any cuts while running her tongue over her teeth to see if they were all right. She did all this while her eyes struggled to get accustomed to the sunlight. When she realised it was just a dream, she sat up and felt the cold on her body as the air hit her nightie soaked in sweat. The shrill noise came again like a slap to wake her up and she rushed to the door instinctively and still out of breath.

"Good morning," the maid uttered two of the few English words she knew and Maya saw the giant white teeth emerging through her parting lips with blinding happiness.

*

"Thank god you called!" Maya said on the phone, sucking on to her cigarette. "The *Happy Valentine's Day* messages on the chat are driving me crazy." She put the cigarette aside and sipped her coffee.

"Well, that's not the reaction I expected from someone who's having her first Valentine after marriage," said Gaurav.

"Oh please, it still disgusts me. Everything is so…red."

"Like your cigarette tip? Blazing red!"

"At least it gives a kick."

"So does *louuu.*"

"Shut up. What's happening? What are your nauseating plans for the day?"

"Oh, nothing much! Every day is Valentine's for me baby!"

"The only thing worse than this day is you. You put the day to shame."

"Haha! Calm down! What's wrong? The day has just started!"

"Dreams, life, etc. Whatever."

"Meet me for coffee in some?"

"Ya. Wear red!" Maya mocked the sing-song tone of young girls foolishly in love and hung up before Gaurav could answer.

Maya and Gaurav's relationship was intriguing. Their togetherness had grown up to a level where they heard each other without words, understood each other without explanations, gave each other what they wanted without asking and knew what the other was feeling without expressions. They had shared t-shirts when Maya needed a too-large-clothing for comfort, shared a shawl in the hostel, eaten out of the same plate in the mess, shared a bed when one or both of them were too drunk, spent nights together watching the stars without speaking a word but they'd never had a *weak* moment. They were platonic and even the closest proximities that sharing a single bed in the hostel room or a shawl to keep the two bodies warm demanded, had failed to change the course of their relationship. They'd even spent several months apart despite being on the same campus when Gaurav got into a relationship with another girl, who clearly despised Maya and the reasons weren't just obvious, they were also measured *correct* by the standards of general belief. Even at that time, there were no discussions or explanations, Maya had quietly distanced away. Gaurav had not asked why and it didn't occur to Maya that he hadn't. They simply belonged together in the most natural way.

"You don't understand sarcasm too well," Maya said seeing Gaurav in a red t-shirt.

"You think so?" he smiled the same smile Maya knew he always did when he'd done something purposefully to annoy her. Nothing about him annoyed her anymore and despite knowing this, he did it anyway.

"The usual?" the waiter asked.

"Thank you," Gaurav replied.

"I'll actually have a green tea," Maya said.

Ignoring Gaurav's mocking laughter, Maya began, "I feel like I've hit a full stop and I simply can't come up with a new sentence. I know the story isn't done, or at least I hope it isn't. But what now? And I don't even know if what's written is good enough, you know? But I do know that I can't trash whatever's been typed, so I'm desperately trying to make that turn where it all picks up and grips the reader."

"By reader, you mean yourself?"

But Maya continued like he'd not spoken. "There's absolutely nothing that I don't like about him. I can't point at anything at all. In fact, it's like a dream come true because the best part about my marriage is that it feels like I'm not married. He has his life, I have mine; I have all the freedom in the world, just like I did before. Then what? I don't know what's bothering me! He doesn't hold my hand in public, he doesn't side with me in every discussion, he takes his own decisions like I take mine, he doesn't lay anything out for me to make my life simpler. I have savings until I find another job, so we're even financially independent! I've contributed to this relationship financially and emotionally as much as he has! It's exactly what I wanted, it's perfect!"

"Then what is it that you want now?" Gaurav asked in a tone that clearly reflected they both knew the answer.

Maya's heartbeat fastened a little. "I don't know! It feels like my heart doesn't skip a beat when I see him in the evening. I love the sex, no doubt. But it's not like we can't keep our hands off each other. It has never been that way. Not since day one. I mean, it's an arranged marriage, aren't we supposed to simply not get enough of each other? Shouldn't I be all dreamy eyed? Shouldn't I smile foolishly during the afternoons thinking about the previous night? You know, all the usual stuff? I have no clue what I'm missing! The spark, maybe?"

"Actually, Maya, you do know what you're missing. Don't you?" Gaurav replied in that rare tender tone full of warmth.

"I hate this stupid green tea!" Maya replied, urging to change the topic least she'd be reduced to tears.

"You might hate it but trust me, it's the perfect thing for you, and sooner or later you'll realise it." Gaurav put it as delicately as the fine dregs at the bottom of Maya's ignored cup.

*

She opened the door and entered her apartment to see Manish standing by the dining table, a familiar blue box in his hand. Six feet tall, well built, clad in blue jeans and a white shirt, eternally messed up hair and frameless glasses; he looked handsome. He didn't fall into the quintessentially handsome segment, but that's what had attracted Maya. She didn't rate well by general norms either and was always invariably attracted to people who were more like her in any aspect. Her heart fell seeing the gift box for Valentine's, but then he said, "Come here" and she smiled at the fact that it wasn't a question instead, inquiring where she'd been. He just wasn't like other men.

She walked over and they exchanged a deep kiss.

"Hi," she said.

"For you." He extended the box to her.

She opened it to see a diamond-studded bracelet with a pink, almost transparent stone in the middle. The shine didn't match up to the shine of her usual smile and this puzzled Manish.

"I love it," she said taking it out and handing it over for him to put it on her wrist. It fit perfectly. Not the jewellery itself but something about that perfection in fitting on to her wrist relieved her, and her smile broadened.

"How about I make you some tea and then we go out for a late dinner?" he asked holding her by the shoulders and looking straight into her eyes. The clear, warm and easy look of his eyes had always left Maya in awe. She felt if at all there's a world of all things beautiful, devoid of all pain, it'd be in those small eyes.

"Yes," she replied.

After the tea, she went in, opened her closet and lazily went through the clothes. She felt tired at the idea of dressing up but focused on how not to go over the top and yet not look disinterested either. She could never understand jewellery. The array of sparkling options at a showroom made her dizzy. She wondered if she's supposed to pick a different one for every outfit? If so, she could hardly remember them all and what would go with what necklines. And going to buy one at a time as and when an occasion presented itself was too much of an effort for her. So she kept it a minimal of studs, a watch and a ring. Shoes, on the other hand, she loved.

She picked a pair of stilettos in a shade of very dark blue. Now that that was sorted, she looked for an outfit to go with it. To play it safe, she picked out jeans in subtle pink and a beige top to tone it down further. She quickly dressed up, left her hair casually open, bronzed her eyes lightly, outlined them in black, slapped on a natural colour on her lips and she was done. She put on her studs and the watch as she walked out of the room.

Taking another satisfied look in the mirror outside, she said to Manish, "Let's go."

"Very pretty," he replied standing up and turning towards the door. This was another thing she admired about him. He didn't go overboard with remarks like "Oh baby, you look hot". But whatever minimal he said, you would know he meant it. She smiled and followed.

As they entered their favourite Italian place, they spotted a photo booth by the corner. They got a picture taken and walked over to their table. The waiter got him a scotch and a glass of red for her. She glanced around her. There were couples holding hands and mumbling to each other, and she wondered what they could be talking about. *Something sexual probably*, she decided and smirked. She then moved on to another table with two guys and a girl. They were clearly friends and their faces were flushed with all the free drinks. They were chatting and giggling uncontrollably.

The sight made her smile. *So much simpler being just friends.*

Every soul that takes a body comes into the world with a set of relationships and you're forever bonded to those people, and if you're lucky, you love them. Apart from that, she felt friendship was the only relationship which not only binds you further, but you invariably enjoy the bonds too. You can be yourself; there are no rules, you can talk your heart out. There's no pressure of doing something special or…looking for a spark. And if you fall out, or just don't connect anymore, you can leave, instead of dragging the relationship for the rest of your life. How simple would life be if society allowed you to just stop at that?

Suddenly she felt Manish's hand touch hers and jerked out of her thoughts. They have been sitting quietly.

"What would you like to have?" he asked her.

"The usual pasta in red for me," she breathed out, still partly lost in her thoughts.

That one feel of his hand on hers put her out. It wasn't just a touch, but a jolt that brought her back to the inescapable situation in her life. Despite everything she loved about her man, she wasn't in love with him. Or probably this life. The difference was blurred. It depressed her to think her life was about work, meals and cafes. Nothing was happening, no adventure, no change, nothing at all.

A few more similar years and she'd have a baby if she didn't go insane. A new member would spread some excitement for a few months, but once again there would be work, baby, meals and cafes. She was finding it hard to deal with this sense of permanence that kept coming back. And what after the baby? *Then there would be nothing at all!* Would the next 40-50 years be the same? Would she merely die one day while going in circles?

"Excuse me," she said and headed to the washroom least the dreaded tear escaped her eye. She went in, bent backwards and fanned her eyes with her palms. She took deep breaths to calm her senses.

"A night at a time," she told herself and splashed some water on her face. Surprisingly, this shoebox of a bathroom felt wider where she could actually breathe and dare to think the thoughts that have been doing the rounds in her head more freely than under an open sky. She didn't have to worry that the expression on her face would leak out or the absence of words that would make people wonder about her silence if she thought for too long. All she wanted at that moment was to just be there. Thankfully, as a bunch of girls came in to dab on some gloss on their ready to drip lips, she pushed herself out.

Walking back to the table, she saw their food had arrived. She must've been gone too long.

"Everything okay?" Manish asked in genuine concern. She hated this even more. It would've been so much simpler to accept that she wasn't in love with him if he were a little more flawed.

"Yeah, I got my period a day early," she lied.

"Oh. Okay, let's finish quickly then. I'll make you a hot chocolate at home and we can watch a movie."

"Yes, that'd be great," she replied, actually feeling relieved to escape from the world and into the one of fiction. However, if she kept escaping such times, what memories would she have left?

At the exit, the manager gave them a framed picture—the one they'd taken earlier.

Back home, they snuggled up in a light blanket and watched a movie on the laptop. The unconditional love of *50 First Dates* made her cry. It wasn't the love she cried about and how sweet and yet painful it all was. The ability of the character to love someone so clearly is what broke her heart. She wondered if she would ever have that. Given her long history of relationships and breakups, she doubted the blessing of being in love to ever be showered on her.

Before marriage, this had never bothered her. It was always moving to another man after a breakup. There were options, and she believed eventually she'll find the right one. But post one failure after another, she decided she'd let her family decide for her, and they'd done the best job—something she could've never been able to do herself. Surprisingly, Manish met every single of her odd ideas of how her partner should be and whenever he fell short, a simple discussion would set it all right.

She loved and respected him as a man; he was indeed one of a kind. He would say unique things to her, like: *"thank you for going to bed alone for all those months"* when he got promoted, something he'd worked very hard for. This reflected on the sense of attention he gave her, without saying much. He was the kind of a man she had always wanted to get married to. And yet, she couldn't fall in love with him. Something was amiss, and she blamed herself. She constantly longed for things that included her not being married. She wanted the sense of freedom that being single brought in…it was exhilarating.

The relationship seemed to grow heavier with each passing day of her married life. She probably knew the reason but didn't allow her brain to think of it or Gaurav to say it. And in all the conundrum, she found herself wanting the easier way out—to fall in love with Manish one day. She longed for her to fall in love like lovers long for each other's bodies after a long separation. She'd never imagined it would be the other way round for her.

CHAPTER 2
Vaidehi & Vinod

V aidehi looked like a bundle of red, sitting on the bed with her mother-in-law and others around. Chatter regularly peaked and erupted into laughter, died down and happened again, in a vicious circle. Vaidehi's eyelids got so heavy, she found it difficult to hold them up. She hugged her knees tighter to her chest and lightly rested her chin on the knees so that her head wouldn't bobble if she fell asleep.

It was a chilly November night of 1982, and the ladies cramped in the room made it warmer while a thick, enclosing, sedating sleep blocked out their shrill voices. Suddenly she felt the bed dip with somebody's weight and her eyes opened. Through her translucent red veil, she could make out it was her mother-in-law.

"Finally even you'll have help now in the house. You should get more rest here on," a high-pitched lady remarked.

"Yes, yes, I hope so. But you know what our astrologer said! He said my son's palm clearly shows two marriages. His first wife would die," the mother-in-law replied plainly. Vaidehi now was wide awake.

"Come now. Let's go out, it's quite late."

The mass of women went out, leaving Vaidehi in a shiver. She didn't even realise when Vinod came in, as the little visibility that the veil provided was lost in the tears that welled up.

*

She was ready by 6 the next morning. After breakfast began the ceremonial couple games and the redundancy of a marriage. The couple was pitted against each other in simple games, reflective of who would dominate the other in life ahead. An affair might take years for the couple to figure each other out and make a decision on compatibility, but an arranged marriage clearly has far superior ways. She won all and took that as a good omen. When the faith in the known falls, it's the belief in the seemingly absurd that helps one go on.

"Do they make you uncomfortable?" Vinod asked, looking at Vaidehi take her deep red bangles off once they were back in their room.

She looked up at him and replied, "Not really. I just thought since we're travelling, I'll wear lesser."

"They look beautiful. Unless you're uncomfortable, you should keep them on. In fact, mix them up a little." He walked towards her.

Her toes curled behind her saree as Vinod came closer. This was their third day of knowing each other. First was when Vinod had gone to Vaidehi's house to see her, they'd then met each other on the day of their marriage and this was their third day when they were making their first conversation. On the day of their wedding, Vinod had stolen a glance towards her, but all he could see was her slow, shy walk towards him with her head lowered. Throughout the ceremony she sat beside him, head down, not saying a word, not making a single movement unless the service required her to. It was only when he was putting the vermillion in her hair that he'd lifted the veil ever so little and that's when something had struck. It was something about those small eyes which had so confidently looked up at him, starkly contrasting her shy body. They weren't fierce, but very strong.

This was the first time Vinod had made a remark on something personal about her and it was too soon. Her heart beat faster, the blood rushed, and the smile from her heart lost its way to her lips somewhere in the nervousness. But her eyes were bold and didn't look down. They followed Vinod's steps and stayed on him decidedly. He walked over to the dressing table and bent over to the intricately carved wooden bangle stand, whose many hands held different coloured glass bangles. He took out 3-4 from each colour and stood back up holding them towards her.

"Mix them up. It'll look nice." He said again.

She looked at the bangles held in his fingers uncertainly for a moment.

"Trust me, they'll look nice," he urged her to take off some she was already wearing.

She smiled, took them off and slid them on the bangle stand. Vinod then handed her the ones he'd picked and she put them on. He turned towards the mirror and held Vaidehi's hands by the elbows.

"Beautiful," he said.

She looked in the mirror but couldn't really see her own hands, overcome by a rush of emotions as varied as the colours of her bangles. Vinod could feel her breath go faster and her body shrink.

"Let's pack and leave," he said, turning away.

Her bags were still unpacked since she'd come into the house just the previous night. She opened one of the bags and transferred some clothes into a suitcase, next to Vinod's. It was a dingy room and the light was dim, making it difficult for her to see. The house had just one room and kitchen, and while the newly married got the room, the mother and father-in-law brought out bedding every night to put on one side of the kitchen floor itself. With every meal that was cooked, their room filled up with the smell of hot spices with no window to let it out.

Somehow none of it bothered her. Coming from a background only slightly better, she was taught to be quiet, to accept the situations and yet, to be strong. This aspect of strength is precisely what reflected in her eyes. Yet, it wasn't the upbringing that kept her smiling these two days; it was a sense of love, or the idea of having that one person who was hers, exclusively. And so, in this tiny dark house, she stood smiling, unaffected by the surrounding or the people who had predicted her husband's second marriage on the day of her wedding night as she now looked down at the companionship of her and Vinod's clothes in the small suitcase. They looked equally cramped, like the actual couple in the house, but at least they were happy together.

"Let's hope it shuts. Push it down." Vinod directed, flipping the top on the bottom part of the suitcase.

They pushed together and it closed with a soft click. He heaved it from the bed and carried it out, Vaidehi following him closely.

"We're leaving, Ma," Vinod said, bending down to touch her feet.

"Take care," she replied, blessing him.

As Vaidehi bent down to do the same, her mother-in-law slightly turned her feet sideways. Still bent, she looked up. Her mother-in-law cast a dark look and averted her gaze, hands firmly at her back. Vaidehi stood up, her heart beating faster from the rejection. The shiver from last night slowly crept up on her. Gathering strength, she walked over to the father-in-law to get his blessings. He touched her head without saying anything. Vinod was already at the door and she walked out hurriedly. There were numerous houses on the floor and the neighbours had come out to peer at them as not many couples went on a honeymoon in their community. They didn't say anything nor did they smile or wave. They just stood there by their doors, staring. It was as though they were watching in anticipation for something to happen.

"Come, let's go." Vinod urged.

They walked down the stairs and Vaidehi stopped.

"I'll just use the bathroom," she said and walked towards a shared bathroom that half the building used. She stepped in and her bones cringed at the smell. She wrapped her saree around her nose and tried to breathe in deeply to calm herself down. There was nothing to hold on to and she just stood there as if her muscles were holding on to her bones for support. Her fists clenched as she urged herself to be stronger. Finally, she opened her eyes and relaxed. Suddenly, the floor moved. For a split second, it stupefied her and as a reflex, she was out the next second, walking hurriedly to Vinod.

"The floor shook!" she whispered to him.

"It does. The construction isn't good. It shakes." Vinod replied.

"Okay, let's go," she said and walked ahead.

The foundation of the family seemed much looser; she knew a shaky bathroom floor would be the least of her concerns.

*

The merciless cold of Shimla seemed to have frozen out Vaidehi's memories of her new home and she came back refreshed and feeling stronger. It was still dark when they reached home and went straight to their room to sleep. As Vaidehi closed her eyes, she could feel the bed move. But was it the loose floor or the motion sickness, she couldn't tell. All she knew was, if she made even the slightest movement of opening her eyes, she would throw up. So, she kept her eyes shut, preferring the dark of her own being instead of the one surrounding her, and slept.

She woke up to a loud knock.

"It's 6," said her mother-in-law's curt voice.

Vaidehi got up with a start and her head throbbed immediately as if the bang on the door had hit the back of her skull. She felt dizzy. Falling back on the bed, she grabbed the dustbin by the bed and threw up. She sat on the bed for a while, breathing heavily, and then got up. Grabbing the dustbin bag, she put her saree over her head and walked straight out of the house, down the stairs to the bathroom. Dumping the bag in the common bin there, she entered the bathroom and splashed some water on her face from the basin. It was piercingly cold, but it made her feel better. She couldn't feel her nose anymore. She then turned the tap on and stood there hugging herself to keep warm, staring at the bucket as it filled with water. Once full, she stripped and poured a mug on herself. It was only then that her mind de froze and the first question that popped in was, Already!?

Her heart now sped up. First with excitement and then with worry. She scrubbed on some soap, washed it off and watched the water drain away slowly. It looked black. Was it because of the dark cement floor or the dust on her body, she couldn't tell. You can never see things clearly in a place like this. Probably that's why people who got here always stayed here, for generations to come. She shivered at the thought and instinctively wrapped the same saree and went back up to her house.

Still wet, she crossed the kitchen in a flash, head bowed.

"Half an hour she was in the bathroom, and now she has gone to change and get ready. Forget it, I'll only make tea and breakfast!" her mother-in-law grumbled loud enough to wake up a few neighbours.

In the room, Vaidehi grabbed her towel with shaking hands and dried herself. Just as she was ready to strip, she realised Vinod was staring at her.

"Is everything okay?" he asked.

"Yes. It's just the cold." But as the lie slipped past her lips, she realised this won't do. In a new state, with no friends and seemingly hostile family, there was nobody else but her husband who could help.

"Actually, there's something," she said hurriedly.

"Yes?"

"I threw up this morning," she replied.

"Oh! Are you feeling alright?" Vinod asked moving over and touching her forehead to check if she had a fever.

"It's not the fever," she said. Vinod looked into her eyes and understood what she meant. As their eyes met, she searched for that spark of happiness in his. Finding none, her gaze fell.

"Maybe it's because of all the travel," she said.

"Hey, whatever it is, I'll come back early today and we'll see a doctor.

"Okay," she looked up, holding on to the care in his voice.

He walked out for a bath. She stripped and got ready hurriedly and walked into the kitchen.

"It's 7. Vinod will leave in half an hour!" her mother-in-law boomed in anger.

"I'll get to it right away," she replied, hardly audible, and started cooking.

As Vinod entered, she looked up, almost panic in her eyes. Their eyes met and he gave the slightest ever reassuring smile and went into the room. He came out, ate and left, and Vaidehi felt like she'd finished a massive chunk of work. She looked at the clock. It was only 8.

"Already in the kitchen?" A voice boomed, ringing off the walls of her home and Vaidehi found a woman from across the corridor standing there.

"So, what else is there to do?" her mother-in-law replied as she sat against the kitchen wall, sipping on tea.

"Arre baba! Give her something else to do. What is all this cooking and cleaning?" the lady said, walking over to Vaidehi. "Look at her hands, the henna hasn't even worn off...oh such soft palms," she said taking Vaidehi's palm. "You haven't worked a day in your life till now, have you?"

"No, of course, I have. At my mother's I used to cook, draw water and carry it home, keep the cows and get milk." Vaidehi replied.

"Hah! we used to do so much more and look at today's generation, a little work and they talk like they've crossed mountains!" her mother-in-law said and Vaidehi's heart sank.

"Oho! Give her something like weaving a sweater for Vinod. Don't make her wash dishes in this god forbidden cold," she said, sitting down.

"No no, I can work. What else will I do?" Vaidehi replied.

"Do you know how to stitch? Make something. Or make a sweater; it's still only December...start with something smaller if you're out of practice," the lady said smiling knowingly.

Vaidehi looked at her in shock. How could she probably know?

"I saw you were carrying a bag this morning." She smiled widely.

"Okay now, it's 9. Don't you have any work to do? Go home," her mother-in-law said and the lady walked out mumbling.

"Go and rest. Here, make a sweater." The mother-in-law said turning to

Vaidehi and handing over the materials from a trunk nearby.

Vaidehi smiled, detecting a hint of care. She took the things and left for her room.

*

7 pm sharp Vinod got home and took Vaidehi to the doctor. On the scooter, he asked, "Ma didn't ask where we were going. Did you tell her anything?"

"Nope. But she knows. Probably the whole building does," she mumbled.

"Oh! You've made friends already?" he asked.

"Na, I just puked. The sound, I guess, pierced the walls," she joked.

"Well, it didn't wake me," he laughed.

"Really? I wonder what were you dreaming about?" she asked teasingly.

"A bigger family."

Vaidehi didn't reply to that but Vinod could feel her hold go tighter on his shoulder. He wished he could see her face.

The next morning, she was in the kitchen, not needing the rest.

*

"You seem okay?" Vinod asked Vaidehi that evening in the room.

"I am. But so are you, aren't you?" Vaidehi replied, looking into his eyes. Her stare always made Vinod stumble a little. Such strong eyes.

"I would be happy no matter what," he replied.

"It didn't seem like it. You don't want a baby now, this soon, it's understandable." Vaidehi said.

"Do you?" he asked and Vaidehi didn't answer.

"Look," he said, putting his arms around her. "I want a baby too and if we were to have it now, I would be the happiest man on earth. But I won't say I'm disappointed that you aren't pregnant. I want our children Vaidehi, but..." he stopped.

Vaidehi knew what he was going to say, but she wanted to hear it still.

"We don't want the children to live here, do we? Where it's always dark and the floor shakes? I want a much better world for them, the best I can do and more. You don't know me, you don't know the struggle I've been through, and I don't want my children to go through the same. So, if we were to have a child now, I'd take that gratefully as god's blessing, but if not, I definitely want them to come into a better world," he said.

Vaidehi's eyes went moist. "I agree," she whispered.

Vinod smiled and they went to sleep.

My child will come into a much brighter world. Our generations won't live here, she thought decisively.

And her heart beat like it had never beaten before.

CHAPTER 3

Maya & Manish

"I feel like my heart doesn't beat anymore," Maya said.

"It will soon; your mother-in-law is visiting," Gaurav replied.

"Oh please! Are we still living in 1982?" Maya couldn't help but roll her eyes despite being on the phone.

Gaurav laughed. "What's the matter?" he asked.

"The same thing!! If only I could pick out the problem."

"Okay, dude, I think we both know what it is," Gaurav said and it silenced Maya.

"It's not a problem. It's just the way you are made! You'll have to come to terms with it! Marriage won't be the same happy state that it usually is because you will only and always find happiness in the forbidden! But you should know that you are in a life that's best for you. You just have to start accepting that this is how you are; from there on we can try and figure how to change it." Gaurav blurted it all out, impatient.

"You're right! I knew it all along. But then…that just means I've made the biggest mistake of my life by getting married, I have ruined this man's life! Not because I'll falter or stray, but because I will never be whole with him!" Maya replied, almost in tears.

Maya had always been like that. She would spot someone who'd take her fancy and as if magically blessed, she would end up with the person by putting in no effort at all. She had always gotten men like that: she wouldn't flirt, she wouldn't bat her eyes or do some hair flip. All she'd do is talk. Talk of the life she has, of the life she'd want, of the things she loved and the passions she had. A few conversations later, the guy would simply fall for her. Probably more for the sheer life force she exuded in her eyes, voice and being in her conversations. *"You're a breath of fresh air" "you're so incredibly full of life" "You liven me up"* were the kind of things she'd always hear. And yet, the absolute attention that she'd shower on the man until she got him, would diminish after a mere few days of the relationship.

Everything from afar seemed perfect but once she had it, it was nothing to her anymore. The excitement would die because everything that she dreamt of doing with the person would now become obvious and she could never settle for anything obvious. So, she hopped from relationship to relationship, never learning her lesson. This also seeped into other aspects of her life — when she'd achieve her career or academic goals, instead of boosting her confidence, they would seem 'easy' to her. And this sense of easy would kill her sense of achievement. She'd always been like this, the difference was, now she realised it more clearly as she suffered the consequences in depth.

"No no, don't say that. You aren't whole with him now, Maya, but that doesn't say anything about your future! You have to realise and accept this flaw completely and then it's just about training your mind, teaching it to focus where it should, that's all. Trust me." Gaurav tried to reassure her.

"So, what you're saying is, you can make yourself fall in love with someone, technically? That's shocking on so many levels! I might've been married to a male chauvinistic pig and I could've fallen in love with him? What does that say about love? If it is a matter of training the mind, why is love so hyped? It clearly has no effects of its own!" Maya burst out with questions.

"My god! Why does it have to be so complicated? You chose Manish because you saw something in him. After all, he met the pointers your partner needed to have. Still, if you feel you haven't fallen for him and the reason behind it is what it is, then just train your mind! How does it matter if love has its effects or not? Just do it, you'll be happier." Gaurav was unable to understand Maya's need to question everything, even after all these years. He wished she would stop, breathe and live happily.

But he knew that would never happen. She was carved out a certain way. With her, *don't think* just couldn't work. She questioned, at the risk of being unhappy, on finding the answers but it seemed like it wasn't in her hands to stop. She couldn't turn away towards happiness when there were elephants in the room. It was this aspect that had made her into this uneasy, uncompromising, unhappy human being. But it was also this which had made her a girl with a mind, a person with depth, someone who could understand humanity layers deeper than the rest.

"No! How could you be okay with something like that? It almost seems like it isn't true! It's forced. I can't do that!" Maya retorted.

"Fine! That's enough for now. We'll just take it one day at a time and figure this out. Calm down." Gaurav said with a sigh.

"You know you should never tell a person to calm down when they're angry," Maya said, put out.

"And particularly when you've made them angry," Gaurav replied. "You go, we'll talk again soon. Don't harass your mother-in-law."

"Shut up."

"Don't question her if it's untrue & forced to make round rotis using a mould."

"Alright then, bye!" Maya said and hung up.

She was actually quite excited to have her mother-in-law over. It was to be almost a year of her marriage and she'd still never gotten to know her well as they didn't live in the same state and this was the first time she would be spending quite some time with her. It wasn't like the olden times when the mothers-in-law were scheming, mean ladies, with 'unhappiness of the daughters-in-law' as their only purpose in life. It was the 21st century, the mothers-in-law were educated, outspoken, and in many cases, like herself, belonged to the same field education wise.

Maya was sure she'd have a nice time and for a week, she'd been getting the house in order. Getting the remotest corners cleaned, getting the bedding in order, doing up the guest bedroom and other things. It was strange. Her ideas, be it questioning things or looking forward to building a relationship with her mother-in-law, were modern, while in spirit she was traditional. She'd gotten all her bindis, jewellery and dupattas in order too—all ready to play the daughter-in-law. She'd also learnt a few new recipes she could cook. Times had changed from women doing these things out of necessity to them doing these things optionally…and every time a woman did these out of love, you know times had changed for good.

*

"There she is," Maya said pointing at her mother-in-law. Manish steered the car in her direction.

Suman stood waiting at the airport with mixed feelings about staying with her son and daughter-in-law. A literature student and a certified teacher, her personality was a strange mix. Milky white skin, short in height and plumpness made her look like a cuddly soft creature, but her eyes spoke a different story. They were confident, something that a hostel life sort of instils, for being independent from an early age, and part vacant, from the experiences and broken relationships they'd seen in adulthood. The mix of these made her face look a little strange and nobody could ever guess what must be going through her mind.

After having not so great relationship with many a relative, she was now hoping this one, with the new daughter-in-law — she had one more, as Manish had an elder brother—would be better. Would she be kind or rude? Would she treat her well or not? Would she make her feel welcome?

"Welcome, Ma!" Maya got down first and touched her feet, smiling broadly.

"Bless you, dear. How are you?" Suman said, smiling back. Silently searching Maya's eyes. They looked happy to her and that relieved her, but she didn't put her guards down just yet.

"I'm good. How are you? How was your flight?" Maya asked as Manish came around and bowed down.

"Bless you, *beta!* The flight was good! Come, let's go home." Suman said to both of them.

That night, Maya slept smiling, thinking she won't wake up to an empty house tomorrow.

*

"Morning, Ma! Here's tea." Maya said the next morning, serving breakfast to Manish and Suman.

"Thank you! Oh, it's such a beautiful day! This is such a beautiful house and what a view! Everything is so green!" Suman said, looking out of the glass balcony. The house indeed was beautiful. The room they currently sat in had a bookshelf on one wall, an arty woodwork showpiece hung on the opposite one. The third had a crockery shelf and the fourth was the glass sliding door to the balcony, with a view of otherwise empty grounds far as the eyes could see, with a soaring pagoda in the distance. Monsoons had rained them with lush green growth and overall, it looked like a wild green expanse of land. Just then it started drizzling and one could see layers of drops in the air to a distance. It looked magical.

"Honestly speaking, given the tremendous woodwork and the empty grounds beyond, during the night I felt the place to be quite depressing. I even wondered why would you choose this. But now, with the sun out, I love it. It's beautiful," Suman said.

"This is one of the best places we saw. Only one other was equally good; it had much contemporary work as compared to this. But the idea of not having to see through another balcony right beside yours is what made us pick this. Soon a building would come up here too but doesn't look like it'd happen any time soon. A little seclusion is a luxury." Manish said.

"Yes, that's true," Suman replied.

"Well, excuse me, girls, I'll have to get going," Manish said and got up to leave.

"Try and get back soon, we can go out for dinner," Maya said, walking him to the door.

"Yes, I'll be here. Be ready," he said and left.

Maya got back to find Suman cruising her bookshelf. She started clearing the table while Suman went through shelf by shelf, her reading glasses on.

"Rabindranath Tagore!" she exclaimed with a tinge of surprise.

"Yes, I love him. Feels like I can actually finally be at home that I was born too late for," Maya said.

"Well, yes, that's a perspective. For me, it's living my past. Life doesn't change much far as people and relationships are concerned. The setting, well, obviously now!" Suman said. She took *Chokher Bali* off the shelf.

"This seems interesting. I'll take my medicine and rest for a while and read this," she said.

"Alright. I'll shower and get ready till then," Maya replied.

This was probably the longest Maya took to get ready. She took out her suit, wore lenses, lined her eyes, put on a bindi and even wore toe rings and bangles. She knew she wouldn't be able to take it through the day and probably get rid of the dupatta and the bangles mid-way but nonetheless, this was the day she truly felt like a married Indian lady and the excitement was high. She stepped out to see Suman at the table with a cup of tea, looking out at the greens.

"Oh, so dressed up! Dear, please feel free to wear shorts or whatever you're comfortable in. You don't have to do this for me," Suman said, looking at Maya.

"No, I like to. Living alone here I don't even feel like I'm married, you know?" Maya replied.

"Haha! Okay, well, you look nice!" Suman said.

Maya sat down across her at the table. "Why didn't you get papa? I really wish he'd come too." Maya initiated the conversation.

"Well, we can't leave the house locked for this long," Suman replied. "And what are you reading?"

"Just Between Us by Cathy Kelly," Maya replied.

"Oh! What's it about?"

"Umm, it's a light novel. I'm just taking a break from the heavy stuff."

"Right. Good. You know, again, your father made excellent arrangements for the wedding. It went really well; all the relatives were happy," Suman said. Maya simply smiled. Was she supposed to say thank you?

"You know, I spoke to your grandmother at the wedding. Very sweet lady. She told me you have been brought up in a very warm, protected and lovable environment and that we should take care of you likewise," Suman continued.

Maya again was at a loss for words. Making conversation with your mother-in-law is harder than it had seemed. She was struggling.

"So, I told my cousin about it. Do you know what she said? She said, 'You should've told her that it's good she's lived this life. Maybe now she can see the other side!'" Suman said and laughed like it was a joke.

Maya felt something cut through her insides. Her smile dropped and so did her shoulders. Usually, in such situations with her peers, she'd given it back without blinking. But here, even the thought of standing up for herself couldn't tear through the surface of shock.

"Oh, I think I'm disturbing you. Why don't you go to your room and read in peace? I'll shower and get ready by then."

Maya stood up and left without saying a word. Back in the room, she started reading. After a couple of pages, the story drew her in and the incident was lost somewhere at the back of her mind. She didn't move and kept reading unblinkingly as if scared to stop, for then she'd have to process the incident and she'd not know what to do about it and might end up doing something drastic.

"Maya," Suman called out to her from the kitchen.

Somewhere in her mind, the anger from the morning and the sound now that disturbed her reading combined and she called back loudly,

"Haan!" She then got up and walked into the kitchen where Suman was chopping vegetables to get things ready for cooking.

"Haan? Even to my maids, I say, 'Always say *Hannji*,'" Suman gave a short laugh.

Maya had never felt so degraded in her life. The sheer audacity and heartlessness of another person to speak this way to her own daughter-in-law shocked her. She just stood there. Her heart screamed inside her but the voice somehow couldn't be set free. The independent, fierce Maya who questioned everything, couldn't raise her concern for the first time in her life.

"I know it's a little early and it's annoying to let a book go but I start cooking in advance to ensure everything gets ready on time. So come, let's start." Suman said.

Maya took another chopping board and started. Strangely, her enthusiasm to cook and please had diminished greatly. Her mind kept playing things on loop. Brought up in a loved and respected manner, in a second she was sort of reduced by this complete stranger who thought it her right to speak that way. *What was happening? Was this for real?* She failed to comprehend.

Just then, Suman started updates on family politics and history. The elderly lady, chopping veggies after veggies, recollecting how she felt mistreated in so many relationships in her life and somewhere while sharing them, she got overwhelmed. Emotions of anger, helplessness, frustration welled up as they would in anybody who wasn't able to live their life their way but had also clearly realised it was all too late now. It wasn't anger on any particular person or incident that made her so bitter, but probably the knowledge of a wasted youth, doing rounds from the kitchen to bedroom. And it all culminated into one sentence, said a little too loudly: "I don't want anything from you. I don't want your money or anything else, but a good relationship."

The younger in line, who was still coping with the earlier cruel remarks, stopped in her tracks. The emotions of the older lady got lost somewhere and culminated into an unnecessary statement for the latter. For Maya, it was a statement that implied that she'd expect her mother-in-law to be a scheming gold-digger and hence she'd felt the need to state herself out. She couldn't wait to get out of the kitchen; she'd tasted too much spice already.

During lunch, the conversation was lighter — about the economy, prices, travelling, weather and other such nonsense that every human has to grudgingly partake in. Somewhere midway, Suman brilliantly recited a poem and asked if Maya knew who had written it.

"No, can't tell," Maya said, drawn in.

"John Keats. You must've read him in literature."

"Yes, I have. Although, I'm very bad at memorising. I can read, understand, appreciate and discuss it at length but I can't remember," Maya replied.

"Ohh. I, on the other hand, remember a lot of things. Of course, it's been ages now since college but I remember certain things so vividly." Suman replied.

Lunch hence, took an interesting turn until it ended and Suman retired to rest. Where was this brilliance lost? A woman with such vast knowledge of literary beauty was today nothing but reduced to bitterness and longing for a life she wished she had. How could life be so cruel?

*

"Brooooo! Are you serious!" Gaurav said on phone.

"Yes!!! I don't get her. She swings, goes on highs and recites classics and then stoops degradingly low and becomes a...mother-in-law." Maya shared the incidents of the day with him in a hushed tone.

"Mother-in-law from 1982, you mean?" Gaurav chuckled.

She ignored it and continued, "But you don't understand. She is learned, educated, a teacher! How then does she talk of such things and behaves like that?"

"Really, Maya? Education?"

"What do you mean?"

"Don't be naive. Education has nothing to do with this! This is the irony staring in our faces with shamelessly glaring eyes. Education has always been about the technicalities, to help you become a writer or a doctor or an engineer. It doesn't mould you as a person. Or else all the educated would be perfect and others, murderers," Gaurav said.

Maya went quiet. Gaurav was correct and this changed everything. The education graded the students on their technical understanding of the subject and helped them carve out a career path, sure. But it definitely didn't carve better individuals, and neither did it promise to. So, when arranged marriages are made keeping factors like financial stability and education in mind, it nowhere implies that they will be compatible with each other otherwise. For instance, such statements which Suman made would make for a very common conversation in a certain culture and environment, but for Maya, it was rude and degrading. Her father's philosophy of going into a known family now seemed shaky.

"Okay, speak later," Maya said, mentally making a note to speak to her father.

As if Gaurav could sense it, he said, "Maya, relax, whatever you do, think twice. Don't blow things out of proportion. I'm not saying keep mum, speak out if you have to, but don't do things beyond that. Think you know what I mean."

"And I think you know I need to know," she replied and hung up.

She decided to speak to her father at night. She felt drained and decided to nap for a while.

An hour later, she was woken up with a soft knock. She got up and stepped out of the room.

"Tea?" Suman asked smiling at her.

Maya saw the table was ready with snacks and two steaming cups of tea. For a girl who'd lived in a family of six and was the youngest, to suddenly live all alone and prepare every meal herself, was daunting and only the dazed and dreamy air of being newly married could pull her through it. Seeing a table ready to be binged on, was hence, a relief she didn't even know she missed. She smiled and walked over. Just as she was sitting down, the bell rang. She walked over and opened the door to see Manish smiling down at her. Suddenly, the second half of the day looked better.

"Oh, I hope there's some for me or else one of you isn't getting a cup." He said, brimming with excitement that comes with motherly love.

"I made extra. Sit down," Suman directed.

"I'll get it," Maya said getting up.

"No, you sit down too, I'm getting it," Suman replied and walked into the kitchen.

"How was your day?" Maya asked

"Good but couldn't stay there for long. You don't know this but the seven years that I've been away, Ma has come to stay for the first time because now you're here," Manish said.

Just then Suman walked out with another cup of tea.

"Ma, we'll take you for dinner at this splendid place for a proper Nawabi meal. You'll love it," Manish said.

"Sounds nice," she replied, taking a bite of the cookie. "These are really nice, you know. I've been meaning to ask if this is a particular brand?"

"Yes, a local bakery here. It makes the best of all kinds of desserts. They're quite particular too, with instructions printed on the box of how and at what temperature should the given dessert be had, what occasion would it suit the best and so on," Maya replied.

"Interesting, not many bakeries do that," Suman said.

And so more frivolous discussions went on at tea until it was 7 and time to be ready for dinner.

Living alone does something to you. It changes you as a person, even if unwillingly. Maya loved mixing with people and being alone equally.

She always strived for a balanced time of both. After marriage, for months she'd been alone, apart from weekend parties, which some time down the line she got bored of too. She was looking forward to having another person over but strangely, as she entered her room to get ready for dinner, she felt tired. Tired of being so up and ready and talking and cooking and just having another person in the house — the chores to any other felt like a task to her. She splashed some cold water on her face, took off her lenses and other adornments. She was too tired of being a daughter-in-law. She picked out her blue jeans and a plain black t-shirt, wore her specks and green ballerinas to add some spunk and she was done. With excess kohl washed away, a fine black line now rimed her eyes, giving a subtle, fresh look. She was herself. Manish got out of the bathroom and looked at her. He only said Nice but the way she caught his gaze momentarily and he stopped what he was doing, said much more.

Soon, they were seated at a table at the dimly lit restaurant, quiet with very light music playing in the background. The ambience relaxed her. She slouched a little and took a deep breath.

"Take Thursday and Friday off, we could do something," Maya said.

"Can't, it's madness at work," he replied.

"She's only come for a couple of weeks," Maya insisted as Suman smiled.

"Exactly, she's come for too less."

"That's unfair to blame it on her. 15 days aren't too less, you need to take out time too."

"For a daughter-in-law, even 15 days are too much," suddenly Suman said.

Maya flinched ever so slightly. Did she say something offensive? She was still struggling to make sense of it, not knowing how to react when Manish said, "Ma, please."

Maybe 15 days were going to be too much after all.

CHAPTER 4
Vaidehi & Vinod

They say you're given only so many struggles that you can take. Hence, every struggle that you're destined to face always comes with an unwavering promise that you can get through it. That is probably why Vaidehi did not walk out of her marriage. Not that she did not understand the magnanimity of the situation, but it's human nature that acts in the strangest of ways. Somehow the shock of it all automatically wired her to learn to cope with the situations rather than thinking of quitting. Also, the first step to dealing with anything came naturally to her: acceptance. Ironically, being brought up old-school saved her marriage. She'd had a life where your mind, body and soul start loving the person you marry. You can't think of a life outside of him, and this simple-mindedness has such power that even a thought of separation can't permeate it. She'd end up spending her entire life with Vinod and also be happy in ways that one would find difficult to understand; but is that a good or a bad thing, would always be debatable.

Around the beginning of the second year of her marriage, the sun seemed to have decided to rise on her already. Her father-in-law and Vinod collectively had managed to save enough to move out of the cubicle of a place they lived in, to a much better, independent house. The first impression of the place on Vaidehi was that the house had so much potential for stories.

It was a kind of a small society where everyone knew everyone else. They were constantly talking over the small boundaries that divided their houses, gossiping, sharing recipes, solutions to household problems, making plans for the next fair and other such things that made the afternoons ripe with hope. The house, to explain simply, was divided into 4 rectangular sections, horizontally placed. The entry gate led to the first, which was a decently big verandah, with a section of square cut out for a garden on the left corner. Right there, the stairs lead to the terrace upstairs. In the garden, the grass was scarce but two swings hung, making indications to the future that made Vaidehi smile.

The two adjacent doors at the end of the verandah led to the second rectangle of space — one to a bedroom and the other to the living room. Post the two rooms, there was another open space that didn't have a ceiling and the sun-scorched the surface. At the right end of the open area, there was a common bathroom and a toilet and an open washing area for clothes and utensils. Ahead of this was the final rectangle of space, divided into a second bedroom and kitchen. It was like a polo with a hole, but square in shape; and for Vaidehi, dimensionless in possibilities.

With getting a bigger house, came the money crunch and Vinod was now working even harder. Working double jobs, he seemed to be always away from home. He would work at a firm as an engineer until 6 pm, post which, he would spend time working at a business he and a friend hoped would pick up. He would get home in time for dinner, eat and study for his MBA entrance exams. Vaidehi spent days after days keeping up the house, cleaning, cooking, stitching, on loop. But there were moments when she felt like a ghost, wandering amidst the walls. Of course, her mother-in-law spoke about things constantly, and Vaidehi, like a perfect daughter-in-law, listened to them very carefully. She wanted to know everything in and out about her new family.

"My family lives further up north. You know, they own about 7 bungalows in a row; one for each brother of mine and their family. Earlier, we were even wealthier; we owned acres and acres of land, as far as the eye could see — it was all ours. But then one spoiled generation wiped a big chunk of it all."

Vaidehi was enraptured in the tale and yet again wondered at the fact that her mother-in-law, even at that age, spoke of *her* family so fondly, while of her husband's, with a clear detachment. She found it strange, as, for her, Vinod's family was already hers. She wondered if her mother-in-law could ever really settle into the family. Or she did in the beginning and all the bitterness had gradually found a way into her life, pushing out all the *belongingness*. Would that happen to her too?

"It's your duty to ensure Vinod never drinks." She was snapped out of her thoughts as her mother-in-law shouted, pointing a finger at her. Vaidehi's eyes were wide with fear.

"Alcohol! That's the demon that burns everything to ashes. They used to have parties every night. Drinks used to flow like water; there was no end to gambling. Fools! So much gone…" her mother-in-law trailed off. Vaidehi stole a look at her. Her eyes were still focused on getting the stones out of lentils but the story that was flashing in them was something else. The look of anger, regret and sadness was haunting.

Vaidehi continued stitching her blouse. If she could've looked up at her mother-in-law, she would've seen how bothered she was by what the time had done and how helpless she felt, for she couldn't undo it. But all those emotions had to erupt somewhere and her restless eyes finally found a destination in the new, shy, seemingly weak daughter-in-law.

"You've been working on that since yesterday? I guess some parents stopped teaching their children well. This is how you do it," she said, snatching the blouse and taking it to her own room. Shocked, Vaidehi was left motionless on the stool she was sitting on. Her mother-in-law came out a minute later with a cloth in hand and an old stitched blouse. She walked over to Vaidehi and snatched the scissors out of her lap.

Vaidehi hurriedly got off the stool. In the next couple of hours, she stood there watching her mother-in-law cut and stitch her blouse. Vaidehi loved stitching. She'd been stitching clothes for herself since she was much younger. She would look at the magazines her father would sometimes get and replicate the designs she loved from it. Now, seeing her mother-in-law stitch, she could tell every tiny mistake she was making and knew the horrendous result they all would culminate into. But she didn't have the guts to voice this and so she watched silently.

Finally, when it was done, she held it up and said, "Do you see this? That's all there is to it. What have you been doing for two days? There's a lot to do and you can't avoid real work by acting busy. Blouse or no blouse, I need that trunk of wheat cleaned."

Vaidehi just stood there, her eyes downcast. She wasn't used to standing up for herself, probably because she'd never had an insult before.

"Take this and iron it. I will wear this day after," she held out the poorly stitched blouse to Vaidehi.

She took it and turned to go to her room to iron the blouse when her mother-in-law called out again.

"We make the sweets at home for the puja." She nodded and went into her room, gladly drawing the curtains.

That night post-dinner, she spoke to Vinod about what had happened.

"It's all starting." That's all he'd said but Vaidehi could see the storm of worry in his head. He was a hard-working man, the kind who would get there despite all odds, no matter how great they were. Nothing seemed to bog him down. But now, his shoulders hung slightly low, as if he felt incredibly tired. Maybe sharing this was a bad idea, for his sake.

*

The next morning after she'd seen Vinod off for the day, she started chopping vegetables for the next meal. She washed a bunch of okra and picked 4-5 of them in one hand. Slicing them in small circles with a knife in the other hand, slowly she lost herself in the activity. The flower-like insides of the okra were so beautiful, sprinkled with smooth seeds, but it had to be chopped off and separated into little pieces for that beauty to come out. But they stuck together with stickiness oozing out, making everything dirtier. They refused to let go, even if they were never going to be whole again. *So much like humans; maybe that's how relationships work,* Vaidehi thought.

"How much time will that take now?" Her thoughts were interrupted by her mother-in-law. She always had this disgusted look on her face — her brows creased, nose scrunched up and sort of hatred in her eyes. Why did she always look at her like that? Vaidehi had a questioning look on her face, when her mother-in-law said, "Where is your tongue? Do you use it for anything other than eating?"

Vaidehi flinched and her palms broke into a sweat. "Almost done," she replied and turned away.

In the afternoon, as she lay down to rest, she forced herself to think of other things. There was a trip coming up for a wedding out-of-station. Vinod had relatives there, a lot of cousin brothers. It would be good to know the people she'd only met at her wedding. Thinking of this lifted her spirits a little. She then glanced at her arms — she needed to wax. She knew of a local parlour nearby. She got up, picked up some money and walked out of the room.

"Where are you going?"

She saw her mother-in-law standing by the door of her bedroom. It looked like she'd walked out immediately on seeing Vaidehi walking towards the gate.

"I need to go to the parlour."

"Parlour? For what? Do you think we have so much money that you can go around spending on enhancing your beauty? There will be nothing of that!"

It wasn't only the words that shocked Vaidehi but also the sheer volume at which her mother-in-law had shouted. She stood there stupefied, unable to understand what to do when someone knocked on the gate.

"You didn't sleep today, aunty*ji?*"

Vaidehi saw a woman standing in the verandah — short, slim, with thick, black braided hair that touched the back of her knees. There was a certain clever intensity in her eyes that were lined with kohl. But there was also an intellectual kindness that Vaidehi sensed in her. What amazed her, though, was that she could read someone so clearly within 10 seconds of seeing her. And she liked people with such strong personalities.

"I was just going to sleep; finished cleaning the utensils. You go inside, meet Vaidehi."

Vaidehi was shocked at how easily her mother-in-law lied about cleaning the utensils. The lady meanwhile quickly walked and came to Vaidehi, smiling.

"I'm Nalini, I live next door," she said, looking up at Vaidehi but her eyes seemed to be judging how she would be, rather than just expecting an answer.

"I'm Vaidehi. Please come inside."

"Were you going somewhere?" Nalini asked looking at Vaidehi.

"Yes, I thought I'll go to the parlour, needed a wax."

"Oh, I'm sorry, I'll come back later then."

"No no, please sit. Will you have some tea?"

Nalini looked at Vaidehi's discomfort for a moment and understood everything. It was a small society with row houses that were constructed exactly the same way. Strangely, the situations in the families dwelling in them matched too. The problems differed, intensities differed, but the dynamics were the same. The walls always failed to conceal things that must always stay within the family, as if aiding the women to gossip.

"Yes. Why don't you make some tea and I'll rush to my house and come back."

"Okay, sure."

When Vaidehi got back inside the room with two cups of tea, she saw Nalini sitting down with a tin of wax and some fresh strips of cloth.

"We'll have tea first and then we can wax. I always wax at home. You know, it's much more hygienic than that parlour. Don't go there for anything other than threading."

And just like that, Nalini won Vaidehi's heart. It wasn't just that little help of hers, but the tact with which she found ways out of situations without embarrassing the other. Neither did she bad-mouth her mother-in-law in any way. There was so much positivity in her. Vaidehi was still wondering if Nalini would understand if she shared things with her when just before leaving, Nalini whispered to her: "Kamla aunty*ji* didn't do the utensils, did she?"

There was such child-like mischief in her eyes that she broke into a hearty giggle. For the first time in days, Vaidehi felt lighter to have finally found a friend.

*

It was finally Sunday and Vaidehi woke up earlier than usual. There was much to be done as the puja was at 12 pm. She bathed and wore a saree that she would change later to a red one, and headed straight to the kitchen. She opened the fridge the first thing and took out the Milkmaid tin Vinod had got her the previous evening on his way back from work. She held it in her hands and smiled. She'd learnt of a new recipe for some coconut sweet using Milkmaid that promised tastier results. This was the first time she was using something fancy and it excited her. Even generally, in a household like Vaidehi's, a festival or a ceremony or a puja brought about a slight wave of happiness. Even if everything else was falling apart, on an auspicious day, everyone smiled. Maybe it wasn't always so and someone some time may have made it a rule and with passing generations, it became a habit.

Vaidehi started with grating the coconut while putting the milk to boil and running other chores in the kitchen simultaneously. She was at it for about an hour and the sweet was finally ready. She spread a thick layer on a plate and set it to freeze. She then started with the meal that everyone would have post puja. Despite having to make an extra dish, she was relieved that she had to make one meal less as no one was supposed to eat until the puja was done. After about another hour, her mother-in-law entered the kitchen. It seemed like she was cruising the slab with a purpose: to pick on something. Finally, she spotted the empty Milkmaid tin and picked it up.

"What's this?"

"Oh, it's Milkmaid. I learnt of this new recipe to make sweets with it. I've already set it to freeze."

She waited with bated breath, realising only now the consequences of spending money on something like that. How could she have forgotten about it in all the excitement while asking Vinod to get it? Kamla took a breath in and her forehead creased like it always did and it seemed like she was about to say something, when suddenly as if something had struck her, she let out a breath, kept the tin back and walked out quietly. Vaidehi stood there for a few moments as if ensuring there wasn't going to be any shouting, then relieved, she got back to work. Maybe she was overthinking things.

By 11:30 Vaidehi was looking in the mirror, ready for the puja. Her sight struck Vinod, who was standing right behind her. She was clad in a simple red saree, hands full of maroon glass bangles and a couple of gold ones bookending them. Just above her red bindi sparkled her maangtikka that she'd worn during their wedding. It made her eyes look even more fierce. Vinod must've been staring at her for a long time as he realised Vaidehi had bowed her head and was smiling. Just like that, a compliment was given and received. They walked out towards the puja room.

Soon it was done and Vaidehi hurried into the kitchen while Kamla set the table. Just as she was about to carry out the sweets, Kamla stopped her.

"Let's have the prasad here." The ladies of the family never ate with the men. As the daughter-in-law and father-in-law never even looked at each other openly, she always made rotis and Kamla served them hot, while the men ate. As per the custom, Vaidehi covered her face with her saree when her father-in-law was around.

Vaidehi uncovered the lid and offered it to Kamla and took one for herself. She took a bite and smiled as she loved the taste and turned around to look at Kamla for her reaction. Kamla saw Vaidehi turn towards her and only then took a bite, and as if she hated the taste, let out a loud yuck. She bent over as if she would puke, then without saying anything, she snatched the sweets container from her and carried it to the dining table.

Vaidehi froze in shock until eventually her eyes welled up. She turned around and started making rotis. By the time the men had finished eating and had gone into their rooms, it was already 2. But Vaidehi's hunger had vanished. Still, with rotis made, she walked to the dining table and sat down to eat with Kamla. The dining table was kept on one side of the living room itself. The rest of the room had sofas and the TV played in one corner. She tried to focus as best as she could on Chitrahar and soon enough she was lost in melodious songs, watching the sarees the heroines wore.

Kamla accidentally dropped her spoon and bent to pick it up, the sound bringing

her back. That's when she noticed the blouse her mother-in-law had stitched the other day. Vaidehi noticed how poorly it had come out—loose from the waist so when she bent, her bra showed and was constantly coming off the shoulders. No wonder there was something so weird about Kamla since the puja started; she was just trying to hold the blouse in place, without constantly adjusting it with her hands.

Vaidehi bowed her head to conceal the smile that was trying hard to hold her giggle back.

*

It was the evening they were all leaving for Vinod's cousin's wedding. They took a train that got them to their destination in the wee hours. Vinod's eldest cousin was there to pick them up. On their way home, her mother-in-law inquired about the usual things: how many sarees were given, the jewellery and money that the new bride was bringing in. It was an acknowledged right of the relatives to know of such details of a marriage.

"I've heard her family has a jewellery shop for decades. That must be good."

"Oho, chachiji, you please ask all this to the ladies at home. I'm just killing myself running around with the preparations."

With that, Kamla sat quietly again. The same creased brows and lips pressed together, as if angry about something. By now Vaidehi had understood that it wasn't really anger, but the life that had left an imprint on her face which now appeared as naturally to her as a smile would to another person.

When they reached home, Vaidehi got down and looked up at the huge house in front of her. They went in and the only daughter-in-law, Padmini, greeted them, along with her mother-in-law, Laxmi. There was the general touching of feet and other greetings, post which their luggage was kept in one of the rooms and Vaidehi and Padmini headed to the kitchen to make tea for everyone.

"Are you settling well?" Padmini asked Vaidehi in a hushed tone in the kitchen.

"Yes..."

"Sshhh..." Padmini cut Vaidehi off. "Talk softly or else she'll get angry," she said. Vaidehi kept quiet, not sure if she was talking about Laxmi.

"Can you pass on the sugar? Please do it quietly."

Vaidehi did so without making a sound. Padmini then started talking about other things. "You know, our husbands are very closely knit. In fact, so are our families. You know the relationships already but you'll get to see the bond too."

Vaidehi smiled in response and Padmini continued. "I'm so excited another woman is coming into the family. Right now it's just me and my mother-in-law," her tone went down even further as she made a reference to Laxmi but the excited way she stirred her tea showed how truly she was looking forward to having another lady in the house. Her bangles clinked merrily. Vaidehi smiled and she was about to say something when suddenly she heard Laxmi shout: "What is that noise you're making? If that is a code to call your husband, let me tell you he's gone out with his brothers. If I hear one more sound, I'll take away all your jewellery to ensure nothing else clinks!"

Vaidehi watched as Padmini held her palm tightly against her chest, trying to calm her breathing. She felt all her excitement draining out from her feet, leaving them cold and her knees shivering. Once they served tea and had something to eat, they immediately got down to prep for lunch. By the time they were done, they had a couple of hours left before they would start making rotis for lunch. Padmini told Vaidehi to take a shower and then come to her room.

*

Soon, the two women were in a room alone and Padmini was making conversation to get to know each other better. Vaidehi liked that

Padmini's room was darker but cool and had a sort of calming effect on her. She felt safe there and could really breathe as if the darkness would conceal her. Being the eldest, and for now, the only daughter-in-law of the family, she was given the biggest room in the two-storey building.

"The house is big but it's all that's left from the previous generations. My mother-in-law and my husband have seen times I would not wish on anyone else. My father-in-law passed away when my mother-in-law was still young and she had five children's education and marriage to take care of. My husband soon left his studies and started working because there's only so much a single woman with no education can earn."

"Do you feel scared?" Vaidehi asked. She'd been building up the courage to ask it and finally, she just blurted it out.

"I do."

"Do you tell *bhaisaab* about it?"

Padmini sighed. She then said, "Look, when I got married, on my first night itself my husband told me what the family's situation was. He also told me how my mother-in-law would treat me. But he also said that when he gets home after work, he doesn't want to hear about any of it. He will be killing himself out there to make ends meet and so I should deal with whatever happens at home by myself, without complaining. Since then, I just take it and keep quiet."

It is intriguing how human brains can be conditioned to anything. Those times were different and so was the culture, where you could tell a woman to take insults after insults, without standing up for herself or even sharing it with her partner. While a marriage is said to be an institution of companionship and creating a life together, this seemed to be a never-ending chore. Padmini was a human being, brought up with love, care and respect. But the day she stepped into another house, she was simply told that she would be insulted and will be miserable and yet she should quietly accept it. And she agreed to this stranger of a man that was her husband. Did she do it out of love? Or out of the conditioning her mind had, seeing the same thing with her own parents? It's shocking how a marriage was reduced to such technicalities, but for

Vaidehi, this raised her bar of respect for Padmini.

The next day, the daughters of the house had come down to attend their brother's wedding that was to take place in the night. The house erupted in laughter and chatter. It's intriguing how a flower manages to push it's way out in a land full of weeds. The wedding went on till the wee hours and soon, the new bride entered the house, with a heart full of hopes. Padmini finally had someone younger to share the wrath with. Laxmi had one more person to pass on the hatred to.

*

"You're exhausted," Vaidehi said to Vinod. They were back at their place. It was around 11 in the night and they were lying in bed, with Vaidehi's hand resting on Vinod's chest. It was something about the way his chest heaved that night that told Vaidehi that it wasn't just the journey that had been tiring. It was probably life and there was so much happening that probably was bogging Vinod down. The exhaustion was taking over. There comes a time in every person's life where they feel their life should step up. And so we set out, looking for possibilities that we should grab. However, when the intensity of our intentions somewhere edges into desperation, that's when we start hoarding. Just like an old woman who stuffs away things like little pieces of wood left back by the carpenter, shreds of cloth left from the last sewing job, or even several empty pens with no intention of getting refills. It gives her a strange sense of security to have these objects if the need ever arises, despite knowing it never would. Likewise, we start hoarding up on double jobs and classes for more degrees, hoping to achieve better paying double jobs, meanwhile losing out on so much our present has to offer. When you're always in a hurry, a hot cup of ginger tea will always burn your tongue, the sound of bangles will become a redundant background score and finishing the lunch box will become a race against time.

"We don't need it, Vinod. I would rather have you home for longer than just a little more money that two jobs bring you. Leave it. I don't ask for anything more. You're earning for a better life while it waits for you to enjoy it back home."

And finally in years Vinod could breathe a little more.

CHAPTER 5
Maya & Manish

Maya locked her bedroom door and undressed. As she took her top off, the familiar smell of her sweat hit her. She felt disgusted. Maya sweated a lot but it had nothing to do with the weather. This is how her body was crafted and she had never really given it a second thought. But over a period of time, she observed how the smell made her feel as she took off her top every night.

At her previous job she was organising an event, a first for her, and the work had drained every drop of energy from her. She'd slept for three or four hours each night for two months straight. After running around through the day and most of the time in the heat, she would drive back home in her car with the AC on full blast. Each night, when she took her top off, the smell of the sweat was different than it was today. The sweat that had dried off some time back and yet clung on through its smell. The kind that made your nose scrunch up with shock, like a sudden flick on the tip of the nose. It was powerful. The smell today, however, smelt like confusion and disappointment. It was as if the ugliness of her bottled up feelings was seeping out through her underarms. It was foul and made her heart sink. It seemed like her sweat glands had their claws firmly clenched into her brain. The more her mind raced, the harder she sweated and the flavour always synced with the seasoning of her feelings.

This morning, like most mornings these days, she thought of the dynamics of the relationships which controlled the weather of her house. Even as a teenager learning the ropes of feminism, she'd stuck on to what felt right stubbornly. However, she found herself confused all these years later. She remembered those aggressive arguments she'd had with her parents about women in Indian middle-class society and the passionate exchanges with her girlfriends about setting their own rules and promising never to compromise. And yet, when it was time to stand up for herself, she found herself holding back. Initially of course, it was a shock. Then it was the benefit of the doubt: 'maybe she'd not quite understood things right'. But now it had truly struck her that even in today's day and age, a woman could treat another that way and actually feel entitled to it. She was at a loss for how to respond. She didn't want to fight or be rude; her mother's values of how to be a bride had after all filtered into her without her notice. It annoyed her, not being able to speak up. It was a strange upbringing failure—etching traditional thoughts into a free spirit. Relentlessly a mother had worked to ensure peace in her daughter's future and had ended up creating a fight in the daughter's mind instead.

She took off her pyjamas, panties and bra and chucked them into the laundry basket. She walked over to her dressing and took out a cigarette from the bottom drawer. As she was getting up, her reflection in the mirror caught her attention and she stood to look. She slid her hand across her chest, held the round of her breasts and lightly pressed the now fattening stomach that once used to be flat effortlessly. She turned sideways as her hands rounded her hips. It had taken her years, but now the stretch marks there didn't bother her as much. The cold that had menacingly eyed her skin when she undressed, now seeped into her pores and made them bumpy and her feet chilly. As a reflex, she put one foot over the other—warming one and further icing out the other and the comfort of one completely erased the discomfort of the other. Just like being in love helps you float through every struggle.

She needed to wax, the dreaded reminder hit again and it tired her. How could a newlywed allow her body hair to grow so much? She loved her waxed body, but the effort even for that minimal maintenance exhausted her. It was too much of an effort to care. She noticed how the thick, long hair on her calves turned denser and curlier on the topmost, inner thigh area. Apart from everything else, to uphold the decision of not razing was such an effort too. She grew colder and the hair stood up. A chill went down her and a shudder shook her out of whatever trance she was in. She tied her hair up in a flash, ready for a shower, when she noticed another thing about her body. Her breasts moved up and back down into position with the movement of her hands. A shock of a thought ran through her mind that physically showed in the worry line that her eyebrows squeezed out and the drops of sweats that ran down from her armpits down the sides of her torso: Sagging already? As if ignoring a show she didn't like, she hit the remote, and swapped to the bathroom in three big strides. She lit her cigarette and blew out, thinking how she hated to hide and smoke. She hated doing anything in hiding, it made her feel weak. It was the same thought that made her feel so restless about the dynamics at her home too—hiding how she truly felt. And from that sprang a deep sense of disappointment which grew stronger each time she kept quiet. A disappointment that scampered about in the brain, nibbling holes into one's sensibility, dirtying the thoughts that leaked and remained half-eaten, infected with the poisonous saliva of bitterness.

The struggle that was much bigger wasn't in her home but within herself. It made her uncomfortable to find herself in her mother's shoes. When she realised that she wanted peace and maybe that's why her subconscious held her tongue, she was in a violent divide within herself. She felt a rush of painful warmth clutch into the nerves of her face as her throat went lumpy and her eyes welled up. The incidents that her mother had confided in her about how her in-laws had treated her came invading into her nakedness. The stories had wrenched innocence out of Maya's heart. She'd found her mothers eyes curtained thickly with tears and yet always pulled back the moment before they would drop. *We're so naive, us humans, thinking it's not crying if the tears don't drop.* The conversations always ended with her mother saying: "but I always kept quiet. And that's why our family is a family today. Together. And that's why I'm respected so much amidst the friends and the relatives." And Maya, lying awake at night beside the grandmother about whom her mother had just confided in, would answer her mother, "But was it worth it? All those years, your youth, gone in trauma. Only getting back respect for not standing up for yourself from relatives who would talk the moment you turned your back?" *But it was a different time,* she would eventually tell herself, trying to fool her mind from racing.

And yet, several years later, she found herself to react no differently than a lady from the generation before. Preferring a peaceful life so badly that she refused to stand up for herself. Then it must be true; every human being desires and expects happiness in money, status, fame and anything else they pursue. She desired it too and looked for it in a peaceful family. Then why is it that she stood naked and shivering on a cold bathroom floor, puffing the life out of her lungs? Maybe because, just like in money, status, fame, or any other materialist possessions, happiness did not necessarily lie in peace either.

*

It was 12 pm and Maya went to the kitchen to knead the dough for lunch. Like a sundry butterfly, a thought lightly fluttered in her mind: Do I smell of smoke? and she was surprised to find how monumentally indifferent she was if she did.

In an ideal world, it would be an obvious consequence of growing up with respect to freedom of choice. Here, however, it qualified for rebellion at least, if not courage. This deep sense of unmendable disappointment at least gave her some liberation. Or maybe it felt so because, even for a wrong choice, she, in her own subtle way, stood up for herself. She scooped out the flour and had just filled up a glass of water when Suman entered the kitchen.

"Oh, you're kneading? Alright, I'll chop the veggies then." Maya just smiled and nodded. She feared her voice would betray her emotions.

"You've taken the water from the Bisleri bottle? You know, maybe you should use the water from the filter for kneading, at least. Bisleri should be for drinking only, you know, it's a big pack of water, must cost at least Rs 70."

Just like that, her rich, artful persona contrasted against a woman that was ripped off her possibilities and designated into a poor household, scavenging to save as much as she could. The woman who then was made to economise on chapatis and spices, not because of lack, but because she was a daughter-in-law.

Something snapped in Maya and she spoke, "How much could we save per glass on a Rs 70 pack? Ma, it's not that bad." But what she actually wanted to say was, "We aren't slum dwellers."

By the time both women finished lunch and retired into their rooms, Maya realised the thing that had snapped in her wasn't her silence, but something entirely different. When she'd married, she'd entered an empty home, except for a couple of plastic chairs, an old TV kept on the floor and a bed in the bedroom. And even though her in-laws were capable of providing a decent living environment, Manish had refused to take any help. Her husband's unwavering self-respect didn't have as much glory as she'd anticipated. She knew that life wouldn't be the same as she vaguely knew Manish's family wasn't as well-off as hers. But this afternoon when Suman voiced concern over something worth Rs 70, Maya's strength in settling down into this difficult lifestyle is what snapped.

She could now feel it in her bones the urban-poor situation that she was in. So, whatever had happened to Suman, decades later was happening to Maya. A sudden regret seized her heart and choked the tears out of her eyes. Did the cycle ever end? Why did she agree to an arranged marriage when she did not believe in it? She should've stood up for herself and not given in. She wasn't forced but somehow convinced and now, even though she couldn't remember the exact moment when her mind transformed, she regretted it. A sense of bitterness oozed inside her, for Suman. She was aware that Suman had only voiced out a mother's concern and yet, Maya felt too shaken at the deficient finances. She may not have thought this marriage proposal through, but she was happy until Suman actually came into her life and said the statement that turned her life upside-down, however unintentionally.

But was this marriage a mistake? It was an arranged one and her parents had always strongly maintained it's always better than love. Then why was she piled up unhappily on the bed, sobbing away in the middle of the afternoon? She thought back to those rare, arranged marriages versus love marriages discussions in her home. Maya had always kept in mind one thing her mother had told her: "If you haven't done wrong, you need not be afraid." And yet, if there was one time when Maya would be genuinely scared was during these discussions. While the rebel in her couldn't hold back, once the words were out, fear would take over. She just couldn't stand up for her opinion of believing in a love marriage over an arranged one. These arguments always turned strangely ugly in a passive-aggressive manner. Her mother wouldn't look up from her plate and seemed like she'd burst into tears any moment. Her dad argued back in a tone that always gave away what he was thinking: *"Why don't you come to the point? If you have somebody in your life, why don't you just say it?"* But he would never really ask that directly. Threats are, after all, more scary than the real attack itself, given the intensity of its mystery. Or was he just afraid that his daughter would actually name a guy she loved? Anger surged in her for her parents, accusing them of her current state. She had been planning to call her father for quite some time. Now she aggressively picked up the phone and dialled.

"Hello *bete*! How are you?" the familiar calm and poise in her dad's voice that had once calmed her, sent another wave of anger through her brain today. She held herself back but couldn't do better than a direct question. "Do you love mom?"

"What? Well, I don't know about love but I do know that your mom, you, Manish and your brother and sister-in-law are my whole world," he replied.

Strangely, she felt like she wasn't speaking to her father. What was this conversation? They never spoke about things like *love*! Amidst the anger and this feeling of strangeness, Maya's mind boggled and out came those words tumbling, "I don't think I love Manish."

The moment just after she said this, a lot of things shocked her. The finality in her words, tone and inside her was one. Another was a slow creeping in of the realisation that she'd actually called to speak of her mother-in-law and this came out of nowhere. Astounded, she froze. She felt no emotion of any kind. She was in a null until the familiar tone jerked her back into life.

"What happened?" the graveness in her father's voice was tentative of what he might hear. This fear deep down that his daughter would say something that would crack his snow globe of a perfect life. There was also a sense of tiredness that shrieked *why can't you just be happy* which angered her so much she started to shake slightly. With clenched teeth, she decided to fight back.

"Nothing. But I don't think I love him!" she defied him.

"*Beta*, love isn't sparks and fireworks. How do you even know you don't love him?"

How could he ask that question when he claimed he didn't know about love? All he wanted to do was to convince her that she loved her husband so that life could peacefully move on. Love, according to him wasn't an absolute presence, rather, a by default assumption in a relationship where everything was alright on a stereotypical scale. But then she could love a friend or a dog by that logic. But *marriage* — that is what was required for the assumption of love to prevail.

"Your mother has been telling me about things your mother-in-law has been doing. I know everything that you have confided in her."

"I don't feel appreciated, loved or respected here," Maya held back a sob.

"But *beta*, you must learn to ignore her. There is no solution to this. If you want to be happy there, you must simply not pay heed to these kinds of things that she says," he replied.

It was that one word that did the trick: IGNORE. If Suman had compared Maya to her maidsearvant by teaching her to respond with a *hannji*, her father was teaching her to ignore the insults, just like the servants do. This was probably the angriest Maya had been in her life of 25 years. She wanted to scream her lungs out, she wanted that calm in her father's voice to shatter. She wanted to tell him how mistaken he was. She wanted to ask him how he could be okay with somebody treating his daughter like that? Where was the fatherly love? Or was marriage bigger than his own daughter's happiness? What was the point of an institution like marriage? Why had she married? Just so she could have children and die eventually? Was she to live life like an animal?

However, "Yes" is all she could manage to say as of now. No matter what she said to him, she knew he won't understand. And what was it that she expected him to say? Could she say it to herself?

"Did you know that they weren't well-off when you married me off?" she asked, her voice surprisingly soft.

"*Beta*, you know how my condition was when your mother was married to me. What if she would've left me because I didn't have enough money?"

The simplicity of his answer surprised Maya. He was supposed to be her father, much wiser; how could he say something like that? Was he really that naive? Or he just wanted Maya to be okay at any cost? She refused to let it go and argued further. "But she came from a similar background!!! This wasn't a struggle to her!"

"I'm there. I have earned my entire life so I can pass it to on to my children. You have no deficiency! It's all yours, you take it," his father replied.

Maya felt so disgusted she thought she'd throw up. What kind of stagnating cultural swamp was she born into? Long as it was arranged marriage, nothing else mattered — whether the girl felt loved or respected or appreciated, nothing mattered. As long as she would stay there. Arranged marriage was never about eventually falling in love, it was learning to be happy no matter what. But was that even possible? Could one be happy if they lived with someone they didn't love? Or where they were demeaned? What was it that held a marriage together? As of now, it seemed like only one thing: societal pressure. It wasn't Maya who felt the pressure, it was her parents and she had to live her life so that her parents could live in the society. Maya hung up the phone. Her father, knowing her too well, didn't call back. She, knowing her father too well, knew her silence would cause him more pain than words ever could. She knew he had a way to take words and nullify their effect so that the situation at hand would seem small. Hence, silence triumphed. If she'd called him for answers, she realised she didn't have the stomach for them.

*

That evening, Maya was quiet. She wanted to rebelliously explode but all she could do was freeze everyone out. To think of it, they were such small incidents, hardly even to be called incidents, but they had such a strong impression on her. Was it really the words that bothered her? Or was it the fact that those words were spoken by her mother-in-law? Was it the financial condition that was finally breaking her? Or was it the fact that she felt she didn't love Manish? She definitely knew that love could've solved a lot of things. Such is the haze of it.

Maya made tea and she and Suman had it in silence. Suman wasn't generally this silent at all. Maya wondered whether she felt guilty and hence awkward around her now after last night's dinner. If it weren't rude sentences, now it was this awkward silence. Her house was indeed slowly transforming into one of those typical households where women could never be at peace.

Manish got home when Suman was in the kitchen, winding up dinner. They hugged but Maya couldn't look him in the eye. She felt tired. Just then Suman came out.

"You're home! Great, today is Gurupurnima; we have to go to the temple. Why don't you too get ready?"

"In a minute," Manish said.

"Umm, I don't usually go to temples. I can't come, you guys go ahead. I'll serve the dinner as soon as you're back," Maya replied. It was true, she never did visit temples but in another time, if things were okay, she would've agreed. But now, the action was getting the inevitable reaction. Manish could sense it too.

"No, but it's Gurupurnima! You must come to the temple!" Suman said, eyes wide. Something ticked off in Maya and she folded her feet on the sofa, making herself comfortable, in a way saying she was definitely not going.

"No, I really don't go to temples," she replied, not looking at Suman.

"Ma, please, she really doesn't go to temples. I'll take you," Manish cut in.

While some love could've yielded anything, just about everything from

Maya, the force could never even have her blink. Boundary issues have always existed in an Indian middle-class households. Members of the family don't just step into each others physical space, but also others' sense of beliefs and values. Maya felt that they just wouldn't let the other breathe their own air! Soon, Manish and Suman left and she felt like she could breathe again. She took out a cigarette and dialled Gaurav.

"I can't comprehend what's happening to me," she said as soon as he picked up. She wasn't sobbing and her voice wasn't weak and yet Gaurav could sense the deep trouble that deadened the spark out of her voice. For once, he didn't joke.

"Tell me what happened."

"All this while I've been wondering about love but I don't think it exists. This afternoon I spoke to dad and you can imagine how that must've gone. For once, he managed to quieten me, rather than have me erupt. He told me to ignore whatever Suman says. How could a father be okay with the way his daughter is being treated? He's my father!! But that's not it. At that moment, I wanted to break that calm in his voice, that poise and that confidence. I wanted to shatter it to pieces and I wanted the shards to stab into his heart to bleed out some kind of rage or any feeling out of it—something that is so so strong, that it tells me to do something...to actually do something, and not just sit quietly and IGNORE.

Whether it was fighting back, talking it out patiently, or even leaving this house for good—I don't care about WHAT he should've asked me to, as long as he would've asked me to DO something rather than take it all quietly. I wanted him to love me more than he loves what society would think. I wanted him to know that I'm stronger than the society's hatred for a divorced woman. I wanted him to know that I'm capable of being happy outside of a marriage and that that kind of happiness also exists. Can you imagine that? Can you imagine a father willing his daughter to be quiet against this situation? Can you imagine a daughter with such rage that she wanted her father to feel the pain she was feeling? Shouldn't he rescue me out of this misery? Should I hide my feelings so that at least he can be protected from the pain? Shouldn't there be unconditional love between a parent and a child? Why isn't it there between us? If there can't be unconditional love between a parent and a child, how can it exist between a couple? How can it exist anywhere?" Maya realised her face was wet with tears when she finished.

"I love you. I'll get you from there right now. Would you come?" Gaurav replied.

Suddenly Maya's body loosened. That's all she wanted to hear. She threw away her cigarette and took a deep breath in.

"What would I do without you?" she said.

And Gaurav knew instantly she was better than she was the previous moment. "Thank god! I thought I'd actually have to get you!" he joked, relief from Maya seeping into him.

"Asshole."

*

The next morning Maya, Manish and Suman went out for brunch. Suman was leaving that evening. So that morning, Maya picked herself back up. Final hours, for now, she thought and pieced her mind, body and soul together to put on a show as good as she could. She wore a bindi, a dupatta, lined her eyes and they all headed out.

During brunch, Suman was talking to them about eating right.

"Eat home-cooked food, *beta*, don't eat out too much."

"Ma, we do, we wanted to take you around that's why we've been out so much. It's for you." Manish replied. The calm in his voice uncomfortably familiar to another man she knew.

"Yes, yes, but I know you don't eat at home as much as you should." Suman was hinting towards Maya's lack of interest in cooking and Maya stiffened just a little bit. Nonetheless too tired to say anything.

"But you have also been eating out for the last 15 days! You've been in our house, not your house na!" Manish joked and burst out laughing. Maya felt shocked, despite everything.

Suman giggled, eyes wide at the shock of the joke. Fumbling at what to say, she replied,

"You're saying this so it's okay. Had she said it, I would've shown her."

Maya felt her jaw clench. She felt like her heart would burst. Why was she being targeted by this woman and blamed and drawn into something that was solely between her and her son? And yet again, the shock was so huge that her muscles didn't yield to words, despite her soul banging her insides.

That evening, as Suman left, Maya pieced her mind, body and soul back together, completely locking out Suman from every cell of her existence. Suman would always be around as her husband's mother, and yet, never truly be even in the vicinity of a relationship with her.

CHAPTER 6

Vaidehi & Vinod

Vaidehi had started feeling her relationships slowly and surely getting more and more complicated. She often wondered if she could see milk getting curdled, would it look like this? The complications of married life were so alien to her that she couldn't even comprehend how molecule by molecule of her being was curdled, one degradation at a time, making her life sour. She felt the space around her was slowly closing in and she could see her own suffocatingly spirit-crushing future dawn on her.

In the beginning itself, there were the blatant bans: she couldn't go out of the house, couldn't spend to meet her basic needs. However, Vaidehi's simplicity of thought process and a crystal-clear heart came to her rescue. They say, what people see in the world is often a reflection of what's inside them. As a result, most of the insults were received covered in the benefit of the doubt and were left unwrapped in the corners of the house, keeping her mind sane. The thing about these words is that they never really go un denting. Vaidehi would, eventually, several years later, unwrap them in lazy afternoons and be shocked at the *presents* spanning all these years. But it would happen when she would learn the brutal, cunning, manipulative and cruel ways of the world. In her present, she walked on, simply observing and disturbed.

She was barred from going out with Vinod. Twice a week, they went to the temple, and those were their only outings. Her own family before marriage wasn't a rich one but being an inspector's daughter, she'd had privileges, small ones, like being able to watch a movie for free in scorching afternoons in a theatre with a tin roof in whatever remote village her father was posted in. Sitting in the theatre with her brothers, sweat pouring down her back, dampening her underarms, the hot air stifling her breathing with the smell of others' sweat, she'd watch rapt in attention the sarees the heroines wore as they went around the trees drunk on love. She would walk back home on foot, movie still playing in her mind, unperturbed by her cheap slippers melting on the hot road. She missed all that. After all, it never really is the luxury that money can buy that we enjoy indulging in, but the sense of freedom of being able to do it. And so, she'd lived, often having unsweetened chai because the sugar would get over mid-month and they wouldn't have the money to buy it, but enjoying the freedom of being able to go about her life the way she wanted.

Now she had a better house and financially — although not sound — it was still much better than what she was used to. Yet this was the house she couldn't open the doors of, given the lock of patriarchy that was so final. She would often dream about the time when her father was posted on the hills and how every morning they would go to a dhaba nearby for breakfast of hot parathas, green chillies sautéed with salt and steaming ginger-cardamom tea. Or the time when they were posted in a broken haveli infested with rabbits and how their infants, soft little balls of cotton, had filled her heart with love. Most of her afternoons were spent in this reverie, lying on her bed, blanketed in her cold room against the scorching sun. A few bedsheets that she had were now patched as she wasn't allowed to replace them. Even the patches hung together with weakening threads. As every aspect of her life was being picked apart, these memories were the patches that held her sheet of sanity together. The strongest patch of news would come soon, but first, it was the summer when her sister-in-law, Poornima came home with her husband Pardeep and two of her four children.

The house was suddenly full and not just with human chaos. This was the first time Vaidehi was meeting Pardeep and Poornima after the day of her wedding. The first thing she noticed was a strange gap between them. Pardeep was tall, fair-skinned, well-built and very handsome. Poornima had beautiful dusky skin and attractive features, but between the two, Pardeep was the one who would turn heads. Poornima was more of a girl next door. But what disturbed her was what reeked from under their skins. Vaidehi could sense a certain bitterness under Poornima's smile — the kinds that come with life and circumstances. She smiled and giggled around the house but a certain cunning lurked just behind the curtain of her lashes. Vaidehi would then catch her train of thought and admonish herself for thinking this way.

As for Pardeep, there was a sense of callous freedom that was a little annoying. Indifference to everything and everyone around him except for himself. He simply didn't care. Maybe Poornima's bitterness came from Pardeep's lack of love. Or from the fact that her parents were devoid of the parental love that pours when a married daughter comes to stay with them, or just parental love in general. Very soon, Vaidehi, to her horror, would realise that Poornima knew precisely how her parents felt for her. But as of now, this gap in Pardeep and Poornima's relationship made her sad.

Then there were the cats with who the two children spent their days of the summer vacation. The mother lazed in the shade while the kittens playfully hopped about her. They said that a cat changes seven houses during the term of pregnancy and post-delivery. This one had chosen Vaidehi's to bring up her kittens. And so, the air was fused with bitter-sweet of innocence and cunning. The effect that the whole affair had on Vaidehi made her heady.

The men would generally spend their day watching television. Vaidehi's father-in-law would take leaves or half-days to be with Pardeep. But they hardly ever spoke. When the TV was off, they would play cards, have tea and snacks, read the newspaper, or just sit in silence. The room would often grow heavy with awkwardness and the pressure of having to cater to the visitors. Marriages are strange that way. The person who would become the closest to your child would always remain kind of a stranger to you. And the parent-child love that is considered the purest of all, sort of stretches out too much, with nothing but a path of memories in-between—a path that you might take, but would never really reach a destination. Hence, the men sat, waiting for this journey to be over.

Poornima sat with her mother, Kamla, in another room. Often clothes were strewn on the floor the entire day, but nothing would ever get stitched. Even though the room would be empty, Vaidehi wondered why they always spoke in whispers. She didn't realise then that it was she whom they didn't want to include. There would always be a frown on

Kamla's face as she spoke and Poornima's forehead would be scrunched up too in concentration. Sweat marks on their underarms, sweat beads forming on the upper lips, the women spoke, relentlessly, every single day. Vaidehi wondered at the intensity of their conversations but also waited to spend whatever little time possible with Poornima, hoping to find a confidant in her. But generally, whenever Kamla saw them together, she would invariably join them.

On the third day of her arrival, Poornima went up to Vaidehi saying, "We'll go to the market in the afternoon, alright?"

Vaidehi looked at her, unsure what to say. She wouldn't be allowed to step out but how could she tell Poornima about the rule her own mother had set? Reading the hesitance, Poornima said, "Don't worry, I've spoken to ma."

Vaidehi gave her a relieved smile. That afternoon, she finished all the work, changed into a better saree and walked out, head covered with the *pallu*, along with Poornima and Pardeep. They went to a market nearby, to buy some bedsheets. Vaidehi knew she couldn't buy any but the relief of being able to step out was far better than the sorrow of not being able to fulfil her needs. Poornima asked for options after options in various colours and fabrics. They sat on the stools, feet on the platform with a mattress on which the shopkeeper threw open bedsheets. Holding them on one side, he would jerk them open, and it would ball up like a semi-parachute, given the fan's air beneath it and slowly float down to the platform, over their feet. Soon, Vaidehi could feel the weight of the bedsheets on her feet. Despite the heat, she shuffled her feet cosily under them. Something was comforting about the stuffy smell of them. They were mostly cotton and in bright colours of red, green, orange and then there were also the dark ones like deep blue, brown and maroon. Now the shopkeeper was ripping them open one by one, keeping the ones that Poornima would approve to the right and the rejected ones on the left. By the end, there were about ten that were approved and this made the shopkeeper very happy.

He shouted to the little boy to pack them, when Poornima said, feigning shock, "Arre! What pack? Wait, wait, I have to still pick from these."

The shopkeeper's smile dimmed a little. The other help at the store was already winding up the huge rejected pile of sheets. Even if he sold 50% of these, it would be a good day.

"No, no, you leave it, I'll see on my own and select," Poornima said to the shopkeeper, rudely waving him off. Vaidehi felt a little embarrassed and bad for him but as if used to it, he walked away in his casual stride. He was a bit relieved, finishing it off with a demanding customer. Poornima went through the pile again, making dismissive sounds and scowling at the finalists as if they were a good looking dish, but on tasting, revealed to have too much salt in them. As the pile of the next batch of rejection steadily grew, Vaidehi felt Poornima wasn't going to buy anything after going through what seemed like a hundred options. Finally, she selected just one, and they went to the counter.

The owner of the shop sitting there stared, first at the mere single bed-sheet and then at Poornima. His unspoken words reeking out like the red of paan from his mouth. Vaidehi quietly stepped out of the shop, head bowed in embarrassment. The shame wasn't about not having money but about the whole experience of the way Poornima shopped. The simple difference between money and class.

"It was just about OK. Now had to buy something because they showed us so many," Poornima was saying to Pardeep as they came out to join her. Vaidehi walked on in silence. Nearby, there was a fair happening and Poornima wanted to go. Vaidehi shifted nervously, knowing it would soon be time for tea. "Don't worry, just some *pani puri* and then straight home. Ma expects us to be a little late." Vaidehi smiled.

The other emotions of fear and anxiety had taken over so strongly, she was surprised how she didn't even instantly feel excited to see a fair anymore. Everyone talks about how your life changes after marriage: new place, new family, new responsibilities, new priorities, but no one ever talks about the new you that you become. This new 'you' creeps in and slowly starts replacing the old you cell by cell so that you hardly even notice the difference. But sometimes, a leak gives way, and you realise how you react and feel differently about certain things and situations as compared to before. You start getting annoyed at the silly jokes you used to find funny, discussions are replaced by angry arguments, and a sense of perpetual sorrow becomes a way of being, punctuated by occasional laughter instead of the other way round. In the end, as if wiser by experience, we say, *"that's how life is"*. But that evening wasn't a sad one. It was one that Vaidehi enjoyed to the fullest, with the assurance of granted permission setting her mind free. Soon, even the conversations became more open with Pardeep. They spoke to Vaidehi about where they lived, their lifestyle there and the people in their life. All the while having a round of *pani puri*, sucking noisily onto the ice cones, even hopping onto a ride and longingly looking at the glass bangles that Vaidehi knew she wasn't allowed to buy. Merrily laughing, they got back home when it had started to get dark. Vaidehi heard Vinod's scooter when she was rolling out chapattis. The dinner was right on time, and surprisingly, she felt more energetic despite the long trip to the fair. That is when she heard the outburst.

"Whole day madam was frolicking around town," her father-in-law shouted on top of his lungs.

Vaidehi's mouth went dry, hands cold on the rolling pin and her heart gave a thud she'd never experienced before. Even the warm floor of the kitchen couldn't keep her feet from shivering slightly with cold.

"If you had given her permission, why don't you say it now?" Vinod shouted back, urging his mother to speak up.

"What do I say? It's between you, your father and your wife. Have I ever had a say in anything ever?" Kamla's voice was the one that sent a shiver down Vaidehi's spine, and not just because she said a blatant lie so fiercely, knowing that everyone knew it to be a lie. It was like nothing she'd ever heard before. Standing in the kitchen, she couldn't sync Kamla's face to that voice. Although not a shout, it was bitter, like phlegm spit out, almost inhuman.

"Why are you asking her to speak up? Ask your wife why she was dancing around town with your sister's husband?"

Vaidehi was numb, unable to understand the words – the mind does to your senses what it does to the body part that is so gravely physically injured that you can't take its pain. As the realisation trickled in eventually, as if being slow would soften the blow, Vaidehi thought she'd faint.

"Don't you feel ashamed saying this?" Vinod's voice wavered.

"Why should I be ashamed? It isn't my character that's rotten!" her father-in-law replied, still shouting for the whole society to hear.

Strangely, Vaidehi stood there, her heart returning to its normal pace, despite the character slander that she'd never faced before. Even though it hurt as her dreams bled out, she felt strong in her wounded self. It wasn't true. How could a lie ever be stronger than the truth? On his way to their bedroom, Vinod caught Vaidehi's eyes in the kitchen. They stood, just looking at each other, helplessness in Vinod's eyes and warmth in Vaidehi's.

That night, Vinod said, "I always knew my parents are like that. It's my fault; I should never have married. You'll never be happy here." The pain in Vinod's voice tore apart Vaidehi's heart.

"Oh, but we'll be just fine. I know it. Don't you?"

"I want to make you happy. Let's move away. Let's separate from them."

Vaidehi was stunned. If they separated, she would be called the reason for that, not anyone else who slandered her spirit and her character. Such was the deep conditioning that even she believed herself to be responsible if this ever happened. How could she separate the parents and their only son?

"No! Don't say such things. And I *am* happy. As long as I have you."

That night, they made love. The kind of love making that heals. Each time their lips found the other's body, they planted such a gentle, long, warm kiss, as if placing a phoenix's teardrop to instantly heal whatever holes were burnt into their emotional and mental beings. In this slowness they felt the time was suspended, they could breathe the other's essence in between the next touch. They drank each other. The essence of their existence blended beyond recognition of individuality. Their sorrows, their struggles, their joys…their very existence, that night truly became one. Neither could ever exist without the other anymore. It was impossible.

*

The next morning, last night's toxicity still hung in the air. Breathing in that poison sat the children and the kitten with the cat, all having milk. Her in-laws went around with a rare calm and an occasional smile flitting on their faces. What kind of a twisted cocktail was this? Words that had disappeared last night, leaving their imprint on the air and humans with a deceiving countenance, cunning throbbing in their veins; Pardeep and Poornima with silent guilt — the power of the unseen had never been stronger. And it clashed so violently with the innocence of the little ones, human and animal merging together in ignorance. It made Vaidehi dizzy. It wasn't what she'd expected. She thought she'll wake up to find her in-laws still angry and cold for the next few weeks at least. She didn't deserve it but the accusation they'd made definitely demanded more anger from them. Poornima went around the house and gave nervous glances to Vaidehi every time their eyes met. She'd not spoken up last evening, giving away her invisible status and hence there was no point discussing this with her. And anyway, there were only two people at fault, and those were her parents-in-law. Or maybe she spoke to them after and that's why they were calm?

In the afternoon, Poornima came to Vaidehi's room and lay down on the bed beside her.

"Can't sleep?" Vaidehi asked.

"Yeah. Did I wake you?"

"Oh no, I was just resting my eyes. Wasn't asleep."

A pause swelled between them mingling with the humidity, as each wondered how to unveil the elephant in the room. The silence might've been for a few seconds but it suffocated Poornima enough for her to choke out, "I can't even ask if you're okay, after last night. Which woman would be?"

The last sentence was like a dagger in her heart. Why did it hurt so much when she'd handled the blow better yesterday? Why was only she the one considered characterless if even Pardeep was linked to her? But then, he was a man and that too, the son-in-law of the house. Despite all her regressive circumstances and orthodox upbringing, the wound from the stab at her character reeked out a little feminism.

"But what happened?" Vaidehi asked. She wouldn't justify herself saying things like *'but you know it's not true'.*

"They are like that only. They like stirring up storms without reason, and then they're done." Poornima replied.

Now Vaidehi understood her in-laws' expressions. They weren't calm, they were satisfied, just because they managed another successful fight. They were just made that way: while most slept peacefully knowing their houses were alright, they slept soundly on the debris of the havocs they created at home. This is how they vented, a life full of disappointments. Bitterness. Anger. While this meant that whatever they would ever say, would never be about Vaidehi genuinely, but just about igniting another quarrel, it also meant that there would never be peace in her home. After all, you can only solve a problem if it exists.

"Just ignore them. That's all you can do." Poornima said.

"Yes. That's all I can do." Vaidehi repeated, not in helplessness, but with a sense of relief.

*

A month after the incident, Vaidehi sat alone in her house. Her in-laws were out to meet some relatives and they'd only return after dark. The sun was on its way home and the silence was sprinkled with twittering birds on the same journey. It was so blissful. Vaidehi didn't take the *pallu* off her head, despite the absence of people for who it was meant for. Or maybe, it was meant for herself, in her love of the traditions. She had even made a cup of tea to pamper herself. It was good, the silence. If only even Vinod was there. His thought made her smile.

Poornima's time here had been such an emotional roller coaster. There had been more fights and shoutings and even tears. Every person in the house with such stark emotions had made her dizzy. Her mother-in-law with her vehement, cruel scheming; her father-in-law's naked rage; Vinod's helplessness and frustration. Poornima, as Vaidehi realised, had layers to herself. She smiled and spoke to Vaidehi simply and genuinely, but never protected her even if she easily could. She never spoke up. She was almost invisible to her parents in terms of having any significant say over anything in their house. She would do things to vie for attention but never spoke up in a fight or defence as if subconsciously conditioned to be insignificant. And so she demanded extra attention, milking it desperately from situations where she knew she was indispensable to. Like, she'd be extra late when she was required to light the lamp in the temple when Vaidehi and her mother-in-law were having periods or in rare times of religious acts supposed to be done by the daughter of the house, she would feign illness but emerge nonetheless after a lot of coaxing. While she was tiring with her layers of complexities, Pardeep was too in his absolute indifference. If Poornima had a voice that was never considered, Pardeep never cared for the importance he had to make a difference.

The children and the cats were the positivity that dwindled pitifully when the others soared. But right now, finally, she had some personal space — a few hours to just breathe. The kittens mewed weakly around her. The cat lazily moved her tail in slow motion, like a rising thread of smoke from an incense stick. Their laziness and laid back demeanour infused in the air and seeped into Vaidehi's pores and relaxed her. She finished the cup of tea and closed her eyes, leaning on the bed for a while. Finally, she took the notebook and started writing a letter to her mother, her hand moving lazily but expertly, just like the cat's tail.

Just as she was done, the cat came over and sniffed over it, as if taking in the contents of it. She looked up at Vaidehi with a jerk of her head, eyes sparkling, or was Vaidehi imagining it? She smiled down at her.

"I'm next," she said, lightly touching her stomach.

CHAPTER 7

Maya and Manish

Maya stood in front of the mirror, brushing her stomach to straighten her crisp white shirt. It was so effortless when her stomach was flat, she thought, trying to tuck in her shirt just right to hide the little paunch. She resolved to join the gym soon. But that was later. As of now, she must focus on the interview. It had been months since her marriage and now she must start working. A new city with strangers that spoke a language she didn't understand. She wondered how different the work culture would be here. The office politics, promotions, the work itself and the colleagues—how would she fit into a culture that was so different? *First, land the gig and then worry about it,* she pushed her mind to focus. She'd assorted her look very carefully this morning. Her nude brogues were the first pick and around it came the blue, ankle-length formal pants, a white shirt, Swarovski studs, a plain fossil watch, stroke of eye liner and a dab of pink on her lips. After fidgeting for some time with her wild curls, she just left them open and headed out, shouldering a bag that matched her shoes exactly.

Forty-five minutes later, she was in her prospective workplace, breathing in the familiar air, realising she'd missed working so much. She smiled, looking through the glass door of the waiting room. There was that familiar play of contrasts between the creatives and the others, the employee who spoke too loud, the occasional balls of paper flying over the cubicles in the creative department, the steaming paper cups of tea and coffee, polished shoes versus colourful kolahpuris, those heads passed out on the tables after pulling an all-nighter and the fresh ones, ready with their presentations. It was relieving to be there, closing out on everything else.

"They're ready for you. First up, into room no. 11."

Maya jerked back to see a man holding the door open for her to pass through. "Yes, thank you," she smiled and strode out.

She entered the room for her first round of interviews and was met with a dark brown, chiselled face with the brightest smile she'd ever seen on a man. Involuntarily and shockingly, her breath fumbled. It was a sensation she'd never experienced before. *Silly,* she thought and pulled her mind back to focus.

"Hi, I'm Ved, please have a seat," he offered his hand and motioned her to sit. Maya found herself appreciating his firm handshake, and then he spoke. "So Maya, we are looking to hire a teacher who has a strong hold on the language and is also brilliant with the students. But our priority is to take up someone who is passionate about their job, as we don't have your everyday students here. These children come from the slums and I see you have experience working with an NGO before, so I don't need to tell you the unique challenges you might face with the students. Why don't you tell me about your passion for teaching and the journey you've been on, and where you plan to head."

Maya was fascinated with how the words marched out in elegant fluency from his mouth. There was so much ease in the way his palms met in front of him on the table, the way his shoulders rested in assurance, his blue shirt hanging on the round of them.

"Umm...you okay? Do you want some water?"

Maya jerked back, too embarrassed and surprised at herself. But she recovered in a moment and spoke with as much ease and confidence. This was nothing new, an interview like so many others she'd given. She knew she got this. About half an hour later, Ved directed her to meet the VP for the final round. She walked out, making an extra effort to keep her back upright, shoulders square and head high. She let out a breath as the door closed behind her. What was this nonsense her mind was playing her with? *Absolute ridiculousness,* she chuckled lightly, shrugging off the whole thing. She walked into the VP's room and was surprised to find the interview even more chilled out than it was with Ved.

"Well, it was lovely to meet you and we'd love to have you here. The HR will get in touch soon," he said, shaking Maya's hand. She walked out to find Ved waiting for her on the way.

"Hey, would you like an office tour? Check out the work culture, meet a few people, get a feel of the whole thing?" he offered, smiling.

"Sure," Maya replied, strangely happy to be with him for a few more minutes.

They went around the office but it was nothing she hadn't seen before. Stereotypical in the way the cubicles changed depending on the teams, the language labs, a cafeteria dominated by the smell of the coffee, and largely, the closed cabins lining the space, with open cubicles in the middle defining hierarchy. It was just about okay, but exactly what she needed.

On her cab ride back home, she eased into the seat, thinking of the pros and cons of the place, despite knowing full well she just needed to jump into this to get away from it all. But her head strangely kept popping up Ved's face. She dialled Gaurav.

"How did it go?" he asked soon as he picked up.

"Aah, fine!"

"You want to take it up?"

"Does it matter? I should."

"But do you like the place?"

"Yea, I do."

"Then be happy. You're making it sound like it's bad but you still have to take it up." Maya made an annoyed sound. "*What now*?" Gaurav asked.

"Nothing! What do you mean what now?" Maya replied, unaware of the reason behind her sudden irritation.

"Never mind; tell me what's up?"

"I'm on my way back home from the interview. The HR will call me and then…just, you know, the usual," Maya cut short, suddenly tired of explaining anything further. Tired of uttering any word.

"Alright, sounds good."

"Yeah, it will take my mind off of everything," replied Maya.

"You know, you aren't doing a job just to take your mind off things. It's your profession, it's your passion, so it's so much more. Don't reduce it to something that is just to keep you busy."

Maya knew Gaurav was right. She felt a strange sense of negativity in her. While earlier, even the smallest of things like a lone pigeon's feather lying serenely on her balcony used to make her smile, she felt nothing about this new job that she'd gotten. Why did her head feel so muddled?

"Yes, but you know, whatever. I just can't right now," she replied, tiredness seeping into her voice.

"You don't sound well. Is something the matter, Maya? Why don't you tell me?" he asked with such kindness, Maya teared up.

"I honestly don't know," she replied, her voice giving away her tears.

"Maya, whatever it is, it really is seeming bigger to you than it really is—just know this even if you don't believe in it right now." She was thankful he didn't ask whether she was crying.

"Yea, thanks. Listen, I just got home, let me call you back."

"Sure. And I'm here if you want to meet," Gaurav said, knowing full well she wasn't going to call him back.

She took the elevator up to her apartment and as she was unlocking the door, her phone pinged, making her jump.

That's amazing! I'm so happy for you.

Manish had replied to her text which she'd sent updating him about the interview. The relief that Maya felt was so strange. There weren't any questions about whether she was happy or if she really wanted this job or why she doesn't sound okay. She possibly couldn't explain to anyone the gap that remained unbridged between her feelings and words. It was a blessing to have close ones badger you to ensure you're okay, and sometimes it's a greater one to have those who ease it out from you. Manish, as Maya was slowly learning, was one of those latter ones. So loud and outspoken with the world and embodying this silent watchfulness within. You would know of his presence in the room from some distance, and yet, he would know exactly what not to say. As Maya would burn in restlessness that was her nature, he would simply be around, creating a backdrop of light easiness with his jokes and casual remarks, waiting for her to open her heart out to him. He was the most available person she had, despite not uttering a word about it. Now, Maya wondered how this understanding was slowly taking form between them. How did she understand this about him, without him saying anything at all? More importantly, why did she crave fireworks despite having this deep silent love within her? Suddenly a voice in her head popped: *But is it love?*

Maya let out a tired sigh with the exhaustion her brain was sending her body in. Her bones felt heavy with these questions and doubts that her back was carrying for she didn't even know how long now. She unbuttoned her pants and unzipped them halfway to let her stomach breathe. She took off her shirt, soaked around the underarms, and chucked it into the laundry basket. She made herself some tea and lit a cigarette, sitting down with a mugful. Her bra was almost wet with sweat, and a drop ran down her stomach. She cut herself a slice of her birthday cake Gaurav and other friends had got her the previous night. She cut off half of 6 and the number didn't make sense anymore. The ambiguity of the number now better represented her age. Just then her phone rang. The screen blared her mother-in-law's name. She sighed again but picked up, putting on her jovial voice. She never could be especially happy about her birthday no matter how much she tried. It came every year and yet nothing much really changed with age, except growing complications. It came every year and one fine year, it won't; that's how it is supposed to be. Then how do you celebrate something so obvious?

"*Namaste* Ma, how are you?" she spoke into her phone, trying her best.

"God bless you, *beta*, happy happy birthday! May all your wishes come true, I wish you all the happiness, progress and peace in the world," Suman replied.

Something about her genuine blessings and truly happy voice made Maya smile. "Thank you so much, Ma! What are you doing?"

"Oh, we're on our way back home from meeting the prospective tenants for our new flat," she replied.

"Happy birthday, *bete*, god bless you!" her father-in-law shouted from the background. Maya giggled at his jolly voice.

"Thank you, thank you, Papa," she replied, still giggling.

"Okay, now let me talk to her in peace," her mother-in-law told her husband.

"Hahaha! Yea, so then, did you finalise everything with the tenants?" Maya asked, her spirits lifting slowly with all the wishes and joy delivered over the phone.

"Oh now, what do I say? We thought we'll have the meeting today because it's your birthday so it'll be a lucky day for us. But the deal didn't go through; we have to keep on looking." Maya felt as if she'd been hopping around, eyes closed, smiling widely, and hit her face in a wall she didn't see coming. She was silent, and Suman continued, "Oh it's alright now. It isn't easy to find good tenants and good value for the place. We're almost home, *beta*. Oh and I forgot to tell you, yesterday we left the gas knob open and by the time we got home, the house was faintly smelling of it. Carefully, without touching and any light switches I went straight into the kitchen and it was reeking of gas. I turned the knob off and opened all the windows and doors of the house."

"What! That's crazy; it's incredible nothing happened! Thank god, I shudder to think of it!" Maya replied, horrified. The shock took her mind off Suman's birthday wish.

"Yes, I know! We were shocked. But thank god nothing happened or else everyone would've said, this new daughter-in-law came and look what happened. Bad luck!" Maya was dumbstruck. At her silence, Suman continued, "*Beta*, we're home now, we'll speak to you later. You have a beautiful, beautiful birthday."

As her own small rebellious act, Maya disconnected the phone without saying anything further.

She put the phone aside and picked up the fork. Sliding her slice away, she digs into the cake instead.

*

Maya woke up the next morning in a strange way. She didn't have a nightmare, she didn't wake up slowly and gradually. Her eyes just randomly flicked open. As if it was her mind's cue to unravel the unprocessed happenings of yesterday. Slowly, the memories of last night crept their way back into her. The dinner with friends, flowing wine, the jokes and laughter. And yet, everything was a daze. She remembered it all, and yet she didn't really feel any of it in her skin. Like wearing a plastic wrap around your face, with holes pierced out so you can breathe without feeling the air on your face. And as if that plastic was ripped off, the realisation suddenly hit her, making the tears gush out suddenly. She made her way to the sofa outside, at least she woke up Manish. As if a door was unlocked in her mind, specific scenes from the past started playing in front of her. She recalled when she was a child, how her grandmother had said casually, "But you're only a girl, he's a boy," while giving her brother a few extra nuts. And in class 8, her brother was allowed to go to birthday parties and she wasn't and when she'd asked, desperately, "But why can't I go too? He goes all the time," to which her mother had replied, "He's a boy!" In her early twenties, her brother's room was being extensively renovated and hers wasn't, because she would marry one day and move out. So, what was the point? She lay there, poker-faced, cheeks wet with tears, shrinking inside.

She shut her eyes, wanting to escape all of this—parents, siblings, husband, in-laws, jobs and friends—the world itself. It wasn't fair. It wasn't right. She scrunched up her eyes, pulled her stomach in and her fist crushed the cushion cover and she let out another, painful cry. Silent, except for the sound of her snake-like breath being pulled out of her gut slowly. She wished she could pull every inch of her body inwards until nothing of hers remained. She wanted to skip to the end. The moments that had filled her a little with pride, like the time when her father had told her mother to teach Maya only basic cooking, as he believed she wasn't meant to be in the kitchen, seemed too bleak a branch to hold onto, as this quicksand of realisation of the rotting knowledge inside her finally started to seep out.

Maya's parents had let her run into the world, but their leash of progressiveness only allowed her to go so far. And here she was now, so many steps closer to her free life but stopped a few steps before she could grab on to it. Would having an orthodox upbringing been better than left squirming mid-way to a liberated life? Or was this just how generations worked? Getting closer to independence but only a step a generation? Was she supposed to stop here, only to pass on the baton? How far would her leash of progressiveness stretch? Would she truly be able to give complete independence to a generation that would demand things out of her cultural comfort? By the time she was 25, the silent and hidden desperation of her parents wanting to marry her had started flowing out. The pressure they thought they were in was never given away by a shrilling whistle, but Maya had lived very much in the middle of its stifling heat. There was a point when the astrologer had asked her parents to make her sleep in the drawing room sofa instead of her room, as the room's vastu would delay the prospects of her marriage. It was one of the most hurtful moments of her life when her mother had asked her to do it. Recovering the next second, Maya had strongly defied her. Where was that girl now? What happened to her? More than anything else, it was the pain of losing her older self that made Maya restless. What was this transformation? Was it for good? Where was she heading? She felt her body sinking into the sofa more and more until her bones got too heavy for her body to lift and carry them over to the bed. Was she really out on the sofa? Was she really married and in her husband's house? Or was she still the girl wondering why she didn't deserve everything that her brother did?

Making sense of these rules that didn't feel *right* even if they were still laid out by her parents and grandparents, and forgetting the fight that was seeding inside her the next moment when cartoon came on the television. Where was she and what had happened to her?

*

Maya's eyes flicked open when she felt Manish's lips lightly brush her forehead. Her reaction must've been delayed, as by the time the vision came on, she heard the door click shut. The clock said it was 8.15 am. She'd never felt so exhausted in the morning. She got up slowly, the memories coming first and only then the feeling in her body parts. It was like reentering the body.

It was the first day of work for her. A sense of defiance came over her as she bathed and slowly got ready, dragging her limbs from cloth-to-cloth and room-to-room. The truth of her upbringing weighed on the realisation of the life she could've had.

I don't care. I don't want any of this. Just. Work.

Something took resolve in her which only grew stronger as each rotation of the cab wheel added more distance between her life and the one she was escaping into. As she entered her office and a sense of hurry and urgency in the air hit her, she suddenly felt light. She headed inside and placed her bag at her desk. There was no one there yet. She walked over to pour herself some coffee. She took one sip, turned and looked up. And there was Ved.

CHAPTER 8
Vaidehi and Vinod

Two years into her marriage, Vaidehi's house had become her entire world. She still remembered the train ride which had put so much distance between everything that was known to her and the new life she had to start from scratch. Now, lying in bed, tired to her bones but ecstatic in her soul, heavily pregnant, she thought of how her life had changed. There had been so much struggle, she thought without feeling unhappy. Not a single experience with her in-laws had been a happy one that she could think back as a good memory. Vaidehi as a wife, a daughter-in-law and a mother-to-be, was shamed at every step possible. And then there was the character slander. At that thought, she made her brain stop. She couldn't think of such things, especially now. She struggled to think of happy thoughts. But that's the thing about happy thoughts—they invariably rely on happy memories. Not only that, they demand happy memories that are recent and relevant. No single memory is ever happy enough to support a person's lifetime. This only goes to say that no happiness is big enough.

Isn't that why humans continuously do things that they call living? They think they're doing it all for earning money but they do everything just to earn happiness that their life can depend upon.

Vaidehi got up from her bed and sat on the floor where she'd kept her lunch plate. She smiled and decided to have a happy lunch. She tore a piece of roti, scooped some veggies in it and put it in her mouth.

Just then her father-in-law passed by her room, heading to the kitchen. He glanced at her and commented, "All day long, all she does is stuff her mouth." Suddenly she lost all taste, like the food itself had sucked it back in, angrily. The lump of sorrow in her throat blocked the entry of the food in her mouth. As the tears struck, Vaidehi rushed to the bathroom and vomited the uncontainable hurt. She stayed on the floor for a few moments. She didn't think she could feel any more despair than she felt in those few moments that followed. She'd never felt such darkness before. Such moments were few but so intense.

And then her children kicked and jerked her out of it. She felt her stomach, looked down and smiled. *I don't care about any of this. Just. My. Children.* She resolved. She got up and walked into her room. Drawing the curtains she sat down to eat, taste very much back into her life. So what? A voice inside her head said when she remembered the events that followed when she got to know about her pregnancy. She remembered writing the letter to her mother, informing her about it. But first, she would have told Vinod. He would have been the first to know about it, that very night. The next morning he would have told her in-laws and when the letter would have reached her parents, they would have known too. But things didn't pan out as she'd planned. The men had just finished eating that night and were watching TV, while the women ate at the dining table. Vaidehi reached out for more pickles. This is exactly what Kamla had been waiting for. She'd exclaimed, loud enough for everyone to hear, "Yes yes, please have more, these cravings are normal in such condition!" Vaidehi had jerked her head to look at Kamla, shocked. How had she even known about it? She hadn't told anyone then but the cat and had mentioned it in the…letter. Vaidehi still remembered the cunning smile on Kamla that said so many things: *"Yes, we spoiled your surprise" "you think you can converse with your mother without us knowing the contents of it?" "you're right, we even read her letters before passing them on to you"* but most strongly, *"I am the power in this house and I don't like you very much"*.

It would take Vaidehi almost a lifetime to understand that Kamla was really just a bitterness of broken dreams infusing the air of her house. But in that moment, she just wanted to turn around and look into Vinod's eyes. How would he react? How would the happiness in his eyes look like? The way his lips would reach out for his ears… But her father-in-law was sitting with him and she couldn't look at her husband in front of him. Her chest had felt heavy at the missed opportunity of such a one-of-a-kind moment of happiness that couples shared. Despite her dying hunger, she ate, leaving out the pickle.

But I have the memory of the moment we found out it was twins, she reminded herself, her resolve to be happy for her children as fierce as the force of water. It was in that moment when the doctor had informed them that *"their happiness was double"* that Vaidehi had learnt that magic had nothing to do with sparkling wands and miracles. The magic was inside all of us and it did show up if we allowed it to. The way two heartbeats just formed inside of you and the way *happiness* could replace the very blood that flows in your veins and the solidity in your bones. How underrated was this word happiness —it should be called something so much stronger. Expenses were still tight, but that didn't bother them at the time. They just knew it would all be as perfect as anything could ever be. While at present this was just a faith in Vaidehi's heart, years down the line she would see it materialise in her life. The opened letters, the scorching comments, all the criticising and the shaming, nothing mattered. There was just happiness.

*

"Have a lot of ghee," Nalini said. She and Vaidehi were in Vaidehi's room. Deep in the womb of the hot afternoon, the room was still cool, with curtains drawn and a rickety cooler managing to throw relatively cooler air.

Vaidehi just smiled in response, eyes downcast. Nalini knew what that meant. She withdrew a container full of ghee and passed it to her.

"Here. Keep this in your room. And don't be so innocent; hide it well."

"Oh Nalini, really, there's no need… I can't…" Vaidehi fumbled with her words. Everyone in this society had more or less the same social status and it would be wrong of her to add expenses to Nalini's list who had her in-laws and three children to take care of, and just one earning hand of her husband.

"Relax, I did it because I could afford it this month. And nothing else is more important right now. You must take the best care possible…and don't stress too much." Nalini replied, hinting at her situation at home.

"You know I don't. I'm just so happy. Nothing else matters. Yes, there are moments when something is happening but I'm able to pull myself out of it. I refuse to let anything affect my children." Vaidehi replied.

"The letters, they still read them? I couldn't have imagined anyone doing that."

"They do, Nalini, they always had and they don't even deny it. I have stopped sealing them before sending it, because what's the point? And honestly, I don't know what they were expecting to find. I couldn't tell my parents about all of this anyway. They would die worrying. Never has reading my letters had any problem at home, except that time when they announced my pregnancy before I could tell Vinod. There is nothing in there that they can create an issue out of. Still, they do it."

"And they will continue. Anyway, let's not focus on that. Have you found out about the sex?"

Vaidehi smiled.

"No, both of us don't want to. We are just so happy to have them, nothing else matters."

Suddenly, Kamla's voice boomed from just outside her room, "Oh god, please bless us with healthy boys. That's ONLY what we want."

Nalini and Vaidehi looked at each other smiling. There was no shock about Kamla eavesdropping on them when she had been reading her letters so openly. But she did feel a twinge inside her stomach at the mention of the child's sex. It's nothing she hadn't known before — this want for a male child — and yet, when you're the mother-to-be, it does tug at your heart.

Nalini squeezed Vaidehi's palm, as if following her train of thoughts. She would know. Her eldest was a boy and then she was blessed with a girl. However, it was the third, unplanned girl child that had created the ripples. She would know and guide Vaidehi through dealing with this. After all, she had done it too, and with such mastery.

"*Arrey* auntyji, don't be so greedy now! If you have one boy and one girl, your whole family will be complete na?" Nalini called out to Kamla.

"Don't you give her ideas now!" Kamla replied. Both Vaidehi and Nalini looked at each other in shock and then burst out laughing, suppressing the sound by covering their mouths.

If you look closely, you can actually see hope. Like these women sharing a fit of laughter despite everything in their lives was hope personified. The way it spurts out suddenly in the direst of situations is the very push that gets you out of places that you otherwise probably wouldn't have been able to handle.

Vaidehi looked at Nalini as their laughter subsided. If it was a world where every feeling was put into words, she would've probably said, "What would I do without you?" but it wasn't. It was one of the silent sayings and silent acknowledgements. A world that was quiet enough to listen to unspoken things.

"*Choodi le looo!*" Suddenly, a man's voice rang out, jerking awake the lazy afternoon. It was a glass bangle seller, calling out to the women. The custom of married women wearing glass bangles was an indispensable one in Vaidehi's world. And so, once in a month or two, a glass bangle seller would go around the area pushing his lorry in the scorching sun. The flat plank of wood over the four wheels was actually nothing short of a work of art. There were columns of colourful bangles neatly arranged in a way that one couldn't take eyes off them. Maybe that's what happiness would look like if it had a face: colourful, shining, alluring and brittle. And then there was a vertical board attached to one side of the lorry with endless sheets of *bindis* in various colours, shapes and sizes. The most prominent of them was the red and maroon ones, as that was the colour symbolic of a married woman. The same was the case with bangles. Most women wore glass bangles in a shade of red, bookended with gold ones, their size reflecting the family's financial state. And on one ignored side of the lorry were other things like plastic toys for children, vermillion, cheap lipsticks strictly in the shades of red, brown and pink, and the odd orange that were just considered red. It was amazing how much that rickety lorry could carry, just like the women crowding it.

Vaidehi and Nalini's eyes shined with excitement on hearing the voice. It was a tiny pleasure she was allowed to enjoy. Her spirits lifted at the mere recollection of the lorry she was about to see in a minute. They walked out to it and as they approached the lorry, the women made space for Vaidehi and her two children soon to come. But their arms still brushed against hers and her stomach against the edge of the lorry. She could feel breaths down her back but Vaidehi knew it was alright and she was safe here. These women came closer in protectiveness instead of spacing away. This is just how they stood. Somehow, knowing so intimately about each others' families had brought them strangely closer, their closeness permeating into physical proximity too. Their houses had doors that just blocked the view of what happened within them, not the knowledge of it. From a slightly ajar window or the slit between the closed door and the floor, or probably the air inside the house pregnant with information, flowed out from the cracks in the walls and seeped into other houses, whispering into their inhabitants' minds. Vaidehi slid her fingers on the bangles and smiled. Once in her arms, they spoke of hers and Vinod's relationship.

"Very nice choice, *bhabhiji*, these will look so good on you. Should I pack 12?" the seller hard sold.

"Oye, you shut up. She has just come, let her see properly and make a choice. Stand aside, give some space to us, and here, have some water," another lady replied. Reprimanded and cared for at the same time, the seller raised his hands in resignation and let out a throaty laugh.

It seemed the humidity was sucked out of the afternoon air because of a mix of all the colours, the children's loud demanding of toys, the mothers shouting back at them—irritated at the disturbance in their tradition of gossip.

These couple of hours once a month were just theirs, stamped-approved by their in-laws. Even the children weren't allowed to disturb them. They wished the seller would stop bringing toys so that they won't hover around. Vaidehi smiled looking at so many women's hands holding a package each of bangles wrapped in newspaper, hiding them with their dupattas, acting like they were still making up their minds about what to buy, just so they can hang out there longer.

The bangles on the lorry were always arranged in a specific way. The same coloured ones were tied with a thread running through them, meeting in a circle in a tight knot that made them stand erect. These were then arranged in a semi circle and placed on the wooden plank in a column so they would catch and reflect the light, making them look much brighter than they ever would, once worn. The women stood in a semi-circle too around the lorry, a thread of gossip running through them:

"Her daughter is doing well but her son...*tch tch*, he failed again."

"I could hear loud noises in their house, they almost rattled our wall... and then the next day, she was hiding marks on her face with her dupatta."

"Her mister comes home for 2-3 days in a week...and drunk senseless... seems he only comes to her to fight..."

"Her father-in-law was coming to visit them for a few hours. You won't believe it, she sent her daughter to my place and told me strictly to not let her out, at least he spots her. What world do we live in, tell me..."

"Her daughter *mashallah* is so talented! You should've seen the henna design she did for me!"

While Vaidehi listened to all of it quietly, Nalini was a better participant during these sessions, responding with shocked sounds and often exaggerated laughter. Vaidehi wondered whether her house was a source of gossip too. Her father-in-law erupted in shouts so often, as is was common in this place they lived in, they would have definitely heard. Her house must be a source of gossip and hence, so would she. What would they be saying about her? And the time when she'd gone out with Pardeep and Poornima? Was her character assassinated just at home, or had become a public mockery?

Even if none of it was true, people would believe a scandal only for its entertainment value. And so, how much of the gossip being said right now was true for the victims in question? But wasn't that always the thing about gossip? These women spoke of them to add colours to their otherwise black-and-blue lives. She felt tired suddenly. Was it the sun? Or the scorching tongues around her that pushed whispers into her mind. She turned and walked back, clutching tightly her classic maroon bangles. That's the only colour she was concerned with.

*

Padmini and Vaidehi sat on latter's bed, talking in hushed tones.

Padmini had taken the train, along with her mother-in-law, Laxmi, and they'd come to stay with Vaidehi for a few days. Last time they'd met at Padmini's house for her brother-in-law's wedding. Even in the rushed stay and the conundrum of the wedding, Padmini and Vaidehi had found time to bond. Pain and struggle strangely break humanity, but brings people together. Now, however, they had even more time to get to know each other better. Vinod had no brother and so Padmini's husband was the closest cousin he could call an elder brother.

Vaidehi sat with her elder sister-in-law, while Laxmi sat chatting with Kamla in her room, a rectangle of an open space separating the generations and their pains.

"Here, I got some for you. Don't tell them." Padmini said, laying out 4 bedsheets on the bed. Vaidehi felt her heart warming up. She remembered telling Padmini about her torn bedsheets and how she wasn't allowed to get more, who had remembered that small helpless complaint and resolved it now, even after all this time. She smiled up at her gratefully. Padmini could sense well how moved Vaidehi was by this small gesture, only to reflect how great her helplessness had been.

"Look, I'm here to help you out with work and take care of you in any other possible way. You just need to relax and not think about the problems too much. I'm here now, we'll see this through together," Padmini said.

"I'm glad you're here… I've been feeling so tired with every small work…and there's been no help…" Vaidehi trailed off, eyes downcast.

"I know, that's why I'm here. Don't worry and don't think about all that now. This is a crucial time," Padmini replied.

Vaidehi felt blessed to be receiving help from these women who knew her problems even before she had faced them and how without asking they came to her protection.

"Come, let's start with changing this thing you have on in the name of a bed-sheet. Here, let's put this one on, it's a vibrant colour, will liven up your mood. These are all good quality ones, use and wash them with care," Padmini said, unable to resist the habit of pronouncing blatantly the praises of her gifts and emphasising the fact that she'd given them. Vaidehi smiled at the fact that Padmini would never know how much greater this act of hers was than whatever words she used to praise it.

Suddenly her room was alive with large, red flowers, on a white background. They sat back, feeling the crispness of the sheet and smelling the new ness of it. To Vaidehi, it was strange how good a bedsheet felt, which further rubbed in the realisation of how deprived she was.

However, Padmini's stay gave her so much relaxation that she couldn't help but feel grateful. Every time Kamla asked Vaidehi to do something, Padmini would find a way and the right words to do it instead. She did let Vaidehi do some chores like making tea so that the older women didn't get suspicious of their plan.

"You're not the first woman in the world to bear a baby. We did it too and worked five times harder than you all do today," was their constant dialogue to Vaidehi, if ever she hinted at tiredness. Hence, the need for this plan that Padmini had devised. How she'd convinced her mother-in-law to make this journey all the way to another state where her house was, was unimaginable to Vaidehi.

"How about another one?" Vaidehi giggled, teasing Padmini about having a third baby.

"If I have to drag through as like I have been, I'd rather do it without a baby's weight making it even more difficult." A tired smile but that of acceptance showed up on Padmini's face.

The two women sucked on to the lazy afternoon air, letting it stifle them.

"What were you guys up to last night?" Padmini asked, turning on her side to look at Vaidehi. After all, such questions' answers always lie in the eyes rather than in words.

"What do you mean?" Vaidehi asked, contemplating how Padmini would know.

"Well, I got up to drink some water and could hear your muffled giggles.

Vaidehi's smiled broadened and Padmini saw her slide her hand lovingly on her swollen belly.

"You know, Vinod finally got into this MBA college. He'd been applying for three years in a row now, but he got in this year. We're so happy! He's going to take up night classes and once he's graduated, his job prospects are going to be so much better... I feel like these children are bringing in good luck already!"

Padmini stared at Vaidehi and the latter just looked to the ceiling, smiling broadly, unaware of the jealousy in Padmini's eyes. Finally, she spoke, "We think studying is a waste of time, and we'd rather bring in money earlier on instead. I don't know what Vinod is wanting to study for."

Vaidehi was familiar with bitterness by now, but it oozing out with such viciousness from Padmini shocked her. They'd not told about these classes to anyone yet. They were waiting for the guests to leave so that when they tell the parents, they could deal with their displeasures personally. The news would spread in the society, but it at least won't travel to other states. However, Padmini had managed to get it out of Vaidehi and, easily too, as she had expected Padmini to be happy and supportive of them. Her condition was worse than Padmini's, why then was she so jealous of her little happiness?

"Oh, it's 5! But I think they're still asleep. Wait, let me quickly go and make tea for everyone. You rest; they don't have to know who made it." Padmini smiled as she left the room.

The shock of Padmini's words had hardly receded when Vaidehi saw this quick transition in her words. It was like a dark shadow had taken over Padmini and left her in the next instant. Vaidehi suddenly felt uneasy with this shifty nature. How could she trust her? Were her smiles ever real? The helping hand that she'd extended, was it really genuine? If not, what could the reason be? Vaidehi could never see through the answer to that question—she wasn't built to think that way. By the time tea arrived, she'd already let it go, deciding never to rub a piece of good news into anyone's face who themselves weren't doing so good. It was, after all, human to feel fallen behind when someone takes a step ahead of you in this seemingly important race that human life had become.

CHAPTER 9

Maya and Manish

It was a strange morning. Maya woke up with a sinking feeling.

A waterfall of everything wrong that had happened to her or was happening to her came crashing on her. As her brain tried to battle through these storms coming from any surprising corner of time in her life, it spilt over a bottle of a range of negative feelings in her. She felt anger, helplessness, anxiety, hopelessness and so many others that she couldn't even name them given their fast transforming nature. She felt like she'd fallen behind in life, in every aspect of it — be it work, or success, social and financial status...and love. It felt like whatever threads she and Manish were bound by, were fast weakening. She was scared they would snap, but as of now, this was one thought she pushed harder to throw out of her mind. It was strange how her relationship with Suman was affecting hers with Manish. After all, in an Indian middle-class family, a marriage could never be between just two individuals. She'd started feeling this blinding despair quite often recently, but unlike this one, the mornings were always good and fresh.

But these were now getting stained too. Clean-slate of the mornings were chalked by everything that was tumbling down in Maya's life, to the point that the white of the chalk had slowly started to reside in the fine pores of the slate itself. She took a deep breath and tried to calm herself. A few minutes later, she gave up and went out to the balcony and lit a cigarette. The first puff in, with a mix of fresh air and nicotine was like a helping hand that pulled her just a little out of the well she was falling in.

Relax. Manish is a good man, a very good husband, he supports me in everything I do. And that's all that truly matters in the end — a supportive and loving partner. But...do I love him back? Is it enough to be with someone who loves you, even if you don't love him back? A marriage works on love, doesn't it? Will mine work if I don't love him?

But you can love him! Another voice piped up in her head. What do you not like about him?

Nothing! But he's just not my kinda guy.

Oh, grow up, that's rubbish! Marriages don't work on that kinda thing, especially because everyone changes constantly and hence if you'd married someone who was 'your kinda guy' he would've changed and then what?

I would've adjusted because we would've changed together.

So, do the same now! Accept him…because he is good!

Maya didn't realise when it had happened but when she opened her eyes, she was sitting down on the balcony, her knees hugging her chest, her forehead resting on the knees. If Manish was a good husband and a good person, why couldn't she love him? She went and sat down at the dining table. Only now she heard some sounds coming from the kitchen and before she could ask, Manish came out with two cups of coffee.

"You look tired. Are you feeling okay?" he asked sitting down.

"Yeah," she replied, hardly audible.

"Okay. Listen, so I was thinking, I'll book tickets for Diwali to go home for a week or so. Could you check if you'll get those leaves?"

"Sure," Maya replied automatically.

There was an uneasy silence after that, while Maya fidgeted with her cup handle.

"What's on your mind?" Manish asked sensing it.

That question was like a knife that ruptured a balloon almost bursting with water.

"Really, Manish? You're asking me what's on my mind? What is it that you don't already know?" Maya replied, surprised at her own volume. They'd fought before but Maya had never felt this desperation. It wasn't because she thought Manish didn't understand, but because she knew he didn't quite grasp the magnitude of the way Suman treated her, and also knowing that there probably was no way out of it. But was it truly Manish's fault? The culture and society they breathed in considered these things alright. Long as there were no physical marks or loud voices, everything was normal. These words were just that, words charged at a daughter-in-law, something that was considered as natural as breathing was to be alive. From casually taunting Maya, calling out her relatives for loving her, indirectly calling her bad luck and more — why was she the only one who was getting so affected by it? Why weren't her husband or her parents feeling for her?

They say people shout only when their hearts have distanced so much from the other that they feel no matter what they did, the other won't understand. Maybe that's why Maya continued shouting, recalling everything that Suman had said. When she was done, she laid her head on the table and cried. She didn't remember when she'd cried this loud last. Manish was quiet, but his hands were on Maya's head and her shoulder.

"I'm sorry" is what he finally said.

It broke Maya's heart a little and then her mother's voice popped into her head, "Never spoil your relation with your husband because of your mother-in-law. Don't ever blame him for whatever his family does to you. It's not his fault."

She was right, and yet, it was so hard for Maya to act on those words. She was taught to not speak up against the in-laws, she was told not to fight with her husband. What then should she do? How could she contain this hurricane of realisation of her mistreatment? She sobbed harder.

"Don't worry, I'll talk to her. I'm sure she'll understand," Manish said, hugging Maya.

"No, I want you to *really* speak to her. Tell her everything I told you; I can't be treated like this... It won't work..." Maya added the last bit with some hesitation. Manish was quiet for a few moments, but just a slight increase in his grip told Maya that he had understood what she meant. In truth, they could never really separate. Of course, by law, she was entitled to a decision, but that's just not how things worked. Even if she mentioned the *D-word*, there would be a breakdown. Maya's parents would not be able to take it, She suspected her father would probably have a heart attack and her mother would fall sick too. Add to that, the unimaginable pressure from the relatives. Because that's just how the extended families were linked: every marriage proposal that ever came knew not of just the immediate family of the potential bride and groom, but their extended families too. Just one black spot anywhere in the lineage could affect the marital prospects of anyone else in the same generation, and often at least one more to come. So the couples fought hard to not separate because life would not become easier after; the problems would just be replaced by others, equal in intensity. This was something Manish knew too, being a part of the same ecosystem. His tightened embrace was hence a strange mark of love. Despite knowing that divorce wasn't an option, his heart painfully tugged at the hint of it, because Maya had thought of separating. And this hurricane that his heart was caught in translated into just an intense, "I will."

Manish and Maya then went into separate rooms. She decided to meditate while Manish got ready. It was too long since she'd last meditated and when she sat down cross-legged and closed her eyes, her mind started a whirlwind of thoughts again. She cried silent tears this time, letting every thought just come and engulf her very being, until it got tired and left on its own, to be replaced by another. After twenty minutes Maya opened her eyes, tears now dried on her cheeks, and headed to her bedroom to get ready for work.

When she gave herself a final look in the mirror before leaving, that's when she realised there was a post-it there which read: "I love you. Have a great day!"

Finally, she felt her heart loosen.

*

Maya was looking at the previous material crafted by her company when somebody tapped on her shoulder. She turned around to see it was Ved.

"What's up? How's your day going?"

"Been going good! How are you?"

Ved took the empty chair beside her.

"Isn't it boring reading all of this? Don't you want to jump onto actually *doing* things?" he asked with a knowing smile, slightly leaning in towards Maya.

She smiled, unable to lie and still struggling with an answer when Ved said, "Ha! I get it, it's alright, really."

"Well, good. I really can't be too politically correct."

"Or at all, for that matter!" They shared a laugh.

"Don't worry, we don't intend to waste your talent by having you sit and study for too long. It's just that we do things a little differently, so we need you to enhance our content based on the lines we follow."

"Yes, I do see that. I love that each of your examples to explain anything is so close to real life and situations which will be so relatable to the sect of students that you teach."

"Yes, exactly. I'm sure in no time you'll get the hang of it and then we can start creating, yeah?"

"Sure."

Maya only saw Ved straight at lunch then. She went to the cafeteria with Konkona, her team lead, and they sat down at the table with Ved and others from various other departments. She was soon lost in the conversations about education and novels, and things that were such an integral part of her life. There were so many passionate teachers and writers and ardent readers here—it felt like she could feel at home here in time.

"Do you smoke?" Konkona asked post-lunch. Maya smiled and they headed downstairs to smoke by the street.

"So, are you liking it here? I'm sorry, it's only been a day and I'm sure you must've been asked this question enough number of times by now," she added the last bit as an afterthought.

"Hahah! Well yes, but it's okay, that's just how it is. And yes, I am liking it here. I like the work that the company is doing, I really like the people working here, which is kinda rare. And Ved is very nice too. I didn't know he will be spending so much time with us—you know, he interviewed me, so…"

"I'm glad to hear that and yes, Ved is in the next rung, above me, but he's not so much elder to us. This still being a young company, you'll find many young people at higher positions. He spends a lot of time with us, which is actually good for team bonding. A lot of things smoothen out because of that…but, Ved, haan?" Konkona finished with a mischievous smile.

Maya burst out laughing. "Oh, please now, really!"

They went back to work and Maya poured over some more on the textbooks and assignments on grammar.

"Hey! Can you help me a little?"

Maya finally looked up from the books and her eyes took a moment to adjust on Aditya, a colleague who sat next to her. His laptop screen was turned towards her.

"Yea, sure, tell me."

"I need an example for past participle. Something for grade 4. I've listed 48, can you gimme one, please?" he asked.

"Sure," Maya smiled. She started on a word doc and listed some examples and sent it to Aditya.

"Oh man, thanks, thanks!" Aditya said, going through the document. He had a fresher's gratitude on his face, just glad to have not to think any more.

"It's not a problem at all! Let me know if you need anything else," Maya smiled, knowing full well the tiredness of the task. The rest of the day wore on, with tit-bits of workplace normalcy. It was seven when Ved appeared.

"Coffee before home," he announced.

"Nope, basketball!" Aditya replied, zipping up his back and getting off his desk.

"Mailed them to me?" Ved stopped him, putting his hand on Aditya's chest playfully.

"Did."

"Thank you so much, sir, minus 10 for ditching us though," Ved replied.

Maya smiled. She didn't know much about him yet but his rapport with every team member that he headed was smooth. He was playful with his words and yet had a way to have his work done on schedule without exerting his authority on the face. The security of his position just exuded naturally.

"YES!" Konkona replied.

"You're my star!" Ved replied, pointing a finger at her.

"In-laws, so no," Avinash replied.

"Respect!" Ved said as Avinash headed home to spend time with his wife's parents, who were visiting them for a week.

"Yo!" Navya replied.

Now everyone looked at Maya.

If she went out now, she would reach home only by 9. As she thought this and the word home sounded in her mind, she felt her chest tightening.

"Let's go," she said.

"You chose well," Konkona said to Ved, approving of Maya's decision.

They called for an Uber and it started raining while they were on their way to the cafe.

"Ready to run?" Ved asked, hand on the passenger seat door.

"Don't talk, run!" said Konkona as she opened the door and dashed out of the car and to the cafe door. Navya and Maya followed suit. Just as Maya was reaching the door, she heard Ved go, "Whoa." He was right behind her and she turned to look, not realising that Navya had let go of the swinging door of the cafe thinking Maya held it.

"Watch out!" Ved yelled, going over Maya and blocking the door just before it crashed on her face. They stood there stupefied for a for a few moments, as the thunder roared and the lights went off. In few seconds Maya realised she'd been standing uncomfortably close to Ved when the scent of his deodorant hit her. She turned around and pushed open the door. As she did, Ved took his hand back and they both entered the cafe.

"Bollywood much?" he said, right before sitting down.

"That happened and one goes off the list of that-never-happens-in-real-life list of Bollywood dramatics," Maya replied and they giggled. The generator came on and the cafe was bright again.

"Whoa! That's one hell of a boss-lady chair!" Maya exclaimed, standing up and heading to sit on a particularly funky artwork chair. There was a lady in it, in typical Indian, Bollywood heroine costume, dark-skinned, wearing goggles that had stripes on it and a cigarette dangling from her mouth.

"Is she human?" Navya asked, a little freaked by the artwork.

"She's so cool, I'm not going to sit on her. She's a part of this group, you guys," Maya replied, taking a seat next to it. Konkona laughed, a kind of mature laughter that was one of the first things Maya had instantly loved about her. They ordered and the chatter began, talking about everything, from boss-bitching, colleague-gossiping, discussing vague start-up ideas that could make them rich, the stupidest apps that existed and finally, they came back to the home topic: books. By now, Navya had left and it was just Ved, Konkona and Maya.

"I do believe that, one who is well read and can write well, but it's not just that, you know?" Maya said

"Of course, but it nonetheless is indispensable," Ved replied.

"Neither is it just about the strict grammar, or the number of words either," Konkona added.

"Frustrated with the ER team?" Ved looked at her smiling.

"When am I not? And it isn't about their work — that's something they're supposed to do. But they can be so foolishly blind to the context, or anything else for that matter. And they just check, sentence by sentence in seclusion! It's tiring to argue with them," Konkona huffed.

"It is, because then they would start correcting your communicative language," Ved laughed and the girls followed.

"I think it isn't about how many words you know, but how you use the ones that you do," Maya replied.

"YES! Oh, YES! That's what I'm talking about," Konkona said. At that, Ved started slow clapping, "All hail the wordsmith." They all laughed.

"Baba! So much drama!" Konkona said.

"You can't take advertising out of me!" Ved replied.

"So how is the role change treating you?" Konkona asked and then added to Maya, "Ved has done his MBA, then got into advertising as a writer and now, here he is, into social work and uplifting the society. You know, giving back, good deeds, helping the country, being selfless…"

"Okay, okay now, we get it!" Ved cut Konkona off.

"It's very different, and honestly, very serious…probably because advertising is just too fast, vibrant and you know, fun, so in comparison I find it…too grey."

"Why did you jump streams?" Maya asked.

"Because I wanted to do something more meaningful. Writing headlines and scripts, moving on to handling the brands, etc is all good, but after a point, you start feeling what are you doing selling another brand of biscuits…you know?"

"Sure, yes," Maya replied.

"Oh please, the pay sucks in advertising." Konkana added jokingly. They laughed again.

"And if it's better here then I can't even imagine what they were giving you in advertising," Maya said.

"Ooohh!" Konkana and Ved exclaimed together.

"Already complaining about the money!" Konkana said. Maya just laughed it off with, "No, it's about you, not me!"

"No no, of course. No, all I'm saying is, I do find it grey and a little boring here, but the overall experience of satisfaction when you see a child from the streets getting a scholarship…just can't be put into words," Ved said.

"That is incredible. The only reason why I do this and will, for the rest of my life." Maya said and Konkana nodded in agreement.

"Well, don't know about you guys but I'll be a rich and famous writer one day," Ved joked. They laughed and added, "No, that? Me too!"

When Maya finally noticed the time, it was 9:30. With rains, traffic and the distance, she wouldn't reach home before 11. They rushed out.

"Hey! Hope you're not drenched! The dinner's ready!" Manish said opening the door and leading her inside. Maya saw the dining table covered with food, waiting to be devoured.

"Thank you so, so much!" Maya said, truly grateful.

"Change and come soon, I'm famished!" Manish replied.

Maya went into her bedroom and locked her door. Manish had not called, only texted once and didn't ask the reason for being late. He knew she'd be hungry and kept the food ready. Where else would she find a partner like that? And the same question came banging in her mind: *Why can't I love him? But I never said he wasn't good and that's why I couldn't love him. He's just...he's just not my kind.*

And Ved is?

Maya stopped abruptly, shocked at what had popped in her head.

Don't be a fool, this kind of charisma doesn't last every day of the marriage. It's just attraction.

But I'm married, shouldn't this stop now?

Why would it? Do people become robots after marriage?

No...but straying is probably the reason why their relationship becomes robotic. I have someone who is so much more...but will I LOVE that 'so much more'?

CHAPTER 10

Vaidehi and Vinod

When Vaidehi had fallen in love with Vinod, she never thought she would love anyone else as much as she loved him. She didn't think it was possible. But now, as she watched her two little ones crawl on Vinod as he read his MBA book, she felt her heart would burst. Could there be any day she could love more than this lazy Sunday? What was this feeling she experienced when they touched her face with their tiny palms? What was this language she'd suddenly found she knew, for when they gurgled, she seemed to understand? How could her heart be so laden with love and yet feel so light she seemed to float through her days. But this was just one side of her.

There was another one, that wasn't so sunny. Days after her children's birth hadn't been easy. This was mostly because one of them had been a girl. And while she'd been in bed, her love had been forced to be partial between her children. Vaidehi knew this would happen in case one or both of her children would be girls, but she'd failed to imagine how much it would hurt—like someone was squeezing her heart, but only enough to drain just one drop of blood at a time, to a slow and steady death. From the first moment onwards, it was the boy who had been picked up first, and then on, it was him who was always passed on to Vaidehi first when both of them shrieked out of hunger. And it was him who was hurriedly moved out of wet discomfort. Every incident, and each time it happened, tore Vaidehi's heart just a stitch more. And of course, there were constant comments:

"God has put us in a strange situation. Do we celebrate? Or not?"

"This is all that talk of having a girl that has led to this. I should've been stricter about allowing only boys in this house. But what to do? You can't tell too much to the daughters-in-law these days. One word and you'll be chucked out of the house."

Vaidehi and Nalini had laughed at the irony of that comment.

Finally, the presence of a girl had pierced through the thick bitterness in that woman: "Whatever is destined to be, will be. Not everything can always be good."

With these and more comments that her daughter's birth was regretted at, Vaidehi had held her tighter, longer and closer.

There there was also that day of the *kua-pujan* — a small pooja, followed by dinner and celebrations. It was a ceremony restricted to the birth of a boy. By being twins, it was impossible for her daughter to not be a part of it as much as her son. How strangely an infant had forced justice. This infant who had just started to see and recognise her mother's face, had rendered all her haters helpless. The frustration of this had gone on building, stifling, ready to burst and yet not finding a way out unless the occasion arrived, so much like the milk in Vaidehi's breasts. It must've mounted a great deal a particular day when Vaidehi had reached out to Kamla, asking with great hesitation and awkwardness, for bigger bras and something to pad it with, to conceal the excess motherhood that inconveniently kept oozing out. All of that frustration had erupted that morning in a bitter whisper, "New bras for what? They'll be a waste soon no? Wear the ones you have. We've also birthed children and that's what we did too. And if they don't fit, then blouses are just enough."

It had been both embarrassing and difficult for Vaidehi as she wet the tips of her blouses, felt her breast weigh her chest down even more without support, with her back sharing the pain of it. She was scared that the muscles holding her breasts up would tear. She couldn't ask Vinod for help — such things weren't asked from the husbands. Anyway, if she did, it would lead to bigger fights, worse heartbreaks and end up landing on her daughter for being such an unlucky addition to the family, has brought even more disputes between members. So, she'd struggled with it alone for days on end, as the milk pushed forth, wet her clothes until they were permanently spotted yellow, as the children refused to wake up and ask to take it in. For her doctor's visit, she would stuff her blouse with as many handkerchiefs as her already about to rip blouse would allow. She would then pleat her pallu, always choosing the thickest sarees she owned. And then, as the sweat wet her body under the suffocating garment and her stitches burned, she would pray and pray hard right from taking the first step out to taking the first step back in, that she wouldn't embarrass herself, while the sun-scorched down on her pain and prayer.

On the morning of the *kua-pujan*, Nalini had found Vaidehi distressed. Nerve-wrecked at being around so many people for a whole day without having a moment to change. How would she manage? Then Nalini had told her another secret solution that these women had somehow come up with for centuries. The secret solutions that weren't mentioned anywhere, but hushed into the ears of new mothers by the older ones. The secret solutions that were tied in their pallus, one knot at a time, their secret shields to protect them from their very homes.

"*That's* what's bothering you? *Haay*, how were you managing till now? You should've asked me earlier. Here, take this comb," Nalaini said, picking up a spare one from Vaidehi's dressing table, "take it in the bathroom and comb over your breasts lightly. As you will reach the tip of your nipple, the milk will spurt out. And don't do it over the drain directly, it's inauspicious to throw away mother's milk. Point at a wall and do it, it'll dry off in some time." Vaidehi took the comb from Nalini's hand and rushed to the bathroom. Sure enough, the milk spurted out with each comb of her hand and it relieved her, at least for some time. If it weren't for her previously wet blouse, Vaidehi would have gone to the extent of hugging Nalini. And if she had, hormones, for once, would've freed a woman.

The kua-pujan had gone smoothly, with the relatives and friends picking up her daughter as much as her son. Indifference was strangely kind; it did not discriminate. Vaidehi couldn't help but wonder how this little infant girl had taken what was hers by being a part of the ceremony — something that was unheard of. She'd compelled everyone to celebrate her birth as much as they did her brother's. A new mother, ridden with hormonal effects, young of age and struggling under all the injustices that her girl was already starting face, Vaidehi prayed that her girl would fight just as she was now against all the mistreatment that would be served to her for being a female.

Growing up, Vaidehi's girl seemed more and more headstrong. She seemed to take what she wanted, toys and affection alike. During the day, the girl's grandparents would pick up her brother and play with him but she wouldn't mind, however, in the evening, as soon as she'd see Vinod, she'd shriek and extend her tiny hand even before her brother had turned his head to see his father. Whether encouraged by the cute shriek, or consciously to right the day's wrongs, Vinod always picked her up first, throwing her in the sky as she giggled wildly. As if sensing where she was wanted, she would only invariably ask either Vinod or Vaidehi to pick her up. During the day, as Vaidehi resumed her household duties, the twins would be on her bed, just gurgling and moving their hands for gestures in tune with conversations of their own world. This would go on until Kamla would come and take the boy away to play with him. Initially, the girl had cried and Vaidehi's soul had ached, but soon enough, both had gotten used to it.

Now, as Vaidehi sat looking at her children crawling on their father, both in their clear territories — girl over Vinod's heart and the boy over his legs — her heart balanced the joy of motherhood and the sorrow of knowing that her girl was already getting used to the injustices done to her, cutting off the wild and wide edges of her life that had just begun, slowly, strip by strip, to eventually fit the frame of this society.

She stopped herself on the tight rope of emotions that she was on, took a deep breath in, cleared her vision and sent out a prayer for her daughter's spirit to never be bound.

*

Vaidehi stood in front of the gods in the tiny wooden temple in her house and lit a matchstick. As she lit the lamp, she had nothing to offer but a heart full of gratitude. There was a mix of pictures and idols in the temple. Each picture was multi-hued, the ornaments in shiny golden colour and all of them put together made the carved wooden box a sheer bloom. Each god had a pet, said to be their medium of transport, that was the only way an elephant (god) could ride a mouse. All the colours were balanced by the small brass idols. The biggest picture in Vaidehi's temple was that of *Khaatu Shyaamji*, an avatar of Krishna. Vaidehi joined her hands and closed her eyes but her glowing face didn't bow. After a point, it was difficult to tell whether the lamp was reflecting the glow to her face or vice-versa. The flame and she were a mirror image of serenity and strength, except the lamp rhythmically wavered as she lightly breathed out. Finally, she rubbed her palms together lightly, pressed them against her face and opened her eyes. Her children ran out of their bedroom, freshly bathed and dressed, excited that now they could play. Vinod was still in the bedroom and Vaidehi went to look for him. She saw him pouring over a paper that she knew was a list of schools in the area. This was the only topic of discussion between them. The schools nearby were not English medium and that's what bothered her.

"Tell me what you're thinking," Vaidehi said, sitting down on the bed opposite him, the sheet between them.

"I haven't studied in English medium, and yet, I think I'm doing fine. Do they really need this?" Vinod asked.

"I understand that, but the struggle will be eased so much more if they knew the language," Vaidehi replied. Her opinion wasn't based on research but a deep-rooted instinct and her experience within her family.

"You're right. But I'm wondering if it's absolutely necessary."

"Okay, we will talk about it once you're back from your interview."

Vinod had been approached by a huge company, asking him to come over for an interview. He had been doing exceptionally well at his job and with so much passion, that the word had gotten around. He met various people from different companies quite often who came to his workplace to see their product so as to work as partner companies. And yet, he had never thought this to be a way to grow personally and expand his career. However, after one of his meetings last week, an executive from another company had slipped him his card, not masking his attempt at poaching. Vinod had told Vaidehi about it the same night and at a time when getting a decent job was a challenge many simply didn't win, risking an existing one where you're doing so good to make a jump for something higher was not just a surprise but also a risk. But they'd finally decided to give it a shot and particularly so because it was a Sunday and no one in Vinod's company would question his absence. They walked out of the room to the dining area, where Vaidehi served breakfast to everyone. Before leaving, Vinod went to the temple and joined his hands in prayer and Kamla put a vermillion dot on his forehead as a mark of auspiciousness and luck.

Post breakfast, there was a small lull until the hustle of lunch and Vaidehi went to her room to pick up some stitching for the TV cover she was working on. Her children ran into the room to her and she took away the cloth just in time to avoid the needle pricking their fingers.

"When will Papa come back?" her daughter asked.

"He just left, beta, he will be back at lunch," Vaidehi replied.

"But on Sunday he never goes out," her son pointed out.

"Yes, but there was some extra work today and so his friends at the office asked for help."

"And you should always help people in need," her daughter completed Vaidehi's statement, who smiled and said, "Yes."

"I will wrestle him when he gets back," the boy declared.

"No! I will arm wrestle him!" the girl replied, louder.

"Both of you can do what you like! You can think and decide what all you want to do today," Vaidehi said.

The children then turned away and walked off, discussing what all they wanted to do with Vinod who mostly only spent time with them on Sundays. Most often, they would be asleep by the time he got home and he'd already left home by the time they got up.

As the children left to play with their grandparents, Vaidehi's mind travelled to a far-off time. Her father being in the police force, they'd constantly moved and had studied in schools with tin roofs, where, while the teachers of any other subject were present and sometimes were also really good, English teachers were mostly absconding. Vaidehi had aced in Math and Biology, dissecting frogs with absolute clean precision. Despite this, or, because of the fact that that was the only subject she didn't have the access to learn, every time they moved, she longed desperately for the new school to have an English teacher. However, it never happened and while, like Vinod, her brothers learnt the language to an extent with their exposure to the job market as they travelled to different cities, Vaidehi could never do the same. She just silently wished she could learn too. Eventually, all of them were married and had children, except her youngest brother who was still a bachelor, had never moved out of home and owned a small shop that always sold different things because nothing really ever got sold there. When Vaidehi was about to get into college, they were moving again and amidst all the commotion, her school certificate was misplaced, or so the rich, competitive aunt with who they were sharing the house with said. When the aunt's daughter refused to do better than Vaidehi at school, she constantly devised plans to make Vaidehi's studies suffer. But everything failed and Vaidehi continued to score better. While she was still cooking up more ideas to hinder Vaidehi's progress, they had to move again. In the beginning her aunt had felt helpless as she'd never been able to do anything if Vaidehi wasn't living with her. And so, as the final step, she destroyed Vaidehi's school certificate and mark sheet, without which admission into a college was impossible. This final strike had worked. Vaidehi only realised her documents were missing when they'd already settled in the new place and when they contacted the aunt about it, she said that they'd lost them probably in all the moving and shifting. Because she was just a girl and would be married anyway to be a homemaker in a few years, no one fought to get them back. Now, two of her elder brothers had placed their children in English medium schools. How did that impact a person in the future, Vaidehi had at best, a vague idea, but she knew in her gut that by the time they grow up, it will be another world in which knowing this language will be indispensable. So, she did for her children what her mother had not, and insisted upon the best for them that they could afford. And an English medium school was one of the first steps.

"Hey!"

Vaidehi woke up with a jerk. She'd fallen into a deep sleep while working on the TV cover. Her thoughts of her past had merged into dreams and she couldn't tell at what point. Vinod was sitting in front of her, holding her palms in his lap. Her children's sounds filtered into her consciousness and grew louder. What was this intoxicating sleep that the world took so much time to pierce in...like slowly turning on the Television sound.

"You're back! It must be late, oh no, I should serve lunch..." Vaidehi replied. Was it the panic of serving lunch late, or the realisation of a dream too big to come true that hindered her to ask Vinod how the interview had gone?

"Relax, relax. It's not that late. I got done early. I'm through, Vaidu, my palms are still shaking. I'm through. I resign this Monday and start next month. And the salary, it's unbelievable!" Vinod replied, excitement snatching itself from the voice that he tried to keep down.

"What? Really? But you said it wasn't going to...what? Really?" Vaidehi fumbled. Was she still dreaming?

"Oh, Vaidu, now I'll be able to give you all a much better life!"

Still intoxicated with her sleep, Vaidehi embraced Vinod tightly. They stayed that way until the children came running in.

"Papaaaa!" they shouted.

"When did you come?"

"Why did you go?"

"I want to wrestle with you"

"I'm going to defeat you today!"

The children bombarded Vinod and this was a picture of such happiness that Vaidehi would remember for the rest of her life. A father pregnant with the knowledge of an unimaginable future—something he couldn't explain to them in words; they wouldn't know what it meant and so communicating it all with an enhanced spirit, laughter and just play.

"We can now afford to as well," Vaidehi said that night, lying in bed, children asleep between them.

"We can manage finances much better now, but even otherwise, I would've somehow managed. But is it that necessary?" Vinod asked the same question. Their whole life had been about doing what was really needed, because that's all they could. Despite this new bump in the wallet, they would take a few more years to get used to the basic luxuries that money could offer.

"Look at me," Vaidehi began, opening her heart a little more. "I feel so embarrassed every time your friends come and you all speak in English. I have no idea what is going on or what you all are talking about. Even when I'm standing in another group with their wives, the same happens. And I know they know it and I know they think of me as a small-town woman and not in a good way. I might've completed school and aced at other subjects but simply not knowing the language makes me...smaller, or lesser than the rest. Imagine how the world would be when they grow up, Vinod. There's a class difference that has nothing to do with money or anything else, but simply being able to speak in English. And no matter how competent or intelligent one might be, being able to speak in English will be an indispensable edge." Vaidehi felt sad for herself as she spoke of this. Vinod's heart shrank on the realisation of how his wife had been feeling and that he had no idea about it. His heart burst with so much love to heal her pain that words fumbled to explain it and died somewhere on the way out. It was decided; his children would attend an English medium school, not because he thought it was important, but because his Vaidu thought so. Because she was important.

Chapter 11

Maya and Manish

As Maya stuffed her bag, she felt suffocated. Dresses complete with kurtis, churidars and dupattas, her vanity bag swollen with bindis and jewellery, footwear that would leave her feet cold, and shawls after shawls that would perfectly match each outfit, completing her look like the newly married daughter-in-law visiting her in-laws for the first time after her marriage. She didn't have to wear all that but she decided to nonetheless, wanting to make sure to avoid any kind of issue from her side, given all the festivities, dinners with relatives and whatever else might happen this Diwali. She remembered a time when she wanted to wear all of this out of choice, for her mother-in-law and for herself, as a step towards becoming one with the family. But now, everything was different. She felt dejected. Every effort she had put in when Suman came to stay with them was simply not acknowledged. On top of which, comment by comment, her love, respect and hopes of her marital life were cut down, with her dignity and self-respect being collateral damage. She suddenly felt herself welling up and shocked at her loss of control over her emotions; she stopped abruptly. Standing inside her wardrobe, hands over the undergarments she'd forgot to pack—forgotten essentials while focusing on outer vanity—trying to calm herself.

Maybe it isn't that bad, maybe you're over-reacting. So many such things happen, even at your own home, with your mother and with your friends and relatives…it just hurts more when a mother-in-law says it. And it's okay; that's how probably it always is, so why to dramatise over something that most girls probably go through… Maybe just ignore it.

As her mind churned these thoughts, trying to convince her to see things positively, the last part was like a tight slap to her face. Wasn't this what she'd always hated about her own home, about the society she lived in and about her country? This mantra: *Just ignore it or zyada mat socho.*

Don't think about it too much. How and when did people even start thinking this way and made it a way to justify and bear injustice? Maybe it began with the wives, exactly like her, who couldn't find a way out of the degradation they were going through. Stuck with the sole goal that her marriage must survive no matter what, somewhere at the beginning of time, there must've been a wife who did not have a way out, having to live adversities far, far worse than what today's Mayas go through.

Desperate for the survival of mind and body, probably she started blocking out the hurdles, despite tripping on them every day of her life. And then one day, she had a daughter. She brought her up with utmost love, affection and care, and as she grew, the wife trained her. She taught her to clean, cook, organise and keep things running, and such things that one day would come together to make her into a wife herself, capable of building a house into a home. Soon, the day came for the daughter to depart into being a wife and *start her own life* with *her own family* as if until now they were holding on to her SOLELY to prep her for someone else. Isn't that why the daughters are called *amaanat* to this day?

As her days of moving into a new family were nearing, the wife taught her the most important things. Things far more important than cleaning and organising and keeping things running, that essentially, unknowingly made her independent. Except, of course, financially — that was the hus-band's job. And so wives after wives, generations of wives were considered dependents because they weren't bringing home money; but husbands after husbands, generations of husbands weren't regarded as dependent on their wives for keeping the house running, feeding them, building homes they could come back to every evening. If only a wife was made to realise that what she was taught was being independent! Anyway, the wife taught her daughter far more essential things than cleaning and organising and keeping things running; she taught her to always obey her husband and his family, she must never talk back and invariably do as they say because that's what she was born to do. She taught her that even if a day arrives when she thinks of coming back home, the doors of her parents' home shall never be open to take her back in. She taught her that once she leaves her parents' house and enters her husband's, she will only leave the latter at the end of her life. She taught her to be dependent. Strangely, the wives taught their daughters the letters I-N-D-E-P-E-N-D-E-N-C-E and told they spelt *dependence*. Then inevitably came the days when the daughters couldn't bear to be wives. Suffering at the inevitability of torture, they turned back to their mothers. That's when the experienced wives passed on the ultimate secret of survival to them: just *ignore it*. Don't think too much about it, keep yourself busier, have children, this is what life is. Thus, the secret of survival was passed down generations of time itself.

The times and conditions changed, of course, for better and for worse. For better, like the rapes and the burnings and beatings, the suffering came down to mental and emotional degradation. For worse, as, first: the women realised their self-worth and became intolerant even to mere taunts and second, as they voiced in protest, the previous generation failed to understand their complaints given their own far worse experience. Subsequently, it became *normal* for a mother-in-law to disrespect and degrade. When the mothers reaffirmed this by saying *"don't think too much, just ignore it"*, the daughters started doubting themselves, wondering if they were dramatic, intolerant, too feminist, too independent, too disrespectful. And subconsciously wondering if they were giving too much respect and dignity to themselves—if ever there was such a thing. Hence, this generational gap brought in an all-pervasive and yet unspoken sense of wonder: "What does she complain about, despite being lucky enough to find such a good family?"

"Maya, are you okay?" Maya turned around to see Manish standing at their bedroom door, holding two cups of tea. It wasn't until she turned to the mirror on noticing his expression of shock and concern that she saw her face and neck glistening with tears. It was when she looked at her ex-hausted face in the mirror that she realised how tired she felt.

"I'm too nervous about…" she trailed off. Her bones ached to think of what words can do justice to her pain.

"Hey. I'll be there with you, don't worry, you have me," he replied.

"You don't understand," she said, thinking Manish probably understood it as her being nervous about going to stay with her parents for the first time.

"Trust me, she isn't a monster," he said, trying to ease the tension and letting her know that he understood. This surprised Maya. Although, she wondered why. Wasn't he supposed to understand? To listen? Or was it that she was so used to men never really listening that she'd grown to not listen either, and hence, expect the same from her partner? Whatever the reason, it relaxed her a little.

*

Maya woke up the next morning and looked around the room that was supposed to be hers. She remembered how happy Manish's parents were to receive them last night. The way Suman had hugged Maya, she had felt that maybe all the problems were actually in her head. That whatever had happened, whatever Suman had said that was affecting Maya so much were because that's just how Suman was. Like a rude friend who always manages to offend everyone but is good at heart. She remembered when she entered the room that was supposed to be hers and Manish's, and had looked around at how the sheets were spanking new, the almost burnt-out incense stick at the bed-side table along with a bowl of crystals was placed to purify the air. The almirah in the room was full of Maya's sarees—ones she'd left behind as she had no use of them staying in another city sans family and relatives. She had slept well and Manish still slept blissfully beside her, both free of the everyday responsibilities.

Maybe something just had to go wrong, so it did. Maybe it isn't as bad as I thought it is. This was the last thought before she fell asleep again.

There were three loud thuds on the door that jerked Maya awake again.

"Manish!" Suman called out loudly, all her class disappearing yet again.

"Coming, Ma!" Manish called back, also irritated at the sudden sounds that Maya was processing. But he instantly fell back asleep again. Maya saw it was 10 am. She got up hurriedly. First morning at the in-laws and she was late.

"Fuck." She muttered, rushing to the bathroom. 45 minutes later, regretting her choice of attires that had delayed her more, she walked out of her room.

"Good morning, *beta,*" Suman said without any trace of disapproval at her late appearance.

"Good morning," Maya smiled back, and then awkwardly stood there, not knowing what to do next. Manish was still asleep, and she wished he would come out. Just then, Maya's father-in-law, Jaydeep crossed the room, smiling kindly at her and Maya saw out of the corner of her eyes, Suman urging her to wish him.

"Good morning, Papa," Maya said. While she had given in to call Suman 'Ma', this was the first time she had called someone else 'papa'. It was weirder. It rolled off Maya's tongue in an awkward, reluctant way. Like the word was decidedly walking through her voice box, up into her mouth and just as it was to roll off the tongue, it saw it wasn't the usual papa it had seen till now but it had already stepped off the mouth, so it just had to fall. Maya missed how such formalities of the younger one having to initiate a greeting weren't there at her own home. She realised how she'd taken for granted the joyful way her own father had wished her morning every single day. Suddenly that tiny gesture meant the world to her.

"Good morning, bache," Jaydeep replied. Whether it was his kind voice or face, the word or the genuineness with which it was uttered, it felt like home to Maya, a little bit.

"Sit, sit. I'll get you some tea," Suman said.

"Oh no! I'll do it, please, just tell me where..."

"No no, you have just come. Sit. I'm getting it," Suman cut her off and disappeared into the kitchen. Yet again, Maya was divided. Suman was treating her so well; Maya even felt grateful. What had gone wrong earlier?

Suman came back with a cup, and Maya said, "I'll go wake up Manish," suddenly realising Suman had called him in the morning so maybe he was required for some work.

"Oh no, that's okay. He's on vacation, let him sleep for a while." Suman replied, walking back into the kitchen saying something about checking on potatoes that Maya didn't hear. She now realised Suman had wanted her to be up because unlike the son of the house, daughters-in-law are never on a vacation if they're visiting the in-laws. All the good feelings which had crept in, slowly nudging out the bad ones, now were washed away, blurring her vision.

The rest of the day went on, reminding Maya more and more of her own home. The Diwali cleaning, mud lamps, buying lights and crackers and colours for rangoli, fresh bottles of oil and ghee—it was the usual zing of the biggest festival they celebrated—and yet she wanted to do it at her place instead. She wondered how it would be if instead of daughters, sons were to move in with their wives. She would be with her parents now. She wondered where had this rule first formed, the woman having to move in with her husband's family and on what basis had they decided this. But more than anything else, she realised how much she'd taken for granted things at home, despite the knowledge of the fact that she'd be leaving all this behind one day. *Just like one still doesn't live up despite having the knowledge of death.* The thought shocked Maya too.

It was the day before Diwali and Maya had been working on her rangoli for an hour now. As she got up, Suman appeared at the door and looked at it.

"Oh my! Our house has never had such a beautiful rangoli before. Well, at least not from the time I wed into a family!" she exclaimed, unable to take her eyes off Maya's creation. And finally, Maya smiled, grabbing on to the appreciation.

"Glad you like it," she replied.

"Go now, shower. Manish and your father might be coming home any moment with all the jewellery. We will sit together and have a look at it post-lunch. You haven't even seen it after your marriage; you must also feel like having a look at it again."

In the shower, Maya felt even more divided. What was this feeling that felt like accomplishment merely because she'd done one thing right and was appreciated for it? Where was the Maya who had not cared for these things? Who had always found it pathetic that women bent over backwards just to be appreciated by their in-laws? And yet, she also thought of what she could cook for lunch so that she could make her in-laws happier. It was like standing on a forking road, she could take the one on which the wives had walked for years or the one that wives today had started to walk on. But what tore her soul was that she was even contemplating about which way to take.

They all finished eating. Maya could feel the dried sweat on her face despite the cold and felt like taking another shower.

Before getting up, Jaydeep exclaimed, *"Beta,* if you cook like this, you'll make us all fat in no time."

A huge smile spread across Maya's face but then Suman almost immediately replied, *"Haan,* we have made you thinner in all these years, no?"

As the smile vanished and Maya had started to hate herself for not saying anything, Manish said, "Ma, please."

"Ah! No no, I'm just saying, the food was very good, beta," Suman replied immediately smiling as nothing had happened.

That afternoon, as boxes of gold jewellery studded with diamonds and rubies lay in front of Maya, joy alluded to her despite the riches. She just sat there, waiting for it all to be over so she could cry herself to sleep.

"Oh! This is a good one," Suman said, picking up a ruby ring.

"You can have it if you like it so much. Honestly, it's ancient," Maya replied, remembering a time she had loved that ring. Now, it didn't matter. And yet, despite everything, Maya wondered how she could still give anything to Suman who had only given her unhappiness.

"Oh, Thank you!" Suman said putting it on immediately.

"Ah, this I'm never going to wear," Manish said picking up his diamond ring that was too jazzy for his taste. "Maybe we could resize it for you," he said, looking at Maya.

Just as she was going to answer a 'yes', Suman said, "No, no, keep it back. It will come in handy later."

What she meant was to save it for Maya and Manish's children. For once, along with tears that took all her strength to suppress, Maya also felt anger. Anger at Suman for refusing to love her despite deciding on bringing her into her family, and tears because of her confidence in the permanence of bad financial condition that they were in. She felt anger at her parents to have sent her into a house that lacked not only financial security but also love and acceptance. She felt like breaking down because her parents were supposed to treat her like the beloved only daughter of the house, and they had failed to do so while getting her married.

*

Maya would've been glad to get out of that house, except on the airplane, the incidents played like a film in her head and tears rolled silently down her cheeks. She remembered how one morning, Suman had just heated a cup of milk, added sugar, put a tea-bag in it and given it to Maya to drink. She said she did it since Maya liked milky tea, while she stirred a boiling pan with tea for Manish, Suman and Jaydeep. Yet again, she had felt degraded and separated from the rest of them. The same evening, she wanted to add half water half milk into a bowl, heat it in the microwave, add a tea bag to it and give it to all of them, instead of adding fresh cardamoms and ginger with the tea leaves and brewing it on the stove, to make a point. Once again, she hated herself to not have the courage to do it.

She remembered how when Maya had told Suman that some of her relatives wanted to visit her the evening after Diwali, she had sighed deeply and said, "Okay beta, since you've married here, we'll have to maintain the relations." Maya wanted to retort, "Not really, I would be glad enough to leave."

She hated herself for not having the courage to do so. She remembered how the night before they were to leave, Suman had called Maya near the temple in their house and extended a baby Krishna's picture to her, to keep it in her home. It was a sign of blessing a daughter-in-law to have a son. Maya had retreated a few steps, saying she couldn't hold it as she was on her period, but Suman had kept coming forward as Maya had kept retreating, and said, "I understand you believe that but in our house, once you've crossed the third day and have washed the hair, it is okay," implying that Maya should change her beliefs to suit their house. And again, Maya hated herself for finally taking the picture, she hated herself for not talking back and being firm on her beliefs, she hated herself for not standing up for herself.

CHAPTER 12
Vaidehi & Vinod

It was only one night and yet, Vaidehi was sweating uncontrollably. Her breath was short and palms were cold. She lay down on her bed but didn't switch off the light just yet. It felt wrong to her. She could feel her heart throbbing against her chest. *Relax, it's not that big a deal. What has happened after all? Nothing!* A voice tried hard to communicate with her but circumstances were too overpowering. It was basically a culmination of a few factors that had Vaidehi so nervous. It was a new, two-storey house, with nothing but overgrown vegetation in the back due to lack of care. Her children were asleep with her in-laws on the first floor — they had started sleeping with them for quite some time now, as decided by Kamla. Vinod was travelling out of the country for a 45-day training, made mandatory by his new company. The new company had afforded them a new, bigger house, but also loneliness for Vaidehi. She reprimanded herself for thinking that and reminded herself to be grateful. *It's just one night. Poornima will be here in the morning.* The voice tried again but in vain. She took a deep breath to stabilise her shivering fingers. The new job was good, the pay was good and so was the environment, the boss and the work. Vaidehi remembered the day when Vinod had come home excited and told her about this training.

He spoke simply, "Vaidu, they're sending me to England, for 45 days, for a training," but his eyes shone with the enthusiasm of realising how big the world could be and the possibility of stepping into it. She'd smiled with difficulty and simply asked, "When?"

"A month later," he had replied. And they'd just looked into each other's eyes and smiled. Vaidehi had wondered if Vinod could see the pain that had already started to eat her up inside. After all, there was a layer of looming success in his eyes and a concealing curtain of a smile in hers. She smiled every day, as her own fear ate up the days faster and faster but she could only hold on to Vinod's hand tighter through the night, in the hope to slow her life down. Where had suddenly all the money come from? And this house? And now this trip? How was it all happening? More than any-thing else, she remembered the excitement in Vinod's eyes and wished terribly that she also had the courage to adventure into the unknown just like him. But she was just so scared.

Her daughter had caught her one afternoon almost welling up and asked, "Mummy, are you crying because papa will go away?" Was it because she was feeling it too, or just plain logic that this knowledge came to her so naturally?

Nonetheless, Vaidehi was reassured to share the understanding of the feeling with someone, even if a child. "Oh no, beta! Why will I cry? It's a good thing papa is going. And remember what Nani had said? Women in our family don't cry." And just that had convinced little Meera. She was still too young to understand that rules were fated to be broken. Vaidehi smiled as she thought of Meera and her mind drifted away to the time they'd decided their children's names: Manav and Meera. Vaidehi had thought long about Krishna and Meera's relationship—unconditional, eternal love that was rewarded with something much bigger than the culmination of it, bhakti, i.e, blessed to be able to love as Meera did. It was considered bigger than enlightenment itself. Manav meant man or human in the sense of a bigger meaning. Manav and Meera together symbolised this relationship bound by bhakti between man and the divine. Even how they'd come together in her life was perfect. But when it was time to officiate the names, a tag that would carry them into the outer world, it made Vaidehi uncomfortable. Manav was perfect, being human in the human world. Meera, however, was just not meant to be for the world, Vaidehi had felt. So last minute, she'd changed it. The world would call her something else, but she, her family, relatives and friends, called her Meera. A place that was perfect and safe for unconditional love. As if the memory relaxed her, Vaidehi fell asleep.

*

"Here, *beta,*" Vaidehi said, placing a paratha in Meera's plate.

"Can I have half?" Manav asked, his hand already proceeding towards her plate.

"NO! It's mine!" Meera replied sharply, shifting her plate away from his hand. Vaidehi caught it just in time to stop the paratha from sliding off.

"Meera, I always see you eat one and a half paratha every morning, why don't you share half with your brother?" Poornima said as Manav giggled merrily. It was something that happened every morning at the table. Manav had an insatiable appetite for parathas and Vaidehi had to stop him at least he upset his stomach. Then, he would stare longingly at Meera's plate, asking for half or even a bite from hers.

"No, but it's mine, I'll eat as much as I want and share when any is left afterwards," Meera replied firmly.

"It's okay, I'll wait but can you be quick?" Manav said smiling. Manav and Vaidehi's eyes met and they smiled at each other while Meera ate in the middle. It always made her wonder how different the two of them were growing to be. Their very eyes spoke of their differences: Manav's were calm, happy and content, while Meera's were all things intense, be it anger or happiness.

"Uff this girl is too stubborn. I'll make another for Manav," Poornima said, getting up.

"No no, *Jiji*, don't. She'll share when she's done and Manav has had enough already, it's okay." Vaidehi replied and Poornima sat back down, lips tight with helpless disagreement. Vaidehi won dered whether Meera was really stubborn or just sure of what she wanted, fierce in keeping what was hers and sharing in a way she was comfortable with? Vaidehi had sworn in her heart to build Meera to become an independent woman, different than how she herself was. But was she going wrong somewhere? The signature parental doubts plagued her often, particularly when it came to Meera. Why was there a confusion in her head between stubborn and standing up for oneself, con fidence and defiance? She often wondered if same questions would've popped in her head if this behaviour was of Manav's. Was she just not used to seeing a girl like this? Or was she going wrong somewhere? But now, Vaidehi only wished Poornima could see Meera as the little girl she herself once was.

"Okay, you can have it now." Meera said to Manav, putting half a paratha in his plate and then looking at Vaidehi, added, "Mummy, apple please." When Vaidehi saw the confidence in her eyes that she herself never had, all her questions disappeared.

They'd almost finished breakfast when a shout made Vaidehi jump. Even after years and years of fights, she never got used to them and always flinched.

"Why would you tear another saree for your useless mats? You can't wear them, can you!?" her fa-ther-in-law was shouting at her mother-in-law.

"I have enough to wear, not that it's your concern anyway!" Kamla shouted back.

"You think I have some treasure with which I can keep buying you clothes?"

Manav got up and went into his room. Meera jumped down from her chair and ran into the other room where the fight was happening and animatedly shouted on top of her lungs, while clapping her extended hands together as if they were a clipboard, "Dadi, your turn, ACTION!"

"As if till now you've spent a treasure on my clothes," Kamla said, ignoring Meera.

"Dadaji, your turn, ACTION!"

"Oh, so you think your rich son will be willing to spend even a penny on you?"

"Dadi, ACTION!"

"Oh, why don't you shut up and go back to your room!"

"Dadaji, ACTION!"

"I'll go upstairs but who will support your nonsense? No one in this whole world will, leave alone in this house!" Vaidehi's father-in-law shouted and walked out.

"Dadi..." before Meera could finish and Vaidehi could get out of the shock at what her daughter was doing, Poornima had ran out of the room and was now returning carrying the little one in her arms, controlling hard to stop laughing, while Meera giggled wildly.

Vaidehi was starting to smile as her shock melted, but Kamla finally shouted, "I don't need anyone to support me. My brothers are enough for me." Vaidehi's father-in-law's hearing had deteriorated considerably and he'd already gone upstairs so this last remark was meant for her.

By moving into this house, Vaidehi had become the villainous daughter-in-law whose hunger for materialistic things never ended and hence had forced them all to move into a bigger house in a rich area. She would also blackmail her in-laws in near future to throw them out on the streets, the in-laws felt. And so, defensively, they'd already started proclaiming they were independent and in no need of any kind of help. When Vinod had bought the house, his parents had refused to move into it. Fear eating away at them at the thought that the owners would be the son and the daughter-in-law that they'd tortured. With time both Vinod and Vaidehi had understood that it was a hoax and that they'd never live alone to struggle over having a comfortable life that they could show off to their relatives. Hence, after discussing for several days as to how to convince them, one Sunday afternoon Vinod had gotten up suddenly and loudly announced to his parents that they were to move today and if they wished to join, they should start packing. And just like that, they had all moved by nightfall. The very next day, Kamla approached Vaidehi to talk about something. Vaidehi had been dreading what fight would break out now but she'd been shocked to see Kamla almost in tears and saying, "You both have this room, the children's room is the adjacent one and they sleep with us anyway. Vinod's father has taken one room upstairs, which one would I take?" Vaidehi was baf-fled at so many levels: Kamla asking for permission from her? Kamla crying in front of her? Kamla showing her vulnerable side in front of her? But instead of asking her to share the room with her husband as every couple did, she'd said kindly instead, "Take the other room that's upstairs, it's all yours. Or any other room that you like." It was only when immediately Kamla had smiled her wicked smile and turned instantly and walked away, that Vaidehi realised it was just an act to get the second room also upstairs and hence the whole floor.

"You know, she could've just had it. She doesn't need to play politics here, she's the elder of the house," she'd said, confiding in Nalini who had visited her one afternoon.

"She doesn't get that. Isn't that why these problems exist? Our elders trying to snatch what they can simply take, as it belongs to them anyway."

Vaidehi missed Vinod even more so when things like these happened. Once, shivering with rage, Vinod had said he would ask them to move out when Vaidehi had shared an incident that had happened. This had shocked Vaidehi so much, she'd stopped sharing anything with him fearing he would separate from them. Nobody, even his parents, deserved to be deserted by their only son, Vaidehi believed. Yet, just his presence made her feel so much better no matter what had passed through the day. Vaidehi juggled and managed the house brilliantly. From the children's school, their homework, to fighting off Kamla's small battles like when she would refuse to chop and let anyone else chop veggies on time so the whole house went hungry, to make-do with the cheap and on the verge of rotting vegetables that her father-in-law bought, to Poornima's demands to go shopping—she conquered each day, one battle at a time, only to reach the end when Vinod would be back. Until then, she refused to breathe freely.

Then one night, Meera came downstairs crying. Vaidehi woke with a start hearing a dissonance of knocks and wails. Poornima slept unperturbed beside her. Vaidehi ran and opened the door, praying it would be something she could handle without Vinod.

"What happened, baby?" Vaidehi said, extending her arms, as Meera came into them. Between a few moments when she finished asking and Meera gathered the strength to reply, Vaidehi's heart started to tear yet again.

Meera's fierce intensity broke as hard as it made Vaidehi's pride. "Mummy, Manav was teasing me, sleeping on my side of the bed so I went and slept on his side. He rolled back, started pushing me to go back to my side. So I said no because he first took away my side of the bed. So Dadi said, 'Manav, you hit her if she doesn't move,' and she kept saying it over and over again." Meera managed amidst uncontrollable sobs. Vaidehi's grip around her tightened. She picked her up and walked around the house to pacify her.

"What did Manav say?" she asked when Meera calmed a little.

"He stopped and moved beside me and said, 'It's okay, you sleep here,' but I came downstairs."

Finally, Meera was identifying the prejudice she was facing. She didn't know what it was yet and that the reason behind it was that she was a girl, but she was definitely feeling it. Unshielded by the wisdom of age, Vaidehi wondered how much worse it would feel pure and unadulterated. But the irony of a woman speaking against a girl while a boy spoke for her didn't go unnoticed either. Patriarchal play could be so unpredictable. Vaidehi's heart tore for her daughter and yet her son's actions mended it stitch-by-stitch. It was one of those moments when she realised she could never protect Meera from anything; she would have to teach her to be stronger.

While Vaidehi's knees were almost buckling under the roof of generational battles, her arms refused to let go—habituated to never give up on family, her bones waited for their cracks to be cemented by Vinod's love. It was during those days, Laxmi came to stay with them.

When Vaidehi first heard about it, her spirit almost gave up, thinking there was no possibility of her being able to take anything more. But once she started staying at home, she saw a completely new side to her. The woman who relentlessly tyrannised her own daughters-in-law was actually fun and easy in someone else's home. She took a special interest in what Vaidehi cooked, what sarees she wore, what she stitched in the afternoons and to Vaidehi's absolute delight, told more and more details of her and Kamla's families. Her stories explored roots so deep Vaidehi didn't think even existed, given how Kamla always turned to her brothers for any kind of help. Due to her constant presentation of her maiden family as her only support even after all these years, Vaidehi didn't think her in-laws were connected to their roots so deeply. The only thing that bothered her was Laxmi's constant taking of things, quite literally. She discussed it once with Poornima when Laxmi had gone for a bath and Poornima informed her that Laxmi's visit to anyone's house meant two things—no decided date of return and simply taking of things that she liked.

One afternoon, Laxmi said, "Bedehi, open your almira, let's check your sarees." She always called her Bedehi. Vaidehi looked up a little surprised while Kamla looked down and smiled knowing what was coming and Poornima just looked from face to face, wanting someone to say something but not having the courage to say anything herself. Vaidehi opened it, and Laxmi got up and went through it, saree by saree, touching each of them, rubbing the material between her fingers, even taking some out and placing them against her navel to measure their length. Finally, from Vaidehi's already humble collection, she took out five sarees, that she folded, kept in front of Vaidehi on the bed and said, "These are my favourite." She wanted Vaidehi to offer her to them, she would never ask for them herself.

Before Vaidehi could say anything, Meera said, "Okay, now you can keep them back." There was silence in the room and Vaidehi saw Laxmi's green-grey eyes fixed on Meera and Meera's defiant black staring back.

"Taiji, then please, please take them; they will look nice on you!" Vaidehi said in a raised volume, as if to erase the memory of what Meera had said from everyone's minds.

Laxmi smiled, "Oho, okay, you're too kind," she said, while picking them up and immediately walking to the other room to store them in her suitcase. That night Vaidehi sat down with Manav and Meera as they drank milk.

"Beta, what you said today to *badi dadi* isn't nice. We should share, no?" Vaidehi said.

"But why does she take away your things?" Meera replied.

"She gives a lot also. She gives us her blessings and she loves us."

"And also, more things come to us once they get finished, Manav added.

Surprised, Vaidehi looked at him. In her fight for herself, Meera was losing a sense of security, while abundance came naturally to Manav.

"Yes…" Meera said thoughtfully, "papa always brings so many things for us."

Meera looked at Manav as if to say "I know now what you mean" and they both smiled.

Soon, days went by and Laxmi and Poornima left, and Vinod came back. That night, Vaidehi told him about the incident with sarees.

"I like that she's fierce. She's so young that her boundaries are blurred. Protecting yourself versus sharing or being rude, these fine lines only get clear with age. I can still tolerate her as a rude child than have her grow up to be a demure woman."

Vaidehi wondered if that was something Vinod wished she had too. Did he not like it that she was the silent kind? But didn't he see that if she weren't, this family would have fallen apart a long time ago? Would he have rather preferred that? But she couldn't be that now nonetheless, some things can't be built after a certain age.

So, all she said was, "Manav had a much wiser thing to say than I did. I'm glad he was there."

"Yes, I'm so surprised," Vinod replied. And they slept, marvelling at how wisdom can surpass the boundaries of age.

CHAPTER 13

Maya & Manish

Maya had trained her mind to fall into deep thoughts as soon as a flight would start moving, and continue thinking with closed eyes until her body would fall asleep. This was to avoid the nausea and headaches that air pressure often caused. Also, there was nothing anymore to be awake for in the flights now.

She still remembered the first time she'd travelled on a flight. During her school years, she, her brother and her mother would go to her maternal grandmother's place for a whole month. Her father would show up during their last week there and take them all back home. His arrival tore Maya into two—she disliked it because it signalled the end of their vacation and she loved it because it was the only time when she had her father all to herself all day long. He wouldn't wear his usual pants and shirts when there but crisp white kurta pyjamas that strangely relaxed her mind. She still remembered how his pink palms, perfectly cut nails and white soles further softened his personality. Even his thick eyebrows and stern moustache failed miserably to give him his rest-of-year stern look. She loved sitting with him and would have wanted to even sleep with him during those days, but at night, only her mother was allowed to sleep in the room with him.

The sleeping arrangements were always the same because the house was always the same, as her uncle never really got rich. The oldest mother, her daughter and son, the daughter's two children and the son's wife and one child all managed to fit in one room. Mattresses, broken at the places where they were folded and kept for years, lumpy but comfortable with familial love, were laid down every night, just like generations in the house. Even they were broken—the oldest was the point of folds, devoid of any cotton inside; just thin, almost torn, holding the cloth of the next generation on both sides together, as they carried little lumps that must be uncomfortable but were the personification of love.

However, when her father came, the single, small room on the terrace would be opened and made ready with cots and mattresses and the best bedsheets the house had, for father and mother. And then, at night, a half of one generation would miss, leaving the rest naturally incomplete. It was for one of these trips that Maya's father suggested they'd all travel in a flight. So, on the day of the travel, they all dressed in their finest, unlike for the trains where they dressed in the most comfortable given the long hours. It was the most perfect flight with genuinely friendly and helpful air hostesses who gave them chocolates and delicious, free food. During the landing, Maya was told to sit away from the window and so, her father sat there instead, with her in the middle and an air hostess beside her in an empty seat. She thought Maya was upset for changing her seat so she went and got her two big Five Stars and two big Bar Ones. Still seeing no smile, the air hostess inquired and Maya's father said that was her signature expression—a serious, I don't care one—which years later would be termed as Resting Bitch Face. But Maya was happy with the score and mentally gave the air hostess five stars, big ones.

Maya had loved the flight, her father was used to flights, her brother never really spoke anything and her mother hated it. For a week to come, the discussion was only about their experiences of the flight. Her mother told her mother how much she'd hated it and how her ears had shut, had a severe headache which had made her eyes and nose water non-stop, which was so embarrassing, and she felt terribly nauseated all the time. Her mother's mother had ridiculed her experience by simply saying, "Huh! Who feels nauseated in a plane?" Maya had thought that the embarrassment part was the problem, not other things. Since then, however, once Maya grew, she had travelled more and more in flights, until they became her only mode of travel. Because they were safer for women travelling alone, and flights were cheaper.

Once Maya was so exhausted, she'd fallen asleep on the flight and had woken up as it jerked when the wheels touched the ground. Like the accidental, unexpected first kiss between a young couple neither of who knew how to use their lips and tongues and bumped their teeth and noses. Since then, Maya decided to sleep on all her flights because it was much easier and comfortable. She'd put on her eye patch and start thinking, until she fell asleep.

Often, these thoughts would be sexual. Of some boy she was crushing on, from college or from the movies. Sometimes, she'd just pick someone she wasn't even attracted to but had strong arms and would strictly only imagine how his arms would confine her, pull her towards him, crush her in his arms, completely darkening out the face into oblivion. There was a phase in college where she only thought of foreigners. White skin, blond hair, wearing denims and white t-shirts, really really tall and named Steven. She had loved that name for years. Steven didn't have a face, but stood for all white American men, whose white skin would blush red on the neck and face as they kissed her neck passionately. That was all the face they ever had—red. She would think detailed sexual rendezvous and she would always be the nervous, scared girl. Which was so different from how she actually was otherwise. And just like that, thinking, she would cross her legs and press her thighs together as she got wet. Eventually, she'd fall asleep and wake up just before landing, her mind picking up the threads of thoughts from where the sleep had snatched them. This had continued even after marriage and Manish was never the man in her dreams. It was still someone from work or from films, or a foreigner. The dreams now were detailed, not just kissing and necking. In fact, they were wild, sans any of the frivolous foreplays or displays of love that we 'normally' associate sex with. They were truly passionate, independent of love or other meaningless decor. Presently, they were about Ved.

Now, on her way to her parent's house for her brother's wedding, eye mask on, lights off, wheels starting to turn, her thoughts started to take off. She thought back to so many presentations and team meetings that Ved had headed, speaking to them about current scenarios, about their competi-tors, about the schools they were working at and the struggles of the children. His sheer dedication towards his work, his true passion to make those children's lives better, his resolve to make a better life for them, his words, his mannerisms, his teeth—every inch of him was awe-inspiring. Slowly, over the passage for time, Maya was attracted to not the face anymore, but his passion to the cause. It was inspiring, it was infectious, and pierced right through her, and she knew he felt the same way about her. Because they'd spoken about it, about how he found her work brilliant and how he was excited to see what more he could do with her talent.

More than that, however, Maya knew she was for him an idea of a woman that he hadn't encountered before. She was married but she smoked and didn't have to get home at a certain time, or cook, or wear marital adornments. There was no marital/love daze on her face and the stupid smile that a marriage brings. She didn't wear red *chudas* or red *sindoor* or even a red bra that spoke of the bedroom where a *pati-parmeshwar* was to be pleased. Her straps, whenever showed, were always white or nude. She knew all of this because he asked certain kinds of questions about her not-so-domestic life, with a slight wonder in his eyes. From group outings, their meets outside the office had come down to three, with Konkona, and then to two. However, not in a planned way. It was just that when others cancelled, they still decided to go ahead alone with that coffee. Like he also did with Konkona or Avinash or Navya. But Maya never wondered if he was with others like the way he was with her. Not out in the open, for despite no marital adornments, there was still an invisible barrier of *married* on Maya. Slowly, though, they had gotten too comfortable and had gone on to discuss what a marriage meant. That's when she had come to know he was in a serious relationship but wasn't monogamous. Maya said she still didn't know what her opinion would be on monogamy, but that if a couple was polyamorous then she wasn't to judge. In fact, she had often wondered whether humans were made to be monogamous in the first place. What was a wedding? Just something humans had devised so two people could have children and not have sex with any other person anymore. Why though? What if there was a world where there was no marriage at all? Everything would be the same, except for a marriage. There would still be a parent or parents—if both decided to stay—there would still be school and jobs which would help the parent pay for the school and food. Wouldn't everything be the same? In fact, wouldn't relationships be stronger if the couple stayed together without any kind of enforcement? And of course, women's hair would fall out lesser without the vermillion. Everyone would be truly independent. A wife wouldn't be dependent on a man to give her dignity that came from his surname. A child wouldn't be called a bastard if there was no marriage in the first place. Fewer complications, more independence. Or was it this very independence that the society was so scared of?

Imagine: a labelless world, where there were no words like wife or husband or any versions of the in-laws in the dictionary. Who would be what then? A woman would be a woman, a man would be a man, a child would be a child. Simpler, independent…scary. Scary just like a label less container with a white liquid in the fridge, or a building without a name or on a map, or jeans without a brand. So unknown, so credit less. But it was simpler, like eating an apple without the knowledge of it being called a fruit or an apple. Just knowing it was edible by nature. So pure, so freeing. And some where down the line, these philosophical discussions had led to one thing and another and she'd admitted to wanting to "try it with someone else". She'd confided that it was only physical, but she possibly couldn't take on anything more than that. She couldn't possibly handle any more emotions, giving away just a peek of what she was going through. That night when she'd got home, she'd told everything to Manish. She wouldn't hide, she wasn't scared. She didn't want another parent to hide things from (smoking, affairs, sex). So, she'd told him all of the discussion, despite a small tiny thing — that in the end. Ved had asked her, "Me?" and she'd stared, knowing that it was leading to this and yet being shocked. Shocked of the expected. Shocked of the known. Like a brother you've grown up with, who does a *BOO* from behind the door you've just entered. That knowledge, she'd kept in her chest, sealed and slept hugging it. And now she fantasised about him in the plane, 36,000 feet in the air. If there was to be a crash, she would die fantasising about another man. A label less man. What a wife, five stars, big ones.

She imagined his fingers tightly pressing her wrists above her head against a wall. She imagined him coming really close to her but stopping short of kissing her, just taking in her nervousness of a virgin. Ripping off her top instead, that jerked her eyes open. She jumped and slid forward a little bit. A hand across her stomach gave her the support and she opened her eyes to Manish, and land. At the conveyer's belt, she decided against it. In her head, getting physical with another man didn't seem unnatural to her. So freeing, so simple, so independent. She could have it and yet, she couldn't. Manish's touch had snapped something in her. So, she picked up her luggage and together they went to her parents' home.

*

Maya and Manish were at home. At her home. And strangely, Manish acquired a sense of alienation that Maya always felt when at Manish's home. So her parents took extra care to always make sure he had company, he had food on time and that he was always comfortable with things to do and warm blankets to sleep in. Before he knew he wanted something, it was brought to him. He was, after all, the son-in-law of the house. So different than the daughter-in-law of his house.

The house was alive with an urgent buzz. Maya's brother, Mannu was getting married after being engaged for over a year and now, they had only so many days before the wedding. Everything they did was in a sense of urgency. No one was ever getting late or falling short of time, but more than the task, the idea of the task to be done was so big that they lived the present in a fast-forward motion. They woke up and didn't sit in their beds for a few minutes, they jumped into the shower, they had breakfast quickly, then they sat with people making suggestions as if their answers were time bound, and then they distributed the executions among themselves and headed out, only to meet for lunch next—a quick one of course. These distributions of executions were the most natural things: choosing by women and booking by men, be it food, venue, or clothes, even the ceremonial items. As if the chores had labels on them of who would do it—MAN, WOMAN, GIRL, BOY. There were variations, of course, even to the stereotypical, for example, the jewellery shopping. Here, the budget was picked by the father, and mother and their daughter went to shopping for it.

The November afternoon was hot. Maya's underarms had sweat patches just from the walk between the AC car and the AC jewellery showroom. The staff welcomed them with chilled lemonade. Their memory of a staff getting promoted just some time back when they'd shopped for Maya's wedding jewellery was still fresh. Maya's memory was fresh too—after lemonade, as the afternoon was to go into the evening, they would be served coffee. But their lemonade was legendary and coffee was average. And another one of her memory was refreshed now as she found herself in the same seat as she'd been during her wedding. Of how she'd said she wanted a bigger gold set for her bridal wear and her mother had said, "Then instead of many, we'll buy you just one." That had shut her up.

Now, the staff unveiled bigger and bigger pieces. Now it was the son's wedding, so bigger pieces of jewellery were acceptable. They had invisible labels too, BOY on bigger pieces, GIRL on the smaller ones. Maya suddenly felt out of it. Like a little girl, she wanted to cry in her room because mummy loved her brother more. But she sat. They all sat. For four hours they swept through the entire two-storey showroom to select the jewellery for the bride-to-be and one set for Maya — customary for a father to give his daughter when his son got married. And the set was a big one too. You see, that way, in that scenario, a big set was a must because the daughter of the house was a mark of auspiciousness and good luck for everything to go smoothly, so she must be honoured. But for her own wedding, the jewellery should be less than what the boy's side would give her because she was a girl. Smaller. Is that how God must feel? When we offer It things for our betterment in return? It must feel shitty to be God. That evening, while on the way back with all the jewellery, nervousness fused into the urgent energy made everyone uncomfortable. Maybe that was the reason why Maya snapped. Maybe it was because she saw the truth. Or maybe she didn't like her label of a GIRL anymore.

While her parents were discussing the amount they'd spent, Maya spoke, "For my wedding, you'd only spent 7 lakhs for jewellery." She was taken aback at how much her voice shook and she looked out the window so that her father wouldn't see the tears in her eyes.

"Beta, that's not true... I don't remember the amount exactly now, but I'm sure that's not true," her mother said in a pacifying voice.

"But I remember. And it is true." Maya said, further angered by the discrediting of her statement.

"Arre beta, so come, we'll buy you more, so what?" her father said.

Now Maya was infuriated. They thought she was being greedy? "It's NOT about that! It's about me saying that what you guys have done is unfair." Maya said.

"Bete, we both love both of you equally," her mother said.

"Maybe. But still, you have bought me less because I'm a girl and he's a boy. That's how this is unfair." Maya replied, containing herself from shouting.

They were all then quiet. Maya felt her chest burn as always, by the feeling that everyone always misunderstood her. Even now. She was either wrong or she was greedy. She was, a GIRL. She wondered whether they really thought these things of her, or was it that they knew the truth behind it and had to curtain with something.

Was it because it was always in her subconscious or because her mind was further dragging her down now that she was already on the way, but as they got home and Maya went to shower, a thought popped up from the darkest corners of her mind. Corners that nobody knows exists until a boogeyman pounces on them from there. The art of *boogeymaning* is generally called overthinking by those who still believe they don't have dark corners. Or that there are no boogeymen. As the water rushed down her body taking the sweat with it, Maya thought of that afternoon when Suman had opened Maya's cupboard in her house where she kept all the heavy sarees and laid out one red silk one on the bed. She'd said Maya could wear this for her brother's wedding. At first, Maya had wondered why would she go through the trouble of cruising through her clothes and take out one that wasn't even good enough for one's real brother's wedding. So, she'd replied, "No, I'll be wearing a *lehenga.*"

"Oh, okay sure, you're right; you can wear your wedding lehenga," Suman had said. Now Maya understood that she was doing this so that they don't ask for money to buy a new outfit. Maya's insides shrunk and her heart shattered.

"No, I'll buy a new one. It's the same guest list so I can't wear my own," she'd replied.

"Yes, that's what I thought, and that's why I was saying wear this saree."

That was the time when Maya had realised how strong she was. When she had kept quiet, nodded and put the saree back in her cupboard.

She stopped the shower and took up the shower gel. She thought back at when in the showroom that day, they were done shopping and were cruising through the showroom and Maya had liked a diamond ring. As she pointed it out to her mother, she'd said, "Yes yes, *beta,* it's good, come, come, come now let's go," pulling at her arm lightly. As if, if she wasn't led away, Maya would shop more and they would have to keep paying for it.

Now she started crying. Sweat replaced by water, replaced by tears. I don't want anyone's money. Her brain shrieked the same words that Suman had once said to her during her first visit. She kept squeezing the shower gel bottle over her head with one hand and kept rubbing the other hand all over her body vigorously until the bottle was empty and she was full of lather. From head to toe. Scrubbed until her nails scratched her skin. Cleaned through the deepest layers of her skin. But sadly, not though her mind. The thoughts, black and grimy, remained. She then turned on the shower and scrubbed her body until it hurt and her feet were covered in washed-down lather slowly dissolving into water. She turned off the shower. The tears took over.

Finally, it was the cocktail night. One day before the wedding. Maya sat at the table with her in-laws and Manish. On another table, sat Mannu, with his friends. She looked at him and wondered about their relationship. He, so silent in the house all the time. With friends, however, he was different. He was open. He was human. Maya and Mannu had once been close but she couldn't recall now when they'd stopped talking. He wasn't a part of selecting a husband for Maya. She couldn't recall any incidents that had happened because of which they'd parted and he'd befriended silence. Why did no one ask him why he was so silent? Why did she not go to his room anymore? Why did she not think of him when wanting to share any of her problems? It was literally like he existed in her life just as a body. She was so involved in his wedding because of her parents and not because of him. And that's where her thoughts ended — that she probably wouldn't have attended his wedding if they weren't the products of the same womb. She didn't even know what else to think of her own brother. A chest of regrets inside her opened where there were regrets for her relationship with her grandparents and to that, she added the regret of her absence of a relationship with her brother.

She walked to another table where the bride-to-be was sitting. Maya loved her. In fact, whatever she knew about her brother was through her. It was strange whenever her sister-in-law would tell her what all happened on their dates. The words he said, the jokes he cracked, the food he ordered—Maya couldn't connect anything to the face of her brother or his past when he was familiar to her. This unsettled her. It felt like he didn't grow up, he got accidentally replaced by another man. A stranger. Their talks felt like two girl friends' gossip session, where one told the other about her newly acquired boyfriend and would one day make him meet her if it ever got serious. And this knowledge became a tumour in her brain that ate away at her sanity. The deeper she went into this thought, she realised how much was wrong with her family. Like a model with perfect make-up and body but with anxieties and jealousy and eating disorders inside that no one knew of. Maya and her sister-in-law were talking when Suman joined them. Something died inside Maya but she CPR-ed herself, forcing a breath of patience, second-chances and benefits of doubt down her spirit.

"Namaste aunty. How are you?" Malvika said to Suman.

"Namaste beta, you look so nice. Are you all prepped for the big day tomorrow?" Suman replied, so perfectly natural and nice.

"Well yes, but you know how it is mentally and emotionally? That strange feeling somewhere inside about this huge change in life… That will take time to go I think," Malvika replied.

Or, it would get worse, Maya thought.

"Yes yes, true for every bride, *bete.* But you need to just accept this change and the smaller changes that it brings with it. Acceptance is the key. Know that all this is happening because you were destined for it. See now, even we thought we would get a girl for Manish who would be in the same profession as him, but then whatever we are fated for, only that will happen to us. Can't do any thing about it," Suman said.

There was silence on the table as Malvika struggled with words and Maya exploded inside. Thank fully, Mannu and Manish came to the rescue, whisking the girls away for a dance. Maya was glad to be on the dance floor, for its inhumanly loud music. It distracted her from thinking. It was like when you bang your head against a low ceiling and someone tightly puts their hand over it, to temporarily subdue the pain from rising. The four of them danced along with other cousins. The floor was crushed under too many people, reminding Maya of a fat man's paunch that would send the shirt's buttons flying the moment he breathed in. The young college cousins showed off their effort lessly flat stomachs wearing the blouses one could wear. Too young to be of marriageable age but old enough to understand sexuality. Young college-going boys were there too, hair standing perpendicular to their heads, stiff like rods no matter how hard they danced. Then there were the newly-married *bhabis*, red *chudas* on arms, the saree *pallu* loose, feeling superior and mature to the college girls. But occasionally they would collect their *pallu* and put it on their shoulders to reveal their flat stomachs, just to make it clear that they weren't 'aunties' yet. And then there were aunties so desperate to get their daughters married that they looked hawk-eyed for potential boys who can be man enough for their daughters. Man-enough generally meant financial status. These girls of marriageable age and yet unmarried were easily spottable. They stood in stark contrast with the heavy make-up faces with wannabe attitude of the college girls and superior faces studded with newly-acquired diamonds in the marriage of the newly-married girls. These were the simple-looking, minimal make-up, earring without a necklace, body-parts covered, demurely smiling (forcibly or willingly) girls. Their eyes were downcast because of broken confidence that came from eluding marriage or just in prayer that no one selects them for they didn't want to be married yet. Either way, they were sketched perfectly to give an idea of they would look as married women, to potential mothers-in-law. Because too much make-up at that age would mean cheapness and too little would mean the *behenjis*. It was a fine line. An art, to walk perfectly on it. Surrounding the dance floor sat mothers who wanted to be mothers-in-law. One with daughters wore desperation and one with sons covered it with a layer of supreme smugness. The potential daughters sat in wait and the sons as yes-men to their mothers, almost seeming to leap and feed at their breasts if they took motherly love a step ahead.

Every wedding was like a disease, celebrating the death of individuality of every couple. And more they happened, the more the disease spread, infecting the minds, dimming the soul, battering the hearts.

*

Maya woke up with a headache. She had had too much to drink last night. It had started with some wine but then as the music had quieted and Suman's words rang in her head again, she had started drinking more, often passing the table where Suman sat, as a rebellious act. At one point she saw her sitting with a particularly familiar aunt of Manish's. Then she remembered how in Maya's wedding her grandmother had told Suman to take care of her and this aunt was the same one who'd said maybe Maya should try and live the other way now. This time, Maya took a glass of wine so that it would be clear what she was drinking, and joining them at the table, said, "Namaste aunty, how are you?" The two older women had looked at the glass.

"I'm good, *beta*, how are you?"

"I'm good too. You know, I never really drank at weddings before, but you know, I was thinking I should try and live the other way now," Maya had replied and smiled. They both were stunned. She left. After some time, Manish had walked up to her and taken her into their hotel room. Suman had told him everything. Manish had just asked why and Maya had exploded. She didn't remember what they'd said to each other in the showdown that had happened. A showdown that probably everyone had heard outside their room as the voices had travelled, of Maya's mainly. But now, Suman was again knocking on the door, calling out to Manish, and Maya remained stubbornly in bed. Every knock felt like her head being hit with an iron. She finally opened her eyes and realised that Manish was in the bathroom. She opened the door. Suman was smiling, she'd heard too then.

She came in without an invitation.

She stopped at the bed and said, "You look tired, *beta*, are you okay?" Maya just nodded. Ideally, she wanted to say nothing so as to be as rude as possible. But she nodded.

"Okay, so you know Kaur aunty who lives in the neighbourhood? She'd come home the other day and was telling me how her daughter-in-law's brother was getting married and she'd given her Rs 30,000 for a saree. Here, I have got the money too for you. Of course, I understand it's your brother's wedding; you must need new clothes. Come now, freshen up; most have finished breakfast," she said and left.

Manish came out some time later. They exchanged looks, both aware it wasn't either of theirs fault. Anger had banged, raged and burned a hellish fire in their relationship, but one tired glance is all it took to repair the damages. It was soothing.

"What's this?" he asked.

"Thirty thousand. Your mother gave it to me for clothes," Maya said, wanting to say more but tired bones refused to pick this battle.

"Oh! She told me last night that Kaur aunty had…" Manish said, realisation creeping in.

"Yes, I know. She told me." Maya replied. His knowledge and understanding was enough.

They both looked at each other and suddenly started giggling. This escalated to a laugh. Tears rolled down Maya's cheeks. It was probably the most painful laugh she'd laughed. She had already bought her dress, spanking new. Backless. Tummy revealing. Daughter-in-law stereotypes defying. In-laws rebelling. This dress was her. The *her* that was lost.

CHAPTER 14
Vaidehi & Vinod

Vaidehi was lying down for her siesta but couldn't sleep. Tighter she closed her eyes, faster the thoughts in her head ran. Meera was one of the reasons. She was increasingly becoming defiant even of Vaidehi. The twins were in class five now. Slowly, they were realising the difference in their genders. Meera was friends with girls only and Manav with boys. Vaidehi still remembered how they'd gone to school every single day with their tiny palms entwined together. They sat with each other, ate together and came back home together. They always spoke to other children, played with them, participated in activities in the school with other children, but they did all that together too. And now, as they were growing, so was the realisation of their one big difference. Eventually, this one big difference would make everything different in their lives, leaving behind the tag of twins but as of now, Vaidehi didn't want to think of that time. She noticed how they shared the happenings at school with restrictions, carefully omitting things their friends had said or thought or done, as if they would give away big secrets of manhood and womanhood itself. They'd then look for opportunities to find Vaidehi alone and share these things with her. But she felt that Manav did so less because he felt his mother was a girl too and Meera had started to not agree with everything Vaidehi would say.

Just the week before she'd come home, waving a party invite and jumping with happiness.

"Mummy, it's Sneha's birthday. She's invited all of us girls to this restaurant for dinner at 6 pm on Sunday. Her parents will be there too!"

Vaidehi took the invite and read the details. She knew about this restaurant; it was close to their house. But she also knew the men who hung out at the paan stall nearby. The way they eyed girls, young or older. They never did anything because it was a busy street, but their eyes ripped through their clothes and shattered their innocence, as the girls obliviously bit into their paan.

"How many girls are going?"

"12."

"Beta, you can't go. Sorry."

Meera was quiet for a few moments. This was probably her first experience of 'convincing.' Until now, whenever she wanted something, she would just act stubborn and throw a tantrum. Now she was older even though not an adult. She was graduating from throwing tantrums to trying to convince, which would end up in arguments, until she was old enough to have discussions.

"But why?" she asked. How could Vaidehi tell her.

"You question too much, Meera; you should sometimes just listen to the elders."

"But last week you allowed Manav to go to a party," she argued.

"Yes, but that was at his friend's home."

"So what? My friend's parents will be there."

It was true, but Vaidehi was still uncertain. Two adults with twelve girls wasn't a good parent-child ratio. A slide of hand here, a grope there, a whistle here, a comment there would simply go unnoticed. And that was all that was needed for a woman's realisation to crack into the shiny glass of a girl's innocence. All those news articles of rapes of little girls started popping in Vaidehi's head.

"But he's a boy and you're a girl!" Vaidehi blurted out in a tone higher than she'd intended.

Now Meera was quiet. Her eyes slowly started drowning in water. She left the room saying "I hate you" but only through her eyes. Actual words would pour out later, after years of going through the same thing.

It broke Vaidehi's heart. She felt sillier than Meera. Everything that she'd wanted for her daughter she'd shattered herself. But how could she have let her go? How could she have let someone touch her, or send her into the danger where this was even remotely possible. So all the eleven girls had gone and spoken only about the party for days, making Meera feel left out. She'd sulked for days, thrown attitude (also graduating from tantrums) and just acted difficult. Vaidehi wondered now where she'd gone wrong. Was it her upbringing where she defended Meera and encouraged her for equality? Or was she wrong now by being over-protective? The other girls had gone. And still, Vaidehi couldn't imagine sending her. She would gladly take her child's hatred instead. Or is it just the kind of difficulty that comes with age combined with lack of maturity?

Meanwhile, in another room, Manav and Meera sat opposite each other on Meera's bed, with chocolates between them. Vinod had started travelling frequently now and with every trip, bringing back chocolates was a staple. And diving them equally between them was a ritual. But it was never simple. Manav always stole and hid a chocolate here, a candy there and Meera could never spot it. The only thing that would give it away was Manav's uncontrollable giggle. Such was his innocent cunning. This would get Meera very angry and she'd ask for the whole thing to be done from the start. It was a one whole afternoon's task. By rule, none of them could eat any unless they were divided, because then keeping a track was difficult. So eventually, too overcome by temptation, Manav would stop and do the task honestly but first, the temptation to tease his sister was to be satiated. Vaidehi could hear their softened voices in the other room. They knew they couldn't be loud when their mother was sleeping as this rest was essential to her health, so they tried to keep their voices down as much as possible, until the sound would lose its way in the conversation and rise. But today, it didn't matter, Vaidehi couldn't sleep anyway. Not by raised voices, but her children kept her up anyway.

"Here, two Kit-Kats for me, two for you. I'll take the Milkyway as you don't like it, so here, you can have gems. And now, for the Toblerones, one for me, one for you. This third one is what we will eat when we both want to, half-half."

Even in their division of property, there was sweetness, Vaidehi wondered. Half-half. Maybe that's how she should have brought them up. Not encouraging Meera so much; but she was a girl, the one who is naturally suppressed should be encouraged more. She loved her children equally, but some-where her injustices found a way to revenge through her daughter. Then why had she not stood up for her, against all the paan-stall men and allowed her to go? But what if something had happened to her? She realised in her the same fear of the unknown that had crept in when Vinod had gone out of the country to train for the very first time in their lives. It was still unjust to Meera, especially when Manav was allowed to go. She should've been allowed too, or he shouldn't have been allowed either. Simple. Half-half.

"I'll take this bitter chocolate," Manav said.

"Okay, but what will I get for that?"

"We can do half-half of the bitter chocolate, but you don't like it."

"I don't want to do half-half for that. Gimme half gems instead," Meera said.

"That's not fair! This chocolate is extra, do half-half for this or else give it to me."

"No! But then I can't eat it, and if I don't then you'll have more than I do!"

"Sssshhhh!" Manav said before Vaidehi could. It made her smile.

Bitter so often came in Manav's life too. Vaidehi thought back to years ago, when they lived in their old house. The children were learning the English alphabet, rhymes and numbers. Meera was just naturally sharper, whereas Manav faltered often. They would both be given time to study by themselves and in the evening, Meera would recite everything at one go but Manav couldn't. Some times, the whole evening would go by, Vinod would often scold him and yet he wouldn't succeed. Vaidehi regretted the things said then, comparing the two: "Look at her, she recited it at one go, when will you manage to remember it?" Of course, those were mistakes every parent committed, in frustration and tiredness, in desperation for the child to learn well and do well. But in hindsight, they always evoked such pain. Once, Manav, while reciting the alphabet kept forgetting one particular letter. It was always, every time, invariably, the same letter that he would miss because of which they would have to start all over again. Vaidehi, already exhausted from her chores, draining more in the afternoon heat and worrying about getting Manav to learn the alphabet on time, before her next cooking time, had hit him. She'd taken a rubber slipper and hit him with its edge so that it hurt more than the broader bottom side of it. Tears rolled down Vaidehi's eyes as she thought of it now. It was as if demons she didn't even know existed had come out that one time and haunted her with the memory ever since. It was easier to be rough with a boy. For Meera, she worried how she'd protect her from the world, and for Manav, she worried how she'd protect him from herself. Bitter. For both, she hoped they'd have equality. Sweet.

"Mummy, you're awake?"

Vaidehi realised her eyes were open and Meera and Manav were standing by her bed.

"Here, you can have this chocolate," she said, extending the bitter chocolate that couldn't fit in their equal division of assets. Vaidehi took it without saying anything. The children stared at her, trying to find whether she was happy or sad. Bitter or sweet.

"And this from my side," Manav said giving up his Bar One. Five Stars for the behaviour.

Unable to judge how she was feeling, they gave her a bitter and a sweet to balance her emotions. Half half.

*

Days nearing a particular Sunday had a very uneasy feeling about them. Like something was going to happen. Manav had started bringing home incomplete classwork, so getting his homework done was beginning to be a struggle. He always got home and completed the classwork from Meera's book, for all the subjects and then started his homework. Meera by then would finish her homework and had to wait for Manav to get his homework done.

Their friends were different, their secrets were different, their parties were different, things that they were allowed to do were different. And Meera noticed all of this. Apart from seeing these growing differences, she also started realising the differences between them that were always there, like their bodies, the clothes they wore, the way they kept their hair, the way they sat or walked and how she always slept with their grandmother and he with their grandfather. So much was different, that she felt the twin she had so intimately shared the womb with, the twin whom she lived with before their life had begun, was slipping out of her fingers. She felt angry at the moment when it had begun—when they had together slipped out of the womb. It was like the whole world was trying to pull them apart. It was only a matter of time when their bond would snap. This scared her, like anything taken away from her or kept away from her did.

And now, when the parents had finally realised that Manav's incomplete homework wasn't laziness or disinterest to write, but weakening eye sight, Vinod had taken him to a doctor for a checkup. Somewhere in Vaidehi's heart, the guilt worm had squirmed again for not having understood her son sooner, better. Why did she always give Meera her ready support but always doubted Manav? It was like a disease in the blood that she wasn't able to wipe out. Meera was denied the doctor's visit so she had waited so many hours for him to get home. It was a strange pull and push between them. She hid her great womanhood secrets that she and her girlfriends shared from him because he didn't tell her his great manhood secrets either. But she wanted to share. She wanted to be more like him. She wanted them to be alike and open and one, like how they were in their womb-life: naked, same, sans the knowledge of differences. Manav got back wearing specs. Meera stared at him, loneliness creeping in to fill the space where their oneness once rested. She started complaining too about not being able to see the board, bringing home incomplete classwork, and yet the doctor gave her a health nod, much to her disappointment. And then when she heard Kamla taunt Vaidehi, saying, "We took care of our babies but now the serials are so important that child's health is a small price to pay for it," she started watching more and more TV. Often Vaidehi would find her nose almost touching the TV.

"What are you doing?" she'd asked.

"I also want specs like Manav."

Vaidehi had sat her down and smiled kindly at her. "It's a good thing you don't have specs, it means your eyes are healthy."

"But I like specs!" Meera had said.

"How will you look with specs? Imagine, when you grow up, you will put lipstick and kajal and all the makeup and in the end wear specs over it?"

Meera imagined herself doing all of this just like she'd seen Kaishma Kapoor do in a movie. Coming out of the shower in a towel, with body still wet. In a silk robe in the next shot, hair and skin dried. Sitting in front of the dressing, applying something on the eyelashes, a line of liner, brush strokes on cheeks that made them blush, and finally lipstick. And then, the movie ended and she put on glasses in the reality of her imagination. It looked fine. She looked fine.

"Yes, it will look good," her stereotyped mind said.

"No, you're not getting specs. Now sleep," Vaidehi replied.

Meanwhile, Kamla was trying hard to blind Vinod. It all started when Vaidehi had told Vinod about controlling the children from watching too much TV after Manav got specs. Vinod had argued that they spent one hour in the evening watching cartoons, which was okay. When Vaidehi had argued further, Vinod had dug out the real reason and found out that it was Kamla's taunt.

"Why are you so bothered? Haven't you heard her say a million times that she used to leave her children wailing, because she was busy working?"

No, it was because she already felt guilty about not taking as good care of Manav as she did of Meera. But Vaidehi's heart ached again, imagining an infant Vinod, calling out for his ignoring mother's milk. She'd felt the pain even more after she had become a mother. She had walked out quietly then, to get Vinod some tea, only to find Kamla listening in on their conversation. She'd then heard her telling the neighbour about how daughters-in-law these days poison the sons against their mothers. Vaidehi had been uneasy since, because in a few incidents that followed, Vinod had come home to find Kamla crying, and when asked, had said that Vaidehi had threatened to throw her out of the house because it belonged to her. In all three incidents, spanning 6 days, it was the same act. All three times Vinod had just told her that it was her home too and she needn't worry, but hadn't confronted or comforted Vaidehi. But it was clear that something irked him. Whether it was his mother's tears, her scheming, or just the dramatics of the whole thing, Vaidehi couldn't tell. She only wondered what would a man think if he came home to his mother crying every other day? And the logical reply wasn't very favourable to her.

But it was a particular Sunday morning, that was the most unsettling. It was a combination of a lot of things for Vaidehi. Guilt worm still scrawled in her heart every time she saw her beloved son's bespectacled face; Meera had hurt her eyebrow while swinging her water bottle, had bled and the knowledge of stitches that the bandage hid made her ache some more; and finally, Vinod's friends were to come for dinner that evening. His English-speaking, Vaidehi-fun-making, modern friends with short-haired wives, were coming for dinner. And all of this, while she battled Kamla's scheming moves and wondered whether Vinod could see things clearly. She finished making *kheer*, kneaded the dough for making *puris,* soaked the *chanas* in hot water and chopped onions, tomatoes, green chillies for making the curry in the evening.

She took a shower and made lunch that they all ate together, except Kamla and Vaidehi. Vinod's parents fought over how many *rotis* to eat. Meera and Manav shared Manav's specs for one-one roti each until Vinod told them not to. Meera asked why. Vinod told her if she wore his specs, her eyes would weaken too. Meera smiled at having found a new way to get specs and resolved to wear them more often later. Vinod thought how delicious the meal was but as always never said it to Vaidehi. After they were done, Kamla and Vaidehi ate together. Kamla complained about the food. Vaidehi kept quiet. Soon, there was a lull, with everyone having gone off to a siesta. As if some god, sitting somewhere (in the colourful pictures and brass idols of the small wooden temple, mounted on the wall in Vaidehi's kitchen) was giving her a time out. And to Kamla, some time to scheme some more. For the men to shut their eyes, and the women to wonder whether they could see them for what they are. For one child to be happy to see the blackboard again, and for the other, to wish she didn't.

They all woke up at 4, yawning, stretching, lying down for five minutes more before slowly descending their feet on the floor, dragging them to carry their bodies to the bathroom and switching on the geysers. And just like that, the bustling energy tricked the peaceful one, slowly and sneakily, infusing itself in the air, pushing out the peace from the molecules until there was none left. The house was filled with the sound of showers and cupboard doors opening and closing, the contents rattling against each other every time someone opened and shut the drawers, the occasional speaking on the phone of "Haan, where are you?" or ringing of the phone asking for directions, of clicks of lipstick lids and chain locks, of the rubbing of cloth against each other when belts of the frocks were tied, the sound of velcro of the sandals being opened to receive tiny feet. Even the silences were filled with raised eyebrows asking for approval of looks and nods giving them, of fingers put on lips asking for silence to eavesdrop before entering and of eyes pleading to lend the specs for some time before the guests came.

Then three things happened at once. The cooker's whistle announced the cookedness of curry, the doorbell announced the arrival of the guests and they both together silenced the eruptive energy of the house. As a result, the house assumed a graceful mannerism of an energy that one assumes in front of guests. A general voice of *"welcome, welcome"* *"namaste" "kaise ho" and "arre yeh itne bade ho gaye?"* went around among the hosts and the cool uncles with jeans, t-shirts and cool rudraksha beads neckpieces and chic aunties with cropped hair, high heels and rouged cheeks. The children mostly hid behind their mothers, sandal-clad, bespectacled and frocks with bow-knot belts. Vaidehi could already feel a sense of something descending inside her. It dripped from her smile, made its way through the middle of her breasts and fell with a thump in the pit of her stomach. Her saree, lightly twinkling gold earrings, delicate chain and multi-coloured bangles didn't belong. Her Hindi language didn't belong. Her reddened hair parting didn't belong. Her absence of education didn't belong. She didn't belong. So, she got up and left, to bring back some drinks. Rasna, orange flavour for the kids and the kids in the adults. There was a general aah from the relief of the iced drink.

"C'mon, Vaidehi, add some fizz of cold drink; don't be sitting with bowed head demureness of a rasna!" a cropped haired, high heeled, rouge-cheeked aunty commented. Vaidehi realised she'd been indeed sitting with her head bowed. She looked up and her lungs managed to throw out an awkward laugh as her only response. But soon the aunties and uncles started talking. Uncles with uncles and aunties with aunties, with their children still clinging to their arms. Until one of them ordered to play together in another room and they dragged their feet to leave.

"Nice earrings, Vaidehi. Did Vinod give them to you?" one of the aunties asked.

"Thank you, yes. He'd gone to Madras, got it from there."

"Ooh, how nice! Good to see you wearing them, I mean otherwise, who wears gold these days, you know, and that too for an evening get together at home like this." Vaidehi's eyes lowered, her grip on her glass tightened and her other hand fidgeted with her earring.

"C'mon now, Sheila, don't be mean!" another aunty commented, thoroughly enjoying the show.

They all giggled, drinks swaying, rouged cheeks high, lipstick lips revealing mean teeth, artificial rings clinking on the glasses.

"And, how did Rinoy do in his exams this year?" Vaidehi asked, torn between running to her kitchen's shelter and being a host. However, her innocent question shut the aunty up. Nothing can beat a child's shame that a parent feels, however small. The boy had failed and so the aunty struggled with the reply. Now, all the teasing eyes were on Sheila, mean teeth ready to come out. Her rouge darkened, her mascaraed lashes lowered.

"Arre! Why is no one having the snacks?" Vaidehi exclaimed, getting the gist and suddenly, all eyes turned to judge the food instead.

The clock struck dinner-o'clock and the aunties, plates full of food, ran after their children, feeding them a spoonful here, a bite there, as they turned for a moment from their busy games. They had mixed like they'd known each other for years, unlike the adults, who had known each other for years. Meera had someone's specs on, Manav had hooked another boy with his story, three girls played *ring-around-the-roses* on loop and a couple of boys loudly shot each other with their palms shaped like guns. Vaidehi could breathe in this crazy hoopla.

Finally, the adults sat back down to have the dinner. Men and women dined together after the kids had. The sounds were merrier now, with some kids asleep and some in its toxic trance. The spoons and plates clattered softly, the conversations were relaxed and controlled by the mouthfuls of food, the aromas rose from the rice and mingled with the *chholas*, the *puris* oiled the fingers and made them shine like gold earrings. The teeth were less mean, the heels were grounded, the rouge lightened and the lipstick wore off with the intake of food. Even Kamla's gossips about Vaidehi and claims to have cooked all the food seemed calming.

"Get dessert," she said to Vaidehi, as the plates emptied. Aunties got up to clear the trays amidst the hosts' protests, but their bellies were full and smiles kinder, so they did it anyway. Kamla joined them reluctantly. Vaidehi went to the kitchen and saw Kamla hovering over the rice pudding.

"I'll get it, don't worry," she said and Kamla jumped. As she turned, Vaidehi saw the lemon skin in her hand. She'd already squeezed the juice inside and was stirring it with a spoon. Her hand's movement was so slow and graceful it was difficult to believe it existed, despite seeing it move.

Questions and panic collided in Vaidehi's eyes. Kamla snapped out of being caught by high-heeled sounds of Sheila coming into the kitchen. In a flash, she put the squeezed lemon in her mouth, chewed a few times and gulped it.

While Vaidehi stood there comprehending, Kamla said, "Haay, the milk was good, how did you even manage to curdle the pudding?"

Sheila went over to see it. The milk, just starting to turn, gave away the culprit's name, the last word uttered with its last breath.

"But didn't you make all the food?" mean-toothed Sheila asked.

"Everything except dessert," Kamla replied curtly, the line finding its place between her brows, the eyes narrowing and the cheeks turning out their signature scowl as if they'd come home. Kamla left the kitchen and Sheila raised a brow and followed as if on a mission. Vaidehi stood there, on the verge of tears, tired of cooking and getting ready and being a host and of just seeing all of it. Somehow the news must've spread because Vinod came into the kitchen carrying packs of ice cream.

"Hey, it's alright. I'd got the ice creams, just in case, you know."

Vaidehi searched his eyes for more, whether he knew. She couldn't tell and yet she wanted him to know. The ice cream was served. The scowl and silence remained with Kamla for the rest of the evening.

"Aunty, the ice cream is really good, did you make it at home?" one of the aunties asked, knowing full well the truth now. Vaidehi wanted it to be over.

"Oh no, Vaidehi got it. She doesn't serve rice puddings anymore. With desserts, she's modernised." Sheila commented. She'd seen it all to crack a good mother-in-law, daughter-in-law joke. Joker hosts for the evening.

"Oh no, even otherwise she has! Don't you remember the twins' first birthday? In *lehenga*, head covered with the dupatta and...and a *maangtikka*! So...exotic!" another aunty replied. Vaidehi was partly glad that Vinod wasn't around to see her demeaned, because what if he loved her less? And partly, she wished he was there to support her.

They all left, leaving behind melted left-overs in transparent bowls. Kamla and Vinod sat down at the dining table, after seeing the guests off. Vaidehi's father-in-law had already gone upstairs and she started clearing the table. Finally, she sat down at the table too, waiting for Kamla to leave so they could go to sleep. But she stayed, without uttering a word. None of them did. Strange energies mingled at the table — Kamla's anger, Vaidehi's hopelessness, Vinod's ambiguousness. The atmosphere curdled.

Manav got up from his sleep and came over to Vinod and said, "Papa, I can see clearly now with specs."

Vaidehi realised Vinod had been so busy, Manav hadn't had a moment with him to speak to him. She wondered if Vinod even remembered. Whether he even cared enough to want to. Whether he cared enough to want to follow up with her either. Thoughts escalated in Vaidehi's head. How did he see her? Like the way his friends did? Long-haired, flat-heeled, plain cheeked; how could he even like her? Amidst all the English-speaking, modern haired, made-up faces and scheming minds that always looked down upon her, could he see her for what she is?

"I see, good," he said, looking at Manav, answering Vaidehi.

CHAPTER 15

Maya and Manish

The battle that was happening inside Maya was slowly turning into a full-fledged war. She didn't know that though. She was engaged in battling the cannon ball events shooting at her, she didn't even realise her mind was preparing defence troops of its own. There would be a war leading to no winners. Just like wars are. What began as a struggle with her in-laws, led to decaying knowledge of unanswered questions for her own family and in a way, all of it questioned her whole existence. Everything felt wrong. More than that, everything felt alien. She felt like an outcast. Despite having three houses—her parents', Manish's parents' and her own with Manish—she didn't feel at home anywhere. Her heart ran amuck, berserk, like a mad man, looking for shelter and food.

Feeling alienated for the first time in her own house at her brother's wedding and having done a rebellion of sorts against Suman, Manish and Maya were to spend some more time post-wedding at her parents' place, and Manish's parents had decided to stay back as well. The thought of it made her head spin. She longed to be alone but there was no escape from the circus, so she put her clown cap on. Again, there were no big events that happened, only the small ones that always happened. The inconsequential ones. The general, usual ones. The ones that the mothers-in-law were entitled to. The ones which if you'd talk about, you'd be labelled an overthinker. The ones that needed to be ignored. Ones that tore her apart in ways she didn't think was possible to tear a person.

Like the time when Suman went out shopping and brought things for everyone but Maya or when Maya asked Suman if she could get her ring fitted since it kept slipping off her finger and Suman waved it off saying when Maya puts on weight it will fit. These small, everyday incidents made her feel unwanted, uncared for and unimportant. Like a sudden rude slap after being brought up with love at her own parents' place. This made her heart go running back to her parents, as if crying, complaining about the children who were mean to her on the playground. At these times she wished she hadn't married. Then her memories would pop up suddenly, reminding her about the shopping trip she'd made to buy her sister-in-law's jewellery. At that, her heart that had almost reached her parents, would retract, come running back and mid-way wouldn't know where to go. Like an orphan on the streets. She would then try and wonder if she could think like every other daughter-in-law, accept the insults as just how the world is, and live on, wait for her turn to be a mother-in-law one day. As she would do this, Suman would do something else. It was like Maya was attracting it all in her life. Like the incident one morning, when Maya and Manish were in the room with Suman. Manish mentioned one of the rings that Suman had asked Maya to buy for herself but hadn't paid half of its cost. It wasn't a gift, it was a custom where a mother-in-law would gift her newly wed daughter-in-law a ring on the first morning after the marriage. They said it symbolised that a daugh-ter-in-law would forever be bound in the mother-in-law's fist. Maya had often found herself blam-ing these customs for all her problems, before physically jerking out of it.

Hence, that morning Manish told Suman, "Ma, why don't we give the rest of the money for this ring? Since we're here, we wouldn't have to make a transfer online."

To which Suman replied, "*Beta*, now the marriage is done, whatever happened, happened. I can't keep going back to the accounts, it's too tiring."

Cheat! the word rose from Maya's heart, lumped her throat, wet her eyes and employed in her head, because she couldn't open her mouth to let it out. To think she was married into this household made her knees go weak. Her heart again went wailing to her parents. But the complaints now were against them. For choosing a home like that for her, where she could never feel at home. For mindlessly pushing her among these people who suddenly seemed so alien to her. Including Manish, because of his silence.

Then, one evening, they were all sitting together, discussing reminiscing about Maya's wedding, when Suman said to her parents, "But see, during the lagan ceremony, when I asked you why you didn't bring Maya along, you said I'd told you not to! In front of all our guests!" Everyone fell silent, their minds coping with what she said, and back to the most controversial moment of Maya's wedding. The ceremony was hosted by the boy's parents and traditionally, the bride-to-be wasn't supposed to be present. However, with time, it had become more of a party that the bride-to-be had started attending too. But during Manish's ceremony, Suman had called up Maya's parents and told them they were holding the function in a place where more than fifty people aren't allowed — "Not even one person over fifty," she'd said — and so the guest list had to be cut down tremendously. After all of this, Suman, in front of everyone had said to Maya's dad that he should've at least brought Maya, making it sound like it was their decision to bring fewer people and not because Suman's family couldn't afford to host more. To which, her dad had replied, innocently, that they didn't because they weren't allowed to. However, a manipulative mind could only see the same in everyone else. She simply wanted Maya's father to go on with the charade to hide their relatively weak financial status. Maya's heart ran to her parents. To hug them. To tell them she loves them and that this woman can go to hell. But she kept quiet. Later, her father declared, "All this happens in relation-ships, *beta,* just ignore it."

Maya wanted to shout *I can't ignore* it but her heart retracted instead and decided to cry itself out in the shower.

It was finally time to leave. Maya was sad and yet glad. Her parents saw everything and did nothing. Her parents-in-law would never be her family. Mannu was honeymooning but his presence would have been like absence anyway. Manish had kept quiet. Just like her parents. Just like her. And this was it. There was no escape from her strongly acquired sense of loneliness that came from being around her closest ones.

*

They were packing and Suman was generally listing the jewellery so that Maya could check all was in place.

"Okay, you have everything, so there's just one heavy necklace set with us in the locker, back home," Suman summed up.

"Yes, and one more. The *Hansli*," Maya replied, panic rising, thinking if it was misplaced since Suman didn't say it was in the locker.

Suddenly Suman started laughing. "Yes, yes, your *hansli* is with me, don't worry. We'll give both to you so you can keep them in *your* locker."

"I just asked because I thought I misplaced it," Maya replied, voice weak with the sting. Manish stood there quietly. Maya was suddenly nauseated looking at the jewellery in front of her. How and why did she come across greedy when it came to jewellery? Maya thought. Not just with Suman, but with her own parents too. She didn't want any of it. The diamonds and rubies and the gold and platinums she'd once wanted and worn with so much love, now seemed too heavy. She was just a girl and just a daughter-in-law, she didn't deserve so much heavy jewellery. She couldn't take it. For now, she packed all the jewellery that her parents had given her, and gave it to her mother asking her to keep it since she didn't have a use for it anyway. All the jewellery that Suman had given her, she packed and took with her to her home and locked it away in the locker. Lockers that stored wealth. Her wealth-tainted green emeralds for greed, red rubies for anger and white diamonds for everyone's silence that passed as peace. All of it disgusted her.

*

Maya felt light as a paper that morning in her office with a paper weight of relationships on her chest. Holding her down. Stubbornly pinning her to the ground, while her corners fluttered desperately to fly away. But it was one of the good mornings as she realised her paper self, compared to only feeling the bone-shattering paper weight's weight. However, she knew it wasn't a permanent feeling; soon, she would go back to only feeling the weight and then have spurts of moments of feeling like paper, and she would oscillate, draining herself. Realising this, she was already starting to feel the weight when Ved tapped her shoulder. Her eyes jerked open and she realised she had passed out, her head on the back of her chair.

"You alright?" he asked.

Maya looked at him as if taking in him after the two weeks break.

The way he asked that question—feelings coming out contrastingly from that body clad in corporate clothes—made her heart flutter. Why couldn't she go with it? It made her feel good. So what if it wasn't going to lead any where? She didn't want it to lead anywhere. She just wanted to feel that flutter of her heart again. A crush, an attraction that made the world disappear. Like a breath of oxygen, but purer, as if in the mountains, needed not just to stay alive but stay alive healthier. Or was it like a cigarette? Giving just an illusion of a high?

"Yes, I'm fine. Just a little…exhausted," Maya replied.

"I know, families, right?" he said. He understood and yet didn't.

Maya was contemplating what to say, when he said, "I think you need some coffee, you're zonked out. Come, cafeteria, quick 10 minutes."

He turned around and started walking away without waiting for a reply and Maya followed like she was tethered to him.

"I take it that the vacation was good and bad?" Maya just sighed. "Okay, more bad than good."

Maya dropped her eyes and prayed that tears wouldn't escape her eyes.

"Wow. Okay. Well, you're here now, Maya. You'll find a way to deal with it. Give yourself time, you can think better when you're away."

Maya nodded. He extended his palm and kept it over hers on the table. This jerked her eyes up. Her heart beat faster with nervousness tinged with a drop of excitement.

"It'll be alright. I promise." Maya smiled, nodded and tried to take her hand back, but Ved pressed it in place under his.

"Ved, everyone's here. Not safe," the words tumbled out hurriedly from Maya and she wondered why she would feel that way. Of course, there were office policies, but they were close friends. Even if they weren't, Maya, in another world, wouldn't have cared. Why then was she scared now? Was it really because of people and company policies or because she was afraid people would know the thing that she was still gathering the courage to jump into?

Ved let her go and sat back. "It's alright, Maya, I can comfort you as your team lead and a friend, you know." He said it with such genuineness Maya wondered if she was really overthinking everything. She looked around; a few eyes were already on them. She wasn't overthinking. Maybe Ved presently was what Maya once was. She sat up and took a sip of her coffee.

"The only thing bitter that is good," she said. Ved smiled.

"Bitter coffee. Feet poking pebbles on a beach. A cactus. A kitten that scratches. All good." Ved said.

"The pain of defilement," Maya added.

"So then what, Maya?" Ved asked.

"So then what, Ved?" Maya asked puzzled.

"How are you going to make your bads, goods? Solve them, use them. This is your world, but still have to MAKE it your own," he said and got up to leave. Maya followed, going back to being silent, but a different kind of silent. Even more tethered to him.

The entire day at work was spent in a haze. Maya worked and constantly exchanged messages with Ved. She was a college kid again, floating on the high of a new crush, butterflies fluttering in the stomach, silly smile on her face. A smile that her newlywed status could never bring. She felt what she had never felt with Manish. It was silly, stupid, immature, but it was essential. It was the first step to either making or breaking of a relationship, but it was an essential first step. A seed that a plant struggled to break and then worked hard to grow through the soil, to see the light. For Maya and Manish, the plant was planted, a life given on a platter and guaranteed, meant to be. Already steps ahead. In a way, a beginning that was already an ending. An ending with no memories of beginnings to feed on. So, Maya latched on to what she couldn't have. It made her smile.

But back at home, this addition to her life changed everything with Manish.

The first to take a hit was their sex life; it ended. At first, Maya refused Manish's initiatives, being tired. While actually, her mind had filled itself with so much Ved to run away from everything else, that Manish's face didn't seem right in bed. While his presence was always home, his sexual touch didn't seem right. Eventually, sensing she needed to be away, Manish stopped too, giving her space. And then came the other things. Small things, things that need to be ignored. Things you needn't overthink about. Like she would look at him but not really see him. She would be on her phone so often, she wouldn't even remember what shirt Manish was wearing that day. She would wake up and her hand that once reached out to Manish, now reached out to her phone. So many times, her thoughts would drift away to her conversations with Ved, mid-way talking to Manish. Manish saw all of this and said nothing. He thought the trip had been too much and that if Maya needed her space, needed to do what she needed to do, then so be it.

And then came the intolerance. Every time a conversation went wrong with Suman, Maya who used to be quiet with shock, would now be quiet with such blind rage that didn't know words at all. She'd not respond to her, but soon as the conversation was over, she would wage war at home with Manish. While earlier she felt pained at his sandwiched status between the wife and the mother, now she didn't care. Head too full with attraction for another man and discontentment with the one she was bound to, benefits of doubt, pain for your partner that comes from love, all vanished. They would have fights after fights and went to bed exhausted.

While earlier Maya woke up with depression, now she did with new found passion tinged with guilt. Guilt, not because of anything else but because she felt terrible for shouting at Manish. The fact that he never shouted back killed her even more. And so, every morning her head would swing between Manish and Ved—what she had and what could've had—and die a little more inside. She was made of two halves, both so incomplete, they couldn't even make her whole together. Another realisation that enhanced considerably was the fact that she didn't love Manish. What was earlier a pebble on a smooth sandy beach, now became a thorn etched in her foot, going deeper and deeper until it gave her enough pain to look at it, confront it, want to do something about it. When she tried to, it only dug deeper and it started to show. It showed when her laughter started to erupt but died down immediately by the weight of the knowledge, or when her candid pictures showed her lost in nothingness and her eyes an intense shade of sad, or when she could never not be restless anymore, constantly searching her phone screen for what she wished was also at home or when she woke up and dreaded the day ahead. It was as if her life had a background score of broken incompleteness and it played even louder in case she forgot about it for a moment.

And what she thought was happiness with Ved, was merely a weak, temporary escape.

Still up? Maya's screen blared bright. There was something about seeing Ved's name on her phone screen. The way his name's letters turned and curved. It had come to mean so much that no human being should mean to another. The way that flash on her phone filled her with hope and happiness reflected such desperation. She knew it but she still held on to it. One demon at a time she thought.

Yes. What's up?

Nothing, just thinking about you. Someone was thinking about her at 3 am and had bothered to say that to her. She meant something to someone. Someone valued her the way she was supposed to be valued.

:-) me too. She replied.

What were you thinking about me?

Maya thought about it. Of course, she thought about his flamboyant personality, the charm, the support, their friendship, but why did it mean so much to make her desperate? What was so different about him that set him apart from Gaurav? It was months since she'd spoken to him, and yet, despite all his missed calls and unseen text messages that she'd not deleted either, why was it so important to answer Ved's at 3 am? They were both her friends but only one had the probability of being more, looming just around the corner. And it made her dive into another world when hers was particularly unbearable. Just like walking out of a room.

Your smile. Your passion for those children. Your laughter. The way you dream.

Then this is only appropriate, he replied with a picture of him smiling.

Haha. Helps, she replied.

Wow, you sure can't compliment.

I did. A big one right now.

:) I'm glad I can. Have you thought about it, Maya? He asked, picking up the question he'd asked before she'd left for the wedding.

It feels like a college proposal. But tiring. Why do we tag and ask and need answers? She might be desperate enough to cling on to the happiness she got from Ved but not courageous enough to admit to anything, yet.

Then how about you send me a face for a face? She smiled. This was simpler. No questions asked. No positions defined. No labels stuck. Just...nothing.

She sent him a picture of herself. Wild curls bellowing around a tired face. Desperate eyes, trying to hide their nakedness behind a translucent smile. Lips, reluctantly doing a job they would rather not. But one would know that if they looked closely. But we don't look at anybody closely enough, be it in person, or a picture.

Beautiful. That's the first thing that had struck me when you had opened the door to that interview room. He replied.

How about a barter? He sent another text, along with a picture of his naked torso.

Suddenly, Maya's body was aflame. She didn't know how long it had been, but she hadn't realized it because her urges had died at some point in time. Maybe when Ved came along, maybe before. But even at that moment, she didn't want Manish, she wanted Ved even though she could hardly have him. Her heart fluttered, her skin goose-fleshed, her nipples felt tingly and she felt warmth between her legs. The picture, her desperation, or her brokenness — something was too powerful. And just like that, she walked out of the room that Manish slept quietly in.

CHAPTER 16
Vaidehi & Vinod

It was a calm, bright morning. Just like the spanking new, white Maruti 800 that Vinod had recently bought. Vaidehi loved it; it was something that neither of them had even dreamt of achieving. This morning, they sat in their backyard with two cups of tea between them, last night's happiness of car-arrival still crisp in their hearts. There was a mildly cool breeze flowing that would later rage with heat. Vaidehi liked her tea milky, mild and almost unsweetened. So, Vinod had it like that too. Mugs full, a plate of Marie biscuits in the middle, they breathed in contentment and were grateful for it. Vinod read the paper and Vaidehi spoke to him.

"We'll go for a drive on Sunday," she said.

"Come, let's go now," he replied.

"No, no, I have just this time of calm before all the work starts."

"Yes, so we'll go on a slow, calm drive."

"No, I can't replace this chai-time with you with anything."

"It's the best time of the day indeed."

"I'm so grateful. We have a beautiful home and a family."

They both looked at each other and smiled. There were still Vaidehi's insecurities and under-confidence. There was still Vinod's pain of seeing her in pain. There were her in-laws creating a new hell for her every day and at every chance. Despite this, they felt grateful, not in a *think-positive and your life will be positive* kind of way, but in a way that was so natural, they couldn't imagine it any other way. They loved each other, completely and absolutely. They had two beautiful children. What else could they have asked for? It's strange how love can find a place despite most adverse circumstances. The point from where Vinod and Vaidehi's love story had begun—their day of marriage—had such an inhospitable environment that love was impossible to ever grow there. Parents hell-bent on making lives miserable, dwindling finances, a one-room house which you were never allowed to leave. Even if an arranged marriage would've tried to force love, how could it have survived in the incidents that followed? How was the family still thriving? How was Vaidehi happy? Maybe an arranged marriage of that time provides not just companionship, but a sense of finality, that with acceptance comes love as an eventuality. Maybe for Vaidehi and Vinod, there was no other way of how life could be lived. *Aisa hi hota hai.* That's how it happens.

"We indeed do," Vinod replied. Although his words didn't, his eyes said thank you, and Vaidehi read it.

"What time will you come home today?" she asked him.

"Somewhere between 8 and 9."

"I hope your timings get better; having dinner so late isn't healthy."

"Aah! Yes, but the work is at its peak. And it's going to be like this for quite some time."

"Have a heavier snack in the evening at least."

"Yes boss!"

Vinod had started to call Vaidehi 'boss' in an affectionate way but they both knew what it actually meant. That one word meant thank you in a world where such open communication was unheard of. It meant he was grateful for Vaidehi, the way she had kept this family together, the way she was bringing up the children, the way she was dealing with his parents, the way she took care of him. The way she had completely transformed his life, given him direction. And also the way she kept things to herself that were thrust on her, knowing they would hurt Vinod. A decision that she'd taken long ago of not telling him things that happened at home had now become a habit for Vaidehi. Vinod asked how her day was but never probed deeper. But of course, he knew things couldn't have been going so smooth. They say the key to a good relationship is communication. Yet, this one thrived in silent understanding. Did it come from love?

Soon, Vinod and the children had left for work and school, respectively and Vaidehi had had a shower. Her bangles were now all maroon. Multi-coloured ones were for a young bride. A very weird kind of feeling snaked into her, like something bad was going to happen. She lit a lamp in her wall-mounted temple again and said a prayer, not for good times, but for strength, as if she had to be prepared. However, even the lunch went by quietly, with Vinod's parents coming downstairs and eating in silence. They didn't even murmur. This made her uneasy even more. Once they left, Vaidehi tried to giggle and sigh out of her overthinking. Meera and Manav, after finishing the food, sat down to do their homework.

Vaidehi wound up the kitchen and lay down for her siesta. She swept into a deep sleep like she was intoxicated and had the same dream that she'd not had in a few years now. Dream that she'd dreamt many a times in her teens. She saw the same pair of legs wearing heavy silver anklets, like the ones she'd seen her mother wear. They were naked till mid-calves, above which was fluttering a plain yellow *lehenga*, heavily layered, a kind that women in her village wore. The legs were running to save the girl they belonged to. It was extremely windy and the girl was running against it, making it even more difficult for her as the Rajasthan desert's sands kept gushing into her eyes, mouth and nostrils. But she still ran, ran for her life, her honour. She could then hear several men chasing her, shouting things, words of which were muffled by the wind, but their dangerous intentions seeped into the very particles of the sand that the girl was struggling against. Her very land was against her. And yet, Vaidehi could hear the girl think as she prayed and begged for help from the land, as there was nothing around her but huge dunes—this she didn't see, she just knew. She then saw men, their whole bodies but not their face. Men who were chasing her, wearing Rajasthani *juttis* that curved upward at their tips to block the sand. Their *dhotis* still crisp white despite the sand blowing like the wind itself, their wrists encircled with heavy silver *kadas* and palms encircling huge sticks tightly, sticks thirsting for blood in this blowing sandstorm. Vaidehi saw the behind of the legs of the girl again, now she could occasionally also see a red *bandhani* dupatta fluttering over her *lehenga* and she knew it had come off her head. Without seeing, she knew the girl was trying to hold it around her, fighting the villainous wind off that was violently trying to strip her naked. Now, she could hear the thuds of the men's feet against the sand even louder, they were getting closer. So the girl ran faster, her lungs exerted more force but they were fast getting choked by the sand accumulating in them. The muscles in her legs ached so each nerve inside took over to force a faster speed, but the sand below her feet became looser and refused to stay under the foot that dropped. The more her body bent forward, trying harder to force ahead, the more solid the wind grew and held her back. The men, they came closer and closer, *thudThudTHUD*, she could hear them so close now, there was no hope but surrender. She saw one of their hands extend and almost touch the girl's shoulder, their sticks rattling with the excitement of almost-caught prey. The skin on her back tingled with the anticipation of the touch.

Vaidehi woke up, inhaling a breath sharply. The girl was her. The men were gone, the sand was gone, the wind was gone, another version of her was gone, but the *thudThudTHUD*... That remained. At first, she thought she was still not out of her sleep, but when it persisted, she realised it was actually happening. Someone was banging on the door. It was the one near the steps, the one to the room where her children slept. She rushed to their room through the second door and saw Meera about to open the door and heard her father-in-law shouting from behind it.

"Stop. Don't." Vaidehi shouted in a panic that scared her children. The three of them stood for a while, Vaidehi wondering at her own words and instincts and the twins wondering why their mother won't open the door to their grandfather.

"Khol darwaja!" Open the door! Her father-in-law shouted again, in a rough bark-like voice, with thuds that rattled the door at its hinges.

Vaidehi snapped out of her deliberation and in an instant, ushered the kids towards her bedroom. Meanwhile, her father-in-law's thuds grew stronger, "Open it or I'll break it down! You think you can kick us out of the house?" he roared like a maddened lion.

"Stay here, don't come out," Vaidehi instructed the kids and went back to their room with the thudding door. Quietly, she slid the lock into the door and turned the key, locking it. She then went to all the other possible entrances to the downstairs area and locked all the doors while her father-in-law howled to rattle the entire society off humanity's hinges.

"*Khol*, you want to rip the children away from us! You think you can turn Vinod against us?"

Vaidehi stood at the door, looking at it, frightened the lock would give away, the wall would crumble, the men would catch her. She started trembling, her palms started sweating. She thought of calling Vinod at the office but she forgot his number. And no matter how much she thought, she couldn't recollect it. Next, she thought of shouting, but her voice refused to come out, her mind warning her. SHAME. Everyone would hear. What then? No one will blame this elderly man, only her, the woman. *Aisa hi hota hai.*

"*Bahar aa*, I want to talk to you right now!" he shouted again. *Come outside*, he was calling her out and not trying to barge in.

Those words gave her a little strength and she shouted, for Kamla, "Mummy, *dekho bauji ko le jao!*" *Please take father away,* she shouted. There was no response. Of course. Vaidehi wasn't surprised; somewhere she already knew it was all a plan. Kamla's plan. Everything that she'd done: trying to get the children (at least Manav) to her side, trying to turn Vinod against her, trying to get her out of the house, she'd twisted it all on Vaidehi and told Vinod's father. He could hardly hear anything for years now and had no way to listen to the truth. There was no use calling out to her. She just needed to ensure the kids were away and that her father-in-law doesn't come in. She would have to stand and let it die down.

"Manav asked me to not pay the *panipuri wala last evening. Yeh sikhati hai bachon ko? Chor banaegi inko?*"

Manav and Meera went every evening to have panipuri nearby with their grandfather. Given the tremendous rush, it was very easy for the customers to just slip by without paying. Manav, in his innocence, had asked his grandfather to just quietly leave after eating, with a wink and swift of a palm. Meera had been taken aback at the thought of cheating and had come and told Vaidehi this. Her father-in-law was shouting randomly about anything he could to extend his theatrics and said about just this now—*do you teach this to your children? Do you want to make them thieves?*

Instinctively, Vaidehi turned towards the entrance of the room, worrying Manav shouldn't hear this shaming. She saw Manav standing there. A look of someone from whom the trust was just snatched away. His face saddened and his eyes welled up as he walked over to Vaidehi.

"Sorry, Mummy, I thought it was okay for me also to do because over there everyone does it."

Vaidehi's heart tore when her son hurt, as much as it had when her daughter was picked on. "I know, beta, I know. Meera told me. It's okay, it was a mistake and you have learned now." Hugging him, she didn't see another sense of realisation of snatching away of trust that crossed his face on hearing that Meera had complained about him. So, this is what she talked about when alone with mummy.

The shouting went on for 45 minutes more, post which tired, her father-in-law went back upstairs and slept. Vaidehi lay down between the twins as they slept, one more distant now than the other. In the evening, Kamla came downstairs to make tea. She did so in silence as if completely unaware.

"Mummy, *bauji* had come downstairs shouting for an hour, why didn't you come and take him away?"

"What? When? What are you talking about?" Kamla didn't even feign ignorance, as she said so smilingly.

"Arre, the whole society heard, didn't you?" Both Vaidehi and Kamla looked up in surprise. The elderly lady in the adjacent house was saying. "Does it look nice? He came in banging the doors, all of us woke up. She was alone downstairs and he kept shouting! Why didn't you help?"

Now Kamla was pissed. "Where does he listen to me? Who listens to me in this house? I'm a nobody here, like a piece of furniture. And if he wanted to talk, you should've gone and spoken to him! What were you afraid of?" Kamla replied.

"How would I have spoken to him, Mummy? I cover my head in front of him. I haven't shown him my face my entire life! How can I suddenly go and talk to him? I was afraid of his temper! He was raging! You heard him!" Vaidehi replied in tears.

"I will speak to Vinod directly," Kamla replied coldly and left.

Kamla sat on the sofa in the living room that evening, directly opposite to the main door. The twins sat watching cartoons on the TV, at the dining table. Vaidehi sat there too. 'Tom and Jerry' was something one can watch at all ages. Both parties could see each other from where they sat but chose not to. And then Vaidehi's eyes drifted to Kamla, wondering yet again how could she. What did she really want? Did she hate Vaidehi so much that even today she wanted her out of the family? If yes, why so? Did she really have a reason or she was just being a mother-in-law?

Then, Maruti 800's lights flashed through the living room, drenched Kamla and turned away as the car did. Kamla adjusted the saree on her knees- as if preparing for her act. Vaidehi saw and resigned at that moment. Kamla bent her head down and pressed her palms against her face and by the time Vinod entered, tears were rolling down her cheeks. She started with a loud sob as he stepped in. Vaidehi told the twins to go inside their room, shut the door and study. Confused about why their TV time was being replaced with studying that they didn't have to do- they left and closed the door behind them. Inside, they went up to their study table and stood there lost, wondering what they had to study.

Outside, Vinod asked, "What happened, Ma?"

This was like a gun shot that Kamla was waiting for and she sprinted as she heard it. "Ask her, why are you asking me? Do you even care? Would you even believe me if I told you what happened? No, you won't, then why don't you ask her what happened!" Vaidehi sat quietly.

"You're crying, I'm concerned and so I'm asking you what happened,"

Vinod replied.

"This woman, this wife of yours, she threatens to throw me out of this house. But that's no news! Now she says I'm trying to turn your father against her!"

"Why would I say that? What did he do for me to even realise and think that you're turning him against me?" Vaidehi spoke for the first time, calmly.

"Just look at her!" Kamla shrieked and her voice tore as her volume went higher on the last word. On *her*. "Now, she's talking back! What respect do I have left now?"

"No, Ma, she's only having a discussion. We all are. Please, calm down," Vinod said and put a hand around Kamla. She relaxed. "Now tell me, why do you think Vaidehi thinks so?" he asked after a few moments. Kamla was silent. She hadn't anticipated Vinod to ask any questions and she hadn't anticipated Vaidehi to talk at all. There was silence for a few moments and then Kamla blurted out, "She says he came downstairs banging on the doors, asking to talk to her about god knows what! And says that she called out to me. But I didn't hear any of it! How would I know? And even if I had, where does your father listen to me? What could I have done?"

Vinod was visibly shaken. His hand slid off her mother. He hung his head and Vaidehi's heart broke with regret of speaking at all. She should've just taken the blame instead; Vinod wouldn't have believed any of it anyway.

"You're a woman too, how can you let this happen to another?" he finally spoke, his heart bleeding words.

Aisa hi hota hai.

While this pained Vaidehi, it struck Kamla's ego and she shouted, "Okay, so if she's a woman just like me, ask her why she had her father-in-law knocking on her door in the afternoon when nobody's around?"

"Bas karo!" Vinod shouted. It was the first time Vaidehi had heard his

voice at this volume so close to her. She physically jumped. Kamla looked shocked too. "You want to live with us in peace, you're welcome, or else there's the door," he said and walked into his bedroom.

Once he shut the door, Kamla looked at Vaidehi, tears in her eyes with hurt ego in front of the lowly daughter-in-law and said, "Congratulations on your achievement, hope you're happy." Kamla went to the kitchen, took food for two and went upstairs. Vaidehi first stopped near the children's bedroom and put her ear to the door. She heard nothing, so she went to her bedroom. Vinod sat on the bed, head lowered and a silent tear rolled down one of his cheeks. Vaidehi sat beside him and put her palm on the back of his. She wanted to be with Vinod. She wanted some time to herself. But there were children, so she went into the kitchen and started serving food into plates. Vinod followed her and their eyes met as he entered the kitchen. As the plate in Vaidehi's hand tilted dangerously, Vinod held its other side just in time.

*

Manav and Meera slept downstairs in the guest bedroom the night of the fight. The grandparents didn't take them upstairs. The parents had fed them and put them into bed. They weren't completely unfamiliar with this room. They stayed here in the daytime with their study table there and two single beds on either side of the room that were joined together when a guest came to stay. But it still felt strange to be there in the night. To sleep with no adult around. To add to this strangeness, the air was infused with the remains of the bitter fight and heartbreaks that bled thick sorrow, and the twins breathed it all in, without knowledge. It loomed heavily over their faces making them uneasy and unable to sleep. But neither of them would call out to their parents because of this unexplained understanding of not disturbing them tonight. Or any other adult for that matter. And this do-not-disturb wasn't the usual kind where they accidentally bumped into the angry mother who took it out on them. Like this one time when a particularly loud fight with the help had put Vaidehi in a foul mood and when Manav was walking by, she'd called him, scolded him for not paying attention in class and sent him to study. Meera who was a little behind, had heard it and retraced her steps. Or the time when Manav was being his once-upon-a-time annoying self and Meera had playfully shouted, waking Vaidehi from her siesta. They were both made to redo their homework, Manav of English and Meera of Math, subjects they detested. But this do-not-disturb was of another kind. It was a result of a certain kind of knowledge that children learn without anybody teaching them. Like, Meera knew she should sit with her knees together even if Manav sat with his apart. Or, like they both knew not to disturb Vaidehi when they found her sitting staring at nothing with her eyes too wet. Or like flipping channels if their parents were around and Micky kissed Minnie. Or, while they can help fold the underwears, they shouldn't touch Vaidehi's bra. It was that kind of knowledge that isn't imparted in a middle-class family, but is learnt by the children somehow. Like an heirloom handed down by invisibility.

Finally, Meera spoke, "What do you think they were fighting about?" Manav was quiet. Meera asked again, "Are you asleep? What do you think they were fighting about?"

"I don't know yaar," Manav replied, his answer tinged with irritation. Meera didn't understand this behaviour of his. Manav was getting quieter and quieter these days, especially with Meera, and if she repeated herself, he would get annoyed. In turn, when Manav tried to tease Meera, she'd shout and get angry to an irrational degree. She would scrunch up nose, squint her eyes and twist her lips, in a way that reminded Vaidehi of Kamla, and give Manav a look that meant she was disgusted by him. In fact, if he threw even a one-liner on her, her lips would curl upside down, her brows would create lines between them and she would look away from him. This quietened him even more. Whether his quiet started first or it was led by Meera's disgust for his joyful teasings, no one knew. But it had become a circle and it pulled them further apart. The bitter and sorrowful air took its place in the space created between them.

"Why do you talk like this? You don't respond first and if I ask again you get irritated." Manav kept quiet. Ideally, he could've put forth his issue with Meera too. Like why did Meera respond so bitterly to his fun and play? Why did she tell Vaidehi about his not wanting to pay the *pani-puriwala*? But that's just not how he was made—by God, or

Vaidehi? They were two ends of a see-saw, one quiet as silence and the other vocal as her own head. They grew further apart by each complaint and each silence.

Manav turned towards the wall, his back against Meera. As he did, a few notes fell out from under his pillow. Twin torsos suddenly stood erect on each bed.

"Is that money?" Meera asked, disgust already forming on her face. Manav looked at her and got down to pick it up.

"Where did you get it from?" she asked now. He didn't answer. "I'm talking to you!" Meera raised her voice.

Manav panicked and said, "Sssshhhh! What's wrong with you? I took it okay, from papa's wallet." Meera sat in shock. Her young mind had concocted Bollywood theories as he'd stolen from someone or somewhere outside or had found a wallet on the road with the money in it. But she couldn't imagine he could've stolen from his own home. She couldn't imagine anyone doing it. In her righteous mind, that was… well, disgusting.

"I'm going to tell mummy." She said, the same disgusted expression clawing her face.

"Of course, you will," Manav said, looking at her with a poker face with a hint of accusation in his eyes. *You're not on my team* they were saying and Meera read it. Like the way, only a twin could have. She fell silent. What should she do?

"What will you do with it?" she asked, hoping it was all for a reason. Manav looked at her, reading her thoughts, the way only a twin can. His face softened, as if they'd found a thread of a twin bond, that had felt lost for so long.

"Just…nothing, chocolates…and this," he said and walked over to his side of their study table. He bent down to the bottom-most shelf. Meera could see his shoulders heaving lifting everything in there to get something out from the bottom. He whisked it out, stood up and walked towards Meera, books in hand. Meera took them and glanced at the cover page of the matte, poor paper quality magazine of sorts. A blonde girl with Barbie hair sat on a beach, stark naked. Meera was taken by the large roundness of her supple breasts, hair at the nipples. It reminded her of the bearded goat she'd seen in Aladdin. She watched silently, completely taken, like one would be on revelation of a hidden truth. She flipped pages after pages, but by the time she finished one, she felt disgusted.

"I don't want them," she said suddenly, thrusting them back to Manav. He watched her taken aback. The same disgusted expression back on her face, but not so confident anymore.

"Throw them or I'll tell mummy."

Torn between confusion and hurt, he said, "You watched it when you wanted to. And now that you're done, you're threatening to tell mummy?"

Meera was silent. As Manav got up and went back to hiding his stash, Meera realised he was right. What made her uneasy was that the only thing disgusting was her attitude. He was right, she had wanted to see it, and had done so. In fact, even now, as the pukey feeling that had come from watching too many men and women nude had receded, she wanted to see more. If only she hadn't been rude to Manav she could've asked for more now. But what would mummy say? And the realisation of knowledge that she can never know this came to her. It was wrong to do this. Should she tell mummy? But what was that thing, between that man's legs? Would she also have hair on her nipples? How nice it would be to have such a large, round chest! But mummy would probably slap them both if she found out. She might go into one of her silences, staring into nothing with wet eyes. Thus, divided between curiosity and righteousness, Meera fell asleep. Manav did too, with the realisation how everyone used his secrets against him—baba (his grandfather), Meera, and even mummy (she hid the fact that she knew about the *panipuri* incident).

Before drifting off, his last thought was, *aisa hi hota hai.*

CHAPTER 17
Maya and Manish

Maya and Ved's relationship was just like any other affair she'd had in college. The fire of passion had not just burned but raged on both sides, except all that they could do, was over the phone. Never did either mention anything about taking it forward. Maybe neither of them wanted to make it too real. Strangely, their coffee meetings reduced to nil too after their action over the phone began. They always went out in a group and always avoided meeting each other alone outside of the office. When they did occasionally have a coffee or lunch or a cigarette alone together, they spoke naturally of everything else but what was between them, like they had before any of it had started. Why were they together? What is it that they wanted from each other? Maya's relationship with Suman pushed her out of her marriage, looking for a distraction, but why couldn't she recognise that she had something so much more in Manish. Why did the boundaries of the *bad in-law* disappear between Manish and Suman? What had Manish done that she couldn't just go to him instead? In one word the answer was, *Escape.* Escapism was a phenomenon much deeply rooted in Maya's mind than just her recent situation with her family. She had grown seeing it, observing it, absorbing it, making it her own. Starting innocently when she was distracted with a chocolate when she fell down and scrapped her knee, right to the point when she'd seen her mother's eyes welling up and then see her shrug it off and turn the other way. In fact, when asked about it, her mother had said, *"Aisa toh hota hai,* these feeling keep coming, you just have to strictly shrug them off and continue with your work." It was the simplest solution to depression. Or any other problem—just find an escape into something else. What struck her was that she felt no guilt despite it being an extramarital one. Her desperation for happiness was justification enough. But was it right? It's definitely not right to continue being unhappy, not just in terms of a philosophy, but in the sense that you owe it to the life you're given. But in this scenario, was temporary escape justified?

"So, this is what you've been up to?" Gaurav asked. Maya had finally spoken to him when he had threatened to call Manish and tell him about her absence. They were now having drinks together. She'd specifically chosen a loud place, to avoid as much conversation as possible.

"And if you thought any kind of loud music can stop me from dragging secrets out of your chest, you've truly forgotten us." He was validly hurt. Now that Maya was with him to actually see his pain, she realised what she'd been doing was wrong. Not the affair part, the ignoring your best friend part. But she knew the other couldn't exist until this one left.

"What do you mean *been up to?* I mean, it's like a small, sundry whatever thing. And I'm working and just...like...everything is normal and usual." Maya tried.

"What exactly do you think you're getting out of this, except for an escape?"

"Argh! Please, relax, just...I don't know, Gaurav, whatever!"

"Well, after your insightful explanations, I realise you know that it's nothing more than a distraction too."

"NO! No, it's not, okay? It makes me happy!" Maya protested. She could feel her cheeks warming up.

"Maya, really? Do you think this tingling feeling of new foolish love is happiness? You know it's going to die. And then what? Someone else? And until when?" Gaurav's tone soothed as if he'd felt the warmth of her cheeks. Maya felt grateful to have him.

"But there's no other way! There's nothing else! And I didn't go looking for it!" Maya replied, voice shaking. "Look, I don't want to do this. I don't feel guilty at all because I was drowning and this was the rope that was thrown at me. I HAD to take it but I don't want to do it! And if I leave it, I'll drown! There's just...so much unhappiness."

The sheer pain in her voice pulled Gaurav out of his ideal righteousness and shoved his feet in her shoes. "But, is there nothing else? Can't you talk it out with Manish and kind of sort it in some way?" he tried, desperately looking for a solution.

"You think? You know everything! I have spoken to my father, to Manish, he has spoken to his mother several times, but she just again… What is the solution? How do I handle this? How do I make it all stop? Why is this even happening to me?" This last question surprised Maya too. She re-alised then that even acceptance of the situation hadn't come fully to her, so the solution was still far away.

"Maya, do you want to see a doctor maybe?"

"So now a doctor will help me fall in love with my husband?"

"Why does love have to be ideal?" Gaurav asked, feeling tired.

"Ideal? Me? Why does a marriage have to be so ideal, as to be monogamous! Okay, I'm sexting, yes and I know it will end soon. So what? So, my marriage isn't a marriage? Who, apart from this society, says we have to be monogamous? And if my round marriage doesn't fit in its square hole, it isn't right?"

"And what about your ideas on falling in love? What do you even expect love to feel like? Like, you'll have more sex or wait for him until he comes back from work, or think about him all the time while he's away or roams around with a silly love-daze smile on your face? Maybe love doesn't feel like that! Maybe you don't always fall in love and then marry, maybe you can find love in Manish now, since, you know, he's a great guy! But no, for you, it HAS to be the traditional way, the way they show it in movies, perhaps?"

"Are you seriously blaming my unhappiness springing from not being able to fall in love with my husband from my arranged marriage?"

"Well, shouldn't I? Please remember that it was an arranged marriage, but not a forced one. You think if instead of your parents introducing you guys, if you had met instead on a blind date or something, you wouldn't have been able to fall in love with him? Do you really not love him for him, or because they way you met? And the finality of it?"

There was a long pause.

"We are together. Now if only I could love him too." Finally, Maya replied.

"Maybe that's what the doctor can help with, love. Not to make you fall in love with him, but just to make you realise that you probably already do."

Was it this chat or the guilt from not treating Manish the way Maya knew he deserved, or just the natural death of a passing fling? Maya and Ved's relationship had already started to dry up. The only thread that was still between them was Maya's fear. Fear of going back to her life completely, waking up with nothing to look forward to, not being able to lose herself in something else after a call from Suman, realising how alone she was after speaking to her parents about her problems. She just didn't want to feel. However, there came the last straw and she just called it all off.

Maya and Ved had finally decided to meet for drinks. Alone together. They were a few down, music was loud and nobody around seemed to be in their senses. Maya always debated that being physical with someone was over-hyped, when actually, it was the shallowest level of intimacy one could have. It was just about sharing your physical being, while a human is so much more. She didn't know if what they had shared was equivalent to actual love making, but despite that, this meeting — which they were too scared and confused to call a date — was a situation that the word awkward was invented for.

"So…are you enjoying your work?" Ved attempted.

"Yea, I guess, it's alright. Oh, I love this song." Maya feigned excitement and immediately regretted as Ved might ask for a dance. This made her realise how much she didn't want to be there. Why had they even met? Ved had simply texted her asking to meet for drinks, but that didn't mean she had to agree. She could've easily made an excuse, or just been honest and said she didn't feel like it. But she'd come. When Ved didn't ask her to dance, she was relieved but she also wondered whether even he wanted to be here. Maybe he'd just asked her out of the pressure of never having asked her. Why were they doing this if they didn't want to? But then again, why was she still married if she was so unhappy? Why had she agreed tto an arranged marriage? Why had she not demanded that her future family to be financially secure and respectful? But don't we always do this? Do things that we didn't want to. Be with people we didn't want to. Even when we aren't forced. Maybe that's where the sense of loneliness seeps in, dampening our lives. When we choose to be alone together.

"Forget about the song, tell me about you," Ved said with that look in his eyes.

Suddenly, Maya wanted to end it then and there. Everything about Ved that had attracted her to him had changed. He was even distracted from his passion to make a change and only severely focused on her. While most women would've loved this, Maya found it repulsive. Even the confident, radiant look in his eyes when he smiled was replaced by this weaker attraction-haze look reserved only for her. It had lost its charm. Now it was her, her, her all the time. Even their conversations that she'd enjoyed so much had died. Was he still the version that she'd liked so much? Where was the intelligent, sorted brain of his that had once understood her without explanation and had offered smart solutions that pushed her to focus on the right things to make her life work? She wanted someone with whom she could grow together while holding their identity. Being two people together but not becoming one. Or was she so broken that she didn't value whatever became completely hers? Whatever the reason, was it the same one that kept her from being able to love Manish?

After a long silence, Maya finally spoke. "Look Ved, I don't want any of this anymore. I was… I am, I am in this crazy crazy situation at home and I'm so out of my mind that I jumped into all of this. But I…but I can't, I don't want…"

"It's not doing for you what it did for some time in the beginning," Ved articulated for her.

"Well, yes," Maya realised how difficult it was for her to say that. After all, it was like saying no, except, Ved had said the 'no' for her; she just had to affirm it. 'No' is what so many of us struggle to say, but always feel inside us. Maybe we feel it snaking our insides so much because we never let it out.

"Hey, it's fine. It was anyway never meant to be anything more. Relax, we're good." Ved said suddenly, his eyes changing back to normal. All looks from it was gone. Strangely, instead of acquiring the earlier attraction, now they looked just empty to Maya.

So, that night ended with a final cigarette together. No drama, no complications, no nothing. As Maya sat in her Uber, she felt a sense of emptiness. But good emptiness, the kind that makes you free and light. There was still sorrow. Of going back home, to the life that had no way out. But it never had a way out. The closest way out that there was, was her hope for it.

"Maya, imagine the D-word. And if it happens. What then? I'm sure you've imagined what it would be like after. How does that make you feel?" Gaurav resumed over the loud music.

"Of course, I have. Feels terrible. I won't be just breaking my house, I'll be breaking my parents' home too, going back there."

"And?"

"And just living with the same, constant unhappiness, while they recover from the shock for years to come, and somewhere along start to find other guys for me."

"There is no escape," Gaurav thought aloud.

"Listen, it's just like how Indian families are. We don't just live together; we owe our lives to each other. Parents to their children and children to their parents. And this exchange extends to as many generations alive as dead. You see, the dead have their specific days where we are supposed to cook for them and give it away to the temples. It never ends. And the alive, for them owing their life to each other means wearing the clothes that makes everyone happy, pursuing a career that makes everyone happy, marrying the person who makes everyone happy, having a child because it makes everyone happy, behaving a certain way with your families because that makes everyone happy. And sure, you can be so NOT okay with that, but you can never truly break away from them. Because then, that makes them severely unhappy, often making them physically, gravely ill. What do you think my divorce would do? And then the only way out is to become so thick-skinned that none of it matters to you and you move out, stay alone and keep living your life. But that's when your mind rebels against you, because no matter what exposure you have had and how modern you've become, something inside of you will always and forever be unsettled, uneasy and unhappy if your family is unhappy. So you can't move out, stay alone and keep living your life. That kind of isolation comes only and only with final and absolute cutting off of the ties with your family. I don't want that! And hell, if my own mind can't support me by being happy after doing things that won't make my family happy, why should I do them? The only hope, in fact, is the dead. We might cook for them still because we owe them, but here's hoping that they don't give a fuck and are released."

"Until then we live together, alone," Gaurav mused knowing exactly what Maya was saying.

"Well, sometimes together together, sometimes together alone," she replied. They smiled.

"Listen, it's over. And it's okay. One day at a time." They toasted to that and called it a night. A dark, hopeless night, with no way out.

That night as she got home, Manish was sitting in front of the TV, with a glass of whiskey in his hand. He still had his jeans and shirt on which meant he'd got home some time back. As soon as she opened the door, Manish looked up at her and smiled. That's when the guilt kicked in. Not for what had happened between her and Ved, but the way she'd treated Manish for so long. She couldn't love him and that wasn't her fault, but she had made him miserable otherwise too. She'd taken out all her fury on him every time Suman had done something, she'd been disconnected with him so much that Manish would often stop talking between a sentence seeing her disinterested face. Every morning on leaving for work and the moment he got back home, she'd looked into her phone than at him to say goodbye and hello, every morning she'd woken up and reached out for her phone as if it were an addict's cigarette. Worst of all, she'd confessed she couldn't love him and she knew it broke his heart. And yet, now when he looked up at her, he smiled the same old smile with eyes seeped in love and a feeling of home. Unlike Ved's that had changed like a switch went off. Maya broke down in tears.

"Hey, what happened?" Manish said, rushing towards her and enclosing her in his arms. But she was sobbing so hard, she couldn't talk. He walked her over to the sofa and sat her down. And then they just sat for a while, Maya crying into Manish's chest.

Finally, when she recovered, she said, "I'm sorry."

"For what?" he asked.

"For everything. What we became in the last few months was because of me. I drifted too far away. I'm sorry."

"It's alright. Sometimes you need to go away to come back."

Maya looked up into his eyes. She didn't want to be misunderstood. She had always respected Manish and tonight, that had gone up to another level. The feeling of being at home around him had come back stronger than ever before. Maybe the sex would come back too. But love... She might've moved further from *"don't love him"*, but she was still at *"I don't know if I love him"*.

"Listen, I feel better in ways I can't explain. There are still a lot of disappointments but something good has also definitely added to those feelings. Honestly, I'm not completely there...I..." Maya trailed off, realising how she must be sounding.

"You don't think you still love me. But you do feel better than before about being with me?" Manish finished her thought for her.

"Yes," she shoved her huge ball of guilt down her throat.

"Look. Ours was an arranged marriage. I don't know why you agreed to marry me. Maybe you had technical pointers to tick off and I fit that criteria and you assumed love would follow. You had no way of knowing it wouldn't. For me, it has come, and for you, it hasn't, it's unfortunate but it's not your fault. Maybe it will come. Maybe it has but you're not able to see it because you have a set definition of how love must feel and you don't feel that. I don't exactly know where you are. But you know, this love, it has no definition. It will feel different, with different people. A lot of times there will be that tingling and those fireworks, a lot of times it will be silence. The only one thing I can request you to try is to separate your idea of love from your idea of wants. Maybe it's already separated, but I'll still say it. Fireworks, spark and such things come from one of many things like materialism which allows you exotic things in life that makes you feel good. Or, things like charisma which gives you butterflies in the stomach. But a relationship can't feed on such things constantly. There will always be silence, a kind of quiet that doesn't mean an absence of anything, it means presence of contentment. I'd personally want to be with a person with who I can live my silence with. The other things be it materialism or personal traits will all come and go and change so often, you won't be able to hold on to them anyway. It'll always be the person underneath all that whom you can truly hold on to. I think that person for me is you. And I'll wait out my life waiting for you to realise that it's me for you."

The first thing that struck Maya was his confidence in saying the last sentence. He didn't say he hoped it would be him for her, he said he will wait for her to realise it was him. Something in her stomach stirred. Suddenly she felt tired of all the things that she'd wanted from a man — charisma, money, exoticness, a knight in shining armour, sweeping off her feet. She liked being on her feet instead. That night, they slept peacefully, hugging each other tightly. They might still be mid-way, but they were strongly moving towards each other. Or was it just that hour of intense talk?

Whatever it may be, tonight, they were together. Together together.

CHAPTER 18
Vaidehi and Vinod

After that morning, Vaidehi would develop a fear of early morning phone calls. They would sound like someone is trying to reach out to her, to haunt her for life, bearers of bad news, ringing in of sorrow, of eternal loss, the omen of death itself.

It was 5 am and Vaidehi and Vinod slept. They both sat up with a start, and Vinod picked up the phone. She read shock take over his face, followed by sadness. Vaidehi's father had passed away. As of now they only knew some nerve had burst in his head which had made him fall on the road when he was on his way to get some milk. He had been in pain for some time and the few passersby had called an ambulance. However, he had passed away quickly, much before the ambulance arrived. Vaidehi just sat there with a blank face, hearing all of it but not registering anything. She listened to it all with an indifference of listening to a movie from the kitchen. However, slowly but surely, the information raped itself inside her mind and the tears fell. And then, they didn't stop. She poured her heart out and everything stagnant from the past, of all the injustices, all the degradation and insults that she'd suffered, all of them came gushing out with a force. They sat hugging each other for the longest time, until Vinod had to get up and make arrangements for them to travel. He started making calls to the agent to book their tickets urgently. At some point in time, Vaidehi had slid down from sitting up to crashing on the pillow when Vinod stood up, to the bed sheets and finally now, she was on the floor, sitting with her back against the bed and knees touching her chest. And she wept. At some point, she heard Meera's footsteps and hurriedly dried her eyes, face and wiped her nose. She saw Meera staring at her and knew Kamla had told her.

"Go brush your teeth quickly and have breakfast, it's 11," Vaidehi said. They were still so young, they must only be allowed information of death, not the sense of loss behind it. So Meera was sent away to the bathroom, then to the kitchen and then back upstairs so Vaidehi could cry in peace. Later that day, Vaidehi left for her mother's with Vinod. This would be the only time she would see her parents apart from the once-a-year summer vacation. Except there would be one parentless. Half of a generation. Half of the whole that she was made of. The children were left behind with their grandparents because it would be traumatising for them to go to a funeral. The whole that Vaidehi came from might be half now, but she and Vinod still had to be a perfect whole for their children. A complete whole, without the cracks of salty tear-line running down the children's idea of real, indestructible superheroes.

Vaidehi broke down at every point since she came into her city. Her brother who had come to pick them up didn't welcome them with a joyous smile. As the house came into view, she didn't see her parents standing outside at the gate to welcome her. Instead, there was a crowd. Neighbours in white, dotted with policemen in khaki. Every neighbour she'd known since she was a child hugged their daughter as she wept. Every khaki-clad man joined his hands to her and made way for her to pass by. It took so much longer for her to cover that small distance from the gate, to her mother's bedroom/living room in that small house she'd spent such blissful summers at, taking a break from everything in her own house. She wanted to shout at the people to disperse and just get there to see her father, while also glad they were there to postpone the visual for a few more moments. The women wailed around her, on seeing her. Finally, she reached inside. Her mother sat there, bare. In complete white. Without the red vermillion, or bangles, or a red bindi on her face. Just white saree and black frame glasses. Black and white. She cried, but she didn't wail. She just sat there, sobbing, her strength refusing to leave her. Vaidehi sat down beside her and the two women wept quietly and deeply. The sorrow was seeped into every molecule of the air from the mourning which the women breathed in and with every sigh let out, it went right back into the air. It was an unending circle of grief. Vaidehi certainly felt she would never be happy again.

Her father lay in front of them, covered in white sheets up till his neck and two white balls of cotton stuffed into his nose. Black and white. Vaidehi suddenly felt like she couldn't breathe either, looking at them.

His hair was still half dark. We often consider dying as meeting death. But it's not true. There's a difference between being dead and meeting death, and you only come to realise this fine line by experiencing the death of someone so, so close. For something that sounds as big as meeting death, the situation wasn't so extraordinary. This was it, the difference of being horizontal and vertical, of the stuffed nose and open ones, of breathing sorrow and being the cause of it, of being dead and meeting death. Simple. Clear. Black and white. The people came and went and so the crowd refused to thin. Soon the body was moved out and laid in the open area so everyone could sit down to mourn.

The women walked in, sand flying till their knees, ruffling their *ghaghras*, and as the view of the assembly came into view, they burst into howling cries and covered their faces to hide the absence of tears. They weren't actually crying, but the etiquette required them to. As they got near, their speed increased and they broke into a run in their last 5-7 steps and dropped down on their knees as they got to the body. Good thing the floor wasn't concrete. Their foreheads dropped to the ground too and they wailed. Finally, they lifted their torsos back up and wiping their non-existent tears, went to the female side of the gathering. They would hug Vaidehi's mother first and then her, before going all the way back to join the women. Then they would sit and discuss about how kind he was, and how he made everyone laugh. Again, although it sounded like an etiquette to talk good about the dead, it wasn't untrue. Vaidehi's father was a mellow, good-hearted, very kind man in the society, famous as an honourable local policeman. And he always, made everyone laugh, children and adults alike. Every summer when Vaidehi stayed there, he would come home every evening bringing Melodies and Kismi toffees for the children. The famous tagline "*melody itni chocolaty kyun hai*" kept the children's attention away from the not-advertised Kismi and what the word actually meant and the merging face of a woman and a man against the red background of the toffee wrap. The woman in white, the man in black. Black and white. If Vaidehi thought about it, she could almost feel his hand over her head lightly sliding from front to back, to bless her. She could feel the khadi of his kurta when he hugged her and the rough feel of his feet as she touched them for his blessings.

Her mind played tricks, making her feel that if she just blinked, all of this would disappear like a nightmare, and he would be there, blessing, hugging, bringing chocolates. But when she did, only tears fell from her eyes, making her vision of his dead body even clearer. This day, he made her cry. Suddenly, they heard another howl but they all turned their heads because it was a child's. It was Vaidehi's youngest brother's daughter. Surprisingly, her head was shaved because of the death of her grandfather, even though she was a girl. Usually, only sons and grandsons shaved their heads. Maybe because her brother did not have a son. Out of two others, one had a son, whose head was also shaved and the other had two daughters, who were too old to be shaved. So this young child, fat like how babies are, bald-headed and unsupervised, had walked a little away from the gathering and was now walking towards them, breaking into a run as she was just a little away from the body, howling like the women did and crashing down completely, until she got up and joined the group. This, she did on loop. She was mimicking the women, right down to wiping the invisible tears. And just like that, sprouted the first giggle, sending a chain reaction. Even in his death, the loving father, the honourable policeman and the kind human, had made them laugh. Parting the black sorrow, emerged the white teeth.

Later, one by one, they all took a bath. There was only one bathroom along with a toilet downstairs and one toilet on the roof, along with one room there. Once all were done, they sat down in the living room/bedroom of Vaidehi's mother, on the floor. All in white, with their long and short black hair open and drying, slowly. Food and hot chai lay between them. They always ate like this at home—on the floor, in a circle, with food between them. It was one of the best feelings Vaidehi had experienced growing up. Today, the circle seemed incomplete as it mourned the loss, but also came closer together and more tightly in their shared grief. She wanted to be there and also not at the same time. They tore open food packages and started eating, sipping tea occasionally. As Vaidehi shoved the food down her throat, her stomach wanted to throw it up immediately. Grief always does come tinged with a non-sensical guilt. Death as an occasion demands from our sub-conscious something much greater than mourning, it demands the alive to be *punish*ed for being alive when their near one dies. So much so that the body believes to punish itself. Maybe that's why people often come closer in their shared grief, to save each other from drowning, to justify continuing life.

But no one really realises this as it happens silently. Just like this silent circle, where one person started the process of eating, allowing others to feel it's okay to do so themselves too. Eventually someone will start the process of being able to talk about the dead, allowing others to follow suit. Someone, even after days of the death, will let a tear pass, allowing the other adults to allow themselves to pour as children do. Then one fine day, when everyone has forgotten it, a giggle will escape someone's lips, pushing the guilt out and allowing the right to happiness back into their lives. And then, the smiling picture of the dead hanging over a wall, overlooking the mournful faces, won't be so weird after all.

Seven days passed, and it was time for Vaidehi and Vinod to leave. Vaidehi was packing her bags, her heart full of emotional baggage of its own. Her mother entered the room and placed a hand over her shoulder. Vaidehi turned around and saw her plain face, empty parting, and white clothes. She broke down in tears. She cried for her dead father who she'll never see again, or speak to again. She cried for how lonely her mother had gotten and so soon. She cried imagining her mother's life will be like how her life would be if Vinod were to be taken away from her. She cried for even she couldn't be with her mother forever to keep her company. She cried looking at her mother's long life that lay ahead. A black and white life while they all had already moved back to colours. She cried until she realised her mother wasn't. She looked up at her.

"*Bas kar, jo hona hai woh toh hona hi hai. Rote nai hain.*" *Calm down now, whatever has to happen, will happen. We don't cry.* She'd said the same thing to Vaidehi as she was leaving for Vinod's house after getting married. But today, to say it in the face of her husband's death was formidably strong. Vaidehi stopped.

"I wish I could stay back more," Vaidehi said.

"No! That just can't be. You must go home, take care of your family. Your children are waiting for you. They need their mother."

And sometimes, the mothers need their children too, she thought but didn't say. With forced normalcy, she helped Vaidehi pack.

On the train back, Vaidehi sat close to Vinod. She felt like the gravity had lost its power a little bit, she felt loose and unstable. One man down. The first-ever man of her life down. Taken. And yet the life refused to stop; onwards it ran, whistling, on track, on time, sending nothing but black smoke behind that will eventually make the past hazy. Vinod bent down to take out dinner from the basket. Vaidehi closed her eyes, dreading having to eat again. She looked away, out of the window and let the breeze hit her sharply. She felt a few drops on her face. Was it her tears or just water chucked out from the window before hers, she didn't know but hoped it weren't her tears. Mother had said we don't cry. She felt cold steel on her fingers and she turned to look back in. There was her father. Smiling up at her, framed and perfect looking. Like he was alive.

"What's this?" She asked Vinod.

"For our room. Wouldn't you want to put it up?" he replied.

Vaidehi subdued the lump that grew in her throat. Kamla would hate it—a daughter-in-law's dead father's picture should hang in her brothers' houses, not in Kamla's. But Vinod was ready to defy all of that scandal. One man down. But the other had stepped up. Her roots took hold again.

*

Manav and Meera sat in the bus on either side of the aisle. She with the girls, he with the boys. Gender teams clear. They didn't speak to each other. Meera was angry and Manav just indifferent. The morning their maternal grandfather had passed away had brought in a series of very quick decisions. Their parents were to go away for the funeral, they were booked for a mild five-day camping trip nearby which the school had organised. The bus was a noisy one with excited children. By the time they were about to reach, the sun was on its way home and the children were tired and asleep. It was pitch dark by the time they got down from the bus and the excitement was now mingled with the mysticism of mountains and fear of the forests. A bonfire was lit. Food was passed around. All emotions tossed away, now there were just butterflies in the stomach from seeing your crush across the fire.

The twins, however, didn't want to be there. They wanted to go back home, to their parents and with them, to the funeral. For them, their grandfather had not died, he had disappeared without goodbyes. When the ghost stories started, Meera wondered if his ghost would visit them here. Soon, the music played and the dancing started, first in two clear teams divided by gender and then slowly, as the teachers' attention started relaxing, the circles kept getting closer. The twins stood at the edge of their respective circles. Meera was looking into the mountains now completely hidden by darkness, when a boy from her class tapped her on the shoulder and said, "Want to dance?" She was completely taken aback. She knew that he was crushing on her through rumours that the girls just giggled away. But this, was real. As a reflex, she looked at Manav across two circles. He was staring at her and his eyes said a clear "no". So, she went ahead and danced with the boy.

She was walking towards her tent when it all ended and Manav caught up with her.

"What was that?" he asked, his voice level but eyes angry.

"A dance! What's your problem?"

"My problem? I'm asking a question. What's your problem?"

"Why are you upset I danced? Will you tell mummy now?"

"No, I'm not you. But everyone was laughing…and at me," he replied, uncomfortably.

"Well, you were laughing too at *nanaji,* weren't you?" Meera replied.

Manav stood silently. The morning of Vaidehi's father's demise, Kamla had come upstairs with the news. Manav was sitting with Vinod's father at the time and she'd broken it to the two of them. Vinod's father had laughed, Kamla had smiled, Manav's heart was broken. And then Kamla had said about how Vaidehi was sitting on the floor, crying her eyes out. And this, had shocked Manav. Something that Meera had not seen, Manav had in his imagination. His young brain hadn't known what to do, somewhere his mother's crying and his grandparents' laughter had mingled in his mind and he had started to giggle.

"I saw it. I woke up because I could hear them laughing and then as I passed by the room, I saw you giggling too. *Nanaji* passed away and you were laughing?"

For an innocent Meera, Manav's confusion in the complex situation he was in, with his parents mourning and his grandparents laughing at it, was unfathomable. Her innocence only knew black and white.

"It was not like that... I just...they just started laughing and I just..." Manav couldn't explain what was wrong because he couldn't understand it either.

"You're a monster," Meera said and went into her tent. Manav stood there, a mountain of a distance between him and his twin, and heart as dark with sorrow as the forest.

The twins never spoke to each other through the rest of the four days in camp. Meera was miserable with all the adventurous rock climbing and rappelling, the only thing she liked was to walk through the forest. Strangely, no matter where she turned, the boy who she'd danced with would be standing there. While in the beginning she danced and spoke to him only to rebel against Manav, eventually, she also felt her heart flutter and her body ache for something she had no idea about. Manav always watched them silently, having his right to speak to his twin taken away. The boys giggled and this angered Manav. On the last day, he saw the boy slip a piece of paper in Meera's bag, just as they were getting down from the bus, to head home.

At night, after readying their bags with books according to the timetable, Meera finally took out the paper. She opened it and it read, *I love you*. No name, no number, nothing. Just that.

"What is that?" Manav asked, snatching the paper from her hands.

"It's mine, give it back!" Meera shrieked.

"What is it now? Good god, I can't wait for your mother to come back!" Kamla shouted and the twins quietened.

"Give it back," Meera whispered with clenched teeth.

"Throw it away. What if mummy sees it?"

"How will she? Will you tell her?"

"What is wrong with you? What do you think you're doing? STOP IT. There's always that stupid smile on your face. *Pagal ho rahi hai kya?" Are you losing your mind?*

"You lost yours when you laughed that morning, who are you to say anything?" Meera spat out bitterly, the expression of disgust already on her face.

"Just shut up. I love him too."

"Oh, is that why you shamelessly laughed, you monster?"

Manav went quiet again. "Don't call me that," he said.

"You're a monster," Meera replied.

Manav walked away, always the silent one. Meera did too. Walking into separate rooms, the boy with his grandfather, the girl with her grandmother. Gender teams clear.

The next day, the twins got home to see Vaidehi waiting for them at the lunch table. Vinod was at work. They all sat together and ate. Vaidehi asked about their camping trip to normalise the air. The twins didn't ask about her father's death for the same reason. They could see that something was off and Meera gave Manav a disgusted look as if to say "See how she's suffering and you were laughing at her loss."

"Come in here a minute," Vaidehi said to the twins, calling them to their day-time room.

"What is this?" she said holding the paper in her hands.

The twins stood, heads hanging.

"Whose is it?" she said then, her volume rising. Manav stood quietly, not able to tell on his twin. Meera stood quietly too, a kind of unknown shame eating her away.

"Answer me!" Vaidehi shouted. They both flinched.

Was it because in her head, the girl couldn't do it, or just turning away and assuming the better of the two worse situations, she held Manav's wrist and pulled him forward.

"Is this yours? Is this why I sent you camping?" Manav looked at her in disbelief, unable to understand why she'd picked him. Meera looked at Vaidehi and her eyes reeking with rage. She tried hard, very hard to gather the courage to say the truth. Meanwhile, Vaidehi went on, "SHAME! Shame on you! Your TV should be cut off completely; isn't that where you learn all this from?"

"What will your father think of you? You don't score good, we don't say anything, you want a new bicycle, your father gets you that, you want pocket money, we give you that too! And all for what? So, you can do such shameful things?" she shouted.

Manav hung his head low and heard every word quietly, without crying, without defending himself. Just like that time when he kept forgetting one letter from the alphabet and Vaidehi had hit him with the edge of a slipper. Tears rolled down Meera's eyes, too scared to tell the truth, too hurt for her twin.

"Ahaaa, see how you assumed it's his? Guess what, it's hers!" Kamla, who had been hearing everything from right outside the room, came in and spat. She had heard the twins' conversation last night and had seen where the paper was hidden. In the morning, just before Vaidehi and Vinod ar-rived, she had kept the paper in plain view in the room and as planned, Vaidehi had found it.

The room was silent now. "Come with me, *beta*," Kamla said, dragging Manav out of the room. The white-haired knight in shining armour to the rescue. Vaidehi took the longest few minutes to recover from the shock. From the astonishing distance, Meera had travelled on the path of progressiveness, unintended by Vaidehi. From the kind of woman she was on the way to becoming, a deceiving one. From the kind of mother she was to her, seeing the fear in Meera's eyes. The kind of mother she was to him, directing all her doubts and accusations on her son by default. And the kind her son was, taking it all silently.

Meera stood silently, her chin almost touching her chest. Experiencing fear like she hadn't ever before. She remembered Vaidehi telling the twins that they should never fear anything if they haven't done anything wrong. But if she had felt the need to hide that paper, if Vaidehi was so angry, then she must have done wrong. Why had it not felt wrong in taking the paper then? And thus, in the crystal clarity of rights and wrongs, that can only come from an innocent mind of that young an age, infused the societal ideas of rights and wrongs. The blacks and whites of thoughts, merging to becoming various shades of grey confusion. Vaidehi pulled her and thrust her to sit next to her on the bed.

"Shameless girl. How could you? No more. No more birthday parties, or friends or phone or group projects of any kind. School and home are your only two worlds. And I will speak to the teacher and change your class." Vaidehi only said this much but with such bitter intensity that something in Meera broke. She felt naked. Her face acquired its signature look of disgust but for herself this time. She couldn't lift her head or move from her place for an hour after Vaidehi left. When she did move, it was because of the pain she felt in her wrist, where Vaidehi had held her. She looked at it. To see a deep blue wound against her white skin.

By the time Vinod came home that evening, the house was already infected by the darkness of dejection, shame, and failure already blotting the pristine white grateful perfection of their lives.

CHAPTER 19

Maya and Manish

The taste of his lips felt like home. Like kissing your lover after a long separation but with just one taste of his tongue the familiarity comes rushing back. His broad shoulders, encompassing Maya spelt comfort. They went on kissing for a long, long time. Long enough for Maya's fire to slowly die out. And her heart sank. It was such a conflicting feeling inside of her. Maybe that's the difference between lust and love? Love could feel like home, but lust has to be something more, like your heart wanting to rip out of your chest, your muscles wanting to tear your skin out to feel him, and your insides wanting to turn your body inside out to have him touch the deepest of corners. If love was home, lust was breaking away from it.

After losing their sex life, getting it back had been a challenge. But Maya forced herself. She di-rected his head to her neck and the dying embers sent out some weak sparks that failed to light up a fire. Manish moved slightly to kiss her throat and Maya directed him to the side of the neck. Again, he came back to the front and Maya directed him back. Why wouldn't he read what she wants despite her clear indication? He went down to her breasts. Maya's body ached. She couldn't remember how long it had been. But Manish moved slowly, almost dispassionately. As if he was going to fall asleep anytime. Maya's nipples refused to harden and she let out a sigh. As if awakened by it, Manish hurriedly moved further down. Right down to the point. His tongue pierced her lips and Maya let out a sigh, of passion this time. Just five or six pokes and she felt she would come.

Had it been so long? Why would he keep going when he can feel I'm about to come? Doesn't he want to come inside me? And why is he so dispassionate? Why isn't his body as hungry as mine? Is there someone else?

As Maya's head exploded with thoughts, she pulled Manish's up.

"Come," she said. She saw him slowly take off his shorts. It annoyed Maya to an unreasonable amount. Relax. Make it work. She told herself. But her body wouldn't agree and by the time Manish touched himself to her opening, she was almost dry.

"Slowly. Very slowly," she said. A one-year virgin. The more he entered, the more it hurt. *Just breathe and relax. The more you relax the less it will hurt. The body will kick in and it'll get wet soon. Breathe. Breathe. But Manish kept coming in. Why is he coming in when he can feel I'm hurting?* "Slower," she said and he slowed down. Maya could feel him going ever so slightly softer. If he pushed, she felt him bending against her and hence barring itself from entering.

"You lie down," she said. Maya rubbed him with her hands. Reluctantly, pathetically. *The worse girl to have sex with in the world*, she thought. And the worse man. Two worse people to have sex with, thrown in together by this cruel fate. She positioned over him and started to lower. She took him in, slowly, completely, but she wasn't wet yet. So she moved in circular motions. When she couldn't take the pain, she came up for air. When she tried to lower herself again, he had gone softer again. She moved off him. "I can't," she said.

"Okay, come here, let me..." he said.

"No," she said, a little too sternly. Sexual frustration building. She hated that they couldn't have sex. Then Manish had started satiating her by other means. But even that now felt like charity and she refused to take it. *Why isn't he frustrated too? Not only calm, how is he so dispassionate? Is he not attracted to me at all?* Maya thought again but stopped just short of saying *Like I'm not attracted to him.* She didn't want to admit it even to herself. Maybe if they had sex right, one thing in her life would be going on track. Right now, there was nothing else. Manish had already left the bed and now came out of the bedroom dressed. He kissed her on the forehead as couples do after having satisfactory sex. It almost felt like he was glad it was over. He then went out, back to his laptop. He wouldn't talk about it. Their non-existent sex life not only didn't bother him, but he also felt like there was nothing to talk about. After getting refusals a lot of times, and failing the other times, Manish now hardly ever initiated sex. When he did, they failed, again and again. Earlier, it was just Maya and her inability to get turned on. But this time, she had felt Manish also go limp. While otherwise they felt more and more comfortable with one another, sexually, were they drifting apart?

Their relationship never had love, at least from Maya's end, but there was a lot of respect and sex, but now, even that had gone. Were they becoming friends while acting like a couple? Were they too at home with each other? Maya, depressed and exhausted, dragged her naked self to the bathroom and lit a cigarette inside. These days, that's where she liked to be, in the bathroom. Where she didn't have to pretend to be working, or be a wife, or be a friend, or a daughter-in-law. This small bathroom that she could never keep spotlessly clean, was her territory. Her solitary hide-out where she felt more at home than anywhere else. Where the absence of everyone allowed her to be her. Where no one entered her being. Where she didn't have to fight, and could mourn the death of everything in her life, in peace. But now, Suman was coming to stay with them again. Even her bathroom time won't be as peaceful. Then Maya thought, how strange, when one feels like they've lost everything, they find peace in the sadness. How could loss be so liberating? Maybe exactly how the man with tattered clothes on a bicycle laughs his heart out when the rain drenches him.

*

Suman's first morning after Manish had left for work, began with purging. Maya had taken a leave because she was a woman and her job wasn't important enough, particularly when it was up against the visiting mother-in-law. She spoke about every relative out there, until Maya couldn't keep a track of who she was speaking of anymore. She craved a cigarette.

"You know, my mother-in-law was the strictest anyone could've ever seen. She would lock away all the masalas, ghee and all that, so I wouldn't waste them, but what she meant was steal."

Maya looked at her with compassion. A learned woman with a degree denied a job, made to put up with things at home, how would she become? Wouldn't Maya herself become that way if faced with things that bad? Thinking of things that bad reminded her of her problems again. How every-thing was going bad in her personal life. Manish and she had not really been able to connect again. There was a sense of comfort and respect between them, but that was all and clearly it wasn't enough. If this was indeed love—the comfort in silence, the feeling of home—why couldn't their bodies connect? Didn't sex come naturally and hungrily to people who loved each other? If not, was it the case that you might love but not be physically attracted to each other? If so, what would be the difference between that kind of love and one that you have for a friend? Lust being as important in a relationship as love itself, why was it so underrated? Why were all the films about love? Why were all the Hallmark cards about love? Why was everyone in search of just love? Eventually, the conversation turned to Manish.

"He is a little frustrated, He worked exceptionally hard this year and got a fabulous rating, and yet, no hike. More than anything, he's now just really dejected. His heart isn't in the work anymore," Maya said.

Suman sat silently for a moment, really worried. "It's natural to feel that way. But I constantly feel that he isn't rewarded according to his experience and his performance. He should be earning much more; he's good at what he does, he works honestly and diligently and yet, there are no results."

Despite having never worked, Suman's reading of Manish's career was quite accurate.

"But, if we have to see overall, he isn't where he should be because he stayed too long at his previous company. Everyone advised him to make a jump, but he kept waiting for an on-site opportunity, that never came," Maya replied.

"Well, it's also *nazar*. During your wedding, your uncle kept announcing the amount your father was giving you. On and on and on he went, so loudly. Obviously *nazar lagegi*." And there she was again. All logical sharpness out of the window, replaced by marital facts. Of course, after marriage, it isn't about the husband's actions or luck, it's the wife's good luck that brings him success and her fault, or her relatives', that brings him failures.

"I need a shower," Maya said and left the room without waiting for an answer. Finally, she was in her zone. Alone. She sat down on a stool, took a puff and dialled Gaurav.

"So, my uncle is responsible for Manish not getting a hike this year," she said on the phone.

"Hmmf, bad uncle," Gaurav replied. Maya smiled surprising herself.

"No, you are supposed to ask me how or why or what am I talking about!"

"Tell me then, na."

"Manish's mother thinks that my uncle announced the amount my father was giving me for my wedding in front of everyone. So, you know, the evil eye thingy."

"Wow, how much did your father give you?"

"What! Besides the point!!!" Maya giggled.

"But if the amount was so enviable, why do you need to work? If not, how do you explain the evil eye?"

Maya laughed. "What are you on?"

"On my sense of humour; you wouldn't know but there exists such a thing!" They both laughed.

Just then, what was supposed to be a loud knock, opened Maya's bathroom door. Maya shrieked. The cigarette fell out of her fingers as she pulled the towel to hurriedly cover her nakedness. The phone was somewhere in her hands, in the folds of the towel. Suman stood at the door shocked too.

"What are you doing?" Maya said to her a little too loudly than she intended.

"Sorry, I thought I heard...are you smoking?" Suman said flabbergasted. She had intended to knock but Maya, used to just the two of them being there, had not locked the door and so it had opened.

"Can you please close the door?" Maya said, this time with an intended fierce intensity. Suman's face looked stricken but also realising her mistake, she immediately closed the door.

"Hello?" Maya heard from somewhere around her chest.

"Shit, hello, dude!!!!"

"Bro what happened?"

"So, I'm in the bathroom, completely naked and she knocked but the door wasn't locked so it opened and I'm trying to cover myself with a towel and she asks whether I'm fucking smoking. What the fuck!" Maya was raging and there was a moment's silence.

"So, you were talking to me while you were butt naked?"

"Wha...are you...you idiot!!!!" Maya said and burst out laughing. "Fuck I'm suddenly so sick of it all again. I don't know how to go out. So weird."

"Are you mad, these things happen. It's called living in a family. Just...I don't know how you're going to handle the smoking thing."

"I don't care about that at all. And I don't think I like living in the family. God, they're all just always stepping on each other's toes. And living two lives you know, one for everyone and one in hiding. I have done that already; I don't want to do it again. I just want to be able to do what I want, live as I want, without offending and hurting other people, or worrying about what to say, or having to hear shit and keep quiet. It's all too much!"

"Yeah, and after you've lived together long enough, each one has seen the other naked at some point in time. Can you imagine that?"

"Go to hell!" Maya giggled.

"Don't go too hard. Relax. Meet me. Blow off some steam. Go back. Just a matter of a few days."

"Well, thanks, pointers to remember!"

Maya hung up and took a shower. By the time she got out, it was lunch time already and she went into the kitchen. There are often certain words or songs that you hear, that remind you of some long-lost memory. But sometimes, the silence does too. Like now, Maya had almost forgotten about the whole incident but Suman's strict silence reminded her of it again. And of course, the cigarette. Strangely, Maya didn't feel scared unlike she would have, in another time, if her parents would've caught her smoking. She felt anger rising in herself but she kept quiet and started chopping the vegetables Suman had kept on the slab.

"It's okay, I'll do it," Suman said.

"Okay, I'll knead the dough then," Maya said walking over.

"No, I'll do that too. It's okay, I don't need help."

Maya knew what was going on. She was being frozen out, out of her own kitchen! At Suman's house, Maya didn't have so much of a say as to what curtains to use and Maya didn't mind. It was Suman's house after all. And yet, now, Suman was freezing her out of her own kitchen? Maya knew in Suman's head it meant much more than it was. The right to kitchen was a daughter-in-law's pride, it meant belonging to the family, it meant being respected and loved and cared for. It meant becoming truly one with the family. Maya smiled as she realised everything that Suman was trying to say by getting her out of the kitchen was anyway true. She didn't feel accepted, respected or loved or included in the family. She was just included in kitchen duties and not what it stood for.

"Cool," Maya smiled and walked back into her bedroom, this time shutting the door behind her and locking it. After two hours of reading, Maya went into the kitchen to get some food, only to realise Suman had not made rotis for her. Just then, Suman entered the kitchen. Her face changed to a kind of satisfaction at seeing that her disapproval was finally hitting Maya. She stood there, expecting Maya to respond but the latter just opened the fridge, took out the dough and started rolling out rotis for herself. Suman couldn't be quiet anymore.

"How could you! You smoke?" Suman's voice was laced with fury. Strangely, this gave Maya more strength. She turned around and said,

"Yes, I do."

"I'll tell Manish."

"He knows," she calmly replied. But this infuriated Suman even more.

"Oh! So, do your parents know? Should I call them now?" Suman's voice came out high-pitched, as if inviting Maya for a duel. It reminded her of a doubles wrestling match where the partner of the one being hit badly leans in with the hand extended for a tag so he could rush in and destroy the opponent. But she stopped short of smiling, that would be rude.

"No, my parents don't know. And sure, you can call them now." She replied and turned away to roll.

"I will speak to Manish," Suman replied after a moment's silence and left the kitchen. Maya cooked and sat down with her food, satisfied. She had finally rebelled, not with arguments and loud words, but with something even more powerful—silently. Calmly. Without challenging or being rude or getting excited. Maybe she had come back to being herself but in a better, transformed way. A circle was complete, a perfect one, like her *rotis*.

That evening, Suman kidnapped Manish into her room as soon as he came in, giving no time for Maya to explain things to him. Maya heard muffled sounds from Suman's room but she could catch Manish clearly saying, "...choice....adult!" She didn't need to explain herself after all.

The next day, Maya went to work despite it being a Saturday. Surprisingly, Suman was normal again, behaving as nothing had happened. She even insisted Maya take another leave and stay back with both of them but Maya cited an important meeting and left. By noon, she was glad she did because the most awaited mail announcing a promotion came. Ved was the first to come over and congratulate. Their relationship had transformed drastically in a year. From attraction to weirdness and then finally to pure friendship. Now, they shared a kind of honesty that could never be before, when you're getting to know each other but also want to be in the good pages hence conveniently leaving out an honest word or two. Usually post a physical tryst that the two briefly had, people often lose respect. But be it circumstances of having to work together or just maturity from both ends, they had eventually found a place where the respect was at first consciously given and then became a way of working together. Eventually, they had both come to square one, of getting to know each other all over again. Maya again became this person who was brilliant at her work and Ved went back to his passion towards bettering lives. However, this time that didn't lead to attraction, but tremendous respect for each other. The same respect that they had started with. But then, don't we always value something much more if we lose it and find it again?

"Party on Maya tonight!" Ved announced on her behalf.

"No, no, just early kinda dinner, that's all! I have a mother-in-law at home!" she replied.

Maya was smiling by the time she reached home. Life can be so strange that way, often instead of finding comfort and relief with our most close ones, we end up finding it with people who are distant. Finally, there was one thing going good for her in life. Manish opened the door and hugged her immediately. She entered and saw there were cupcakes for her on the table. Suman stood there too, smiling. Maya walked over and touched her feet like a good daughter-in-law.

"Congratulations beta! I'm so happy for you! At least you are getting to pursue your hobby! It's like, I always wanted a big book shelf in my house. And now I have that...because of you, of course."

Struck, Maya turned around, picked up a cupcake and left for her room.

By the time Manish came into the room, she had finished the cupcake, smoked two cigarettes, texted her father about what had happened and received an elaborately decorated "ignore her" and now she sat with a glass of wine. Silent and calm rebellions don't always work. That's when cigarettes and alcohol come to the rescue. Manish stood there for a moment, silently disapproving the glass.

"You know, I'm trying to talk to her. But you didn't have to be that rude either."

"Excuse me? I was rude? What would you rather have me do? Smile and say thank you? I don't talk back but that's the most I can do!" Maya raged, teeth clenched. "She thinks my promotion equals her fancy for a bookshelf? Really?"

"But she gave you credit for that, right?" Manish said.

"Wow! Wow, she's smart and you, like any other man, you're just…"

"Dumb?" Manish replied.

"No, Manish, you don't get to turn this around on me. I'm sorry but I'm done. I can't, I can't do this anymore. I can't find happiness here. And I'm tired of trying. It's not gonna work." Maya said tearing up.

The circle had come back, but it hadn't stopped moving.

"What is it that you want?" For the first time, Manish's voice was tainted with irritation. Maya felt like this nagging wife who was unhappy for no reason. This angered her even more.

"I want her to stop talking shit to me. I want to be financially more stable. I want to be able to have sex again because God knows I'm desperate. I want to be attracted to you. I want to be able to love you."

"I'm working on her. I'm working on the finances, I'm sorry my family isn't as well off as yours, but this is how it is. The rest, Maya, you married me, I'm open and honest and this is who I am! This is it. This is all. Know that this is how it is. Now, what are you gonna do?"

"I want an open marriage." Maya blurted. There was a long, shocked silence.

Finally, Manish walked over and sat down on the bed with Maya. He put a hand over hers and said, "Really, is that what you want?"

Maya's heart broke a little, but the alcohol gave her the strength. "Yes, I think so."

"Why do you want it though?"

"It could be either of the two things. I'm very unhappy here, be the family, the situation between us, the finances, all of it together is just pouring down on me. And I…" she cut off, feeling shameful.

"Go on. Wherever we are in our relationship, we can make it work if we can talk openly. And you know you can tell me anything, Maya."

"I just want to feel that butterflies in the stomach feeling again, like in college. Secondly, it could also be that this is the way I am. I'm not declaring that I don't believe in monogamy, but I am starting to feel that I'm probably not monogamous. And I didn't know this always, I'm just realising it now. Or else maybe I shouldn't have married." As Maya said these words, a strange feeling created inside her. Imagining her life without Manish felt hopeless. She still didn't know if she loved him but she knew for sure now that he couldn't be in her life. Is this it? Was it love? If so, why did she still feel like seeing other people? Is this how polygamous relationships work?

"Listen, I'm glad you didn't realise this before, or else I would've never got to marry you. About open marriage, I'll never be able to say I'm 100% alright with it. Of course, it bothers me that you want it. It would bother me if you went to someone else. I'm honestly scared that you might find someone and would want to leave me. What then?"

"No, no, don't get me wrong! I'm not looking for someone to move on permanently with. Listen, I don't know if what we have is love, but I do know that I can't do without you. I respect you so much and I could never break your heart, but I'm not saying I want to be with you forever because of those reasons. I want to be with you for me, for myself wanting to be with you and you only. This other thing, it's just…it adds some spark to my life. The crushing, the flirting, the silly things. I feel like I need them. And I know I'm not making you happy either, don't you also want something more?"

"Well, I know I love you and I'm sure of it. Yes, physical incompatibility is there but I'm sure we can make it work. I understand the kind of stress you are in with my parents and finances and not getting support from your parents and just about everything else, and I know that because of that we can't translate our sex lives for the better. But I still feel that it can be worked out. And well…if you crushing, flirting, having an affair or just whatever, can help you be better at home and with me, maybe it's okay? But Maya, I can never be a 100% cool with it. Flings are still okay, but finding a permanent solution in them really scares me."

"I don't want a permanent solution in them. I have a permanent solution in you, even if it comes with defects of its own. I know that this is for me. I'm really not looking for anything more."

"Okay then, I think for one thing in our lives, we are on the same page. And I promise you, Maya, we will work out everything else too. I believe in us. Don't you?"

"I do," Maya replied, believing in them now.

Maya hadn't thought she would ever say it out loud. She had never thought she'd ever want such a thing for herself that she had always thought shameful. But now, having life thrown her in a situation that she was in, she felt she couldn't live without it. Or was the situation to be blamed at all? Maybe it was all her, the kind of person she was. And for a person like Manish who did right and went by the rule book to agree to this did mean that she had it good after all. Maybe he agreed to it because it wasn't so wrong in the first place. Maybe it was ingrained by the society for it to be considered wrong. It all came down to labels. And Maya was ready to rip them off.

In another aspect of her life, she had come back a full circle again.

CHAPTER 20
Vaidehi and Vinod

A tug of war had taken over Vaidehi's home. It penetrated every relationship without the members even realising it. One of the matches was between the simple good-s and bad-s, like in every person's life. The intensity with which Kamla had been scheming against Vaidehi had gone down considerably after she had realised Vinod's unwavering loyalty and love towards his wife. But her unreasonable hatred and wish for them to separate was stronger than ever. Even Kamla didn't know what she would achieve if Vaidehi left their lives or how the children would be brought up; she just hated her with a loyal ferocity. She still kept her husband brainwashed about how Vaidehi wanted them out of the house and how, while he was the eldest and the head of the house technically, it was Vaidehi who held the reigns.

If she knew nothing can hurt a man more than his challenged ego, she was also smart enough to tug the children on the love nerve. When Manav was younger, she would feed him with her own hands casually mentioning it to him that his mother wasn't free to do it. Now that he was grown, she still did motherly things for him liking giving him an oil massage, serving him food, hovering over him at home when he got back from school, asking him about his day. Now she didn't use words, but still made it seem like Vaidehi was too occupied to be doing her job. But her failure was evident, not only with Vinod, but also with Meera. When she was younger, Kamla would do little things like asking Meera to tie her hair and sleep if Vaidehi had asked her to leave it open through the night. Or, when Meera was learning to make *rotis*, she would immediately come over and start instructing her before Vaidehi could. These really small chores were taken over by Kamla so as to get Meera on her side too. However, she was failing for two main reasons: Meera was now more than clear that her grandparents never wanted a girl child, which they had made clear quite often in passing comments. Secondly, Vaidehi had started opening her heart out to Meera about how she was treated by Kamla ever since she got married, in ways that she never could with Vinod. So Meera knew her grandparents in ways that Manav didn't.

The good-s were Vinod's incredible success at work. He was being made the President of the company and Vaidehi had decided to throw a party, calling all their family, friends and relatives. They now had more money than they'd ever had or known anyone in their families to have ever owned. They also had a bigger car, a better house and a more luxurious lifestyle. Little things in Vaidehi's life had improved, like, she was once never allowed to go to a parlour but now could call the lady home and enjoy the treatments in her privacy freely. Or, the ban on them going out and socialising or travelling weren't adhered to anymore either. She could now do what she wanted, as the older generation slowly yellowed and started to peel away weakly from the tree. Only now, she couldn't. After years of imprisonment, Vaidehi didn't feel like socialising or travelling. Even though the restrictions were no longer binding, the memory of fear that she'd felt when Vinod's father would shout at them for going out had made a home in her mind forever. Not going out now had become a way of life for her. Very few people were allowed in, and absolutely mandatory situations were attended to. However, this didn't bother her too much because the new found peace, power and freedom at home—a given for any other woman in her married life—looked luxurious to her. In its own twisted way, life had beaten her down by giving her the worst and then making it a little better, making it seem like the best of life. Be it through acceptance or ignorance, Vaidehi was happy. Now, as the days of the party neared, she was ecstatic in her preparation for it, and one of these afternoons, Nalini visited.

"After so long!" Vaidehi said, taking in the feeling of a by gone home that Nalini brought with her. Of the home-waxing, the gossip afternoons, the bangle carts, the *ghee* tins, the release of breasts bursting with milk, their children playing together every evening. It seemed like a lifetime ago. Nalini's husband had grown too, and moved into a bigger house elsewhere. But their successes could still not be compared.

"Arre, I know, but our houses are so far apart, it gets difficult to regularly meet," Nalini replied, her hair still long, thick and dark. Her shoulders still square and her chest still out, her eyes still true and her being still genuine. So unaffected and not intimidated by Vaidehi and Vinod's tremendous success.

"I know. And you know all about me and how it gets if I go out."

"Auntyji is still like that?" Nalini looked into Viadehi's eyes and smiled. Nalini couldn't relate any more to Vaidehi's new social and financial status, but her grounded nature, demure being and her silent obedience towards her in-laws' injustices that passed as respect were still relatable.

"It's not so bad. Time changes things, but still, I don't want to take any chance of disturbing this home. I just want some peace," Vaidehi replied.

"*Aur kya!* Peace and prosperity are all we want for our husband and children. For that we have to compromise—which woman doesn't? *Acha sun*, now-a-days, there is this new thing that *punditji* has told me. For prosperity and good luck. A brass Ganesha idol."

"I know, I have always had one. Even you have!"

"No, no, it's not like that. It has to be a stolen one."

"What?" Vaidehi looked up in surprise. It made Nalini giggle. Her simple Vaidehi, who considered lying the ultimate sin, was being asked to steal!

"Yes, yes, it's not the wrong *baba*, that's how it works. You go to someone's home and steal a brass Ganesha idol from their temple and bring it back to yours, do a simple ceremony to place it in your new home and it is said to bring immense prosperity and good luck."

"Haw! But how to steal like that?" Vaidehi asked, wideeyed. She was feeling this kind of shocked interest after such a long time. Only Nalini could do it with her outlandish beliefs, be it releasing pent up milk from the breasts, or releasing much-needed good-luck.

"Hahah! Arre, ask Vinodji to do it. You don't even attempt; I know you'll fail miserably."

They both laughed. No matter how much money Vaidehi had now, luck and prosperity still required stealing.

"Come earlier tomorrow, okay? And bring your clothes here only, we'll go together." Vaidehi said as they bid goodbye for the night.

The next day, Vaidehi's house was spilling over with relatives. It was the day of the party and no one could hear their voice over the conundrum that was not only a gathering for Vinod's promotion but also a get-together for relatives who'd not met each other in a long time. The rooms were full of groups that formed by themselves as people that belonged together found each other naturally. There were Vinod's cousins who sat in careful silence and muted exchange of words, calculating how much he would be making now and how much they could borrow from him. Then there were the sons-in-law of two generations, constantly demanding to eat food and drinks and see people. There were boys—cousins from both sides just hanging together, catching up, looking cool and laughing that brash, loud laughter at possibly sexual jokes. As for the female section, first there were the older ladies, gossiping about the uselessness of their middle-aged daughters-in-law. Then there was Vaidehi's generation, ladies from Vinod's side openly throwing dark glances of jealousy and from Vaidehi's side, smiling proudly but not genuinely. And girls—cousins of both sides, giggling, talking about clothes and shoes. Among these were scattered friends of both sexes, some genuinely happy, some seeing their peer way ahead in the race than they would ever be. It wasn't their fault, they were human. It was a tug of war of relationships, fake and genuine. Vaidehi passed a group and overheard Nalini talking about stealing Ganesha idols and smiled.

The day turned into evening and Vinod and Vaidehi stood together at the evening of celebrations, mingling with the guests.

"Vaidehi, you look nice. And congratulations!" They stood with Vinod's friends—men still stubbornly sticking to cool boy charms with rudraksh neckpieces and open buttons that revealed now greying chest hair and women with short hair, tall heels and mauve-painted lips. This particular group of women were always in startlingly perfect sync with the fashion and hence each other. Presently, they all wore pants with large kaftan kurtis, the same shade of lipstick, the same shade of pink nail polish and huge dazzling earrings and bracelets around left wrists, a huge equally dazzling ring on the right hand, and a bare neck. Anyone who didn't do all of this was, in their terms, *"pu-raane zamane ka"*. Old-fashioned. Vaidehi stood in a white silk sari with golden threads forming delicate motifs and a border. She wore a long gold chain that reached her chest, delicate gold studs, rings in both ring fingers, and maroon bangles in both hands, book-ended with gold kadas. She wore a shade of maroon lipstick, closest to her natural lip colour, and a maroon bindi. She might be wearing the most expensive, but looked the most subtle.

"Thank you, how are you?" she replied, her old self-consciousness not as strong as before, as their synchronised jewellery looked like the lightings on the trees.

"Yes, she does look nice, doesn't she? Without the *pallu* on her head and the shiny border of her *lehenga,*" one of the women said, revealing teeth tainted with escaped mauve lipstick. The ladies giggled.

Vaidehi smiled and said, "Thank you. I do wish I could go back to the age of wearing so much bling and shine." The women, now conscious of their blinding jewellery and medley of painted colours, nodded dumbstruck.

On another table, Meera sat talking with Vaidehi's mother.

"Why are you wearing jeans? You should've worn a suit or even a saree!" Vaidehi's mother said.

"Oh, *Nani* but this is just fine! What's wrong with jeans?"

"It's a celebration! You could've worn something heavier."

Meera just giggled. Her nana had passed away years ago and she loved her Nani. They always met with Meera touching her feet and then her Nani looking at her up and down, inspecting everything from her hair to her toes and she was never happy with what she saw. After a few affectionate words, she would start scolding her about how her hair was too short or how her clothes were not right. Meera loved this open, strong, confident woman who magically made those words also reek of love. Vaidehi came and sat with them and as everyone sat down at their table for dinner, Vinod stood up, calling for attention.

"Thank you all for being here. I'm so thankful for this success, but I'm even more grateful that I can celebrate it with all of you. There's no greater treasure than the beautiful relationships that you build in life, and in that aspect, I feel blessed looking at all of you here today. And here's to the most treasured person of my life, Vaidehi. Your unwavering love and support have taught me what a stable life even means. Your perspective and opinions have taught me much more than the world ever could. To have you at each step as a partner, as a lifeline, as a director and as a person whom I call home is the only reason I am here today. Forever, us."

Vaidehi's utter surprise turned into a smile as the applause dived into a clattering of plates and a happy murmur. She looked down to see her mother's hands full with one of her own and the other of Meera's. Three generations, each a step ahead into the world, on the path laid by the previous' sacrifices, today joined in love.

That night, as soon as Vaidehi got home, she went straight to the temple to express her gratefulness. She took off her footwear, covered her head with her saree pallu, joined her hands and closed her eyes.

"Thank you for giving me so much more than I could even imagine."

She opened her eyes, to see her brass Ganesha idol missing. A tug of war between promotions and regressions.

*

"What are you doing?" Vaidehi asked, seeing Meera lying on the sofa. Her voice was laced with irritation as any parent's when they see their child preparing for boards, resting.

"I'm taking a break, mummy!" Meera replied. Her voice laced with the irritation as any child's when their parents think they aren't allowed to breathe if they're appearing for board exams.

Vaidehi paused, torn between sending her back to her study room and not going too overboard with the board's fever. She chose the in-between.

"Okay, come, help me the kitchen."

"Why is it always the studies or the kitchen? Why don't you ask Manav to do it too?"

"Well, he is studying, and doesn't need to take as many breaks as you."

Meera wanted to say that he takes breaks in his own room, but kept her teeth clenched instead.

"Vaidehi, please let her be," Vinod said.

"She needs to learn!" Now the conversation had escalated from preparing well for boards to preparing for marriage.

"No, she doesn't. She needs to know the very basics, which she does. She can practice when her exams are done. I'm not preparing my daughter to please some in-laws. I'm preparing her to be independent." Vinod replied.

Vaidehi knew the conversation was over. Meera smiled at her father and went back into her room.

"Okay fine. Have you seen the designs for Manav's room?" Meera heard Vaidehi say a little softly to Vinod. Meera's heart sank. Manav and Meera now had separate rooms to sleep in but Manav's was getting renovated to prepare for his future bride. The marriage was still years away, they had not even started looking for girls but Vaidehi and Vinod had already started preparing for both their children.

"We can do this later, Vaidu, why must you…"

"I don't understand my fault," Vaidehi now said, her voice low yet stern, "A girl will come for Manav, so he has to have a better room. And Meera has to eventually leave the house, so she has to learn to cook."

"But you can surely understand how she must see this difference," Vinod said, his voice heavy with sadness. Vaidehi paused. Somewhere down the motherhood road, the road of wanting Meera's life to be different, had merged into following the tread-on route. Of course, she had to be independent, confident and she should be able to fight for herself, but all that should happen in the protective cover of a marriage. Every generation walks a few steps ahead of the previous ones in breaking stereotypes and Vaidehi had walked hers. She had given her daughter education, the freedom to make choices, she had never differentiated between her and her twin brother—as much as those few steps ahead would allow—and now, that was it. With everything she'd taught her daughter, she'd have a different marriage, a different life, a better one.

"Yes, but with and despite everything, we can only afford to do up one room. And logically it has to be his. She would, well, she will be eventually…"

"Getting married and leaving, so why make a room for her?" Meera cut Vaidehi off. They both looked up to see her standing in the room. They didn't know when she had come back and how much she had heard. They didn't discuss all of this in front of her, not because they felt they were wrong but because they knew this talk would hurt her. She wouldn't understand this the way they did. She was a different generation, way ahead of theirs, a result of what Vaidehi had intended.

"Meera, you're misunderstanding us."

"No, it's fine. I don't want your room." Meera said and left. Vaidehi and Vinod looked at each other in helplessness.

That night, Vaidehi couldn't sleep. On one side, things were falling in place with Vinod's success and their financial stability. They could provide a better life for everyone in the family. And yet, problems managed to find their way into the dynamics of the house. Vaidehi had longed for freedom earlier in her marriage but now, when she actually could live her life, she felt like just being at home with her family. She'd wanted Vinod to be home more often and be a part of their family, not miss any special moments with each of them. But now, when he could do that, there only seemed to be problems around. She'd never wanted to differentiate between her son and daughter. But her son seemed to have gone quiet and distant and she had no idea why or when that had happened. And her daughter, who she'd taught to fight for what was rightfully hers and grow up strong and independent, was now fighting against her, for what she thought was hers. Maybe it wasn't so black and white after all. You can teach someone a lot of things, until their own mind takes over and starts making judgements for themselves.

Vaidehi remembered how when Meera and Manav were born, she'd specially picked up her daughter and walked away from a traditional upbringing, giving as much love and importance to her as the world gave to her son. How she'd taught the girl to consider herself as important as her brother. And now, she struggled with the fact that while she had stopped walking on the path of progress just a few steps ahead from how her own mother had brought her up, Meera had left her hand and had kept walking further still, launching another tug of war, between modernism and traditions.

Chapter 21

Secrets

She woke up on her own this morning. It was freezing outside and so dark. It was exactly 6:30 am. Her mother would come to wake her up any minute now. But for the first time, she was wide awake on her own. She decided to head to the bathroom to start brushing her teeth. Her toes curled as her feet slid into slippers that felt like they were just taken out of the freezer. She walked over to the bathroom, hating the morning, the school, her life. What was the point of all of this? She switched on the geyser and imagined those moments between pouring mugs of hot water when the cold air hits you harder and the way her teeth would chatter as she would dry herself with a towel, apply coconut oil all over her body and dress up. And then all those hours, or so it seemed, it would take for her body to get warm under the sweater, feet in the shoes and palms in the gloves. Now she felt like crying. Why did she have to bathe? She started brushing her teeth. Why had her mother not come to wake her up? She then undressed, filled a mug with hot water and stood there, dreading to start the bathing process. She must've stood like that for about 5 to 7 minutes until she shouted at herself in her mind and poured the water on her face simultaneously. As it emptied, the cold hit her. She quickly filled up more mugs and poured them all as fast as her hands would allow, to keep herself warm. Soon she was done and out. Her teeth chattered and her body goose-bumped. She opened the blue plastic coconut oil can that had launched in the market, especially for winters. Its lid was broader so that the oil could be taken out easily when frozen. She dug her index finger and took out a substantial amount and rubbed it between her palms. She wondered how it melted so quickly despite her hands being so cold. She slid them over the length of her legs, hands, then her flat chest and tummy and her back. Lastly, she unscrewed Ponds cold cream and applied some to her face, finally sliding a finger of coconut oil on her lips. Her toes felt frozen by now. She quickly put on her white slip on and then her underwear.

Why had her mother still not come? If only she hadn't woken up, she would've skipped school and simply blamed it on her. She then took her white shirt and buttoned it up.

Just then, her mother burst into the room.

"Maya, quick, quick, your auto has come, you must leave right this moment!"

For a splitsecond Maya wondered at how her mother had her maroon bangles and bindi still on at this hour. And she hated it when she called her Maya—it was a name she used when something was too important or serious to be good. The utterance of her other name, however, always signalled normality. In fact, the sound of her name would predict what was to come. She looked down, to see her shoes and socks were on, but her skirt wasn't!

"But…" she started, pointing out the situation.

But Vaidehi cut in, "What but but? Come on now, your father is travelling, so who will drop you if you miss the auto? Leave! Now!" Meera saw Kamla watch, sitting on the sofa, but not stop her. *Dadi! Dadi!* She called out to her, asking her to stop Vaidehi, but no sound came out and Kamla sat there and smiled.

Vaidehi pulled Maya by her hand and the next moment, Maya looked at her school building, still half-naked and shivering. Her palms, underarms and feet sweated with shame. She looked around and saw peons and students passing by her. No one seemed to notice her semi-nakedness but Maya was frozen where she stood. Everyone would see her naked now. Why didn't her mother let her dress? Why didn't anyone else say anything? Maybe she should turn back and go home. But just then, the peon in grey pants, shirt and cap started to ring the metal bell announcing the start of classes. She turned around to see the gates being closed by the watchman in khaki pants, shirt and cap. The bell grew louder as if forcing her to enter the building with the same urgency as Vaidehi had pushed her out of the house.

Maya woke up with a start.

"Meera, *utho beta 10 baj gaye!*" Vaidehi called from outside as she knocked on her door. Wake up Meera, it's 10.

"Another hour, mummy, please!" Meera called out weakly. She had actually sweated through the dream.

"Okay, okay. You keep watching movies till 3 and then wake up at lunch," Vaidehi replied kindly. *But what else is your parents' home for*, she thought as she walked away smiling.

Meera, however, couldn't sleep now. It was always a strange feeling coming home to stay and having to sleep alone. When she would be with Manish, she would feel like she needed more physical space and now when she had the bed to herself, she felt like she had no support and was drifting away into nothingness. Her body yearned for another's touch. Meera stayed in bed, thinking about her dream. Ever since her grandmother had passed away, she'd dreamt about her too many times. It almost felt like she kept coming back because there was some unfinished business. But this dream was strange in particular. This dream of hers of being naked in public was a regular one that had haunted her countless times when she was in school but now, these two dreams had strangely culminated into one. This was the one where she saw Kamla as she'd always seen her, growing up. In her other dreams, Kamla had visited her looking strange and scary. Once, Meera saw her as a baby, except her hair was silver and long like it had been when she was alive and as she cried, she actually said the words, "I'm not happy," instead of just wailing like a child. Another time, she'd looked like this stern lady in completely black clothes from neck to feet, with brown skin that was also firmer than she remembered from when she was alive, and her hair was black too, tied up in a tight bun. Meera had never seen Kamla with such black hair ever. Other times, she would see her as she'd become when Meera's grandfather had passed away. Without a bindi or bangles and always in wornout sarees. In the dream, however, Meera saw her with unkempt hair and wearing only a blouse and a petticoat, the worn out, almost negligible saree, not there in the dream. Often, Kamla didn't say anything in these dreams but always scared Meera, and now, she'd come armed with her most scary nightmare from childhood.

In her heart, Meera did know that there was unfinished business. She'd just ignored this thought all these years but now felt it more and more and had started to acknowledge this fact. Was it because of Kamla's scary appearances in Meera's dreams? Or because everything was falling apart on the marriage front, so these thoughts too decided to attack at her weak status? Or, was this thought of unfinished business the very cause of Maya's behaviour that led to her marital problems?

Meera's mind went back to the start. At least as far back into her childhood as a mind is capable of. She remembered herself as a child, she and Manav playing together with Kamla. She didn't remember what she'd said but she did remember Kamla saying, "We wanted two boys, but as fate would have it." She remembered looking blankly at Kamla, feeling not right but not understanding what was wrong. She remembered coming downstairs in tears when Kamla had asked Manav to push her from his side of the bed. She smiled at these thoughts. Being a child is so much better; there's so much strength in innocence, survival happens by default. Then she remembered those afternoons when she was grown up. Almost every afternoon, something in Vaidehi would open up, and she would talk about Kamla — how she'd said Vinod was destined to marry twice on their wedding night, how she wasn't allowed bigger bras even during pregnancy and post it; how her character was slashed ruthlessly; how free she was before marriage and how she was hardly ever allowed to go out, after; how all her letters to her mother were read; how Kamla hated her and wanted to separate her from Vinod... And on and on these would go.

To date, Meera remembered each of these incidents clearly, but what she didn't remember was when she'd stopped speaking to Kamla completely. What Vaidehi and Meera both didn't realise was how much her mind was poisoned listening to all of this. Now, every time Meera thought about how she and her grandmother would co-exist in the same house, even the same room and she would just not speak to her. In rare cases that Kamla asked her anything, Meera would reply in a simple yes or no. This had gone on for years and years; how was it even possible? How was it even possible for her to hate someone so much and hold on to it for so many, many years? How was it possible for this hate to become a default? How was it possible for her to feel this was a normal way of living? How was it possible for her to take life, both hers and Kamla's, for granted? How could she not see that this hatred and silence would one day end, but only through Kamla's death? Meera's throat choked up and she went to the bathroom, switched on the exhaust and lit a cigarette. She knew it was but natural to feel animosity towards someone who has done wrong by your mother. But was it still right for her to do that to her grandmother? And if she didn't, wouldn't she be cheating on her mother? Although she hadn't intended to, was she her mother's revenge? She remembered she wasn't even in the city when her grandfather passed away. By the time she had landed, his body was already taken. Kamla had told them then that he'd called for Manav and Meera both and told her that he was leaving. Neither of them had been able to be there. Not even the loyal Manav, who stood by his grandparents throughout their lives. How could have Meera not realised that she had no time, even then? In fact, the last she'd shown any warmth towards her grandmother was on the day of the death of her grandfather. Kamla had sat on Vaidehi's bed crying but had still not allowed her daughter-in-law to console her out of hatred. That's when Meera had fed Kamla biscuits dipped in hot tea, her first meal of the day. She had even urged her to eat "one more biscuit". How had this hatred tied three generations of women so strongly? Is love ever as strong as hatred? And after that day, Meera had gone back to not talking as naturally, as compassion is supposed to exist.

A few years later, she was to be married. By then, Kamla was in a wheelchair. She remembered coming down the stage, Manish following her, to touch her feet. She had smiled and touched Kamla's feet, and when she'd looked up, she'd seen the same angry, wrinkled face. Even then, the hearts couldn't soften. But she'd also seen that when Manish had bent down, her face had transformed into a smile. The anger, the hatred, was only reserved for her and Vaidehi. In the days between her engagement and marriage, Kamla was bedridden and had lost all memory. Finally, Meera could sit on the bed and hold Kamla's hand in hers, as Kamla called out to her mother, delirious. That was the only time she'd heard her grandmother saying Ma. It sounded so strange, for the old-est generation of the house to not only have parents but also to hear them call out to them. Not only this, but Kamla had also gotten Manav with her now, sitting on the other side of Meera, holding her other hand.

When along with memory, her hatred was taken away, all her family had come naturally to Kamla. Manav, the ever quiet, the ever absent, sat across Meera, but by then, they had forgotten to make conversation with each other. Things that happen in innocence can be ignored, but their consequences show up nonetheless. Was it his not standing up for her when she was put down for being a girl? Was it Vaidehi's constant special attention to Meera? Was it Meera's constantly breaking young Manav's trust, being disgusted with him and even once calling him a monster? What was it and when was it that had caused them to drift so far apart? They knew each other before life. But in life, they had become strangers. So, both had sat, with their own memories of Kamla — Manav with good ones and Meera with bad ones — and not spoken a word to each other. Then one day, Kamla's memories had come rushing back, as her body ached with monstrous bedsores, her one breast gone with cancer, like her memories. She had called out to Vinod and Vaidehi urgently as if she had no time. Meera had stood behind them. She'd asked Vinod to hug her tightly. Then she'd taken Vinod's and Vaidehi's hands, joined them between hers and said, "Always be together," blessing them with one thing that she'd fought against all her life. Meera had waited, thinking she'd be called too but Kamla had no time. That was the end of hatred and the beginning of regret, a business that would always remain unfinished. And Meera had to bury the feelings that she had not even completely realised yet, because the cards were printed and the wedding was due. Surprisingly, she had cried once, in the bathroom when Kamla's body was taken away. Post which, she had no time to reminisce. However, the first time when it all had struck her was when Kamla's sister had come on stage to bless her and Manish. The resemblance was uncanny. She realised it could as easily have been her grandmother, but just like that, it couldn't be. While brides remembered various moments from their weddings, Meera always remembered this. How much had Kamla's sister looked like Kamla! The death was recent, the emotions weren't registered and yet, not even for a moment could Meera mistake Kamla's sister for her own grandmother. How did the mind remember and not remind her of it every single moment? She had wanted to burst into tears again but there was no bathroom to hide in.

Now Meera wondered why she could not just put her foot down and postpone the wedding. Vinod would've understood, but she'd also felt strangely numb at Kamla's passing away. It was probably because she'd only felt hatred towards her for so many years, that her mind was dumbstruck when it had nothing more left to hate. And so, with a heart full of death, she began the second phase of her life. It was her first night after the wedding when Meera should've realised something was wrong. But, how could she? These things never come with a warning, but with a slight step and silent breathing. That night, her body wasn't able to perform. No matter how much they tried, she wouldn't get wet enough. When Manish had tried to enter, Meera had borne the ache as much as she could and then she'd asked him to stop. Like her mind, her body too was so numb that she didn't realise how much of Manish had entered her. Then there was the honeymoon and then the in-laws and so many new problems that the deceased was given the least thought, obviously.

Now, sitting in the bathroom, blowing into the exhaust and lighting a second one with the first, some nights where she'd burst into tears came rushing back to her. It was like a chain reaction. One feeling led to another, each opening a deeper, more painful part of her mind. Tears rolled down her cheeks. She realised there was so much she wanted to talk to someone about. Anyone. Manish? Vaidehi? Manav? Vinod? She couldn't share it with anyone. When had she drifted so away from everyone that now, when she needed someone the most, she had no one? Her mind answered her question, popping up another memory. Those times when Manav was allowed to attend parties, and she wasn't. And how Vaidehi had blurted it was because she was a girl. But she also remembered how she'd hurt Vaidehi growing up. Once, Vinod had gotten back from a very long work trip and had promised his children a night out at the movies. Vaidehi, at the time, used to be sick a lot because of her back. As circumstances would have it, when it was time to go, Vaidehi couldn't get up from the bed. Vinod decided to cancel the program. The twins were heartbroken, especially Meera because she wasn't allowed to go out much, because she was a girl. They'd sulked back to their room.

"Kya yaar!" Meera had said.

"She's always sick," Manav had said. This struck Meera. It was true,

Vaidehi was always sick. What was new? Why did they have to cancel a program because of something normal? She'd marched off to her parent's room and blatantly said, "But papa, let's go! Mummy is always sick."

Vaidehi and Vinod had looked at each other. What Meera had thought to be watering eyes because of the pain, she now realised was tears of hurt. Vaidehi had insisted they go and they'd gone.

But then, Vaidehi's concern for Meera, at times, had led her to be hurtfully rude too. Meera remembered the time when her room wasn't done, but Manav's was. Or the time when that *punditji* had come and announced that for Meera to get married faster, she should sleep on the drawing-room couch. Meera had just smiled a smug smile saying, *"As if!"* But to her horror, Vaidehi had insisted she do the same after he'd left.

There was also the time when Meera remembered conversing with her parents and saying, "So this friend of mine, her father works but her mother does nothing; she's just a homemaker." And how Vaidehi had shushed Vinod when he'd tried to object, looking at the cocky defiance in her daughter's eyes.

Were these the reasons why Meera had often seen Vaidehi go quiet and her eyes well up even though they never flowed? First, her in-laws and then the children. Would she get no support? Is this what the members of a family did to each other? Disrespect, hurt, degrade. Like Kamla did to Vaidehi. Like Suman did to Meera. Like Vaidehi and Meera did to each other.

And just like that, torn between her family and in-laws, between money and love, between husband and lover, between guilt and blame, between right and wrong, the darkness firmly dug its claws in yet another woman's mind.

*

This morning, when Meera came downstairs, everything was mostly the same. Vinod still greeted her with contagious joy. Vaidehi still asked whether she'd have breakfast. Manav still smiled his distant smile that took the feeling out of his pet name, Mannu, that Meera called him by. And Malvika was the same loveable, happy face, adding another layer of the curtain to everything wrong in the family. And yet, this morning when Meera came downstairs, nothing felt the same. All she could see was everything that was wrong, has been wrong, as if the curtains had gone transparent. By the time she sat down for breakfast, everyone left for work and it was just Vaidehi and Meera. Despite everything, she felt at home, like those numerous lazy afternoons bearing stories of torture. Ripe with pain and family. Marriage had taken so much away. Her heart warmed and she looked at her mother and smiled. That's when Vaidehi noticed her daughter's eyes, slightly red and swollen.

"What happened to your eyes?" Vaidehi asked. For years, it was the same question, every time. Vaidehi knew that Meera knew that Vaidehi knew it was because of crying. And Vaidehi would never simply ask, "Why were you crying?" She'd ask, "What happened to your eyes?" instead, hoping it would be not because of crying, hoping there would be no problems, hoping their life would be just perfect. How could this be expected if we just repeated the lives of every generation to resemble the previous one?

"Nothing, was awake late at night, so..." Meera replied as she always would, despite knowing that Vaidehi knew that Meera knew that Vaidehi knew she had been crying. But now, Vaidehi was relieved and Meera was unsettled to not let it go.

"I dreamt of *Dadi* again," Meera said. Stories starting to rise like the steam from their cups of tea.

"What was it this time?" Vaidehi asked, showing more concern for nightmares of the dead than her living daughter's real problems. Meera told her about the dream.

"Oh well, so you saw her normally."

"Yea, but it wasn't so much about how she looked or what she said. It was about what she didn't say. I looked at her, and I felt that way..." Meera trailed off.

"What way?" Vaidehi asked, knowing that Meera knew that Vaidehi knew what way.

"Like the way, I felt every time she said they'd wanted a boy," Meera said, surprised and horrified at how her voice was shaking. She'd spoken about this so many times. She and Manav had even joked about it growing up. A few times when a hint of being twins showed. And yet, now she was that little girl who'd gone to mummy crying. Kamla was dead. Meera was married. Years had passed. How did it matter?

"Meera, she's passed away. Let go of this bitterness now, *beta*." Vaidehi replied, instantly enraging Meera.

I'm still bitter because you decided to share all of that with me when I was still young. But you never told me not to hate her. You heard every time she put me down for being a girl. But you never answered on my behalf. And you didn't do it, because despite wanting a girl and loving a girl, you still treated me like Kamla would treat a girl when it came to marriage. You still decided to not let me have an identity outside of my father's and then of my husband's.

Meera thought all this with a hint of doubt. Even though her anger didn't allow her to dwell on the fact, she still knew it wasn't entirely true. She had let Meera go freer when she'd grown up. She had encouraged her to pursue her dreams, no matter what they were and required. She had given her independence and allowed her an identity, but she had always tied it back to family, a husband. It might not be as away from traditions and into modernism as Meera would've wanted, but still, for Vaidehi, they were a lot of steps away from where she had come.

"Why did you share everything with me? I know papa doesn't know most things about how you were treated that I do," she replied, trying to keep the anger out of her voice.

Always so transparent, this child. Vaidehi thought.

"Because if I had, your papa would've separated from them." Meera was quiet. Her shock dethroned her anger. She sipped her tea.

Vaidehi could see more was coming. It was always something about Meera's awkward mannerisms that one could tell she was trying hard to contain the volcano inside her. But she was yet to learn that a force like that can't be controlled. She waited.

"But Mummy, wouldn't that have been…" Meera could get herself to speak it. How could Vaidehi do it?

"Better? No *beta*. They're our parents, they're old. Who would take care of them? Your father is their only son. No one should go through something like that." Vaidehi replied.

"But what did you get out of it all?" Meera asked, knowing full well she shouldn't be heading in this direction.

"How can you not see? Look at the relatives, look at our friends. I have earned every bit of the respect that they give me, because of keeping our family together. Your father today is so successful and yet, the society is able to look outside of all that financial success and social status — at me — and see the good deeds I've done."

"Yes, but at what cost? Mummy, your youth is gone. All those years simply putting up with everything and for what? Respect of those who talk bad soon as we turn our backs?"

"Oh, so naive, beta! But this is how relationships are! A lot is about what's on the face because behind backs, everyone is bad. No other lady in our extended family is respected as much as I am. And you think there are no sacrifices that one makes to earn money and social status? Your papa is a great father, but he has missed a lot of you both growing up. How is that sacrifice smaller than mine?"

"But you were degraded! Tortured!"

"So was your father. Not as much as I was, but these fights, all of it happened to him too. It pained him as much as it did me."

"So it hurt both of you. Then why would you? To earn respect? And what do you do with that?"

"I live with a clear conscious. I could never live in peace if the family had broken because of me."

"You mean because of *Dadi*."

"Enough, Maya, you think you know everything but you don't!" Meera was quiet momentarily. Vaidehi always called her Maya as a way of distancing herself when she was too serious.

"So, there's more? What do I not know? Tell me, I can't possibly hate *Dadi* anymore and she's not here to see it anyway."

Now Vaidehi was stunned. She was aware of how Meera behaved with Kamla, but she'd always thought it was her decision and because of what had happened to her. Only now she realised that it was because of her. And even in Kamla's death, it hurt Vaidehi that she'd hurt Kamla.

"Okay, then I think it's my responsibility to ease that hurt into understanding and compassion. It's too late, but what else can be done?" Meera regretted asking for it. Could she take any more family complications!

"Bete, no one is purely cruel. Please know that we are all humans after all, and as much good and bad exists in each one of us, as in others. I don't know why mummy hated me so much. Or why she wanted me to separate from your father but I think maybe it was because she'd never known what a husband and wife's relationship truly is. Your grandfather had temper issues. When she married, she was openly called ugly by her in-laws. Not only that, your grandfather would abuse her verbally and also beat her up. You know Laxmi *taiji*, I've heard incidents from her. *Bete*, no matter what she did, she's a woman and above all, a human. And no human deserves something like this. But it happened. And when a tortured person does bad things to you, would you rather let your anger and hatred, or your compassion win? And in our family, living in this society, there never is a logical, balanced way out. It was always either the life we had together or them living alone. I chose the former and I know it's right for me as I can sleep at night. Because I'm happy. All her life had been this and nothing more. Of course, she was family but no respect or love was truly given to her. Somewhere down the line, it made her a certain way… She was so full with what she got that she could only give what she had. Don't be mistaken, her attitude towards her own children wasn't that of an ideal mother. But it's all she had to give! You can say that it's not fair. You can say I should've chosen to be happy but what you don't get is that my happiness might not necessarily lie where yours does."

That afternoon, the stories still ran but only in the minds of the mother and the daughter. Vaidehi found happiness in the pain she had endured. And Meera, going beyond right and wrong, realised how through generations, the torture gave way to a respectable life, only and only because one woman decided to sacrifice hers for a better tomorrow for the next daughter. While that was a battle, fought slightly and won quietly, there lay another one in front of her.

As each mother walked a step ahead, so that her daughter could get a world a little better, the tortures she faced decreased too. But even that was not enough, because while each mother stopped a few steps ahead of her life, the daughter walked on, hence being way ahead in knowing how she should be treated, to even endure the decreased tortures. The new daughters-in-law were increasingly learning the importance of self-respect and happiness. As the traditions slowed them down, they realised this might be the same war, and the demon might have mellowed, but it still couldn't be fought silently.

CHAPTER 22

Changes

"It's the end of an era," Maya said.

"It's only the 30s," Gaurav replied.

"Exactly, end of an era," Maya said.

"I'm sure you don't even feel different."

"That's the thing, I don't. Things on the other hand have changed. For the worse."

"Well, it's not like you got to know of them today. You discovered it all through the past few years."

"Yes, and that's how it's changed. The picture is clearer now."

"And what do you see?"

"I'm still not in love with my husband. The only freedom that I didn't have was to date; now, even with it, nothing's changed. As much as I thought I'll be this liberated woman who is above the petty in-laws issues, I'm pretty much that woman with in-laws issues who takes it all silently. In fact, my whole life is being that traditional woman in a traditional life, where I share my problems with my parents, they turn me around back to my in-laws, saying ignore it. From finances, to domestic life and love life, there's no aspect of my life that I'm happy with. Or even okay with."

"Well, your friend-life is sorted."

"You're useless."

"Your birthday party sucks."

"What did you expect a *welcome to 30s party* will be like?"

"With you heavily pregnant and me sitting with you getting sloshed."

"Well, at least I'm fat if not pregnant."

Maya and Gaurav toasted to that, emptied their glasses and opened the third bottle of wine. The other friends had left the party. Manish was travelling for work. Maya had the house to herself and she was thankful to just be alone. Alone now had become a place for her where she could be herself.

"Let the wallowing continue," Gaurav said sitting back down, handing a glass to Maya.

"You know, let's analyse this. Let's go back to the roots of the problem."

"Like, why you were born?" Gaurav asked.

"No, like dreaming! If you only knew what I imagined my life at 30 to be like! Now I look back at the 20-year-old girl and want to smack the fairyland off her fucking brains!"

"Now you want to blame the parents?"

"Of course, why not? The parents—they will feed you, love you, educate you, provide for your experiences and lifestyle—all of it! So nice, I'm very grateful. And then, at some point, marriage comes into the picture and they will want to take all of that away from you! No no, not take it away, but they will ask you to surrender it all. Work if the in-laws agree. Lifestyle, whatever the in-laws can afford. Travel if the in-laws agree. Ignore their insults. Independence and identity? Whatever the in-laws decide about that! It's like, we have to be born again to perfectly suit a new household. Why should I suit anyone? Am I born to keep suiting people and families? I don't think the parents of the world realise that bringing up a child a certain way and then expecting them to change completely to take a more derogatory life, is not only not easy, but also illegal."

"Sure, you're not a clay anymore, you've hardened. You're a vase now, you can't be moulded into a bucket."

"Yes! I'm used to taking flowers, not bathing water!"

"Wow, it's the end of an era."

"It's The End," Maya replied.

*

The next morning, Maya woke up with a headache. She stumbled out of bed and went to use the bathroom. She was to fly back home today and was yet to pack. As she got up to get out, her feet were still unsteady. She decided to sleep some more and walked towards her bed. On the way, she caught a glimpse of herself in the mirror and stopped dead. Her kohl had smeared and gave her patches below each eye, her hair was a mess and stood stubbornly at weird angles, her translucent t-shirt marked the protruding paunch far ahead of her breasts. She turned towards the mirror and stood feet together to notice that her thighs rubbed against each other. *When did that happen?* she thought. She drew her feet apart to see how far apart they have to be for her thighs to not touch. She then raised one hand to the side and shook it slightly, to see that a flab flap where there used to be hardly any fat at all. She went closer to the mirror. Her cheeks defiantly revealed pores through last night's foundation. She saw two lines, running from the side of her nose, to the side of her lips. She saw fine hair sticking upwards from her nose and a darker patch on each side of her cheeks. She lifted her face to see three very dark hairs on her chin, where there used to be one. Her doctor had mentioned hormonal changes while prescribing medicines for PCOD. So, this was it. Her state of mind was finally showing on her face. Suddenly, remembering everything again, a pain shot through the base of her neck, all the way down between her spine and right shoulder blade. Instinctively her head bent, to see cellulite on her thighs, ending at black-yellowish toe nail from running in her shoes. Wherever she looked, everything was wrong. Everything was destroyed. Her knees gave way. She landed on the carpet and cried.

When she woke up again, she looked worse with puffy eyes, but now, she didn't have time to mourn her life. She rushed to the bathroom and switched on the shower. She let her skin burn under the hot water, as if it would wash away not just the makeup but all the signs of her mind's struggle. She scrubbed until her skin was pink and the hot water now burned even more. She got out, ignored the mirror, put coconut oil all over her body and cream on her face. She didn't want a drop of makeup to touch her skin. She dressed, hurriedly threw some clothes in the bag and called for a cab. She was going to fly, from her present, to her past. From being a daughter-in-law to a daughter. From the struggles to simple. From expectations to unconditional. The way to the airport had a long patch of secluded drive and sleeping through it with an unknown driver would be careless. But whether it was the relaxing thoughts of home or a complete surrender to the destructive way her life was heading, Maya relaxed into sleep.

*

Maya stood at the airport, waiting for Vinod to pick her up. She remembered how many times she'd stood there through various years of her life, coming back home from a work trip or a holiday with friends and more recently, from her *new home*, and how every time, she would stand at this very spot in the pick-up lane and watch her father come pick her up. A white Maruti in early days, a champagne Corolla later, then a grey Jetta, and now a signature blue BMW. The home wasn't just that building where she stayed, it was this very land too, where she took off from to always come back to, the colours of the cars, the entire route which had remained the same, except for one hotel, a short distance away from the airport, that kept changing names but never the building. Now, however, she realised she'll always come here to go back. She'll always be a visitor in the town she grew up in because she had decided to leave it. It was irrational to expect marriages to work when a woman is expected to change lands, change what they call homes, add parents, change their complete lives in a snap. It was one of the most absurd things humans had created. So unnatural, so against the nature – how had we forgotten that? And yet, she had decided to leave her town. To marry and move. It had gotten on her nerves, the same buildings, the same people, the same routes, and she'd craved for a new life, never imagining that something new could turn out to be not so good too. Now, she felt at home neither here, nor there. Stranded mid-way of changing lives. The feeling of home curdled into a feeling of familiarity and Maya craved a cigarette.

Just then, she saw a red Beetle drive into the lane. She smiled at the thought of how she'd told her father last year she loved that car. If she was still unmarried and staying with her parents, she would have asked for it, instead of passively expressing her desire. Malvika had heard it and demanded it relentlessly and Vinod had bought her one just to get it over with. As it came closer, she saw Malvika in driver's seat and Manav waving at her from the passenger's seat. The dagger twisted afresh in Maya's gut. The acceptance that she'd married into a home which was poorer than her father's, and that the luxury that she used to get now went to this strange girl who married her brother and hence was entitled to it, just didn't come, no matter how many years passed. In another life, she would've been happy to see a new car in her family, but now, she just felt a piercing bitterness. That's how selfish an unhappy marriage can make a daughter. Manav got out of the car and hugged her affectionately, while Malvika waited behind the wheel. Maya quickly got into the car and Manav followed shortly after securing her luggage.

"Love the car!" Maya said with immense difficulty that astonished her.

"Thanks di, I know you love this car, you'd mentioned it last time," Malvika replied.

"Your favourite cousin is going to stay with us through this marriage… and a week more," Manav teased. Maya had come to attend a cousin's wedding and a sea of relatives were coming down too.

"Ohh god! Why isn't he staying at the hotel? I'm sure his room is booked too!" Maya replied, already feeling tired at the prospect of meeting relatives and, Rahul in particular, who she'd always detested.

"*Haay*! Why would he stay at a hotel *when his brother has a house here*?" Malvika replied mimicking the older ladies whose sole purpose was to find slip ups and make a mountain of an issue. When his brother has a house here…not her anymore. Maya realised with a shocking clarity how the rule that a daughter truly only belongs to her husband's home was ingrained in every sentence. Suddenly, Maya noticed Manav tucking a strand of Malvika's hair behind her ear. It was so strange to see this new Manav. Slowly, over a period of time after getting married, he had magically transformed into this open, more talkative person. He still wasn't what he used to be as a child, when both of them were young and free of anger and grudges, before they were drawn apart and he chose silence. Before, when they were truly twins. And yet, Malvika had changed him, not made him what he was but changed him in a way only a partner could. Maya wondered whether they were the most distant twins, as twins could get. A living irony. She was happy that he looked happy and yet, this happiness in sharing that once was with her, was now with someone else, and even though it was with his partner, Maya's being throbbed with yet another realisation of lack. Of loss. Or was it that for someone to go back to being a version of what they were, they needed a complete stranger? Emo-tional baggage weighed down so much on Manav that he just couldn't stand back up to be himself with people who'd done this to him. Malvika, in a sense, then had been his only way out.

They reached home and Maya looked up at the strange house that her family now had moved into. Her parents had moved into this house after she got married and every time she visited, it felt a little more strange. She entered the house, abuzz with the low rumble of men, chattering women, children running wild as the help dodged them to get tea and snacks on the table. Maya felt like a stranger looking into what easily could've been a banquet hall. She couldn't get herself to walk in. She spotted Vaidehi. Sitting among a crowd Vaidehi easily stood out, with her greying hair, increasingly swelling eyes that always looked tired, bent back as she sat and slow, wobbly walk as she moved around. The idea of time struck Maya with a jolt. Where had it gone and what had it done to her mother? Parents aren't supposed to grow old! Maya's heart melted. Her problems seemed to disappear in a snap in front of her ageing mother. She felt like hugging her and never letting her go.

"What are you still doing here? Come on in," Manav said entering the house with her luggage, Malvika behind him.

The three of them walked in together. Malvika went into the kitchen, Manav went upstairs to keep Maya's luggage and she walked towards the living room. The aunties looked up as she approached the room and spoke together: *"aa gai" "aaja aaja" "Meera aa gai"*.

Maya went straight to Vaidehi and hugged her. Then she went to various aunties and folded her hands in greeting or touched their feet depending on their age and relation. More orders for tea were given as Maya sat down amidst them and the aunties asked her questions and scrutinised her clothes, jewellery and state of happiness.

"Why are your eyes swollen? Didn't you get any sleep?"

"You're not wearing any bangles."

"Put some kajal no! You look so…tired."

"Wear some Indian clothes! So many sarees your mother gave you but you still wear jeans."

Maya looked over to Vaidehi whose eyes were downcast. She looked like she was in another world. Maya felt like even if she wanted, she couldn't reach out to her.

She excused herself and went upstairs to her room and shut herself in. She was just about to light a cigarette when someone knocked. It was a tray of tea and snacks. She took the cup and sent the rest back, locked the room, went into the bathroom and lit a cigarette. She took a deep drag and instantly felt the energy draining from her body. Her body was drained and her mind was too exhausted to dwell. She found relief in numbness. She walked out to her bed, put on music in her ear plugs and slept.

*

It was late evening when she woke up. She sat up in her bed and listened. The house was quieter. She got up, contemplated washing her face before going back downstairs, decided she didn't have the energy to care, and went out of the room. She got back into the living room hoping to find Vinod but her aunt was there instead. It was too late to quietly go back. Malvika, Vaidehi and Maya's aunt and uncle were there. She craved for some alone time with Vaidehi.

"Meera! I invited you to come earlier, club the wedding with some time at home. Why did you still come late?"

Maya was taken aback, listening to her aunt, inviting her to her own house. This aunt had moved to the city and started living near Vaidehi's house and used to visit her every day and now spoke like the house was more hers than Maya's. She looked at Vaidehi for support. Vaidehi smiled back. Too shocked, hurt and enraged to speak, she was saved by another tray of tea and snacks. As everyone turned their attention, Maya turned to leave.

Vaidehi stopped her. "Where are you going? Eat something, you didn't earlier." Maya took a deep breath turned and sat down as away from everyone as possible. There was so much happiness in everyone's voices as they chatted, making Maya gladly feel invisible. Suddenly, her uncle said, "How would the newest person in the house know how anything's done." Maya looked up to see he was teasing Malvika.

Vaidehi replied, "She's my daughter-in-law; don't say anything to her!"

Maya noted with hurt that Vaidehi would take a stand that she craved for her mother to take for her. Everyone started taking cups of tea and passing them around. Her uncle said, pointing at different cups and to the person, they were for, "This is for the daughter-in-law, this is for the mother-in-law, this is for us, who is this one cup for?" Everyone looked at Maya and giggled. Maya looked at Vaidehi, but she looked back quiet and smiling. A heaviness pressed deep against Maya's chest. She throbbed like a child wanting her mother's support. After a hearty laugh, the topic moved on to something else, and Maya quietly took her tea and started heading towards her room. Before she could escape, Vinod entered the house.

"*Aa gai beta, kaisi hai?*" Maya smiled and hugged Vinod. Before she could reply, she saw her cousin Rahul entering the house. Vinod must've gone to pick him up.

"Oye pagal, you're home again? Now you're married, please stay at your home only." Rahul said to Maya in his usual humour. Instantly she cringed by his being. Rahul was tall, dark, had a fit physique with bulging cheeks and an unpleasant smile on his face all the time. Since she's known him, she'd heard him constantly joking about how his sisters were vain, and now after they were married, how they should stay at "their own home". Over the years, Maya had developed a strong indifference to him and his remarks. Now, when he said this again she felt the same cringe she had when she was younger, just more intensely. She looked back at Vinod. He was smiling on hearing the comment but his eyes were sad. Maya knew it was because of everything she'd shared with him. He knew she wasn't happy and yet he couldn't share this with anyone, not even Vaidehi. She wouldn't be able to take it and this was a burden of knowledge that he had to shoulder alone.

"Okay, go show him the house and his room," Vinod said to Maya. She walked ahead and Rahul followed her. He was to stay in one of the three rooms upstairs. There was a room immediately on the left of the landing. It was open so Rahul peeped in and said, "Whose is this? Manav and *bha-bhi's?*"

"No, this is mine. Their's is…"

"Oh, wow really! Well done for the *jugaad!*" Maya was dumbstruck for a moment and then she snapped, "This is my father's house. I don't need to *jugaado* anything; my room here is a given."

"Yea yea, I'm going to my room. Will be down in a bit." Rahul replied and closed the door to his room.

Maya was shaking with anger. She went to her room, locked the door and lit a cigarette in her bathroom. She took a puff and tears ran down her cheeks. She struggled deeply against the fact that all this relatives nonsense was affecting her so much. None of this was new. She had always heard it before and yet now she couldn't take it. It was a deep-rooted insecurity that had quietly taken seed and she'd not realised when it had grown into a mammoth tree. She felt lesser now that Manish's family had lesser money and his father was much less influential than Vinod. She wondered, shocked, that a life of honesty and the pride that that brings along didn't matter to her at all. She thought herself too shallow because of this and hence the hatred for her body seeped deeper into a beginning of hating herself as a person. This then deepened her insecurities. She started seeing herself as a weak, shallow person with no social standing or wealth. And like a vicious circle, the poorer she thought of herself as a person, the uglier her body and face looked in the mirror.

She suddenly felt drained again. Getting up from the pot, she threw the cigarette butt in and flushed. Walked out and gladly crashed on her bed again, readily welcoming sleep, her only escape.

Someone banged her door waking her up with a jolt. "Meera, beta, are you ready? Come downstairs, everyone is about to come." It was the same aunt.

"Yes," she replied in a voice drugged with depression, hopelessness and sleep.

"Still sleeping? Up, up quickly now! Everyone is about to reach!" her shrill voice was starting to annoy her.

"Yes!" she replied, her annoyance ringing clear. Vaidehi would have instead walked in, gently woken her up and once Maya's eyes would have opened, she would've backed off without pushing her to get up right away. Maya longed for her mother.

There was silence on the other side as if reading into her annoyed 'yes' and then she called out again, "Come come, right away. Or else I'm coming in," she said, weird joy in her voice. Immediately the door handle moved, but the door was locked. Maya was angered at first and then resolved into silence. While silence was often her weakness till now, now it became her rebellion.

Maya got up silently and walked into her bathroom for a shower while her aunt called out again. She closed the bathroom door behind her silently so she wouldn't hear it outside. She turned on the shower on full, blocking out all the noise. She stood there for about 10 mins, just letting the water pour and then got out, a towel draped around her body but still dripping wet. She walked like a zombie to take out her dress for the evening, but slipped and fell on the extended wooden board of her bed making a loud bang. Immediately the aunt called out from downstairs, "Arre what happened, Meera! Don't break our things, okay?" followed by her laughter. Anger erupted, tearing apart her numbness. She didn't reply. She sat slowly, nursing her lower back. As the pain eased, she dressed, still dripping wet, messily wrapping a saree around her. By the time she was dressed, her blouse was completely wet from behind because of her dripping hair. She lined her eyes, put on a lipstick and walked out of her room limping slightly from her fall. Her hair was still unkempt and wet but she didn't bother. She walked through some relatives that had come home for one of the functions that was being hosted in the house and smiled and folded her hands with all the strength she could muster. In return, they all commented on her hair and wet clothes and absence of jewellery.

She finally reached Vaidehi who took her to her room and sat her down. She took a ruby-diamond set of Maya's that she'd kept with her. Unhooking and tying the necklace around her neck, Vaidehi asked, "Why are you limping?"

Maya felt tears oozing out, in gladness as if someone had finally looked at her. She blinked them back and steadying her voice, said, "I fell."

Vaidehi's hand stopped. She took in her wet hair and clothes. "You didn't dry yourself and slipped? Are you okay? Where does it hurt?"

In places, I didn't know existed. "Lower back but just slightly. It's nothing," Maya replied. Vaidehi gave the earrings to Maya to wear and meanwhile took out an ointment and applied it to where it hurt. Someone called Vaidehi's name.

"It's okay, you go, I'll be there soon," Maya said. Vaidehi smiled and handing over a comb, said, "If you feel like it." Maya combed her hair taking an elaborate time as Vaidehi left. Finally, she walked out, feeling better with some love and ointment. There were more people and she bent down to touch a relative's feet, an old lady who was best friends with Kamla. It felt strange to not see Kamla sitting beside her, like in every celebration that Maya could think back to. As she was standing up, the lady's daughter-in-law caught hold of her necklace to see whether the diamonds were a cluster of small ones or they solitaires. And then asked, "Your mom gave this to you?"

"No, I got this myself," Maya replied with anger springing from the fact that her in-laws could never afford to buy this and the knowledge of her social step-down a common knowledge and a source of fun among the relatives. It was truly shocking to see how Maya could see her relatives sadistically enjoying the fact that now her financial status had changed so much. She was now the last one to be looked at and smiled to among her family, all the love and pampering she'd received earlier, even fake, was now replaced by their blatant, real feelings. Vinod's success had brought a lot of relatives very very close to the family. Everyone wanted to be associated with them. The aunties flaunted their family to their daughter's in-law's to show off they had rich circles even though they weren't rich themselves. Such pressure and these actions springing from it were a result of girls finding themselves husbands from families that were much richer than theirs. While they climbed the social ladder, their maiden families struggled to keep up, baffled simply because they mistook money for class. Maya, on the other hand, had her life running exactly opposite. She mistook her ease of living with pride because of perfect family conditions as fierceness and confidence. But now, when faced with challenges of turned social conditions, she felt as much restless, under-confident, insecure as the aunties themselves, whose daughters had found rich husbands.

Maya went into the kitchen to make some tea for everyone, to simply escape the circus. Malavika was there, along with her annoying aunt. She picked up a piece of ginger and started to peel it, when Malavika said, "No, no, we don't peel the ginger, just wash and use it."

The aunt added, "Yes, you might be doing it at your place, but here we don't peel the ginger."

Maya put down the knife, washed the ginger longer than required to control her tears. She wanted to scream like a child to Malavika that she'd lived in the family for 25 years while Malavika had just come a few years ago! What she completely failed to understand that it was simply Malavika's pettiness if not immaturity to be so insensitive with her words, while her aunt's actions and words should just be as invisible as her importance in the family. But with insecurities raging already, Maya felt she was crashing again.

"I'll be back, you serve," she said curtly to Malvika and left to get a quick cigarette. Suman called while she was smoking and Maya's first instinct was to flinch. However, she blew out the smoke and said, "Hello, Ma. Namaste." The word 'Ma' irked her. It was too big to be said when you didn't feel it.

"Namaste beta! You're at your parents' home, must be enjoying now."

"Just going to have dinner, what are you doing?"

"We just finished having it. Wanted to talk to you about something. Are you free?"

"Sure," Maya said, not sure at all.

"Alright! *Beta,* now it's time you had a baby, no! It's your thirtieth birthday, I strongly advise you consider having a family of your own!"

She felt like she was only seen in roles and expected them to follow it in the most quintessential societal manner. No one saw her as a person. Her relatives expected to play her part in a much lower financial standard, her parents expected her to now just be somebody's wife and daughter-in-law, and her in-laws expected her to be a mother. All Manish wished for was for her to love him back and that she just wasn't able to. She wanted to play a role too, by not wanting to be moulded into society's expectation.

Maya's hands shook out of anger that was more than her already exhausted being could take and the phone fell on the floor. In a rage, she stamped on it with her heel.

CHAPTER 23

What we pass on to our daughters

It was 3 am and Maya was far from asleep. Anger was raging through her, making her breathless. With everyone telling her what she should do with her life, she felt claustrophobic enough to rebel. Her rebellion had no cause, it was just to run away from the expectations so she could breathe. Suman's voice rattled in her head from their last conversation: "just have a baby for us, your parents and for Manish." She wanted to shout that she was a person and had a choice. But she knew she wouldn't be heard. Maya felt they weren't financially stable to have a baby and that all the compromises that she had to make, she didn't want her baby to make too. What she couldn't tell them was that she simply didn't want a baby. She just didn't feel like she could be or wanted to be a mother. But this reason just wouldn't do, just like lack of love in a marriage wouldn't do for a divorce. These weren't questions. These were steps that one must take in their lives—marriage, baby no.1 and baby no. 2. And then the cycle continues to the next generation.

"Bro, you need to calm down," Gaurav said over the phone.

Meera was in the bathroom again, smoking and speaking on the phone.

"What the fuck, Gaurav. I can't fucking calm down! She told me to have a baby for others. How fucked up is that!"

"Yes, but you also know that's how the society is."

"And so, I shouldn't get angry?"

"No, I'm saying what's the point?"

"What do you mean what's the point? I don't want this. You know I've never wanted a baby!"

"But have you ever asked yourself why? Is there a reason? Maybe there isn't…maybe…"

"If wanting a baby can be natural, why can't not wanting one be too? But please, go ahead finish your sentence."

"Maya, maybe you're just rebelling for the sake of it! Why are you rebelling?"

"When did I say I'm rebelling? Why is wanting motherhood natural but not wanting it is not? I don't want to be that! It's against societal norms… Okay, maybe I'm rebelling by default, but I really don't want a baby!"

There were moments pregnant with silent disbelief.

"Gaurav please, if I wanted a baby, I would have it. Why wouldn't I?"

"Because your mother-in-law told you to. And now you don't want to do it to rebel against her."

"I have always told you I don't want to be a mother."

"That was before."

"And so, you didn't believe me? You didn't believe me then because I was young, you don't believe me now because you think I'm rebelling for the sake of it."

"Maya you have a tendency to just make trouble. Just unsettle things."

"Like what? Not being able to love Manish despite everything being right? Not wanting a baby?"

"Well yes!"

"Gaurav, I honestly don't know what to do if I don't feel how I don't feel. My marriage wasn't forced on me, it was my decision. Manish wasn't forced on me, I decided to marry him. If these things were forced on me and then I felt like I didn't love him, it would make sense that I was rebelling. But if I have taken those decisions and despite that couldn't fall in love, what can I do? What should I do?" Maya's voice shook.

"So then what is love for you, Maya? What do you mean by it? You had a fling. Did you find it there?"

Maya was stung. "No," she replied in a voice that had a finality of an end.

"So then? Maybe you do love Manish but you want to show to your parents how unhappy you are to get out of this marriage. The finances, your relationship with your mother-in-law...are all excuses for the same."

"Why would I want to get out of a marriage if I truly felt love?"

"Yes, but why don't you? Who could you love if not someone like Manish? And I know you've been telling me that you don't want a baby since way before you got married. But maybe all of these things — reasons like not being able to love your husband and that not wanting to be a mother — are all acts of rebellion to seem unconventional. Maybe you want to be a certain kind of a person. But maybe you aren't that. Maybe it's not how you really feel. You feel normal, but that isn't good enough for you. Hence, you're doing all this."

Maya paused as the words fell on a being that slowly turned steely. "You know, I told my father about this too. And he asked me if there is a financial problem, would I rather keep my lifestyle or have a baby. And I picked my lifestyle. So, he said to me, 'So there is a fundamental problem. We'll have to change that in you.'"

"Right, so then?"

"So then, you're not the only man to tell me that I don't know how I feel, that I don't know what I want, that even if they believed I wanted something, that it was wrong."

"Maya come on…"

"I need to go."

Maya hung up. For the first time, she felt a kind of tired that made her want to give up. Give up everything and just tell herself that she loved Manish. Give up and just have a baby. Just be what they said is normal.

But knowing that she wouldn't be happy if she did this made her resist. Not only not happy, she thought she'd further go deeper into depression. And if ending a marriage is difficult, ending motherhood is impossible. What if she hated her baby as much as she hates the circumstances of her life right now?

Her father advised her to have a baby despite knowing how she felt about her married life. Gaurav felt she was wrong. Manish was quiet as she'd pushed him afar silently. Manav was long gone. And ironically, she didn't even think to reach out to the women in her life. Was this a pattern? Were they in the same place once as she is now and were they too advised to "just ignore it" and did they also get so tired they just gave in? Vowing to make it better for the next generation of women? If so, where was that resolve lost now? Did they now realise that raising their daughters to see a better life was young folly? How sad that that silent young folly had done the job, and only their resolve had failed? Why didn't they believe in themselves more?

*

Meanwhile, downstairs, Vaidehi and Vinod were sleepless too.

"Why is Meera unusually quiet?" asked Vaidehi.

Vinod knew everything and yet couldn't tell Vaidehi. She would worry. And why worry her? This was probably just a phase with Meera. Wasn't she always like this? But she also always came around. This was much more difficult but with time she would be okay.

"I can't believe she's unhappy that Manish doesn't have enough money. We had nothing, Vinod. We didn't complain."

"But she had everything and then she went into a different environment. Maybe it's a shock."

"No, but still... Is money that big an issue?"

Vinod sighed. A conflict between morality and money was unresolvable. Mostly so, because we assumed one was the enemy of the other. Wanting money as a pre-requisite made a questionable character. Did Meera not love Manish because of money and the way Suman treated her? He'd asked Meera if Manish was a good person and she'd said yes. Was that not enough?

"She also has clashes with her mother-in-law," Vinod said.

"But I had much greater ones with mine. And she knows that. And still…"

They were quiet again.

"The world will never be perfectly good. She has to learn to deal with it," Vinod replied.

"Yes, for Manish. Manish is a good man. He deserves a good life."

"And for her own happiness, Vai," Vinod added.

Vaidehi looked at him. "Of course. I care about her happiness. Every mother wants her child to be happy."

"Yes yes, of course. But Vai, don't compare her to yourself. This generation is just different."

Vaidehi's whole life passed through her head in an instant. All the times when she'd wanted her daughter to have everything equal to that of her son. At least more equal than she had received in her life as a daughter. Compensating and compensating for all the partiality that the society subjected them to and which permeated into their lives. Until she couldn't do it anymore. Often because of societal circumstances and finally because it was as far as her feminism could go. What had she done wrong? Was Meera wrong? Who was at fault? Where was this unhappiness coming from?

"Is she supposed to be grateful knowing that she has received more than I ever could?" Vaidehi asked.

"Or is she right in asking, for we have exposed her to a world that she can't compromise on now?" Vinod summarised.

"Were we right or wrong?"

And they slept with a question that probably never leaves a parent.

*

The next morning was empty, to Maya's (slight) relief. Even Manav and Malvika weren't at home. Maya, Vinod and Vaidehi were having tea when Vinod started the conversation again.

"*Beta*, think about having a baby. We don't want to force you but the only worry is later what if it's too late?"

Maya didn't bother blinking back the tears that so readily sat waiting.

"*Kya hua beta?*" Vaidehi panicked.

Even at that moment that was the final tipping point, Maya would never tell Vaidehi that she didn't love Manish. She wouldn't be able to understand it, and yet, not be able to take it. Neither could she tell her parents she didn't want a baby, they wouldn't able to take it. What was the way out?

"I have no car," Meera said.

Vinod and Vaidehi's questioning eyes waited in silence.

"You know, you have a Beetle and what not. A bungalow. Diamonds. You can make trips to anywhere in the world. Meanwhile, I often raze my body so I can save parlour money. Do you know this?"

There was silence. Meera continued.

"Am I greedy? I don't know. Did I want to marry some billionaire? No! But I would've been better off at someone who was equal to us. It would've been one less thing to think about."

"*Beta*, our money is your money only no," Vinod said silently.

"Honestly, even this stay feels like I'm a guest. How can I take your money? And why should you give it? So, I can have a baby? Does everything end there? You could give me money so I could have a baby, but why couldn't you marry me into a house that had financial security for MY happi-ness? Earlier, dowries were a matter of pride for the girl, the higher it was, the prouder she felt. Then came a generation that abolished it and subsequently, the youth started looking down upon those taking money from their wives' parents. But if I am to be truly liberal, I should either not take money from either of our parents, or be open to taking it from both—if a girl and a boy in a marriage are truly equal. And yet, I constantly feel like I can't take money from you, you're my parents and now my in-laws should be providing for me. And yet the lack of it bothers me. Why is my wanting money for myself makes me greedy but wanting for my baby is okay? Am I not a person?"

"A baby is for your happiness, Meera," Vaidehi said.

Not everyone necessarily finds happiness in motherhood! Meera thought.

"Between dealing with the finances and trying to ignore my demeaning mother-in-law, I can't have a baby."

"Beta, all these mother-in-law things happen. You can't take it to heart! You know everything that happened to me, it was much, much worse."

Maya's blood boiled at her helplessness at getting her parents to be enraged at her daughter's mis-treatment. *How can you be okay with your child being treated like that? How can you ask her to ignore it? How can you ask her not to be offended by it? How can you kill her self respect like that?*

"How is less wrong not wrong? Why should I accept it? How can you expect me to be okay with that?"

"Because families mean compromises, *beta.*"

"To what extent?"

"Remember my life when you wonder how far you can go."

"If that is what you expect me to endure, why did you give me an education at all?"

"Okay, we need to stop now." Vinod intervened as Vaidehi's being was struck. "There is a problem and we will solve it. We are all in this together and for each other, to support one another. We are a family. I'm going out, you guys relax. We will talk about it later."

Maya went to her room. She felt guilt, regret and anger in turns. How can she talk to Vaidehi without hurting her and yet getting her point across? She tried to imagine in vain why a parent would be okay with her child being in this situation. Vaidehi's shocked and fallen face kept haunting her. It seemed that at that moment Vaidehi aged 10 more years.

What kind of a daughter would do that to her mother! Couldn't I just take some insults, love a man that was good and bear his children? Was it too much to ask for? Why can't I just be normal? Someone that society will accept? At that moment she hated everyone but detested herself. Could she end it and start fresh? Somewhere in the mingling of the afternoon lull and her restlessness, she fell asleep.

It was dark when she woke up. She walked down in a spirit of a person who has given up. Not because they bent, but because the exhaustion took over their fight completely.

"Meera, come in *bache,*" Vaidehi called out from her bedroom. "Papa has gone out and Manav and Malvika haven't returned. Come sit with me."

Meera went and sat on the bed. Vaidehi did look like she'd aged over an afternoon. "I'm sorry," Meera said and with renewed strength, her tears flowed.

"No *beta*, it's alright. But what is in your heart? Tell me." Meera looked up. For the first time, she felt like she could share not out of anger but because she could. She took a good few minutes before starting.

"When I moved in with Manish, there was nothing in the house, Ma. I have lived, ate and slept on the same bed for two months. I didn't expect a mansion, but I didn't expect this either. I'm not saying Manish should've been earning more than that at the time. What I'm saying is that if a family decided to bring a girl in, shouldn't they have cared to provide basic amenities if their son couldn't at the time? I felt unwanted. But I was young and newly married, I took it in my stride. It didn't affect me so much. And then you know how my mother-in-law treated me, the things she said to me. That feeling of being unwanted only grew with time with her treating me like that. How is it that we treat our guests so much better, in fact, they are equated to god in our culture, but a girl who decides to leave her life to take up a new one, finds it so difficult to find a footing in her new family? If a girl leaving her house and going to live with her husband and his family is a norm as old as time itself, why does she always find such struggle? I'm not a daughter-in-law there. I don't know what I am, but the absolute callousness with which I am treated, I don't feel like a daughter-in-law. And top of that, my mother asking me to take it, makes it feel like this is what it is to be a daughter-in-law even today. So why would any girl want to marry at all? Why do we marry? Why do women encourage each other to bear such things? Shouldn't they rather try to find a solution instead of saying the problem isn't big enough? Why must one woman suffer quietly, simply because another had had bigger issues? 'Wrong' has intensities and yours were higher than mine. That can't mean I should be okay with my wrong." Maya stopped as she wept.

"Meera, you will always find people and circumstances that will jostle you. Nothing is certain. What if we lose our wealth? And families are like that. They hurt each other but they love despite everything. Only looking at the hurt is not fair. We marry because no one can live alone for their whole lives, Meera. You can adopt children but nothing replaces a life partner. When you're young you don't see it, and by the time you do, it could be too late. We never want to see you in that situation. We only do what we do because we see some possibility in the future that you don't now. And we anticipate our children's disbelief in our ways, even fights and hatred but we have to keep going with it and hope that eventually they see it. So if children saying hurtful things to their parents is wrong too, should we not take it? And what would that mean?"

"Is it fair to compare a parentchild relationship to that of a mother-in-law and daughter-in-law? Each relationship has specific parameters and is to be lived by those. No child saying hurtful things to the parents is okay. But Ma, I genuinely do not understand why I should be taking all this. You can't compare this relationship with that of mine with my in-laws, the parameters are different. And if I'm to measure them how I measure my own parents, then shouldn't they measure me like they do their daughter? Why is it that a daughter-in-law must only keep on giving? Why can't this be a two-way relationship? When I said what I said earlier, I meant that daughters are brought up so differently now than earlier. If that has changed, why does it go back to being the same when it comes to marriage? Why do I feel like marriage is suffering?"

"Yes, all relationships are different. And we ask you to tackle it a certain way because we believe it's the best for you and your happiness. If you fight back, it will go downhill from there. There is nothing worse than sour hearts living under one roof. Your life will curdle and rot if your relationships aren't good. If there is a dispute between two people, one of them has to be bigger and tackle it in a way that creates harmony. Why can't that person be you? Shouldn't a greater education and exposure teach you that? If fighting patriarchy leads to a worse life then you must be fighting the battle wrong even if the war is correct. Marriage isn't suffering, *beta*. You have seen multiple aspects change suddenly. Lack of financial security, mistreatment, and a general shift from being a daughter to a daughter-in-law. Your marriage is between you and Manish. What is wrong with that? That man is loving, loyal, respectful. Don't let other aspects of your life seep into your relationship with your husband. You are looking at a thousand wrong things and not at one right thing — the only thing that matters."

Would she understand that I'm unable to love Manish despite him being this ideal husband? Maybe not yet.

"But didn't you say that marriages are between a girl and family and never a man and a wife? And that arranged marriage ensures greater happiness because the families are known? Why is it then I'm treated like this?"

"Only you can assure your happiness. To be decidedly happy takes most amount of courage from a person. That's why it isn't easy to do. With an arranged marriage we can ensure security. I know you don't feel secure right now but believe me, you're finding your footing. You are secured. We have ensured that. As for your mother-in-law, beta we can never tell how a person is no matter how well-known the family is. How can that ever be? Hearing you talk about finances and the lack of, I feel like I don't even know my own child."

Maya was stung. "I do not understand what greed is. Struggling and being disappointed because financial security was suddenly taken away from me and wanting it back is greed? You have come up from circumstances that were incomparably worse. But you weren't born into it and have now grown. My life has moved in the opposite direction. My anger also springs from you not understanding that. My shock springs from taking my life for granted and that it will always be that way. But there was also a blind trust that a child has on their parents that they will take care of every as-pect, to make a child's life better. And then when that wasn't the case, it was a rude shock. Money might not be happiness, but it is comfort, it is mental security and it is indispensable. The thing is, you realise all this only when you lack wealth. I don't think wanting that is greed."

"You crave what has been taken away from you. You have an education and crave wealth. I have wealth but I crave education."

The two women sat quietly in the same room but worlds apart.

"All of this created such a distance between me and Manish that I still can't find my way back. Sometimes we feel we both exist under the same roof, he in wait and I unable to find my way to him. It is so scary to feel like a stranger with someone you have spent each day of several years of your life with. All of it together depresses me. I'm going to get help. But amidst all of this, Ma, my clock is running out and I must have a baby. How is that okay? It's a circus. I can't make sense of what's happening. I'm so tired I want to give up and just bend myself to what the society demands. But I'm unable to. I can't unsee the world you exposed me to with education. Now I'm lost somewhere between your principles and what this other world says."

Vaidehi already knew this. So did Vinod.

"What makes a marriage work, Ma? You have just taken and taken everything dished out to you. Is that kind of suffering the only way a marriage can work?"

"I survived on love for your father."

Maya's heart ached on that word. What was this magical potion that made everything worth it? Why couldn't she have it? With more knowledge you question everything. A simple 'I love you' is always met with scepticism while a hateful statement is blindly trusted. How has the world taught us to doubt the good and trust the bad easily? If Vaidehi was happier despite the lack of exposure and Maya wasn't because of it, is it still required? Or is it a few generations that will be martyred in this push and pull of a great change, until a new world is born? Generations that will be lost, suspended into the nothingness of an in-between of a change. A loss that will be labelled 'dramatic' at best because of the lack of blood-spilling and waving flags.

"What is love, Ma? How do you know you love someone?" Maya asked thirstily.

"I don't know, *beta*. No one told us. And we never asked to know. But I do know that I love your father," Vaidehi replied.

Vaidehi possessed a kind of knowledge that she couldn't pass on to her daughter, and Maya waited in desperation, hands stretched, begging to get it.

"Why didn't you ask?"

"It never occurred to. It was never a question. Everything was just acceptance."

"Why am I unable to do that? Forget right and wrong, I would've been happier if I could do that."

"You question because I made you that way. I told you you could have the world, that you were no less. But I couldn't see through it completely. This is my threshold and I can't go further."

Meera thought of herself as a part of this in-between generation. Neither here nor there, struggling to fit into two worlds that constantly fought each other. There could be no choosing, she couldn't live without either. She was told to think, and yet, to be silent.

"Do you remember that one time when I was in school and a couple of boys started following me and my friend as we rode home?"

"Yes," she said. For a moment both women wondered at how they both

amazon.com

SXKYG7FbsZ

Your order of December 14, 2022 (Order ID 111-3024541-1778652)

Qty.	Item	Item Price	Total
1	**What We Pass on to Our Daughters** Yadav, Manisha --- Paperback **9390463580** 9390463580 9789390463589	$12.00	$12.00

This shipment completes your order.

Subtotal		$12.00
Order Total		$12.00
Paid via credit/debit		$12.00

Return or replace your item
Visit Amazon.com/returns

0/XKYG7FbsZ/-1 of 1-/i/MTN2-CART-A/second/0/1216-07:30/1215-22:34

A2-
M2

remembered it still, after all those years. A trauma faced by one but suffered by both. The suffering an ode to the mother-daughter bond.

"I remember after that, dad made some phone calls. He asked me what they looked like. But you never spoke to me about it. Why?"

Vaidehi was silent. No one ever spoke about these things. These weren't supposed to be said out loud.

"You were young, we thought you'd forget."

"Yes, but what if it happened again? How would I deal with it? What I'm saying is, why didn't you prepare me for it?"

"I did what I knew to do, beta. I protected you instead."

"By not allowing me to go to parties unlike Manav? Some random boys did something wrong. Why was I punished for it?"

The word punish stung Vaidehi.

"Every time a parent faces a situation with a child, there are various ways in which it can be handled and the choice that the parent makes at the time defines how the child would turn out. Every way has positives and negatives, but there's no mistaking the fact that one can never tell how it would affect the child. You were so young, we thought we'd give you more love through our actions. We'd protect you and in time you'd forget. We'd try and provide for you a protected world where this doesn't happen to you. Meera, despite my efforts to provide you with an independent personality, somewhere I never thought you'd become this person. And that isn't because I didn't believe in you. That's only because I couldn't imagine it. You're my daughter and yet our lives couldn't be more different. In fact, so different that we could as easily be strangers. And when my efforts bore fruit and you started becoming this person, you rigorously sought to move out of our protective environment. That's why we struggled at every point to let you go, wondering if you were prepared. But we also knew there was no other way but to let you just go with whatever we could teach you till then. You see, I chose the way to not teach you to take action against those boys because what if the next time it happened there were more and you did take action? And also, I chose to make you more independent than I ever could be, not foreseeing you'd walk out of the very same source that made you. A parent just has options, but never a sure-shot knowledge of how it would affect a child. We just have to pick one and face the brunt of it later."

There was silence. Vaidehi said, "Why did you ask this?"

"Because…I don't know how to stand up for myself. I feel like I missed that lesson. Be it the boys on the road, be it a difficult mother-in-law or any other situation in my life—whenever there's a challenge, I become quiet. There's something inside me that bursts with the wrong that it faces and yet something stops it from coming out. Those boys following me back is the first-ever harassment that I remember I faced. I wonder what if my friend and I would've shouted, hit them, called out so loudly for help, that those boys would never do something like that again? But I was too scared and your silence somewhere told me it was the right thing to do as you didn't tell me otherwise. So, every time when it happened to me later in life, I always quietly tried to outrun my harasser, heart throbbing against my chest. Why should I have to do that? And what if the first time my mother-in-law told me something demeaning, I would've answered? I don't know how or what but just…if I would've stood up for myself, would it have happened again? Now whenever we meet, I'm in this constant stress and live with bated breath least at any point she again would say something to me. In one way it's just words and in another, it's my self-respect."

"Why are the daughters not taught to stand up for themselves?" Vaidehi asked, to no one.

"Why does it come so naturally for the men to be confident and aggressive but the women to always be…kind of secondary to them? Why are the daughters not taught this, even though we see history repeating itself generation after generation, to a point where now the bad chapters have become normal and the better ones where we're given the freedom to make our choices, is considered lucky. All of us as a body of women are so broken that we think our rights are supposed to be granted by someone and consider it a big up if they do!" Slowly it was dawning on Meera that the questions she asked had no answers.

After a long silence, Vaidehi said, "If I had to do it all over again, I would still bring you up the same way. Would you rather I wouldn't?"

"No, I don't wish that. Of course, if you would've taken me further it would be better but I'm glad you did all that you have." Meera let out a sigh. "I think that's why it's difficult. Probably for a man to let out his opinion when faced with a situation is easier, just as it is easier for a woman to be quiet. But for a woman who knows better, it will always be difficult to be quiet, that's all this is may-be. It's what men always do but it's difficult for me because I'm a woman. No one said feminism and independence would be easy. In fact, wouldn't they obviously be the most difficult."

Vaidehi watched the very brain she'd created, wriggle in its own questions, grapple with its own existence.

CHAPTER 24

Wife and Husband

It felt different this time when Maya landed at the airport. When she walked out and saw Manish standing there to pick her up, it felt even better. It was like before she could realise it, something about this land, this city, this airport, this man, had become home. Walking towards Manish her luggage rolling behind, she found her feeling this comfort to be strange. When did her feelings change? She hugged Manish and took in his scent. Her hand let her luggage go automatically. Manish took it and they walked towards the parking arm in arm.

"How was the trip?" Manish asked.

Maya paused for a few seconds and then broke into tears. A sense of loss of a previous life, and the surprise of the gain of a sense of home in her new life was all too much for her to make sense of. Loss and gain playing her mind until her head spun. Amidst her warring thoughts, she heard Manish's desperation to console her. But she couldn't make sense of it, until eventually exhaustion took over.

Manish gave her some water and said, "How about we simply list everything that is going wrong with your life right now? It could be a zillion things, but let's list them."

"Loneliness," she started after giving it a thought.

"I promise to be home on time and be with you whenever you need me apart from that," Manish replied.

"Okay. But it's not just that. I've always been lonely and I can't seem to shake that feeling. I have you, I have my friends and work. But I think this loneliness springs from not being able to connect."

"With people?"

"More like, not able to belong anywhere. Every wedding that I attend, I meet my *Nani*. But I feel I'm progressively disconnecting with her. She's my roots. But I don't feel a connect with her. Who is she? What are her beliefs? I feel like I'm from another world. Increasingly, there are differences between me and mom too. And even Manav. I don't feel connected somehow to this modern world of feminism and independence, etc. I agree with their beliefs, they naturally seem right. But do I belong there? Am I really independent? When I feel the need for our families to support us financially, I'm not thinking independently. When I expect you to take main responsibility for our companionship and finances, that's not feminism. I realise I only believe in it in parts, those that are convenient to me. But do I act on all the parameters of this modern, independent, liberal feminist world? No. Similarly, do I abide by the belief system of my mother and her mother? No. Then who am I? Where do I belong? I feel like I'm this in-between generation who isn't able to be either here or there."

"I get that. There's no advice I can give you. But I get that. I'm a traditional man, or so I felt till now. Just following the rules. Studying, then working, earning money, becoming independent of my family financially. Getting married. Wanting children. It all comes very naturally to me. And then I get married to this amazing woman and I can't believe my luck. But I realise it's not all that easy. It couldn't have been, no? Not everything can keep going smoothly. And you bring in all these ideas and ask the tough questions, which I know other women including my mother and sister have swallowed and chosen to live quietly. Even though it makes life more difficult, I admire you for it. Would I have been happier if you would've been quiet too? Maybe. But there's also a sense of release that comes from knowing the absolute truth."

"I didn't realise we've both been torn between two worlds. Me, because I chose to pick the other one not realising how difficult it is to belong there in absolute. And you, because you've been thrown into it. Manish, despite that I don't feel sorry."

"And you shouldn't. It takes courage to say things that you've said and ask for a life that you have."

"You basically only mean open marriage. You're not okay with it?"

Manish paused. "Of course, I'm not. Since we're talking about courage in honesty."

"So...you don't want to do it anymore?"

"No. I will. But you must understand I'll not so easily be okay with it."

"Then why do it? It makes me feel so guilty knowing that you are only in it because of my misery in my circumstances."

"Yes, Maya, but you can't think like that! I'm glad you care for me and it makes you feel guilty. But I have understood that you're just wired differently. You are wired to be polyamorous. It's not just a way of life but I need you to understand that I'm also wired differently than you. I'm wired to be monogamous. What comes naturally to you, doesn't to me. If I can't subject you to my way of things, you can't subject me to yours. Of course, I understand the guilt, but just like I deal with you seeing others, you'll have to deal with the guilt. I feel like this is the best middle ground we can get about this."

"Okay, fair. I always knew you were not okay with it because you agreed without putting up a fight." *Fighting for me.* Maya thought.

"Maya, I am fighting for you. There's not just one kind of fight, baby, where I bar you from seeing others and make promises that you will fall in love with me and be happy. How can I promise something like that? It's unreasonable, illogical. How can someone know if someone else will fall in love with them? They can't. You just have to be you and constantly be the best version of you and the other person will have to decide. Movies have just been feeding us the wrong ideas. The ideas of true love, grand love, soul mates and what not. I am fighting for you by giving you what you need. I know you need to feel free, from societal constructs, familial bonds, marital stereotypes."

"I feel like I'm discovering things about myself that I should've before deciding to get married. I mean, I was so young! We were so young. I changed. And I know how unfair it is turning out to be for you. Honestly, this thing about dating other people—how do I know I'm polyamorous really? What if I'm just unwilling to let a part of me go? The part where you're young and free and feel butterflies in your stomach? What if it's just that? It seems like I'm this person who questions things and shatters the rules. But I'm just really feeling something about myself deeply and I need to act on it."

"I get that."

"And there are so many things that make a marriage. Social circle, family, finances, sexual compatibility and hopes and dreams that we have for our life. But weddings have become a race for your child to *settle* and the system only looks at the facade of a family, like the caste, youth, beauty and that's it. And then, the success of a marriage like that is expected to be the default. Where does that expectation even come from?"

"Because women are trained to be quiet, accept everything and keep going. If she can't think and can't speak what she thinks, a marriage will work. Of course, it won't be a happy one."

"And then she starts realising the problems. Often these problems have no solutions. And even if they do, they are so drastic that one person in a couple can't make it and they compromise to a life of misery. Or if they can't make it the solution, they divorce."

"Do you want to divorce me?" Manish asked, his voice laced with the dread of a question like that.

"No," Maya replied, confident.

"While it's very assuring to hear that, may I ask why? Because clearly I haven't made you happy."

"Because I respect you too much. I believe it to be more important than love. While I doubt whether I love you, or what love is in the first place, you feel like home. However miserable I've been, I know I've been able to speak my mind, however culturally shocking my thoughts were. But I don't think that courage has been solely mine. It came from me knowing that you would listen. That you would truly, truly listen to understand. And it's made me realise that while a dozen factors might make a marriage work, listening has been the most underrated one. I think my respect for you might also be rooted in that — your fiercely fair attitude to listen and make judgements. To hear me and what I feel and what I want and understand the dearth of it to push yourself into doing something that you would've never even thought of in your life. I don't know a lot of couples, but I feel something like this is rare."

Manish paused. "So my fight is working after all."

Maya chuckled. "Listen, me wanting to see other people isn't a reflection on you. Maybe if my circumstances were happier I might've not wanted an open marriage. Or, even if they were, I would've wanted an open marriage. Guess we'll never know. But even if the circumstances are bad, you're not. Even though we fight, I know you're doing your best to make sense of this life that we have been put together in. And I might wish for a lot of things, but I do not wish for another husband. I might be unable to relate to myself or not be able to know who I am or where I belong, but I know if I was in the kind of shit that I am, I would want to deal with you as my partner. And so, while you say you haven't been able to give me happiness, I think I haven't been able to give you happiness either."

"Look, despite any of it, I want to be with you too."

"Okay then. We're on the same page about this," replied Maya, as they reached home.

Maya locked the bedroom door and stripped. She felt exhausted and yet a little light. Distancing from her city felt like discarding her problems too. Whatever they were, it felt like they existed there. In that house. With another morning, another phone call from home or another incident, these problems were going to show up again. But right now, she was here. She was home. She went to the bathroom and lit a cigarette. She thought about Gaurav. And her father. And Manav. How had they one by one, become so distant? How is it that they didn't understand her despite spending so many years of knowing her? And how did Manish understand it despite knowing her the least of them all? How had he adapted to her so quickly? Or has it been a slow process, every year of struggle culminating into where they were today? Is this what love is? Years of hard work, of this undying, want to be with a person so much so that you find a way around every hurdle? But it has nothing to do with butterflies, silly smiles and passionate nights. Wanting to be with this person despite not having these things. Then what did they have? Why did they want to be with each other? Maya wondered why did she particularly want to be with Manish, given how everything in her life had been turned upside down after marriage. Maybe, she thought, *it's not Manish and never was, to be blamed. It was something else.*

Lost in thoughts, she got out of the shower, hair dripping wet. She wore an oversized t-shirt, nothing else, and felt relieved to be able to walk out like that. As she opened the bedroom door, the darkness took her by surprise. As her eyes were still adjusting to the darkness, Manish lit a candle on the table. And then two more.

"Just a tiny bit of timing amiss," he smiled. Two glasses of deep red towered demeaningly over plates of cheap Chinese, glistening in oil. Both her favourite.

"I'm not dressed for a candle light dinner," Maya said, every pore in her body widening by a deep sense of contentment.

"But you're dressed perfectly," Manish said as he walked towards her.

He kissed her deeply. Maya realised a strange sensation in her while kissing him. She felt like she'd known this feel of his mouth and the action they were engaged in, for lifetimes. Like she'd known nothing else but this. As if this moment, action and the feel of it have always been a common knowledge for her. And yet, she didn't feel one thing that the kiss should've made her feel—sexually aroused. She felt the passion in Manish body hesitantly recede sensing a lack of in hers. They parted, smiling at each other. Did she sense a tinge of yet another defeat in Manish? Or was it just in her head as he confidently moved on, holding her hand, walking her over to the dining table?

They sat down. Maya took a long sip of her wine and it relaxed her further. Manish dug into his plate. After a couple of mouthfuls, he said, "I don't think it will be either for us."

"Sorry?" Maya asked puzzled. She'd already washed away the thread of their earlier conversation with shower, smoke and wine.

"You said when the problems arise in a marriage, the solutions are often drastic. In the face of which, the couples don't take them, hence resigning to an unhappy existence or a divorce. I refuse to let either happen to us." Manish said.

"Yeah, I don't want to be those people either."

"We need to drastically change the rules of our marriage. I have struggled a lot after you suggested the idea of an open marriage. I obviously felt insecure, took it personally — all of those things that a partner would go through. But I think I get it now."

"And yet you don't want it for yourself?"

"I don't think so but I don't know. See, I have lived my entire life by the book. I've lived by the rules so much that at some point I started mistaking them for the only right way. I forgot that it's just one way of living life, that probably the majority of the people live by. I still don't think I would see other women. But I do realise whether I did want to or not, it would have to be a personal preference and not because one is right and the other is wrong."

Maya wondered when and how had Manish started talking like her? Isn't this what happens to couples who have been together a long time? They become an amalgamation of belief systems, to the point that you eventually forget who was who. What a strange marriage was hers, everything was a stereotype and yet, in a way nothing was.

"Hence, I don't think ours should be an unhappy existence or a separation. I think we need to bend the rules, break them even so that we both can have happiness. I'm alright with you seeing other people. But I'll need your help and support to lead me through it."

"You mean, you want to lay ground rules?"

"Yes."

"Tell me."

"I don't think I would want to know about the person. I want absolute secrecy. That would depend on who you choose — would they be from our social circle? Would it be from your circle of friends? Would it be a stranger? How deep would your relationship be with them? I don't want to know it all, but I do want you to think about it, because it would require for you also to give back accordingly. What would their expectations be? We need to figure all that to make sure it doesn't disrupt our life."

"Makes sense. I would hold off on anyone from our circle of common friends. Preferably pick someone whom we don't meet very often. And you're right about expectations too. There's only so much we can give them. And they shouldn't indulge if they want more."

There was silence. Maya slurped her second glass to finish. Manish shoved in a heavily laden fork of noodles. Maya pierced into a capsicum piece and felt its juice on her tongue as she crushed it with her teeth. They ate some, washed it down with wine, ate some again and continued the loop. A strange awkwardness dined with them. One moment they were as open as a couple could be and the next, they hid behind their drinks.

"It just doesn't get easier, does it?" Finally, Maya said.

"Nothing great should ever come easy," Manish replied, his hand reaching hers.

"We'll get through it. Neither of us knows how this works, but we'll figure it out," Maya said firmly.

"I know we will," Manish replied even more firmly, squeezing her hand.

Maya kept looking into his eyes. Overnight, he seemed transformed. Or was he transforming slowly and she'd missed it, engulfed in her own problems? He even looked at peace, a sense of comfort about his being. Maya felt he looked like someone entirely new, and yet, someone she's known at the same time. The food lay forgotten beside their intertwined hands and eyes.

Suddenly Maya sucked in sharply, stood up as the chair fell behind her and went over to Manish. She kissed him deeply, hungrily, savagely. Manish did not flinch, as if he knew what was to come. The tongues explored the mouths and the hands ran through the bodies as if wanting to rip the skin off. Maya could feel how hard Manish was, and suddenly the hunger in her ignited to the point where she could give her life to be satiated then. Manish's fingers felt her wetness. Maya stood up a little and freed Manish from his clothes just enough so she could take him in. She sat back slowly, her moans sounding off her relief. Both their heads fell backwards for moments. They sat like that, still, as if they were experiencing sex for the first time in their lives. Then their heads turned back, their eyes met and they could see the intensity coming back simultaneously. Their mouths met as if in combat. Maya ripped off Manish's shirt, sending the buttons flying. Her hands scratched through his chest, down his stomach, further feeding his passion. Manish ripped the neck of her t-shirt so he could see her breasts. Her t-shirt gave way, falling at her hip and his hands aggressively squeezed her breast. He took her nipples between his index and middle finger and shook her breasts rigorously. They hardened and Maya arched her back, needing to be sucked hard. She moved a little up, without letting him out and just allowing him to suck on her. Manish took her breast and sucked on it until she shouted with pain. Then he took the other one. Maya sat back, taking him inside her fully. They were so desperate for their bodies, they just moved in hurried, famished motions, feeling each other. They didn't look into each other's eyes, their hands held the furniture instead of the bodies. They didn't exist for each other in those minutes that went by, but just the sensation they were providing to each other. It was true, pure lust. And then Manish got up, lifting Maya with him, her legs wrapped behind his back and took her to the sofa—it was nearer than the bed. He lay down and she straddled him. She bent down and they kissed until Manish pushed her away and waited. She understood and did what was told to her. Her body moved in circles, then to and fro and gained speed. Their moans creating a symphony that neither of them heard or cared for. She started bouncing on him and the slapping sound of their bodies added another note. Manish's hands sud-denly held her down and their eyes met. She saw an animalistic urge posses him. He shook. Then it overpowered him and he got up, still holding her so he wouldn't get out and sharply turned to lay her down. Their bodies parallel to each other. They kissed like savages. And then his body moved up. She could still see an animal in his eyes and knew she had called it forth. Now it was going to give her something that she desperately needed. Manish pulled out almost completely but stopped at the end and thrust inside her with force. Maya's body shook, her head bobbed. He pulled out again and thrust himself in her again with all the force he could muster. Maya shouted in pleasure. He did it again. And again. And again. Slowly pulling himself out almost completely, and then thrusting in with speed and intense force, followed by Maya's scream. Eventually, he picked up speed. The thrusts had the same force, coupled with speed. He was annihilating her and in those moments that seemed everlasting, they both forgot their existence. They only knew the sensation they were experiencing.

*

The next morning Maya woke up feeling weightless. She remembered Manish had to go to work half-day and embraced the empty house with a smile. She looked at her phone. It was 12. She remembered something and jumped out of bed. Her legs ached but there was a renewed sense of energy in her. She felt light, as if walking on air. She caught herself in the mirror. Strangely, she looked young again. She stripped, went to the bathroom, lit her cigarette and took it in deeply. She wondered what it would be like to shower and smoke at the same time. She switched on the shower and stood under it, her hand extended out of the water range so the cigarette wouldn't give out. She poked her head out, took a puff, got back in and exhaled into the water. She smoked the rest of her cigarette that way. Then she dumped the butt into the toilet and looked up into the water running out of the shower. There were no thoughts in her head except feeling the water run down her body. She took her shampoo and inverted the bottle on her head and squeezed it for a while, half emptying it. She then started massaging it into her hair, face, neck, chest, around her breasts—her nipples felt sore—armpits, hands between her thighs, down her legs to the toes. She ran her hands from her head to toe like this multiple times until she was covered in thick lather. She giggled, enjoying how smooth it felt. Then she turned the shower back on and stood there like a statue letting the excess wash off and then scrubbed the rest off her skin and hair. She slowly turned the shower towards hot until steam rose off her body and then slowly brought it back to the middle and went over to the right until it was chilly and then brought it back in the middle. *If we messed with the water temperature, would it matter what season it was out there?* She thought and giggled at the nonsensical thought.

She got out, stood in front of the mirror. She slathered her body with lotion. Applied a face cream. She looked at her face. Her skin looked tighter and for the first time looked at her acne marks like they were art. She applied a subtly shiny golden eye shadow, mascara and kajal. Then lipstick and looked. Then picked up the forever-ignored blush and put some colour into her cheeks. *See you at 4*, the note on Manish's pillow had read. She smiled. The blush, combined with the red acne marks made her face look pinker, messier and she smiled at the confusing complexity of it that she refused to hide with a concealer. *Perfect*, she thought. She took out the flimsiest of bralette and softest of thongs and put them on. She then took out her raging red dress and slipped it over her head. It fell to her mid thighs.

She picked out a corner at the coffee shop and sat down, tucking her dress under the thighs, between her legs and then crossing them. The waiter got her coffee and she opened her book. Her phone pinged. It was Manish.

You're cruel. He'd replied to the mirror selfie she'd sent to him just before leaving the house. She smiled and put the phone face down.

She dug into her book and became unaware of her surroundings, until her phone chimed again an hour later.

It said, **Look up, hotness.**

She smiled and looked up, watching Ved walk towards her table.

Made in the USA
Middletown, DE
15 December 2022